THE
MONKEY'S
FIST

By the author of

Playing the Dozens

The Rage of Innocence

THE
MONKEY'S
FIST

WILLIAM D. PEASE

VIKING

VIKING
Published by the Penguin Group
Penguin Books USA Inc., 375 Hudson Street,
New York, New York 10014, U.S.A.
Penguin Books Ltd, 27 Wrights Lane,
London W8 5TZ, England
Penguin Books Australia Ltd, Ringwood,
Victoria, Australia
Penguin Books Canada Ltd, 10 Alcorn Avenue,
Toronto, Ontario, Canada M4V 3B2
Penguin Books (N.Z.) Ltd, 182–190 Wairau Road,
Auckland 10, New Zealand

Penguin Books Ltd, Registered Offices:
Harmondsworth, Middlesex, England

First published in 1996 by Viking Penguin,
a division of Penguin Books USA Inc.

1   3   5   7   9   10   8   6   4   2

PUBLISHER'S NOTE
This is a work of fiction. Names, characters, places, and
incidents either are the product of the author's imagination or
are used fictitiously, and any resemblance to actual persons, living
or dead, events, or locales is entirely coincidental.

LIBRARY OF CONGRESS CATALOGING IN PUBLICATION DATA
Pease, William D.
The monkey's fist / by William D. Pease.
p.   cm.
ISBN 0-670-85129-9
I. Title.
PS3566.E2425M66   1996
813'.54—dc20   95-47588

This book is printed on acid-free paper.
∞

Printed in the United States of America
Set in New Aster
Designed by Virginia Norey

Acknowledgments

I would like to express my special thanks to Al Silverman for the care and attention he has given to this project—as always, for the good advice, and for the gentle diplomacy with which he manages to overcome sometimes stubborn resistance.

And to Bob and Mary Bradshaw: for their advice and comments on the early drafts, and for their steadfast support and friendship, I am forever grateful.

You pretend that you're my brother and I pretend that I really believe you believe you're my brother.

—*Malcolm X*

Beware of people who believe. They aren't reliable players.

—*Graham Greene*

THE
MONKEY'S
FIST

PROLOGUE

In the beginning, it was not Toddy Grehm's death that occasioned the headlines but the circumstances of its discovery.

It was a warm, wet Wednesday afternoon at the last of April. In an impoundment lot serving Washington's second police district, a stray dog wandering among the collection of stolen, abandoned, and towed vehicles caught the scent and began growling and scratching at the door of a dark-green Buick. That caught the attention of a lot attendant, who shooed the dog away and looked through the Buick's front window to discover the body slumped over the front seat.

The lot attendant reported his find to the officer in charge, which report both interrupted and caught the attention of a local newspaper reporter, who had been arguing the injustice of his brand new Volvo's having been towed for a mere half-dozen unpaid parking tickets. The reporter's interest, of course, turned immediately from the recovery of his Volvo to that of the Buick and how that Buick could have been impounded without someone noticing and calling attention to the presence of a body on the front seat.

The homicide detectives called to the scene, however, were long experienced in the ways of Washington's local city government, and they showed little or no interest in the lack of care or level of incompetence that might have surrounded the body's delivery. They focused instead on the fact that it had suffered a single gunshot wound to the chest, and that clutched in its hand was a nine-millimeter semi-automatic pistol of a manufacture previously unknown to any of them. They noted as well that the victim had either carried no personal items or identifying documents, or such items had been purposefully removed from the body. There was no wallet, no money, no driver's license, no passport or Social Security card. The vehicle's license plates were traced to a rental agency based at Dulles International Airport, some fifteen miles west of the city, but the car itself contained no registration papers or rental agreements. The detectives did find under the front seat, however, the business card of one Trevor Grehm of the Iberia Trading Company, S.A. The card listed the address of the company's headquarters in Lisbon, Portugal, and those of its branch offices in London and above a small bank in a small building on Washington's Capitol Hill.

Inquiring at Iberia Trading's Washington office, the detectives learned that the company was an international commodities brokerage and that Trevor Grehm was known to the local staff only by name and his telephone voice. According to the local office manager, Grehm rarely, if ever, conducted business out of that office, and neither the manager nor any other member of the staff could recall when or if Grehm had last visited. Certainly no one there felt the least confident that he could view the body and say whether it was or was not that of Trevor Grehm. The detectives were referred to the home office in Lisbon.

By midday Thursday, the police had verified through a spokesman at Iberia's Lisbon headquarters that Trevor Grehm, who was more familiarly known to the spokesman as "Toddy," age forty-two, was indeed an employee of the Iberia Trading Company. Grehm, according to the spokesman, was a British national who maintained a full-time residence in London and a part-time residence in the 4500 block of Q Place, Northwest. Grehm's business in Washington was primarily that of client development and lobbying—"wining and dining, as it were," said the spokesman. "Not the sort of thing we leave to the local boys on the desk." The detectives were assured, of course, that the company would do everything in its power to assist the police investigation. They would immediately contact Grehm's family and have the family contact the police.

Late Thursday afternoon, after the morning headline HOMICIDE VICTIM TOWED FROM DOWNTOWN and its accompanying story were published to a morbidly amused public, and days before the body of Toddy Grehm was finally and officially identified, the police found in an overheated room in the house on Q Place a second victim, whose body was grotesquely bloated and blackened by the processes of decay and putrefaction. About all the detectives could say of their new discovery was that it was the body of a woman of indefinite age, probably white, based on the texture of the hair, and that it had apparently suffered a similar single gunshot wound to the chest. There was speculation that the second victim may have been Helen Scott Grehm, thirty-eight, Toddy Grehm's estranged wife, who could not otherwise be located; but it was only speculation, for the woman's body, like that of Toddy Grehm, was days away from being officially identified.

But in other quarters, such confirmations were not needed before actions were taken and reactions were assessed. Hours before the reporter had published his story, and days before the police had any answers, carefully coded and encrypted messages had been sent and received over secured lines and satellite signals across the city and to other states and to other cities in other nations; and not one of those messages or any of the information they contained would ever be shared with police investigators or inquiring reporters.

PART

ONE

1.

Perched on a rise overlooking the upper reaches of the Severn River, some thirty miles east of Washington, the old house seemed as removed in time as it was in distance. But for its patches and repairs and minor renovations, the house remained much as it was that day nearly sixty years before when Eddie Nickles's father put the finishing touches on the master bedroom and carried his bride over the threshold. The house wore its history like the old man had worn his Bay Rum cologne and nickel-plated watch with its cracked crystal and age-yellowed face. It was a history noticed only by strangers, like the scent of summer strained through the window screens or the sounds of the slow-moving river. It was the sight of lilac bushes grown wild in the yard and a bottle of witch hazel gone dry on a windowsill; an Ivory Soap bar split in two, one-half resting on the iron-stained sink, the other in a dish on the scroll-footed tub. It was cracked linoleum and beaded pine and a leaded-glass lamp that had never worked but was never repaired—things ignored but never discarded, like a lock of hair or an unsigned poem cached in some box meant to be opened only after the funeral.

It was morning, and Eddie stood at the bathroom sink where his father had stood each morning for more than a half-century. He pushed away all thoughts of the old man and of the single massive stroke that had sent him to the special wing of the nursing home reserved for those who were "pretzeled," as one nurse had put it when she thought Eddie wasn't listening: where old men and old women shriveled into fetal balls totally dependent upon the meters and pumps and tubing that supplied their oxygen and delivered their fluids and evacuated their waste. No, such thoughts served no purpose, and thus were to be avoided. Instead he turned his attention to the soft, soapy swirl of shaving cream sitting on the tips of his fingers, which in turn reminded him of frozen custard, which in turn reminded him of that old Chevrolet, the one in which "Ain't" Mabel and "Ain't" Alma came to visit most Saturdays, the one with the rumble seat that, if the weather was good and the old ladies were of a mind, he and his two younger sisters would pile into, and they'd drive to the frozen custard stand. Eddie wondered, just as he had wondered as a boy, why the frozen custard didn't just fall out of the cone when they'd flip it upside-down and dip it into the hot chocolate coating. A light tap on the door frame behind him interrupted his thoughts.

"Dad?"

Eddie looked up to see his daughter's hesitant frown in the mirror, and he blushed as if caught at something embarrassing. "C'mon in," he said. "I'm decent." He supposed he was—decent, that is—dressed in a rumpled pair of khakis, T-shirt, and bare feet, but he wasn't altogether certain. It had been so many years, and if he had ever known the rules, he was sure they had changed.

Priscilla had been barely five years old when her mother ordered Eddie out of the house and filed for divorce. She was eighteen now, and in the years between father and daughter had maintained a tenuous hold on one another through sporadic phone calls, occasional dinners, and the rare weekend. Priscilla's mother was remarried and about to move away—whether to her husband's estate in Bucks County or to the winter home in Boca Raton, Eddie wasn't sure—but, with only a few months before Priscilla was to start college, it was decided that she would spend the summer with her father and only a mile or two from where she had grown up.

"So, what's up?" Eddie asked, quickly spreading the shaving cream over his beard.

Priscilla bowed her head, and one sneakered foot pawed gently at some ancient stain on the wooden floor. "Kinda weird, isn't it?" she said softly.

"Weird? Whaddaya mean, weird?"

"Oh, you know, like you 'n' me living here in Grandpa's house, y'know, after all these years."

Eddie shrugged. "I don't know about weird, but I suppose it's gonna take some getting used to." He turned toward her. "Why, does it bother you?"

She shook her head. "No, it's just, I don't know, different, I guess. Why, does it bother you?"

"You mean being here?"

"That . . . and me, and Mother getting married and moving away. You know, like everything."

Eddie studied her a moment. Priscilla was only an inch or two shorter than his own five feet eleven inches, and he could see both his mother and baby sister reflected in her auburn hair and bright-green eyes. But, unlike the women of his family, Priscilla was trim, even delicate, despite her height, like her mother had been at that age, and Eddie was grateful that she showed no sign of his own thick frame and rough features. It bothered him, though, that her entire wardrobe seemed to consist of little more than tight jeans and form-fitting tops that never did enough to conceal her generous breasts, and it bothered him even more that he felt he had no right to say anything about it.

Priscilla took a step back from the door and looked away. "I'm, ah, sorry, you know. I didn't mean to, like, you know, disturb you."

Eddie shook his head and turned back to the mirror. "I'll tell ya what disturbs me," he said. "The end of the summer, you're starting college, and, like, y'know, like you're still like, y'know, talking like you grew up in, like, y'know, Sowfeast D.C.! You know?"

She rolled her eyes. "Do you really want to get into a discussion of grammar and vocabulary?"

His mouth twisted a bit before he said, "No, I suppose not."

Eddie Nickles, recently retired after twenty-five years with the Metropolitan Police Department, had spent most of his career as a homicide detective "working the sewers," as he called it, dealing with street thugs and back-alley snitches for whom "muthafucka" seemed an essential element of the language. Over time his conscious ear had been numbed, and often—and sometimes at the most inappropriate moments—he'd slip into the dialect of the street with its easy obscenities. But since Priscilla had come to live with him, he had been trying as hard as he knew how to break the habit.

She stood quietly, waiting for more, but Eddie only frowned into the mirror and took another stroke at his beard. "Was there something in particular you wanted?" he asked as he rinsed his blade.

"Oh, geez! Yeah, I almost forgot. There's a man here to see you. He's at the front door."

"What?"

"Yeah, I'm sorry. I think he's a lawyer or something?"

"A lawyer?"

She nodded. "I'm not sure, he looks like a lawyer. I didn't ask. He just said that he was here to see you."

Eddie turned toward her. "Did he give you a name?"

"Yes, but I'm not sure I heard him correctly. Bowles, I think, or Balls? Does that sound right?"

"Balls?"

"Something like that."

"Did he say what he wanted?"

"Not really, he just said that he had an appointment with you."

"An appointment? I don't have any appointment."

Priscilla shrugged.

"Well, how 'bout telling whoever he is that I'll be right down."

"Sure. And, oh, by the way, are you gonna need the car this morning? I've got a lot of errands to run."

"No, that's okay, you go ahead."

"You're sure it's okay?"

"Yeah, sure," he said. Priscilla nodded quickly and started back through the bedroom toward the hall. "The keys're on—" Eddie started.

"I know," she called over her shoulder.

"And be careful with it in reverse, it's—"

"I know," he heard her say as she bounced down the stairs.

"Pris?" he called, but she was gone. *Be careful,* he had wanted to say.

🐾

"Detective Nickles?" The man stepped in from the front porch and set down his briefcase, a well-worn and soft-sided affair whose leather sagged like an old dog lying down. "You are Detective Nickles?" he questioned.

"Used to be," Eddie said, shaking the hand that was offered, "but not anymore."

"Ah, well, yes, I understand that you have retired. But that's precisely why I am here. We did have an appointment, correct?"

The air was cool, yet the man was perspiring, and he reached in his pocket for a handkerchief to pat his brow. It was a high brow and broad, accentuated by thick black hair swept back and lying flat as if lacquered to his skull. His long chin hung like a counterweight, and in between, his eyes, nose, and mouth were all small and set close together, as if those features by which he might be judged had circled their wagons in the valley of his face. It was not a handsome face, Eddie thought, and it certainly was not plain; but for all it was not, it was a face that stayed with you.

"An appointment?" Eddie said. "No, I don't think so."

The man looked surprised. "Oh? I was certain my secretary had called to make arrangements."

The man's words, like his manner, seemed so precise as to be awkward, and his accent had a certain unnatural quality, as if it was something he had acquired to match the formal cut and color of his suit. British, Eddie thought, but not quite. "No, no one called," he said.

"Oh? Well, then, of course this must be a surprise. I am sorry. I don't usually burst in on people like this. Obviously there's been a bit of a mix-up. But . . . Well, I am here now. Would you have a moment?"

"Who are you?" Eddie asked.

"Oh dear. Again, I am sorry. How rude of me. My name is Garland Bolles. Here, my card."

"Garland Bolles, Investment Counselor," the card announced,

along with an office address on Fifteenth Street in Washington and a second address in Covent Garden, London WC2. Eddie studied the card as he did this large, heavy-set man standing stiff and erect in a dark-blue suit and hard black shoes. "I was just about to make some coffee," Eddie said, then stopped. "Investments, huh? You're not selling something, are you?"

The man smiled easily. "No, no, Detective, I am not selling anything. Quite to the contrary, actually. I am here to purchase."

"Really? I wasn't aware I was selling anything."

"Well, to be precise, I would like to hire you."

"Hire me? For what?"

"A bit of investigation."

Eddie lowered his chin and looked at Bolles carefully. "I'm sorry," he said, "but I don't do that kind of work. Not anymore."

"Yes, so I understand, but if you'll allow me, you might find what I have to offer . . . well, shall we say *interesting?* And," Bolles emphasized, "we—that is, the people I represent and I—are prepared to be quite generous."

Eddie cocked his head.

"At least hear me out," Bolles said. "You have been specifically recommended to us, and, as I said, we are prepared to offer compensation appropriate to what I am told are your very special talents."

Eddie had not quite gotten around to any serious thought of what he might do to occupy his retirement beyond worrying about money. His pension alone would be barely sufficient, even for his modest needs. But events over the past two months had eased his concerns, at least financially. His father's nursing care was fully covered by an insurance policy whose limits would not be exhausted for another two years—assuming the old man lived that long—and his sisters, both of whom lived in opposite corners of the country, had urged him to move into the old house to take care of things. Eddie was not entirely certain what that meant— "taking care of things"—but the arrangement at least relieved him of any rent or mortgage payments and allowed him the freedom to delay the hard decisions about his future.

There was, however, the matter of Priscilla's high-school graduation, scheduled the next day. Eddie had spent weeks trying to think of a gift that would match both his modest resources and his immodest pride in his daughter's achievements. After all, not only was she the first in the family to be going to a full, four-year college, but that college was Duke University, and her education was being substantially funded by the merit scholarships she had won.

Eddie paused, studying Bolles. Whether it was the man's reference to generosity or that he had been specifically sought out for whatever "special talents" Bolles thought he had, Eddie was at least curious. "Come on back to the kitchen," he said. "We can talk there."

While Eddie prepared a pot of coffee, Garland Bolles stood at the door leading from the kitchen to the back porch, his hands clasped behind his back, his stare fixed on the freshly mowed lawn running down to the marsh grass at the edge of the water, where an old dock limped out beyond the shallows. "A beautiful spot you have here, Detective . . . or do you prefer Mister Nickles now?"

"Doesn't matter. Either way." Eddie came to the table and sat down. "So tell me—" Eddie started, but Bolles interrupted him as if he had not heard.

"Yes, quite idyllic. Where I live in Washington—and in London, as well—it is always so crowded. Always so much noise. Neighbors right on top of you and all that. Here it appears you have this whole point of land to yourself. Is that right?"

Eddie frowned as Bolles continued to survey the scenery. "Well, not exactly. There are neighbors. You just can't see them for all the bushes around the property. But you're right, it's pretty private out here."

"Indeed," said Bolles. "If the day ever comes that I can afford to retire, this would be just the type of place I would hope to find."

Eddie, not at all sure what to say, began again where he had left off. "So tell me, Mr. Bolles, how'd you happen to find me . . . and why?"

"Well, Detective," Bolles said, at last turning from the back of the property to join Eddie at the kitchen table, "I represent the family of Trevor Grehm. Do you recognize the name?"

"No, can't say that I do."

"Hmmm, well, I thought perhaps you might be familiar with the case. It was some weeks ago, in late April? It drew quite a lot of attention in the local press. A man was found in a car after it had been carried off by the police? He had been murdered. The man in the car, that is."

Eddie nodded slowly. "Okay ... yeah, I remember reading about it."

"Yes, well, that man was Trevor Grehm. The people I represent, the Grehms, he was their son. Most tragic for them, as you can well imagine."

Eddie nodded.

"I thought you might still have been with the police department when it happened, that perhaps you knew some of the details."

"No, I retired a month or so before that."

"I see."

Eddie waited, but Bolles said nothing. "Murder?" Eddie asked finally, thinking back to the newspaper articles. "I might not be remembering the same case, but wasn't there something about a gun found with the body? Wasn't there at least some speculation about a suicide?"

"Ah, well, yes," Bolles said with some hesitation, "that's right. There was talk of suicide, but the family doesn't believe that for a moment, and I must say that I agree with them. With all due respect to your former colleagues, we feel the police simply have not given this matter the appropriate attention. We can all understand, of course, the problems facing the authorities in Washington, what with all we read in the papers about so many killings every day. But, still, it doesn't seem quite right that they should arbitrarily decide this matter as a suicide simply to be done with a difficult case. Do you think?"

Bolles's question struck a chord. Eddie Nickles had come up through the department during a time when the homicide squad was an elite corps, when detectives took pride in the quality of their work, when a ratio of eight to nine arrests for every ten murders was the minimum standard, when detectives worked closely with DAs who similarly considered a rate of eight to nine convictions for every ten cases tried minimally acceptable. But over the past decade the politics of race and home rule had split the department from the federal prosecutors, who in the nation's capital—as in no other jurisdiction—prosecuted local crime, and detectives were being recruited more for their ability to fill quotas than to solve cases. By the time of his retirement, the city's kill rate led the nation, a dozen or more police officers were under indictment for everything from drugs to running protection rings to first-degree murder, and the mayor was calling for help from the National Guard. Less than half of all reported homicides resulted in an arrest, and less than half of those arrested were ever convicted. It was a sense of personal embarrassment more than any other factor that ultimately had led Eddie to file his retirement papers.

"Yes, well, the department has been having its problems, I agree," Eddie said. "But what makes you think they're not investigating this particular case?"

"Well, certainly, there's the matter of Helen and why—"

"Helen? Who's Helen?"

"Of course," Bolles said, raising his hands to stop himself. "I haven't explained, have I? Helen, you see, was Toddy's wife."

"Toddy?"

Bolles frowned slightly, then smiled. "Yes, Trevor. The family called him Toddy. In any event, Helen was Toddy's . . . that is, Trevor's wife. She, too, was killed. And by the same gun that was found with Trevor's body. But in the house. Helen was in his house. Trevor's house, that is. It's all rather confusing, I agree, but—"

"Hold on a second," Eddie interrupted. "The gun they found with the husband was the same one that killed the wife?" Bolles nodded, and Eddie considered a moment. "So the police think it's a domestic?"

"I beg your pardon?"

"A domestic. Lover's spat. The husband and wife have a fight, and for whatever reason the husband shoots the wife. Then, because he's despondent or frightened or remorseful or whatever, he kills himself."

"Well, that's what the police would have us believe. But we don't accept that. Not for a moment."

"Why not?"

"In the first place, the Grehms tell me there was absolutely no—how does one say this?—no bad blood between them. Between Trevor and Helen, that is. It is true that they had separated almost a year before. But the parting was most amicable, I'm told, and Helen remained quite close to her husband's family. The Grehms."

"And her family?"

"You mean Helen's?"

"Yes."

"I'm afraid she had no family beyond the Grehms. I understand her own parents were killed in an automobile accident some years ago. Also, Helen no longer lived in Washington. She was American, you see, but she lived in London, not too far from the Grehms, actually. So you see, it would not make sense for her to visit Trevor in Washington just to have an argument, and the fact that she was in the house but Trevor was not there at the time—"

"Wait a minute, slow down here."

"Yes, again I am sorry. I'm not presenting this very well, am I? You can see why we might need your help. This certainly is not my line."

"What exactly is your line, Mr. Bolles?"

"Business and trade. International trade. I'm representing the Grehms as a favor. They're quite old friends. And, of course, their living in London makes it very difficult for them to follow up on these matters directly. You understand."

"Sure."

"Now, where was I?"

"You were about to tell me that this Trevor and Helen were separated but still the best of friends. Correct?"

"You sound as if you believe that's not possible."

"Well, I really wasn't offering an opinion."

"In any event," Bolles continued, "I can't say what good friends they were or were not, but, all that aside, there is one piece of evidence we think very telling, evidence which the police seem either to be ignoring or incapable of following up."

"And what's that?"

"Let me try to make this as clear as I can. First, as I believe I said, Helen was found shot in the house Trevor rented in Washington. Trevor's body was found nearly two days later in his car. And there was yet another day before her body was found. But, in any event, sometime between the time the coroner estimated Helen died and the time of Trevor's death, a Negro was photographed by a bank camera trying to use one of Helen's credit cards."

Negro? How long had it been since he had heard the term "Negro"? Eddie took a second before asking, "Credit card?"

"Oh, what do you call them? Your money-machine cards."

"An ATM card?"

"Yes, an ATM card."

"Did he succeed? Did this *Negro* have the PIN number?"

"You mean the identification code?"

"Yes. Did he manage to get any cash?"

"Oh, no. He did not."

"Did the machine seize the card? I mean, does anybody have it? The police? They checked it for fingerprints or whatever?"

"No, it seems the man walked away from the machine with the card."

Eddie considered a moment, then shrugged. "Yeah, well, he probably knew enough to stop before the machine seized it. Tried once or twice and figured, if he couldn't hit the right code, he might at least sell the card on the street."

Bolles's expression brightened suddenly, as if one small mystery may have been resolved for him. "Yes, well, that would make sense, now, wouldn't it? You see, Detective, that's precisely why we've come to you."

"How did you happen to find me?"

"It was simple, actually. I called an American client who happens to be a lawyer. He in turn called other lawyers. The old-boy network, as it were. After all was said and done, you came highly recommended to us. In fact, I'd say it was more than a recommendation. I've been told that you may well be the only man who can help us. You have quite a reputation, Detective, particularly, I am told, among former prosecutors and lawyers familiar with such matters as these."

"Reputation?"

"Yes, sir, quite a reputation. I'm told that . . . well, shall we say that you have your own unique way of doing things, and, more important, that there very well may be no one, on or off the police force, who has a better network of informants or knows better how to get around in that milieu."

"*Mill-you?* What *mill-you* is that?"

"Drug people, things like that."

"The Grehms into drugs, were they?"

"Oh, no, certainly not. It's just that, with this colored fellow in the bank photograph . . . Well, you understand."

The two men stared at one another for a moment. "You have a copy of that photograph?" Eddie asked.

"Certainly," Bolles said, then stopped. "I say certainly, but in fact it took some badgering to get the police to let us have a copy."

"I can imagine," Eddie said with a smile.

"I virtually had to threaten that the family would go to the press." Bolles stopped as he reached into his briefcase for a red file folder from which he took a photocopy of the bank photograph and handed it to Eddie. "Yes," he said, "the family is quite upset with the lack of cooperation on the part of the police."

"How much time did you say it was between the death of the woman and when her husband was found?"

"Well, it's all in the report that I have prepared for you, but the bank card was used about three-thirty in the morning on April 26. The coroner estimated the time of Helen's death to be sometime during the evening of April 25, and Trevor's body—well, his car, actually—was towed sometime around eight-thirty the morning of April 27, but it was not until late that afternoon that someone actually found the body. The coroner estimated that he had died early that morning, sometime between midnight and six, as I recall."

"A day and a half, maybe more, between them, huh?" Garland Bolles nodded but said nothing as Eddie studied the photograph.

The photograph was not clear enough for him to glean much beyond the fact that the subject was a black male, an adult; his age was difficult to estimate. Medium height, with a thin face, either darkly complected or the photo was badly exposed, and wearing a dark nylon-type skull cap. The only unusual marker was that the man appeared to have at least one seriously protruding front tooth. What was that puppet show? The one he used to watch every night before supper, back in his frozen-custard days? *Kukla, Fran and Ollie?* And Cecil the Seasick Sea Serpent? Yes, that was it. The man bore a striking resemblance to Cecil the Seasick Sea Serpent.

"Exactly what is it you want me to do, Mr. Bolles? Even if I wanted, I'm not sure I could help you. Y'know, the police department doesn't exactly welcome outsiders to their investigations, not even people who were once on the inside. And these days they're more than a little sensitive about their reputation, if that's what you'd call it."

"Which is why we have come to you, sir."

"Oh?"

"Yes, quite. You see, Detective, the point is that the Grehms are quite intent that Trevor's . . . and Helen's, too, of course . . . well, that their killer or killers be caught. I'm sure you understand."

Eddie nodded, then waited.

"And in truth the family is *disturbed*," Bolles said, drawing out the word, "that the police seem to be doing little or nothing to accomplish that task. What we are looking for is someone, like yourself, who might find this man in the photograph. It may not be obvious to the police, but it certainly seems obvious to us that, if this man were found, we will have found the killer. Am I right?"

Eddie shrugged. "Not necessarily. But I suppose you'd be a helluva lot closer than you are now. The police have no leads?"

"Not that we're aware of. We don't even think they're trying."

Eddie leaned back, studying Bolles as carefully as Bolles seemed to be studying him. Bolles's narrow-set eyes were steady, his manner intent and certain despite his being involved in a matter he readily confessed was beyond his experience. Eddie wondered, and so he asked, "You're an investment counselor? International-trade stuff?"

"Yes, well, I'm more of a business consultant, finding trading partners for clients, putting together joint ventures, that sort of thing."

"Do you mind telling me exactly who it was that gave you my name?"

"Not at all. Actually, it was several people. I was given various names to call, but it was a fellow by the name of Stanley Rubinow who convinced me you should be our first choice. You do know Mr. Rubinow, don't you?"

"Yes, I know him," Eddie said slowly, picturing the short, wire-haired former DA who was now a partner in a large Baltimore firm. Rubinow had prosecuted a half-dozen or more of Eddie's homicide cases. "The Badger," Eddie once called him, a man not high on anyone's list for a friendly beer or casual conversation, but among the top two or three lawyers one might hire to bring one's worst enemy to his knees. "Look, Mr. Bolles," Eddie said, "I understand your problem, and I sympathize, but the fact is, I'm not in the business, and, like I said, the department isn't gonna welcome me back as part of the team. It just doesn't work that way."

"I understand. But what I am suggesting is that you work, shall we say, *discreetly,* to find this man without necessarily telling the police anything about it."

"What do you mean, 'without necessarily ' telling the police?"

"Look, we—that is, the family and I—we are quite sensitive to the politics here. As disappointed as we might be in what the police are doing, or not doing, we certainly would not want to antagonize them, or in some way discourage them further. I suspect that, if they knew we had hired our own investigator, they might well feel insulted or otherwise use that as an excuse to do nothing at all. Am I right?"

Again Eddie shrugged. "Who knows what they might think."

"And, too, I can well imagine that you would not want to—ah, what's the phrase—burn any bridges with your former colleagues?"

"Exactly what is it you have in mind?"

"Well, we thought, if we could present the authorities with a *fait accompli,* as it were, something they could not ignore, well, that just might do the trick. What we propose is that you find this man, whoever he is, or where he could be found, and then turn that information over to us. And then we, or I, someone besides yourself, could give that information directly to the authorities. It seems to us they would have to follow up on such a lead, wouldn't they?"

"One would hope."

"Yes, I would think so. And for this, as I said, the family is prepared to be quite generous."

"Define generous."

Bolles again reached for the red file folder. From it he extracted a check, which he laid on the table. "This is a cashier's check for ten thousand dollars, which I'm prepared to give to you right now. That would be a retainer, against which you would charge whatever hourly fee we agree is appropriate. Shall we say one hundred dollars? One hundred twenty-five?"

Eddie said nothing.

"Well, shall we say one twenty-five, then?" Bolles continued: "In any event, if you still haven't found the man after spending however many hours it takes to use up that ten thousand dollars, well, then we would discuss what progress you had made and whether you or the family wished to continue further. On the other hand, if you find the man quickly, you may keep whatever balance is left of the ten thousand, and we would pay you an additional bonus of five thousand dollars. Does that sound generous enough?"

Eddie raised his eyebrows. "Generous? Yeah, I'd say so. But you make it sound like you're looking for a bounty hunter."

"Well, I hadn't intended that, but, yes, I can see why you might think so. But let me assure you that we—again, the family and I—we have given this matter considerable thought. We are not interested in just another investigator. The Grehms have lost their son, and a daughter-in-law with whom they remained quite close despite the separation. I'm sure you can understand what that must mean to them. And they just happen to be in a financial position to secure outside help."

"Why didn't you just hire Rubinow? He'd know all the angles for something like this."

"Because, Mr. Nickles, we don't need a lawyer. We need an investigator. Mr. Grehm may be generous, but he certainly is not wasteful. He wants to put his money where he feels it would do the most good. We wish to match a particular talent to a particular problem, and in this case the problem is to find this colored man who tried to use Helen's bank card. Now, for such a project Mr. Rubinow tells me that you may be the most talented man we could hire. But if you feel that you can't help us, perhaps you might suggest someone who could."

Eddie picked up the check and stared at it. His first thought was Priscilla's graduation. The party had been planned and the arrangements all made without consulting him beyond securing his agreement to use the house and its wide lawn overlooking the river. His ex-wife, Megs, had said that he didn't need to worry, *they* would take care of everything. Megs and her newly retired insurance-executive husband with his summer estate and his winter home. Just as *they* had reassured him about the cost of Priscilla's college education. *They* understood just how much of a struggle it might be for him to get by on his paltry retirement.

They would take care of whatever expenses there might be over and above the scholarships Priscilla had won. He shouldn't worry. His daughter shouldn't worry. *They* would take care of everything. What *they* would not take care of, however, was his gift to his daughter. He looked at Bolles carefully and asked, "You're serious?"

"Yes, sir, Detective, quite serious."

Eddie held the check up to the light. "I couldn't start until Monday."

"That's agreeable."

Eddie took his time, then nodded. "I'll do what I can."

"Excellent. I will leave these papers with you. I hope my report has been thorough, but if you have any questions, you have my number. And, of course, if you need anything from the family, background information or whatever, just give me a call. I'm out of the office quite a bit, but you can leave a message with my secretary and I'll get back to you as soon as possible."

Eddie nodded.

"And . . . well, if it doesn't sound like too much of an imposition, I would appreciate it if I could call you for a report of your daily progress. Given their experience with the police department, the family would appreciate knowing what progress you're making as you go along. I'm sure you understand."

"No problem."

"And what would be a convenient time for me to call?"

"Well, this type of work is usually done at night, when all the creatures come out of their holes. . . ."

"Indeed," said Bolles as if made vicariously nervous by the image drawn. "Well, then, shall we say each morning? Not too early, perhaps?"

"That's fine. Let's say around ten o'clock. And if I need to reach you?"

"Anytime, just call my office. As I say, I regularly call in for messages, and my answering service knows how to reach me at any time." Bolles sat back. "So, are we settled, then?"

Eddie again looked to the check. "Yes, Mr. Bolles, I guess we are."

ɾ

Within minutes, Garland Bolles was in his car and listening to the crunch of the tires on the gravel drive leading away from the house. He stopped just before turning onto the paved road and looked back at the old Victorian encircled by its porches and topped by its red tin roofs, the separate barnlike garage to one side, and the wide-open lawn bordered on three sides by tall trees and a seemingly impenetrable hedgerow of azaleas and rhododendrons which, like the lilacs, had grown high and wild. The fourth side of the property was protected by the Severn River at its widest part, a place called Round Bay, where the nearest neighbor on the opposite shore seemed miles way.

Bolles looked again at the map that had directed him to the spot and marked it with a black-inked circle. It was indeed a beautiful setting, and one perfectly suited to his purposes if the need were to arise.

2.

From the Old Executive Office Building, a hulking gray mound of a structure festooned with columns like a child's sand castle, F Street stretched westward through an eclectic mix of large glass-and-concrete cubes, old apartment houses and small hotels, university residences and Federal-period townhouses, some of which were private residences, some of which were private clubs, and some of which housed a few of the special-interest groups and foundations that sprung like weeds throughout the nation's capital.

One such group was the Percy T. Unger Foundation, whose four-story red brick building appeared large but hardly imposing behind its black wrought-iron fence and the English boxwood which bordered a small patch of kempt grass. If one were to inquire of its neighbors, little would be learned about the foundation other than that its employees seemed uniformly pleasant and well mannered when greeted, which was rare, and that its mission had something to do with the arts, or perhaps it was architecture, or was it the environment? Whatever its purpose, it was generally agreed that the foundation was a good neighbor, keeping to itself and bothering no one. Some, looking at the full canopy of tall oaks behind a high brick wall at the rear of the building, were curious whether there might be a formal garden and whether the foundation, like other such organizations, might rent out the space for wedding receptions and catered cocktail parties. But if drawn to inquire through the small brass speaker at the front gate, one would be told, "Oh, I am sorry, but I'm afraid that the gardens are available only to members of the foundation."

Indeed, about the only outward sign that the foundation carried on any business at all was the dozen or more pieces of mail that were delivered daily and placed in a large box embedded in the brick gatepost just below the small brass speaker and a small brass plaque that read "Percy T. Unger Foundation, Please Ring for Service."

Except for the last two weeks in August, when she rented a cottage on Fenwick Island, and the two weeks each January she vacationed in Florida, Miss Wendy Berksmere spent some part of each day, Monday to Friday, excluding federal holidays, at her desk on the second floor of the Percy T. Unger Foundation making certain that her staff had made certain that the various letters and parcels they had prepared and posted to the foundation days before were later received by the foundation without any sign of having been intercepted or tampered with. It was just one of the many procedures developed by Miss Berksmere in her capacity as chief of internal security for the Special Projects Directorate, one of the most, if not the most clandestine unit among America's intelligence agencies, whose work was, in fact, the true and only mission of the Percy T. Unger Foundation. And in her eighteen years and seven months with the directorate, Miss Berksmere had not once failed to complete that task, not even on the day she had outpatient surgery to excise a small and mercifully benign tumor, of which only her life's companion, the diminutive and reclusive Alice Whiting, and the directorate's chief, Philo Machus, had been made aware. There was no more dedicated or faithful servant than Miss Berksmere, and her special position was uniformly recognized. Even the chief, who never called anyone by anything other than his last name—"Dorfman, come to my office," he'd bark into his phone; or "Ousby, where the hell are those figures?" he'd call down the hall—addressed her always and respectfully as "Miss Berksmere."

"Miss Berksmere, would you have a few minutes?" the chief asked, bowing cautiously—as he would to no one else—through her office door.

"Yes, sir," she answered. "In your office?"

"If you don't mind."

Miss Berksmere stood, smoothed the wrinkles from the lap of her navy dress, and reached for the light-gray sweater draped over the back of her chair. The chief's office would be as it always was, too cool for her comfort.

She followed Machus down the hall, keeping several steps behind. She always kept some distance between them, the difference in their heights being a discomfort for them both. Miss Berksmere was precisely five feet ten inches in her bare feet, which no one in the directorate had ever seen, and her thin, angular features and close-cut graying hair made her seem even taller. She was an attractive woman often thought to be considerably younger than her sixty-one years, whose outward manner and style had a certain grace and elegance that left no doubt that she was involved with the arts. When the occasion dictated, however, one could readily see in her sharp blue eyes the hardened and pragmatic discipline that made her subordinates sit up straight, as if their third-grade teacher had just entered the room.

The chief, on the other hand, was a small man, barely five feet five inches. Still, but for the hint of a paunch and a certain darkness about the eyes, at age fifty-five Philo Machus looked nearly as fit and robust as he was reputed to have been when he was the youngest Marine ever to have reached the rank of colonel; when, it was said, both the secretary of defense and the director of the CIA had personally, but quite privately, commended him for his work with the Military Assistance Command Surveillance Group's "Phoenix" program; and when he had directed the activities of the Provincial Reconnaissance Units—America's answer to North Vietnam's campaign of terror—out of offices at 60 Pasteur Street, then the CIA's six-story walkup in Cholon, on the outskirts of Saigon. The pencil-thin scar that sliced his right cheek from the bridge of his nose to the edge of his jaw was said to have been inflicted during a stint in Savannakhet, where everything from whores and opium to threats and philosophy was used to influence the ephemeral politics of Laotian neutrality. It was all legend, however, and nearly a quarter-century old. The chief never spoke of those times, and no one among the current staff knew for certain what was fact and what was fiction—except, perhaps, Miss Berksmere, whom no one dared ask.

"This memo on FROC," Machus said, referring to the Revolutionary Front of Workers and Campesinos, the latest group then trying to foment rebellion in Nicaragua, "I'm not certain that I understand your concern."

Miss Berksmere took it upon herself to be seated in the unoffered wine-red chair in front of Machus's solid mahogany desk. "My concern, sir, is with Pedrito the Honduran," she said.

Machus frowned, and his eyes narrowed. "Yes?"

"Well, other than the issue of which side we're picking here, I wonder why we're even bothering."

"The problem is not which side, Miss Berksmere. Who gives a damn for which side? The new Sandinistas, the old Sandinistas, Humberto and his army, even the Front 380, they're none of them any more than annoying little savages. The problem lies with all these new mandarins at Defense and the NSC. There's talk of cutting funds for Dunning's group. Dunning's been a good friend to us. Wouldn't want to see his budgetary head lopped off just because a bunch of shortsighted Arkansas crackers won't listen to reason. Maybe a firefight or two up in the northern provinces will make them nervous enough to mind their own goddamned business!" The chief rapped his fist once on the desk and then swirled in his chair to stare out to the courtyard. "Nitwits, Miss Berksmere. This town is filling up with nitwits."

"Yes, sir," Miss Berksmere answered quietly.

The chief turned slowly but not entirely back to her and asked, "Besides, what are we talking about here? Three-fifty, four hundred thousand? Pocket change. Not going to cause us to shortchange any other project, is it?"

As chief of internal security, Miss Berksmere also had responsibility for overseeing the directorate's finances. "No, sir, not at all," she said.

In the netherworld of black operations, the Special Projects Directorate was both unique and highly successful in the degree to which it had managed to maintain its near-total anonymity. There were few in or out of the government—indeed, few within the intelligence community itself—that even knew it existed. The directorate had evolved from the political chaos of the 1970s, a time when intelligence was anathema to the press and press-hungry politicians, except as a source of prize-winning revelations and electoral advantage. But whatever else their shortcomings, the likes of Philo Machus and his colleagues were well versed in the tactics of diversion, and quite adept at offering up to the press and politicians any number of marginal programs and bureaucratic blunders that could be burned on the public pyres of self-righteousness. While the hungry hordes of investigative reporters and members of Congress were feeding on their headlines and reveling in their hearings, the essential business of covert operations carried on however the secret-keepers saw fit.

Still, operations required funding, and funding required budgets, and budgets required scrutiny, and scrutiny—at least on Capitol Hill—seemed to require leaks. More and more, the secret-keepers found, long-established front organizations were being savaged by the bureaucracy, and its barely camouflaged line items easily identified by anyone who bothered to look.

Something new was needed, something independent, self-sustaining, and totally secure. The director of covert operations for the Central Intelligence Agency began talking with selected friends at the National Security Agency, who in turn spoke with selected people within the Defense Intelligence Agency and the National Security Council, and in time a group of seven was formed representing the power elite of the covert side of America's intelligence agencies. That group, known as the Joint Operations Committee, had but a single mission: to establish and oversee the generation of substantial off-budget and off-the-books funding which could be used to conduct such covert operations as they and they alone deemed necessary. Philo Machus, who over many years had enjoyed remarkable success in achieving his superiors' objectives by means that allowed them total deniability, was picked to head the project. Thus was born the Special Projects Directorate.

It had taken time and careful planning and even more the careful selection of personnel—managers and salesmen, accountants and agents, brokers and bankers and traders and technicians—but, eventually, the clandestine funding source was established under the guise of a business formed and incorporated offshore, and known as the Iberia Trading Company, S.A. The company started out as a small commodities trader based in Lisbon and trafficking in mace from Grenada, and marjoram from Egypt, and in cassia and cacao and Dendicut chilies. Soon Iberia Trading had expanded its reach from the Ivory Coast to Tsientian, from Pakistan to Sarawak. In time, the spot markets in New York and London and Hamburg and Antwerp began to notice the presence of Iberia and its opening of offices in London and Zurich and New York. Iberia's profile remained low but its profits were high, and those profits were reinvested and supplemented by unmarked and discretionary funds diverted from other agencies' budgets until Iberia Trading had earned a name in the business, albeit a small name rarely heard outside the trading community.

Subsidiaries were formed, and to the spices were added minerals and metals, oil and gas and cobalt and gold and titanium. Profits from those trades were reinvested as well and supplemented with discretion to form new corporations and partnerships controlled by Iberia and dedicated to generating even greater profits to be funneled to the ever-expanding needs of covert operations. All that was required of those operatives seeking off-budget funding for some special project was knowledge of the directorate's existence and the approval of the Joint Operations Committee. No budget proposals or threat assessments were ever prepared, no object statements or policy reviews were ever submitted, no statutory or treaty justifications, no entry or exit briefings. No written document or any oral communication was ever disseminated beyond the Joint Committee, neither to seek advice nor to obtain consent of the legislative, executive, or judicial branches. And nowhere on the lists of government agencies and nowhere on the lists of government employees would anyone find the Special Projects Directorate or the people who ran it.

To those very few who did know, Philo Machus was a genius. Machus, however, knew that it was not genius to which he owed his success, but a simple understanding of how things worked in Washington. Neither he nor anyone else associated with the directorate took credit for its successes but ensured that those public servants and private friends who might gain power or prestige from the directorate's work took credit themselves. Thus, those powerful few who were aware of the directorate and who were its beneficiaries were fiercely loyal to it and jealously guarded its independence and anonymity. Machus understood, too, that, if genius had indeed played any part in his success, that genius was in his early recruitment of a brilliant but disaffected accountant from a Big Eight firm who early on was given the mission of overseeing the daily business and financial operations of Iberia Trading and who almost single-handedly constructed its intricate and very discreet financial empire. That man was Arlis Brecht.

Machus turned full-face to Miss Berksmere and said, "Well, enough of Nicaragua. What I really wanted to talk to you about is this business with Brecht's people."

"You mean the Grehms?"

"Yes, where are we on that?"

"Where we've been from the start. As far as we know, the police are still operating on the theory that it was either a burglary and double murder or a domestic murder-suicide."

"And our people?"

"They still smell an odor."

"Of?"

"They're not sure. They haven't uncovered anything, but . . ." Miss Berksmere stopped herself.

"But what, Miss Berksmere?"

"Well, as we've discussed so many times, the murders hardly seem to have been random. I mean, the circumstances certainly argue against the rather odd notion that the deaths were at the hands of some burglar."

"And?"

"And, well, if not a burglary and not a suicide . . ."

"And we're certain it was not that?"

"From what we know, the probability factor seems next to zero."

"So?"

"So, if it was neither suicide nor a random killing, the obvious concern remains that the killings are connected to directorate business, or at least to Iberia's business."

"And?"

Miss Berksmere, like everyone in the directorate, understood the near-religious importance the chief placed on loyalty, and understood, too, his special relationship with Arlis Brecht. She said nothing, but neither did she shy away from the chief's stare.

"Miss Berksmere?" Machus pressed.

"Well, the concern is that there is little hope of uncovering internal problems at Iberia unless it's through Arlis Brecht."

Machus pursed his lips and turned in his chair to look again out on the courtyard. "And is that considered a problem?"

Miss Berksmere did not answer.

"Are you suggesting," Machus started, his back still to her, hesitating for an instant, "well, that there is some concern about Arlis Brecht's reliability?" He reached for a hard rubber ball on the windowsill and began squeezing it in one hand while he waited.

"No, sir," Miss Berksmere said after a pause, "I'm not making any accusations. No one is."

"But," Machus said, "you have your suspicions?"

"No, sir, not even suspicions."

"But?"

"Well, I think this only points out a problem that's been developing over some time now. If there were a problem inside Iberia, who but Mr. Brecht would be able to find it? The point is, I only wonder if Mr. Brecht and Iberia haven't become just a bit too independent. Or we might pose the question another way. Are we too dependent on him? After all, his strengths are in business and finance, not intelligence, and if there were a problem with the Grehms, would he even recognize it or know what to look for? More important, if there is a problem within Iberia, how do we make sure that it doesn't spill over to the directorate?"

"*If* there is a problem."

"Yes, sir, if there is a problem."

"We're no closer to finding the man in the ATM photo?"

"No, sir."

He suddenly twirled in his chair to face her. "Damn! We can topple entire governments, but we can't find one lousy thief in our own back yard? You've called on our friends at Fort Meade?"

"Yes, sir, but street thieves aren't exactly their strong suit. You understand that we are in no position to be asking around ourselves."

"Yes, yes, understood. But nothing has come back to us through channels. Nothing out of Langley or Quantico?"

"No, sir, nothing."

"And from the committee?"

"No, sir, nothing."

"And from Brecht?"

"Nothing more than what you know already."

Machus turned back, again full-face to the window. "The Cat," as was known the stray calico Machus had adopted years before, which the staff speculated was the only living creature the chief allowed to touch him—his aversion to even the shaking of hands being equally part of his legend—slipped from the corner of the room and leapt to his lap. Machus leaned back and stroked The Cat as if he were stroking his thoughts, and The Cat's tail twitched violently, the animal seemingly uncertain whether it was pleased by its master's touch. "Tell me, Miss Berksmere," Machus said finally, "given that Trevor Grehm's work was primarily independent of Iberia, and given that we have long known and encouraged his dealings with the underbelly of the weapons trade with which Iberia has never been involved, why are we so concerned that these deaths relate to the Iberia operation?"

"Well, the fact that his wife was there—"

"Yes, precisely," Machus broke in, "the man's wife. Doesn't that give us reason to believe that they were together for personal reasons and she unfortunately ended up at the wrong place at the wrong time?"

"Perhaps, but, still, she was family," Miss Berksmere said, referring to the fact that Helen Grehm, too, was an employee of the directorate.

"Yes, but a mere courier, as I understand it. Certainly not anyone capable of or trained for operations."

"On paper only."

"Oh?" said Machus, turning back to her and cocking his head curiously.

"Yes, sir. I don't think we can afford to underestimate what Helen Grehm may have been capable of."

"You knew her?"

"Not well, but certainly well enough to say she was probably far more clever than her courier's job required."

Machus nodded slowly. "I see. And you suspect she may have been part of the problem?"

"I don't know one way or the other, which is precisely my point. I just think we should be doing everything we can to make sure that whatever problem the Grehms had is not related or traceable to the organization."

"And what, may I ask, do you think we should be doing that we aren't already doing?"

Miss Berksmere took a long moment before answering in a quiet and calculated tone. "I think you should authorize my people to go inside Iberia, and at the same time tighten our controls over Arlis Brecht."

Machus sat back and raised his chin a bit, his words chosen with equal care. "Strong measures, Miss Berksmere."

"I agree, but the risks we face if we don't take strong measures are not insubstantial."

"Nor are the risks we face if we do. Our Mr. Brecht and the efficient operation of the Iberia network are not exactly fungible items that we can afford to offend lightly. We must be careful to take our time here. Make sure we are not throwing the proverbial baby out with the bathwater."

"May I ask how much time?"

"A little more time, Miss Berksmere, a little more time. Sometimes it's best to let sleeping dogs lie, if you will."

"Sir?"

Machus leaned forward. "Consider, Miss Berksmere, that all has been very quiet since the incident with the Grehms, and, with all we have done to ferret out whatever problems there are, nothing has surfaced. There is always the possibility that there is nothing more to this matter than what we have already seen. And maybe . . . just maybe, if we leave it alone, this old dog will die in its sleep."

Miss Berksmere sat still and said nothing until Machus leaned even closer and raised his eyebrows to her. "Yes?"

"Yes, sir," she said without expression, "that is a possibility."

Machus sat back. "Yes, it is. And, absent some compelling reason to do otherwise, I think it best that we give this matter a little more time before taking any action that might prove precipitate. Don't you agree?"

Miss Berksmere smiled a gentle smile, the smile she most often reserved for those outside the directorate. "Yes, sir," she said, "perhaps you're right. A little more time."

3.

Arlis Brecht looked across the Grand Anse, where eleven years earlier U.S. Marines first stormed the beach in order to save Grenada from itself. Brecht's focus, however, was not on history, but on the presence of the woman lying just beyond the palms, her long and languid form draped over a chaise, one thin arm dangling to a listless wrist and a lazy hand, one thin finger of which was making slow circles in the sand.

Her bathing suit hardly mattered. She wore no top, and the bottom was little more than a strawberry string settled between her buttocks, and the crest of her hair shone in a shallow sunlit arch over the liquid tan horizon of her back. A light puff of air slipped off the ocean to pick up the scent of her lotion and carry it to where Brecht sat. He lifted his head and sniffed deeply to capture it.

The sun was dead center in the sky, and not a single cloud stood in its way. He could almost feel its heat sting the woman's skin and suck its fluids to the surface. Her back glistened with sweat, and his mind focused on the image of a single bead oozing from its pore, swelling like a tear, and coating itself with her perfumed oils. Oh, to be that bead, he thought, to slide down that flesh, to move ever so slowly down the valley of her spine to the small of her back, where he would pool with the others and wait for her to grow restless, wait for that first perceptible contraction of muscle, that first sign of movement, that first sign that she might stretch and roll and spill him onto the smooth rise of her ass, roll him to its summit and then down its slick slope, leaving his snail's trace as he slipped into the crevice, slipped into the dark warm places between her legs. . . .

"Mistah Brecht?"

Brecht twitched.

"Mistah Arlis Brecht, please?"

Oh, please, not now.

"Mistah Arlis Brecht?"

"Yes?"

"Ah, it's you, sir. Yes, sir, telephone."

"What?"

"Yes, sir, a telephone message for you."

He looked back to the woman, who began to stir. "Yes, I'm sorry, what did you say?"

"A message, sir."

"Well, what is it?"

"What is what, sir?"

The woman reached back and pulled the slight, slick bottom of her bathing suit over the cheeks of her buttocks and sat up.

"Sir?" the bellman interrupted.

Brecht's eyes snapped back, squinting hard over the rims of his dark glasses. "Yes, well, what is it?"

"The telephone, sir."

"You said that. What's the message?"

"I don't know, sir. It's for you, sir."

Again his eyes were drawn to her as her hands spread perspiration and suntan oil over her arms, breasts, and thighs.

"Sir?"

"Oh, for Christ's sake," Brecht spouted, "what is it? What's the message?"

"The message, sir, is the telephone, sir. For you, sir. Inside."

"You mean someone is holding on the line?"

"Yes, sir. Inside the bar, sir."

"Then why in blazes . . ." Brecht stopped suddenly, the bellman's expression obviously divided between fear and bewilderment. "Thank you," Brecht said. "I'm sorry, I was thinking of something else. Whatever." He reached into the pocket of his white terry robe for a tip; the bellman accepted it with a nod and backed away. Brecht then gathered his unopened biography of Henry James and his robe and started gingerly across the bright white fry pan of a beach. "Ooo, ah, ooo, ooo, ah, damn, ooo, ah!"

Reaching the cool tiles of the shaded bar, he called out, "Is there a call for me? Arlis Brecht?"

The barman answered with a silent finger pointed to a phone sitting on a table in the far corner. Brecht nodded. "A vodka and lime, please," he said, as he moved to the table.

"Hello?"

"Arlis, is that you?"

"Yes."

"Arlis, do you have any idea how long I've been holding for you?"

Brecht sighed audibly as he recognized the voice of Arkady Treshkov, former head of West European Operations for the Komitet Gosudarstvennoy Bezopasnosti, the KGB, now retired and turned businessman. "Hours, I hope," Brecht mumbled.

"I beg your pardon?"

"What is it? Why didn't you just leave a message? I do know how to dial a phone, you know."

"Well, we are in a bit of a snit today, aren't we? I do hope I haven't disrupted your tan time."

"I take it this is important."

"Yes, Arlis, it is most important."

"Well?"

"We have a problem."

"Oh?"

"Yes, I'm afraid so. I've received an inquiry from Yury Khavkin."

"What?" Brecht was alarmed at the mention of Yury Khavkin, former colonel in the Soviet Special Forces, who like Treshkov had retired to join the swelling ranks of Russian entrepreneurs.

"Yes," Treshkov confirmed. "From Khavkin himself. It seems the partners in Kaliningrad have gotten wind of the trade."

"What trade?"

"What trade? What do you mean what trade? What trade do you think?"

Brecht took an impatient breath. "I take it you're referring to the scandium?" Brecht said, referring to the rare earth metal mined in central Russia, which, in addition to its more benign uses, was an important ingredient in nuclear-research reactors. Because it could be easily broken down into small, one-pound units, each of which could bring profits well in excess of thirty thousand dollars, scandium was quickly becoming one of the favored commodities of Russia's black marketeers, among whom Yury Khavkin and his agent broker, Arkady Treshkov, counted themselves and their partnership if not the largest, certainly one of the most organized and successful of the syndicates.

"Of course the scandium," said Treshkov. "What's wrong with you?"

Brecht hesitated, then asked, "What exactly did Khavkin want?"

"What do you bloody well think he wanted? They've been told Iberia sponsored the sale. He wants to know if that's true."

"What did you tell him?"

"That I would check, obviously."

"When?"

"When what?"

"When did you get this inquiry?"

"Yesterday. But he had been trying to reach me for a week. He did not sound pleased."

"I see."

"I certainly hope so, Arlis. I certainly hope that you see our situation clearly."

There was a long pause while Arlis Brecht considered his options. "Well," he started slowly, "I think the problem is easily resolved."

"Really?" Treshkov asked with obvious skepticism.

"Yes. Listen to me, Arkady. Simply tell Khavkin the truth."

"What?"

"Yes, I understand what a novel concept that must be, but—"

"What are you talking about?"

"Look, just tell him the truth, or at least so much of the truth as will not compromise us. Tell him that Iberia was not behind the trade. As far as we know, Grehm ran it on his own. You were not aware of the problem, because I had not said anything to you. I was trying to track down exactly what Grehm had done and where the money was before alerting you. It's mostly true. A small lie, but a reasonable one. And, if you think it necessary, tell him that you have talked with me and, if we find that the problem was strictly with Grehm, I can credit their account with what should have been their commission. But you might also suggest that their own people may have been involved. There's no sense just giving away our money."

"Well, I'm not sure that it wouldn't be wiser simply to pay the commission to keep things quiet. We don't want Khavkin's people to start looking too closely."

"Yes, well, that is a point. By the way, have you made any progress in tracking down those account numbers?"

"Yes, which is the second and more serious problem."

"What do you mean?"

"Well, there were two cutouts used, but apparently most of the funds landed in a trading house in Brussels."

"Which one?" Brecht asked

"Barzini's."

"Well, well, that is interesting, isn't it?"

"I would say that it's far more disturbing than interesting," Treshkov huffed. "Grehm used at least one partnership account that I controlled, or at least I thought I did. And the second account he used could easily be traced to both of us if anyone cared to look close enough."

"Really? And no one asked any questions?"

"Grehm had to have had the codes, which raises a serious question in itself."

"I see. And how much are we talking about?"

"About 3.6 million U.S."

"Is that all?"

"I understand it's not much, Arlis, but the problem is not the amount."

Brecht paused. "Yes, I suppose you're right. Are the funds still on account?"

"No, which is why I say we have a serious problem."

"Meaning?"

"Meaning that the funds were wired to a numbered account in Berne."

"When?"

"The day after Grehm's body was identified."

"What?"

"That's right, Arlis, the day *after!*"

"Oh, Jesus."

"Yes, now you see, don't you? The problem goes beyond the Grehms."

"Oh, Jesus," Brecht repeated. "And you heard all this from Khavkin?"

"No, I ran most of it down myself. Khavkin doesn't know anything about the money. Not yet, at least. He only knows that someone out of Iberia brokered this scandium deal using the partnership name and authority."

Brecht thought a moment, then mumbled, almost to himself, "At least that's all Khavkin says he knows."

"What?"

"And Berne? Have you checked with the bank in Berne?"

"I have a contact checking now. Hopefully, I will have some answers in a day or two."

The barman delivered Brecht his vodka and lime, from which he took a long swallow before saying, "The question, then, is who were the Grehms working with?"

"Precisely."

Brecht hesitated. "This *is* serious."

"Yes, I'd say so. Arlis, I think it's time for you to get back here."

"Hmmm, perhaps."

"Perhaps? What the hell do you mean, perhaps? No, Arlis, there's no perhaps about it. Our ship is springing leaks. They have to be plugged. When can you get here?"

"You mean Lisbon?"

"No, I'm in Washington."

"I was planning on heading straight back to Lisbon."

"Then change your plans. When can you get here?"

"Look, I'd just as soon stay out of Washington if I can. Why not meet me in Lisbon?"

"Because I have business here that I cannot leave. At least not yet."

Brecht released a long sigh. "Well, it doesn't matter. That's what the phones are for, after all. Besides, I can get a lot more done in Lisbon without you constantly badgering me."

"Be careful, Arlis. I am not in the mood for your humor."

"I am not trying to be humorous, I am dead serious. I understand the situation, but to deal with it properly I need to be in Lisbon. Now, what about Khavkin?"

"I think I have that under control for the time being, but we are going to have to come up with some answers soon, and I doubt that Khavkin will be satisfied with any answer that does not include what should have been his commission."

"Well, don't even mention a commission unless you have to. This isn't a charity, you know."

"Listen to me, Arlis. This is no time to be niggardly. We can't afford a quarrel with Khavkin right now."

"Yes, well, I suppose you're right, but I wish just once you could understand that it isn't so easy to juggle the accounts. If my people were to come in for a full audit, I'm not so sure how much I could hide. I'd much rather have Khavkin's boys nosing around."

Treshkov laughed. "Yes, accounting and finance never were the strength of our glorious revolution, were they?"

"Not hardly. Anyway, if it comes down to it, I suppose I can engineer some losses on future trades to make up the difference."

"Hmmm," Treshkov murmured, "you always make me just a bit nervous when you say such things. But I understand that you are only joking. Imagine how unpleasant our business could get if you were not."

"Whatever," Arlis said. "And by the way?"

"Yes?"

"What about the man with Helen Grehm's bank card? Any progress in finding him?"

"I've taken care of that."

"Oh, really? You've found something?"

"Not yet, but you needn't concern yourself. I am dealing with that issue. What you need to concern yourself with is finding out exactly what the Grehms were up to and who else may be involved. Understand?"

"Yes, I suppose you're right."

"Remember, Arlis, the Grehms were your choice, your people. Ultimately you will have to take responsibility for them."

"I am painfully aware of that fact, thank you very much."

"So, when can I expect to hear from you?"

"Give me a few days."

"Fine. Shall we say by Wednesday, then?"

"All right."

"One thing more," Treshkov added.

"What's that?"

"I think you should immediately order a change to all the account codes. Obviously there is someone out there who either has been given the access codes or has somehow devised a method to crack your system. You have to cut them off immediately."

Brecht considered a moment. "No, I think that would be a mistake."

"What? A mistake? Arlis, you can't be serious."

"Listen to me, Arkady. We've already blocked the trading codes, so there's no chance of their being used again. As far as the account codes, they're the only chance we'll ever have of tracking down whoever's out there. I'll arrange alerts for all those accounts, so I'll be notified directly of any transfers or withdrawals. We may lose a few dollars here or there, but I don't know any other way to track this down. Besides, I can't very well change all the bank codes without alerting my people in Washington, and that will certainly prompt them to ask all sorts of questions we don't want to answer. We need to clean up our own mess, don't you agree?"

There was a brief pause before Arkady answered, "Yes, well, perhaps you're right. But you listen to me, Arlis, and listen carefully. This is a very serious business. I hope you understand just how serious. You need to do whatever it takes to resolve this matter, and quickly. Do you understand?"

"I understand," Brecht said, as a cool uncomfortable feeling crawled down his back, and without more he hung up the phone. He emptied his glass in a single swallow, then turned and looked out toward the beach. The woman was gone.

Oh, Helen, you and your Paris. What have you done to me?

4.

Eddie Nickles sat in the far corner of his back porch, away from the other celebrants of his daughter's graduation, away from the feeling of being at the center of something in which he had no part. For days he had asked Priscilla what he could do to help, but she had just kissed him on the cheek and said, "Thanks, but you don't need to worry. Mom's taken care of everything."

Eddie looked to the dock and to the repairs he had finished just that morning. Rotted planks had been replaced and rough edges had been planed and sanded. Popped nails had been pulled and new nails driven and countersunk and the holes filled and smoothed over with a waterproof putty so it could be walked barefoot or sat on without the worry of splinters or snagged shorts or scraped thighs. The old Boston Whaler his father once used for fishing had been scrubbed clean and outfitted with a new outboard motor powerful enough to pull the new water skis he had purchased just for the occasion.

That he had been assured the party was to be fully catered had not stopped Eddie from imagining hot dogs and hamburgers and paper plates and soda; maybe even a keg of beer to go with the bushel of steamed crabs he had bought. Kids would go swimming off the dock and ski behind the Whaler and turn the record player just loud enough to annoy the distant neighbors. But he had never imagined this, never the bright striped party tent or the portable dance floor, not the cloth-covered tables and strings of lights and propane-fired grills and steam tables filled with sliced beef and baked ham and fried and barbecued chicken. He had never imagined young men in waistcoats circulating trays of hors d'oeuvres and pink champagne; nor had he expected his daughter and her friends and her friends' friends and her friends' families to be decked out in sundresses and Capezios and madras blazers and Docksiders and altogether oblivious to the Whaler bobbing gently and alone at the end of the dock.

Priscilla had dragged him from group to group, introducing him to all the people he should have known but did not. Eddie made the effort, spending what seemed to him hours straining for conversation until he could strain no more, and he slid into the background, leaving Priscilla and her friends vibrating to the sounds of a live band, which for all the world looked to him like some lost tribe found living under a bridge. There, in his quiet corner, he entertained himself with a cold beer and the typewritten report prepared by Garland Bolles. It struck him in an odd way that the victims Bolles had brought to him seemed very much like these strangers now gathered on the lawn where he had grown up, people from different worlds than his own, people into whose lives he had been invited and with whom he would be involved, but only temporarily and only out of necessity.

Trevor Grehm was, according to Bolles's report, a forty-two-year-old Englishman who had traveled frequently in his job with the Iberia Trading Company, a small brokerage house trading principally in spices and other agricultural products. There was no driver's license or other identification found on his body. A business card found on the floor of his rental car had led the police to a branch office of Iberia located in a small building on Capitol Hill, and after several phone calls, the employees there directed the police to the home office, which in turn directed them to the house where Helen Scott Grehm's body was found.

The people at Iberia reported that they had been unaware of Trevor's return to Washington and that he had not been in the office at any time prior to his body being discovered. Trevor's body—

like that of his wife, who had no immediate family—had been identified by the president of Iberia Trading, one Arlis Brecht, who, at the request of the Grehm family in London, had made all arrangements for the shipment of the bodies for burial in England.

Helen Grehm, thirty-eight, had been an employee of Regent's International, a company based in London which specialized in the leasing and swapping of elegant estates and vacation homes throughout Europe, the United States, and the Caribbean. She, like her estranged husband, traveled extensively in her work. Her employers, Bolles reported, had not heard from Helen for more than two weeks prior to her death, and said that there would have been no business purpose for her having traveled back to Washington. There was speculation, however, that she and Trevor might have been trying to patch up their marriage.

According to Bolles, the autopsy on Trevor Grehm established that he had died of a single gunshot wound to the heart and that there had been a "burn pattern," as Bolles called it, indicating that the muzzle of the gun had been pressed to Grehm's chest when fired. The weapon was identified only as a nine-millimeter semi-automatic, and Eddie wondered that there was no notation of the gun's make or model number. Perhaps Bolles, inexperienced in these matters, considered such information superfluous.

That same weapon, according to the police, according to Bolles, fired a matching nine-millimeter bullet that struck Helen Grehm just to the left of the sternum and killed her. There were no burn marks on the wife's body or clothing, indicating that the gun was fired from some distance—a few feet at least, Eddie speculated, and probably more.

Eddie wondered about the estimated time of Helen's death. No autopsy or toxicology reports were included among Bolles's papers. Bolles did, however, reference what he called a "bug report" prepared by a forensic entomologist from the University of Maryland who was routinely consulted in cases in which the passage of time and the environmental conditions surrounding the body made a reasonable estimate of the precise time of death possible only by analyzing the presence of flies and the developmental stages of their deposited eggs. It was obvious to Eddie, though not explicitly stated by Bolles, that Helen Grehm's body had been found in some advanced stage of decay. Bolles's report said only that the three-day delay in discovering Helen's body and the unusual warmth of the room in which it had been found—the thermostat, apparently, had been turned up high—had turned the flesh black and bloated and rendered her "visually unrecognizable." Eddie imagined that Bolles would consider it an unnecessary exercise in bad taste to impose upon the reader any detailed discussion of the processes of decomposition and putrefaction and the laying of fly eggs in their usual patterns around the nose, mouth, eyes, and rectal and vaginal openings. Bolles did, however, detail the ultimate conclusions of the entomologist derived from an analysis of the generations of larval growth and maggots advanced to their hard-shelled, brownish pupa form: Helen Grehm was estimated to have died sometime early on the evening of Monday, April 25, at least six to eight hours before the attempted use of her ATM card was recorded by the bank-surveillance camera at Mount Vernon Square, several miles away, and some forty-eight hours or more before Trevor Grehm's body was first discovered at the police impoundment lot.

Cecil the Seasick Sea Serpent and the ATM card. Neither one fit. Helen Grehm had been murdered in her estranged husband's house in the 4500 Block of Q Place, Northwest, a quiet middle-class neighborhood nestled between the mansions of Foxhall and the Georgetown Reservoir. Her husband's body was found two days later, an apparent suicide with the same weapon that killed his wife. In between, and just hours after her death, Helen's ATM card showed up at a bank halfway across the city, in the hands of a snaggle-toothed black man.

Eddie wondered. A scavenger? A small-time burglar unlucky or lucky enough to have stumbled upon the aftermath of a murder, who saw Helen's body and split with whatever he could easily and quickly take, such as her wallet?

It was the easiest theory, the one to which the department most probably had attached itself, the one least likely to disturb their murder-suicide hypothesis, and the one that would allow them to close the case without more. But a scavenger, coming all the way across the city to choose a small house in a small neighborhood?

No, it didn't compute; no more than did a man's killing his wife and then, a day and a half later, driving to a downtown location to commit suicide.

Eddie looked up from Bolles's report to see his ex-wife walking slowly across the grass, then onto the porch, where she approached him and sat down without a word. Eddie, almost as if he had been caught at something unseemly, laid the report face down on the floor. "Megs," he said.

She smiled slightly and shook her head.

"What?" Eddie asked.

"Nothing. It's just been a long time. 'Megs.' You're the only one who ever called me that."

"Margaret, then. Sorry."

"No, no, I didn't mean anything. I . . . Oh, it doesn't matter."

A long silence followed until Eddie squirmed a bit in his chair and looked away. "This is quite a bash you're putting on, you and Marty," he said, referring to Megs's husband.

"Martin."

"Jesus, okay, Martin!" He paused, then tried again. "He seems like a good guy."

"He is."

Eddie took a long swig of beer.

"That's not a comparison, Eddie. He's just nice, that's all."

"You must be doing real well, you know, to be able to do all this."

"Is that why you're over here pouting?"

"Whaddaya talkin' about? I'm not pouting. I'm just, you know, relaxing."

"Look, Eddie, it's not only us. The Bermans, the Hartages, the Duttons, we all chipped in."

Eddie nodded but said nothing.

"We thought it'd be better to let the kids have one big party, you know, instead of having them running around—"

He stopped her with an annoyed shake of his head. "It's not that. I just . . . You know, I don't know all these people. I just thought I'd sit down and have a beer, that's all." Eddie shifted uneasily. "You look great, Megs."

She did, too. She was thinner than Eddie remembered her being at their last meeting, almost two years before, and she was tanned, and her hair was styled as he had never seen it. She seemed a stranger, but, still, she was and always would be the same young and hesitant girl he had first seduced in the sand dunes above Thirty-fifth Street in Ocean City, after whom he had never stopped lusting, even long after she had thrown him out of the house. Even now. Megs let her eyes drop to her lap, where she folded her hands primly, and Eddie said, "I don't mean anything, you know. I just mean you look, you know, well."

She smiled without looking up. "Thank you." She took a deep breath and the smile faded. "Look, Eddie, please don't take this the wrong way, but . . . well, I think Priscilla's a little upset . . . about the car."

"She doesn't like it?" Eddie asked abruptly, as if suddenly stabbed. Within hours of his getting the cashier's check from Garland Bolles, Eddie had endorsed it over to the local Ford dealer as a down payment on a bright-red Mustang convertible. The car had been delivered that morning with a large satin bow attached to its hood, and presented to Priscilla as a graduation gift.

"Oh, no, she loves it. She really does. She's overwhelmed. So am I, for that matter. It was really sweet of you. She's . . . well, she's just worried, I think."

"About what?"

"Well, I think maybe she thinks you can't afford it."

"What, she thinks I stole the thing?"

"Now, don't start getting angry at me."

"Why should I get angry? You're just sitting there telling me I can't buy my daughter a graduation present."

"No one's said that. It's Pris. You know how she gets. She's just worried that maybe . . . Shit, let's just drop it. I'm sorry I said anything."

"No, say it. She's worried that maybe what?"

Megs sighed. "Well, she thinks maybe that you're trying, I don't know, maybe that you're trying somehow to compete with Martin and me . . . maybe. You know, that you really can't afford it."

"Can't afford it?"

"Well, being retired and not working, and with your father and all."

"Is that what she thinks or what you think?"

"Eddie, it's not about you and me anymore."

"Is that what you think?"

"I don't think anything. I don't care anymore."

Eddie's stomach tightened, and he looked away.

"Look," Megs said, leaning a bit closer to him, "I don't mean that I don't care, I just mean that it has nothing to do with me. I hope you hit the lottery and make a million dollars, whatever. But, either way, whether you're rich or flat broke, it has nothing to do with me. Understand?"

"What makes her think I can't afford the car?"

"Eddie, please, she's watched the way you've lived all these years. That apartment of yours. She never understood how you could live like that."

"Like what?"

"Barely any furniture, no pictures on the wall, no curtains or whatever. She said the place always looked like you had just moved in the day before."

"What's she talking about? That place was just fine."

"For you, maybe, but she never understood that. She always thought you were down and out, wondering if we shouldn't be sending you some money. I never said a word to her, not once. I never mentioned all the times you'd forget the alimony and child support."

"I always paid."

"Yes, you did, but not always on time. It was like I had to keep reminding you that we were still here."

Eddie blinked slowly, then looked down and brushed a blade of grass from the toe of his shoe.

"The point is, this isn't about us. It's your daughter. She's eighteen years old, and she hardly knows you, and she's worried, that's all. She's always worried about you, like you were some stray dog I shooed off the property."

"That's a shitty thing to say."

"No, it's not. It's—"

"Look," he quickly interrupted, "I got a job."

"Eddie, listen to me. I'm not asking about your finances. Really, it's none of my business."

"I'm just saying I got a job," Eddie protested. "I can afford the car."

"Don't tell me, tell Priscilla."

"She's really upset?"

"Just talk to her, all right?"

Eddie nodded and shuffled his feet a bit. "I'm sorry the boys didn't get back for this."

"Me, too," Megs said, again lowering her eyes. "It just didn't work out, that's all."

Carl, Eddie's older son, was twenty-five, a deputy with a local sheriff's department in eastern Oregon who had never forgiven all the sins he was certain his father had committed. They had not spoken in almost three years. Tom, twenty-three, never held grudges, even if he had cause. He was simply different, someone on whom Eddie just couldn't get a grasp. At eighteen and barely two months shy of graduating from high school with nearly an A average, Tom had found an offer to crew on a forty-five-foot sailing yacht being delivered to the Grenadines more interesting. In the years since, he had found neither the time nor the inclination to get his high-school diploma, nor had he ever asked his parents for help. By all outward appearances, he and his Jamaican girlfriend lived happily in the Florida Keys, aboard a wreck of a fifty-two-foot gaff-rigged schooner forever dry-docked and undergoing repairs financed by odd jobs delivering other people's boats to and from the islands. Eddie wondered if his second son would ever grow up.

A long, uneasy silence fell between them before Megs again leaned forward, as if she were about to say something, and Eddie stopped her with a shake of his head. "I just wanted to do something—I don't know—something special for her. That's all."

"It is, Eddie. Special, I mean. Very special. Like I said, she's just bowled over. She never expected anything like that. Just talk to her. Just let her know she doesn't have to worry about you all the time. All right?" Megs smiled. "I swear, between the two of you, it's sometimes hard to tell who's the parent and who's the child."

Eddie sat back with a sudden frown. "Let me ask you something. Did you know she's set on going to Ocean City tomorrow? Alone, with just her friends? And this boyfriend of hers?"

Megs shrugged. "She's not a little girl anymore."

"Yeah, but . . ."

"She can take care of herself. Trust me."

"But that boyfriend. I mean, that hair and a goddamn earring?"

"Please, don't start. Not today."

"You approve of this?"

"She's all grown up, Eddie. She's not . . . well, she's not a little girl."

"What's that supposed to mean?"

Megs laughed. "I don't remember my virginity being one of your priorities that first weekend in Ocean City. You remember when—"

"Stop!" Eddie blurted out, holding up his hand. "Please. You don't need to say it. You've made your point."

"Same old . . ." Megs said, then stopped and shook her head. She reached over and took the beer from Eddie's hand for a sip. "I went to see your dad this morning."

"Megs, please, don't."

"You really should go see him, Eddie. The day will come when you'll be sorry you didn't."

"What's the point? He doesn't even know you're there."

"How do you know? Maybe he does. Maybe he can hear and understand everything you say, but he just can't let you know it."

"Jesus, you and Pris. The both of you. Why can't you just leave it alone?"

Megs turned her gaze to the water and released a long sigh that trailed into an even longer silence. At last she turned back. "So, you got a job, huh? I thought you were going to take it easy for a while."

"It's just a onetime thing. It'll take a coupla weeks at the most. I got an offer I couldn't refuse."

"Doing what?"

Eddie's expression turned hesitant, almost embarrassed. "Ah, well, you don't wanna know."

Megs nodded, then smiled. "You're right. I probably don't." She stood up and reached her hand out to him. "Come on," she said. "Join the party. Just this once let's pretend we're still a family."

5.

Eddie had been here before, more times than he cared to remember, traveling the back streets of the nation's capital never captured by postcard photographers or Hollywood film crews, where the homes of postal workers and day laborers and government secretaries looked no different from the stash houses of local dope dealers, where the curtains were constantly drawn and the furniture was placed away from the windows, where once-quiet neighborhoods were now free-fire zones.

There had been rules once, but no more. Once, the drug markets were controlled by small local groups whose territories were clearly defined, and, except for the occasional turf war or a "stick-up boy" thinking he could walk off with the bank, the killings were infrequent and of little consequence to anyone but the immediate victims.

Once, the police and the dealers nodded politely to one another, and they stood by their silent agreements. The department ran predictable raids at predictable locations and made the predictable arrests that established their presence and maintained their control. For their part, the dealers kept their activities geographically confined, not letting the street hawkers spill over the boundaries to those neighborhoods where people cared about such things. It wasn't pretty, but it worked.

But the times had changed. Demand was up, and the markets had expanded, creating yet more demand and more competition for more dealers, until the eastern half of the city had become an open drug market attracting the old pros and young Turks from Cottage City to Sursum Corda. They came from New York and they came from Jamaica; they came from Detroit and from Miami, and they conquered. Law enforcement lost all control. It wasn't even a player, except as a service to clear the streets of their bodies. "Operation Clean Sweep," it was called.

Eddie wanted to believe that it was age and experience that gave him the wisdom to be fearful where he had never been fearful before. But it was more than that. It wasn't that the old rules had changed, it was that they had been abandoned completely. Children carried automatic weapons, and cops were fair game, and school yards and playgrounds and a mother's front porch were no more respected than were the back alleys and boarded-up buildings.

He no longer had the power of the badge or the authority to carry a weapon, although both were with him. The jail time he could do if caught carrying these items Eddie balanced against the prospect of working the streets naked and alone. The choice seemed clear. Still, it made him uncomfortable. He had accepted the money and he would do the job, but he wasn't enjoying it, not at all like he thought he might. He didn't miss the streets at all.

It was his fourth night after his fourth day. They had been long days and even longer nights, and he wanted the job finished. He had confined his search for the man with Helen Grehm's ATM card to an area within walking distance of the bank at Mount Vernon Square, quartering those sections of the city like a gundog working a field, searching out old snitches and screening new sources.

It was early, just past dark, and a small group of young men barely out of their teens looked questioningly over its collective shoulder, no doubt suspicious of the lone white man in the beat-up Oldsmobile who had parked at the curb near the Golden Rule Market and who walked slowly to a phone booth as if this was his corner, as if this was his phone booth. The young men turned back to their huddle and exchanged a few words, and a few turned to look again; but no one said a word and no one made a move.

Eddie was accustomed to the reaction. It wasn't his size that gave people pause, although his barrel chest and solid waist and thick hands and forearms made his physical presence imposing. It was the look he carried when he went on the street, a certain dark look about his dark eyes, which were perpetually guarded by a half-squint, as if he suspected everyone of everything, a shadowy look not even his graying hair and ruddy tan could lighten. His mother had once told him that first impressions were the most important. Eddie had taken that lesson to heart. He had cultivated the pose over so many years that he was no longer conscious of making the effort: it was simply part of him. On the street, Eddie Nickles looked exactly like he wanted to look, exactly like he wanted to be. On the street, Eddie Nickles was a man with an attitude, a man who caused others to think twice.

Eddie kept the door to the phone booth open and stood only partially inside as he dialed a number from a small, dog-eared notebook he held up to the light.

"Speak," said the voice at the other end.

"T?"

There was a long pause before the voice said, "Who's askin'?"

"A man with a very long memory."

Another silence followed, and then, "It's a bad time, y'know?"

"Not so bad as that night on Acker Street," Eddie said.

"Shit . . . Look, man, how 'bout tomorrow?"

"How 'bout five minutes, in front of the Golden Rule?"

"How 'bout you kiss my ass?"

"How 'bout you name a place, then."

Another pause, and then the voice spoke away from the phone. "Baby, how 'bout you fixing me somethin' to eat. . . . Awright, then, take a shower, whatever. I got business here. . . . No, baby, now."

"So?" Eddie asked.

"Gimme a minute."

Eddie waited.

Finally, "Man, there's nothin' happening, nothin' to talk about. What's your hurry?"

"Just business."

"Not my business."

"My business," Eddie said. "Tell me where."

"Man, I ain't got time for this tonight, you know what I'm sayin'?"

"Won't take long. Fifteen minutes, tops."

"Shit."

"I'm waiting."

"Yeah, yeah, awright."

"Where?"

"Yeah, okay, the old place, up on the Hill. You remember?"

"Yeah, I remember."

"Just you 'n' me, right?"

"Yeah, just you 'n' me. No hassles, just looking for a favor."

"This favor can't wait?"

"No. Gotta do it tonight."

"Okay, just this time. Give me 'bout twenty minutes. You ride with me."

"Whaddaya drivin'?"

"A Volvo."

"Give me a color."

"Black, like always."

"All right, twenty minutes."

It was just twenty minutes, and Eddie was stepping out of his car, when the black Volvo pulled alongside. The car barely stopped, and Eddie jumped in as it pulled away.

"Nice ride," Eddie said.

The tall man in a gray silk suit and open collared shirt, looked over with disdain. His name was Jean St. Jean Toussaint, also known as Johnny Easy, also known as Johnny Two Cheeks. Eddie, and Eddie alone, called him "T." "Shit," T sneered, "I only use this for running errands. You know, of the unpleasant kind."

"And here I thought we were old friends."

T looked over and stroked his full and neatly trimmed beard. Several small diamonds set in gold on his dark and manicured right hand sparkled in the light from the streetlamps. "Man, if we weren't, I wouldn't be here."

Eddie frowned. "What's that mean?"

"What, like since we haven't talked for mostly a year, I'm not supposed to know you're retired?"

Eddie didn't answer. He simply nodded and said, "Yeah, well, I appreciate it."

"Yeah, man, like you ever heard the word 'please'? Calling me up with that old bullshit."

"Like I said, I 'preciate it."

"Yeah, okay, but, like, don't go makin' this a habit, y'know?"

"No problem. Just a onetime thing, you know?"

"You remember that, what you just said, 'cause like I will remember, you know what I'm sayin'?"

"I understand."

"So," T said, turning off the quiet jazz on his CD player, "what's this all about? Like I told ya, I ain't got time for no chitchattin' down memory lane."

"I'm looking for a man."

"Yeah, well, like that's news?"

"This man," Eddie said, pulling a copy of the ATM photograph from his pocket and handing it to T.

T pulled his car to the curb near the entrance to the Marine Corps Barracks. He flipped on the map light to study the photograph. He then looked at Eddie with a curious frown. "This personal?"

"Nah, just business."

"So, what, you hiring yourself out?"

"Call it a favor."

T shook his head. "Never figured you for that shit."

Eddie said nothing for a moment. Then, with a shrug, "So, whaddaya think? You know the guy?"

T thought a moment. "If I did, he ain't the one you're lookin' for."

"What's that mean?"

"The man ain't no shooter."

"Whaddaya talkin' 'bout?"

"This got somethin' to do with the dude got towed away from downtown, am I right?"

Eddie smiled broadly. "Ya see what I'm sayin'? Like, what the fuck am I doing wastin' night after night shuckin' 'n' jivin' with back-alley trash when all I gotta do is come see my man Johnny T? Shoulda known right off."

"Yeah, well, it ain't like it's no big secret. Word is been lotsa people lookin' for him."

Eddie frowned. "Like who?"

"Don't know who, just know they's lookin'."

"How's that?"

"Shit, black children dying every day, and you gotta get past twenty pages of discount-furniture ads to find it in the paper. But a coupla white folks from Northwest die and suddenly ever'body's innerested."

"Who's everybody? The police?"

"Don't know 'bout the police, but word is been lotsa questions asked. White dudes, strangers, people that don't fit, know what I'm sayin'?"

"But you got no idea who it is?"

"Strangers, that's all."

"How many?"

"A few . . . maybe the same people over 'n' over. I dunno. I ain't innerested. Not my business."

"And the man, he's runnin'?"

"He thinks he is, when he's awake."

"Meaning?"

"Look, the dude's chump change, you know what I'm sayin'? His whole life he prob'ly never crossed the Rock Creek Park."

"Meaning he's layin' up in his crib, just waitin' for the shit to come down on his head."

"Question is," T said, "why's ever'body lookin'? The man I know'd get lost on K Street. Can't see him lookin' for some house up past Georgetown, and he wouldn't know how to get in one if he did."

"Funny, I was thinking the same thing."

"That's right."

"And?"

"And nothin'."

Eddie thought a moment. "Listen, both victims, the woman in the house and the man in the car, they were both shot with a nine-millimeter automatic. They found it in the car with the husband's body. I know a nine-millimeter ain't exactly unusual these days, but if this was the guy, he ever carry a piece like that?"

"Haw!" T laughed in a sudden burst. "Man, this dude ever got his hands on a piece like that, he'd marry it . . . or sell it. Damn sure he'd never leave it behind."

Eddie smiled. "So?"

"So why's ever'body lookin' for him?"

"Word is he got hold of the lady's bank card, try to run it through the machine."

T chuckled. "Fool prob'ly was lookin' for Michael on the jukebox."

Eddie laughed, too. "So whaddaya think?"

T shook his head. "Shit, I dunno. Don't make any sense."

Eddie nodded. "So tell me, T, am I gonna find him or what?"

"If you do, what ja gonna do with him?"

"Ask him where he got the bank card."

"And then?"

"And listen to what he tells me."

T hesitated, his eyes fixed on Eddie. "Tell me again, what's your play in all this?"

"The man's family. They want to know what happened to their son, and the police can't tell 'em. And, you know, I could use the money."

T smiled and shook his head knowingly. "Yeah, tell me about it. I got a daughter startin' college in a coupla months."

"No shit," Eddie said. "Me, too."

"No lie?"

"Square business. My little girl's going to Duke University."

T grinned. "Imagine that. You 'n' me. We both got blood that's gonna make somethin' of themselves." He shook his head again. "Imagine that." He turned off the map light and handed Eddie the copy of the bank photo. "You know where N Street triangles right there at New York, just above North Capitol?"

Eddie nodded. "Yeah, I know the place."

" 'Bout halfway up from the corner, on the left. Red brick with a metal stoop and a 'Jesus Saves' cross in the window. You're lookin' for the Apple Lady. Anyone asks, that's all you say. You're lookin' for the Apple Lady. When you find her, it's on the third floor in the back. There's a dude layin' up there with a snagged tooth, just like the man in the picture. Go early, before dark. And you might want to bring a little somethin' to keep him down, you know what I'm sayin'? You roust 'im before he's had a chance to score, he won't even see you for all the snakes that'll be crawlin' his walls."

Eddie paused a moment, then asked, "Can you help me out with that?"

T's brow furrowed deeply. "Not so easy being on the outside, huh?"

"Nah," Eddie said, "not so easy."

T nodded and lowered the sun visor. He then slid his fingernails under one edge of the visor and snapped it open to display a half-dozen small, flat aspirin tins. He considered a moment, then took one and opened it. "This'll do," he said as he handed Eddie two small yellow pills marked on one side with a "K" and on the other side with a "4."

Eddie slipped the eight milligrams of Dilaudid into his jacket pocket. "Thanks, man. By the way, our friend got a name?"

"LeRoi. Not Lee-roy, mind you, but LeRoi. You know, like the king." T laughed. "One sorry-ass mutha, but he won't fight you. He'll lie to you up one side and down another, but he won't fight you. One sorry-ass muthafucka."

"He anything to you?"

"Not a thing."

"What's he do?"

" 'Sides dope and runnin' his mouth?"

"Yeah."

"Runs errands when he can find 'em. Mostly got his head in trash cans like an old stray dog. Got an ol' lady almost as nasty as him keeps him dry."

"Will she be there?"

"Prob'ly not. But if she is, won't be any trouble. Give ya some mouth, but she'll walk away from it. Won't be any trouble. Just ask for the Apple Lady. She'll know what to do."

"I owe you," Eddie said.

"Yeah, you do. And don't think I won't remember."

Eddie nodded. "I know you will," he said, and then he smiled. "Like I remember Acker Street."

Eddie rammed the heel of his hand against the top of the window, loosening and shoving it as wide as it would go, hoping some air might relieve the stench of the room. LeRoi sat on the corner of his mattress clutching a gray, grime-rotted bedsheet about his naked body, his back shoved against the wall. He shook as if chilled by the hint of fresh air, and the sweat rolled from his neck and down the center of his sunken chest.

Eddie shook his head. "You wanna take a shower before you go downtown?"

"Downtown?"

"LeRoi, please don't make me go through the bullshit. I know you been inside before. Am I right?"

LeRoi's head bobbed erratically, his eyes squinting, then widening and darting about the room for an answer that just would not come to him.

"You know I'm the man, right? . . . LeRoi, look at me, man. You know it's time, right?"

"Time?"

"Yeah, man. It's time."

LeRoi nodded, then shook his head, then nodded again. "Time?"

"Look, man, I can go through the motions and all. Y'know, read the rights, go through the questions, but, like I say, I've been talkin' to folks 'bout you. You're a stand-up kinda guy, am I right?"

LeRoi's head bounced vigorously. "That's right."

"So I figured, Hell, why hassle the man, y'know? I mean, we get the bullshit over real quick, get you settled in. You know, a hot shower, fresh set of jumpers, three squares, get you down to Lorton, see some of your home boys. Y'know, no hassles. I mean, what the fuck, you gotta pull some real serious time on this one, so I said to myself, Why not let the man do it right? Relaxed, y'know what I'm sayin'? 'Sides, man, like it's nothin' personal, ya unnerstand, but this place—for real, man—this place is a shithouse. You payin' rent here?"

"Yeah, you know, like when I got it."

"I unnerstand. Landlords. Sumbitches take your money, and what do they give ya? Know what I'm sayin'?"

"You right, man. Ain't give me shit. You right."

"Shit, even the man down at Lorton keeps the place clean. Like the Hilton Hotel compared to this joint. I mean, like I'm not tryin' to insult ya or nothin'."

"I unnerstand. You right, man. Shit, Lorton. You right."

"So, whaddaya say, LeRoi? You ready to go or what?"

"Yeah, man, okay . . . Guess it's time, right?"

"It's time, LeRoi. And let me tell ya. It makes me happy we can talk together like gentlemen, you know what I'm sayin'? Like I heard you were a stand-up guy, and I appreciate it. Square business."

"Yeah, okay, that's cool. . . . So, like, it's time, huh?"

"It's time, LeRoi."

"Yeah, well, like I unnerstand 'n' all . . . but, y'know, like I ain't zackley certain what it is . . . you know, like what it is I done so that I gotta, you know, do this time."

Eddie let out a low groan and pulled a bare wooden chair over to the edge of the bed, where he turned it backward and sat down. "Oh, LeRoi, now look what you gone and done. I'm disappointed. Truly."

"No, no, man. Look, see, like I unnerstand. No hassle, man, no bullshit. Square business, I'll do the time. Stand-up, like you say. Yeah, man, gonna do the time. Just like, you know, like I'm feeling kinda sick right now, you know what I'm sayin'? I think it's the flu, kinda got the shakes 'n' all. So like I ain't altogether unnerstandin', you know? Like it ain't no problem my doing the time. That's cool. Just like I don't altogether unnerstand like what it is I done."

"Feeling sick, are ya?"

"Yeah, man, real sick. The flu, y'know?"

"LeRoi, please. I've been straight with you. Am I right?"

LeRoi nodded quickly, his whole body shaking.

"So I mean, you know, like I'd appreciate it if you wouldn't insult me like that. Okay?"

He nodded again.

"You're strung out, right? . . . Am I right?"

"Yeah," LeRoi said, his eyes lowering and his face turning away.

"So, LeRoi, all you had to do is say so. Like maybe I can help. Least make it a little easier until you get settled in the joint. How 'bout a D? Will that help?"

Eddie reached into his pocket for one of the tablets, which he held out to the skeletal remains of a man whose once-dark skin had turned gray and loose, whose arms, hands, and thighs were heavily scarred and marked with sores both old and open. LeRoi stared at the Dilaudid but did not reach for it. His body started rocking with whatever thoughts were shuffling through the haze.

"Nah . . . man, you know . . . you're the man."

"LeRoi, I'm just trying to help. What, you think I'm settin' you up? Is that what you think?" LeRoi continued to stare at the pill. "Look, man, if I wanted, you're already set up, y'know what I'm sayin'? I mean, here you are and here's the D. You think I'd come up here for a lousy dope beef? Man, I just thought you'd want a little help before we went downtown. It's gonna be some time, what with the paperwork 'n' all. You want to go cold, that's okay. Just trying to help."

The man's body started to shake more violently, his sweat profuse, his confusion profound and evident in his eyes.

"LeRoi, you do know why I'm taking you in, don't you? I mean, you know what this is about, right?"

The word came softly, almost childlike. "No."

"LeRoi, you killed two white folks. You shot the lady in her house. Remember? Up there off MacArthur Boulevard, on Q Place. And then the man. You left him in his car downtown. Now, LeRoi, that wasn't a smart thing to do, you know, leaving the man in his car like that. Anyway, we know it was you, 'cause, see, we got your picture when you tried to use the lady's bank card. See?" Eddie pulled the folded photograph from his pocket and laid it out on the bed in front of the man. "See what I'm sayin'?" LeRoi's eyes widened. "Yeah, man, it was the tooth. Nothin' personal, ya unnerstand, but that's a bad tooth you got there. Kinda hard to miss. Lookit there, right there in the picture. You know, when you get down to the joint, like you oughta see if the dentist can't do something 'bout that tooth."

The man's eyes darkened and he began to rock more violently and his arms closed in on his stomach.

"That's right, LeRoi. First-degree, two counts."

"Aaaaaah, shit, man, shit, aaaah, man, sheeeeeit." He doubled over, and his rheumy eyes began to drain.

"Goddamn it, LeRoi! Don't you start puking, you hear me? I

don't wanna deal with that shit. No, sir, you unnerstand me? Motherfucker, don't you dare start puking! Calm down, man. Here, take a D. Shit, take two. Just calm down. Take it easy."

LeRoi reached anxiously for the one pill and then for the second, which Eddie took from his pocket. "Man, it weren't me," he wept. "Hand to God, man, no lie, it weren't me. Man, I never . . . shit, man, never kilt no white folks. No, sir! Okay, like I done things, y'know? Okay, okay, I done things, no lie, done lotsa things, all kinds a shit. And I'll do my time if that's what's gotta be. But—no lie, man—never, never, never kilt no white folks. Weren't me. Hand to God, man, hand to God!"

Eddie shook his head and spoke quietly. "LeRoi, what am I gonna do with you? Man, I got the picture, you got the tooth. Whaddaya want me to do here? Take you home to meet the family?"

LeRoi curled into a tight ball and pulled the putrid sheet over his shaking body, holding the two pills in one fist clutched to his chest.

"Take the pills, man," Eddie said. "Just take the pills. I'll give you a few minutes to come down, all right? And we'll talk."

It didn't take long for the Dilaudid to work its magic, and Eddie took quick advantage of that narrow window between LeRoi's new state of calm and the point when he would most likely nod out. Eddie pressed and LeRoi responded, each seeking some advantage from the other. His story was simple enough, and, measured against the implausibility of this wasted shell of a man wandering west of Georgetown to kill a woman in her home, and then a day or more afterward killing her husband and leaving his body and the murder weapon behind on a downtown street, his story made some sense.

LeRoi had fallen on hard times. His days as a runner for a local dealer were long past. He couldn't be trusted with a package of dope, using more than he'd sell, and more than once coming up short on the cash. Eddie suspected that it was LeRoi's pathetic insignificance that had saved his life. He simply wasn't worth the cost of a bullet. And so he worked the area of the Convention Center and the upscale hotels nearby, snatching a purse or robbing a drunk whenever the opportunity arose, but generally panhandling the tourists and visiting businessmen.

LeRoi remembered that night—not the month, not the day of the week, not even the time—it was just "that night." He was hurting, he remembered, and he had gone to see his woman, Neecy, who was plying her trade east of Thirteenth Street. Neecy, too, had seen better days, and was left to work the darker blocks, away from the whores who had pimps and fine clothes. But Neecy had soul and a bit of kindness left for him, and she'd usually share a rock or a bag of dope, whatever she may have scored that night. It didn't matter to LeRoi whether he'd go up on crack or down on heroin; whichever way, it had to be better than where he was.

It was crack, he thought, but maybe not, who cared, it made him feel better. Yes, it must have been crack, because he remembered feeling better, so much better he felt up to going back to his corner near the Convention Center. He had just started down the street and was passing some words with Teeter—nasty bitch, that Teeter, nasty mouth, never had a kind word for nobody—when a car came by. Had no idea what kind of car, but it was fine, he remembered that. A fine car, with white dudes in it, and as the car passed he heard something hit the ground, and when he looked it was a purse. A lady's purse. So he went for it. Yeah, it must of been crack, because he remembered fighting Teeter for it. Wouldn't have fought her otherwise. One nasty bitch, that Teeter.

And so he grabbed the purse and took off. Didn't even look in it, at least not until he got to the park, the park down there near the Convention Center. So, when he got to the park, he looked inside. He took his time. There wasn't anybody there, so he took his time going through the purse. It was filled with nothing, bunch of crap no good to anybody except for a wallet, a lady's kind of wallet, one with all those little compartments that each had a snap to it. And some credit cards and things like that. No cash, at least not what you'd expect with people who had credit cards and a fine car like that. Maybe forty, fifty dollars, that's all. So he tossed the purse and kept the wallet. Yeah, sure, he tried to run the bank card through the machine. He weren't no fool. He looked over whatever cards were in the wallet. A driver's license, maybe. Maybe not, he didn't remember. And maybe he used a birth date or maybe he used a street number to try to hit upon the right code—people always use birthdays or addresses or their telephone numbers—but he didn't get much of a chance. A cop car came by.

He remembered it slowing down, and he remembered thinking, No sense being a fool, so he took off, with the wallet, with the cards. Plenty of time to try later, or maybe he'd just sell the cards. He knew lots of people who'd pay good money for the cards. But he could do that later. And so he thought he'd just chill for the night. So he headed on back and he saw his friend Mace, and Mace sold him a bag, and he just went home and fired up. It was a good night.

But then it turned bad. Neecy saw the wallet later, maybe that day, maybe later, he didn't remember, but he did remember her ragging on him about the wallet and how he'd better lose it. She read something in the papers about the white folks that were killed and she put the names together. He told her he'd lose the wallet and the cards. But then word got around that people were looking for him. Not by name or anything, but looking for the man with the tooth and saying it had something to do with the white folks that were killed. Some thought they were cops, but some said they weren't sure, and so he figured he'd better lay real low for a while. But that was weeks ago. He thought it had all blown over.

And the wallet? Yeah, well, he told Neecy he had tossed it somewhere, but he hadn't. He still had it. Back in the corner of the closet, under his things. Hell, those cards still might be worth something. Waste not, want not, that's what LeRoi always said.

Eddie left LeRoi with instructions to stay quiet and to stay put, and with enough money for him to enjoy a bag of dope or a few rocks. Eddie took the wallet and the cards and said he'd do what he could to straighten this business out.

When he hit the street, Eddie drew in a deep breath of fresh air and walked quickly to his car, where he opened the trunk and tossed in his badge, his nine-millimeter Beretta, and Helen Scott Grehm's wallet. His took off his suit jacket and tie and opened both front windows for the long drive home. He was a happy man. He wasn't even thinking about the five-thousand-dollar bonus, he was just glad this job was over.

6.

You haven't reported this to anyone, have you?

The question repeated itself, over and over again, as Eddie stared at a gibbous moon riding high over the flat black river. That morning, during their regular ten o'clock call, Garland Bolles had been impressed, even congratulatory, when Eddie reported his meeting with T the night before. He had listened patiently and without quarrel as Eddie told him not to get his hopes up until he had actually tracked down and talked to LeRoi. But earlier that evening, after Eddie had returned home and called Bolles with the news that he had found LeRoi and recovered Helen Grehm's wallet, the man's patience immediately evaporated.

What was in the wallet? Bolles wanted to know. Specifically, what credit cards, what ATM cards, what condition were they in, was there a driver's license, were there any other papers, any notes? Eddie answered Bolles's questions, one by one, as he handled the wallet and its spare contents carefully, his hands in an old pair of rubber gloves he found under the kitchen sink, gloves he imagined his mother had once used to wash dishes and scour the sink's pitted porcelain.

Bolles asked a second time and directed him to slow down as

Eddie repeated the address where LeRoi had been found. Bolles seemed as uninterested in Eddie's opinion that LeRoi was an unlikely candidate for the killer of Trevor and Helen Grehm as he was in the details of LeRoi's story. It was the contents of the wallet that excited his interest. Could Eddie deliver them that night? If not, Bolles asked, could he send a messenger down to Annapolis to pick them up? And, he added with considerable enthusiasm, he would have Eddie's bonus check delivered at the same time.

"Quite remarkable, Detective. Truly. You certainly are deserving of your reputation, and, of course, your bonus. I am quite impressed that in less than a week you accomplished what the police could not accomplish after all this time and with all their resources. Yes indeed, quite remarkable. I know the Grehms will be delighted. May I have the messenger sent down straightaway?"

But Eddie had balked. "Look, Mr. Bolles, I don't think that's a good idea."

There was a brief pause before Bolles said, "May I ask why not?"

"Well, I'm sure the family is not just interested in the fact that we've found LeRoi and the wallet. I mean, the idea here is that the couple's killer be found and a proper case made, correct?"

"The point . . ." Bolles started, but then he stopped himself. "Well, yes, that's true, but . . ." His voice trailed into an awkward silence.

"Look," said Eddie, "I understand that you're not a criminal lawyer or whatever, so you're not familiar with the procedures. Let me try to explain the problem here. You see, if this case ever gets to court, you've got to worry about what's called the chain of custody. Without going through all the legal mumbo jumbo, the point is that the fewer people involved in handling the wallet, the better. For evidentiary purposes, you understand. Now, I know we talked about my not getting involved directly and letting you deal with the police, but I really think it's better if I deliver the wallet to Homicide and run down what I've found." Eddie waited a moment, but Bolles said nothing. "What I'm saying," he continued, "is that it'd make a cleaner case. Ultimately I'll have to testify anyway, which is no problem, and I wouldn't charge you or the family anything extra for that. I just want to make sure the court case isn't compromised. Okay?"

"Hmm, well, I'd really prefer to see the wallet and inspect its contents myself—as was our understanding—so that I can inform the family, you see."

"All right, well, that's no problem. Why don't we meet in the morning, y'know, before I take it in to Homicide. Afterward, if you want, we can take it over to the homicide office together."

It was then that Bolles asked the question. "You haven't reported this to anyone, have you?"

No, he hadn't, Eddie said, but, once again, he was not concerned whether or not the police knew of his involvement. His only concern was that the police be given the information and the wallet so that they could follow up. He was certain they would.

Bolles pressed, and Eddie pressed back. It was not an argument, but it was not without tension either. Finally, Bolles agreed. They would meet the next morning, and Eddie gave him directions to Chaney's, a less-than-elegant bar and restaurant just a few blocks from police headquarters. "Ten o'clock?"

"Fine," Bolles said sharply, and hung up.

Several hours passed, and Eddie was sitting on his back porch, one of a series of beers in hand, his feet propped on the railing, and rocking his chair to the fidgeting rhythm of the crickets and tree frogs and the hum of the old refrigerator struggling in the background. He was bothered by thoughts of Garland Bolles, bothered by the sudden altered tone of Bolles's voice and by his overriding interest in the least significant details. What did it matter what were the contents of the wallet, compared with locating LeRoi and the contents of his story? Had he been Garland Bolles, the first question asked would have been why the police had not been called and LeRoi arrested and the evidence secured. Eddie had answers, of course, but Bolles never asked the questions. Why?

You haven't reported this to anyone, have you?

The memory of Megs's voice came to him suddenly, her soft voice that was meant to soothe but too often seemed framed in words unspoken. "Why ruin tonight worrying about questions that'll answer themselves tomorrow?" she would ask, and *What could possibly be so important?* he would hear in the language of his marriage. It was true, however, that, one way or the other, the questions that bothered him would either be answered or rendered meaningless in the morning, when he met with Bolles and together they delivered the evidence and information to the police. Still, he could not let those questions go.

His chair creaked as it rocked, and the sound captured his attention. It was the sound of his childhood and of those long summer nights when he would lie on his bed, his head at its foot, staring through the window screen and listening to his parents' rockers slowly working their grooves in the soft pine flooring of the back porch. Hour after hour they would rock without uttering a word. He would listen to their silence and look out on this same dark horizon sprinkled with the lights of strangers on the opposite shore, certain that those strangers' lives were different, certain they were never bothered by all the things that bothered him, certain that they never asked themselves when they would leave or where they would go or what they would do. All those years and all those experiences, and all he had managed to do was to come full-circle, back to where he had started, still asking himself the same questions and still having no answers.

Suddenly from the front of the house came the crunching sound of car tires on the gravel drive. He looked at his watch. It was nearly eleven. It had to be Priscilla home from the beach. She had called earlier to say that she was on her way. She hadn't said, and Eddie hadn't asked, but he hoped that she was alone. He was in no mood to struggle through the awkward pleasantries with which her boyfriend strained for a connection. He was a nice kid, Nick, not nearly so strange as Eddie had first thought. If only the boy would get a haircut and lose that earring and quit trying to explain how all of Western civilization was blindly surrendering its intelligence to the numbing influence of computers and the broadcast media.

Eddie went back into the kitchen and for a brief moment again stared at the contents of Helen Grehm's wallet, which were laid out on the kitchen table—one bank ATM card; two credit cards, one of which was in her husband's name, the other of which had expired nearly nine months before Helen Grehm's death; an English driver's permit; a badly worn and dog-eared Social Security card; and a crumpled slip of paper inscribed with what appeared to be telephone numbers located outside the United States. Again he donned the rubber gloves to return the contents to the wallet, which he sealed inside a plastic sandwich bag and tossed to the back of a small cabinet above the refrigerator. No sense trying to fathom the unfathomable. Tomorrow morning he'd turn everything over to Bolles and the police, collect his bonus, and be done with this business.

He took off the gloves, then gathered Bolles's report and the several sheets of paper on which he had made his own notations, and slipped them into Bolles's red file folder. He started to reach for his holstered Beretta, lying at the edge of the table, but stopped when he heard the strain of the front screen door and footsteps starting across the living-room floor.

"Priscilla?"

There was a second set of footsteps in the hallway, and he shook his head at the prospect of having to entertain Priscilla's boyfriend for however long it would take before he could politely send him away without offending his daughter. "Pris? That you?"

He looked to his left and stopped. In the doorway stood a short, stocky man with a wide, flat face that lacked any expression whatsoever. Reflexively, Eddie's right hand made a slight move toward his Beretta, but he stopped when the man quickly raised a black semi-automatic pistol toward his face.

"Please step back," came a voice from his right, and Eddie turned toward a second, taller man, who stood at the opposite end of the kitchen, next to the door leading to the hall. He, too, pointed a semi-automatic and, like the first man, had on a pair of thin, black leather gloves. The tall man nodded to his companion, who motioned with the muzzle of his pistol for Eddie to drop the file folder on the table.

Eddie did so and stepped back, raising both hands to his shoulders, palms out. "Gentlemen, listen—"

"Quiet," the tall man said.

His suit was of a gray, shiny material, his shirt black and open-collared, and dark-rimmed glasses with dark-tinted lenses covered his eyes. The short man, in black pants and a black windbreaker, stepped up to the table and took Eddie's gun, which he slid across the counter to his companion. The tall man took the gun out of its holster and stuffed it in his belt. He then nodded at the red file folder, and the shorter man stepped forward to inspect it. The short man nodded, as if to say that it was what they had expected.

"Is that everything?" the tall man asked.

"Whaddaya mean, everything?" asked Eddie.

The tall man smiled and raised his pistol toward Eddie's head and fired, exploding a large jug of brewed tea on the counter behind him.

Eddie dropped to the floor and froze in a tight, wincing crouch. *"Jesus Christ!"* he blurted out, peeking hesitantly over his forearm, which he held protectively in front of his face.

"Stand up," the tall man ordered.

"Jesus, man," Eddie murmured between quick breaths, "take it easy." He started to rise very slowly, struggling a bit against a sudden quivering weakness in his knees. "Look, man, whatever you want."

"Precisely," the tall man said. He stood erect and still. His hands were steady and his eyes emotionless. "Now, once again. In the file, is that everything?"

As quick as thought itself, Eddie understood his situation. He had seen their type before, if only rarely. These men were none of the mindless, drug-wasted street gunsels that had so overpopulated his career, none of the vermin to whom killing came without thought for cause or consequence, none of the stupid, quixotic killers ruled by fleeting moments of fear or ego. These were not men whom quick talk might dissuade or draw into mistakes. No, these men were here on business. There was no emotional content. This was a job and nothing more, and Eddie well understood that whether he was to live or die had been determined by them—or been determined for them—even before they had set out. The odds favored the latter.

You haven't reported this to anyone, have you?

Eddie raised his hands higher. "Yeah, man. That's everything."

"You're sure?"

"Absolutely."

The tall man motioned his partner to slide the folder over to him. Looking through its contents, he asked, "No other notes, papers, whatever?"

"That's it, everything, except . . ." Eddie pointed to his back pocket. "In my wallet I've got the business card of the guy who hired me." He shrugged his silent question whether the man wanted him to reach for it.

The tall man again nodded to his companion, who stepped forward and took the wallet from Eddie's pocket. The short man retrieved Garland Bolles's business card and then emptied the rest of the contents on the table and stepped back.

"Look, man," Eddie said. "Like I'm just hired help, y'know. I got no stake whatever in this. Nothing, man. Whatever you want."

"Quiet!" the tall man ordered again. "Now step forward and put your hands on the table." Eddie did, taking several deep breaths trying to calm himself.

"Now the other wallet."

"The other wallet?" Eddie asked, and the tall man began to raise his pistol. "All right, all right," Eddie said quickly. "No games. No bullshit." He took a deep breath, his mind racing. He needed time. He needed an opportunity. He needed—Priscilla! She could walk in at any moment. If only he had some time.

"You mean Helen Grehm's wallet, right?"

"Where is it?"

"It's locked in a safe."

"Oh, please," the tall man chuckled.

"No, really—"

"Don't fuck with me."

"I'm serious."

"You got the file and your gun here but you stopped off to put the wallet in a safe? Don't test my patience. You'll learn very quickly that I don't have any."

"Man, I'm tellin' ya, I just put it away and was sitting here making notes and whatever. Look in the file, look at my notes."

"And where's this safe?"

"Out in the shed behind the garage. You want the combination, you got it. Three turns to the right to fifteen, two to the left to thirty-seven, then back to zero."

There was indeed such a safe, but he altered the combination slightly. If the tall man sent his goon out to the shed alone, Eddie didn't want the man opening it to find only his second pistol. He wanted them to have to take him to the shed to open the safe. Maybe there would be an opportunity there. "But you'll need a flashlight. There's no light in the shed."

"And of course," the tall man sneered, "you wouldn't have put the folder in with the wallet."

"Man, I'm tellin' ya. I was sitting here making notes. Serious, man. Look in the file. You'll see."

"A safe in the shed."

"Yes."

The tall man smiled. "And I suppose you'll swear to that?"

"Man, right now I'll swear to anything you want."

The man's smile widened. "Yes, I know you will." He seemed to enjoy Eddie's squirming, as if it might just heighten his pleasure at the inevitable ending to the play.

Eddie took another and obvious deep breath. "Look, whoever you are, I don't care. Understand? Like I said, I'm just hired help. I got nothing personal in this. I did my job and got my money. Well, most of it, anyway. But what the hell? Just business, you know? You take what you want, and we both walk away. Just go about our business like none of this ever happened, and I don't know from pea turkey jackass. You know what I'm saying?"

"Why don't we all take a walk to this shed of yours. All right?"

"Fine. You'll see. I understand who's holding the cards. I just want to walk away, that's all."

"I like your attitude, Mr. Nickles," the tall man said, and nodded to his companion, who took a step toward Eddie's side. "But let me warn you—" He stopped abruptly at the sound of the front screen door opening and then shutting with a bang.

"Dad?" Priscilla called from the front of the house.

The short man wheeled to his right and Eddie seized his opportunity. He lunged at the short man and grabbed for the gun with his left hand while driving the fingers of his right hand into the man's eye. *"Priscilla!"* he screamed. *"Run!"*

The short man's piercing wail was cut short as the right side of his face blew apart. Eddie did not hear the tall man's gunfire until he felt the shot man's dead-weight pull them both to the floor. He wrenched the pistol from the dead man's hand and fired randomly toward the other end of the kitchen. Two, three, maybe four rounds; he wasn't counting. He rolled to his right, holding the dead man like a protective pillow, and fired another round, maybe two, before he looked up. The tall man was gone. He tried again to scream some warning to his daughter, as if the gunfire were not enough, but he had no breath, choking on the effort to get out from under the dead man and feeling a sharp pain in his chest. He struggled to his feet, but one leg buckled and he fell against the counter. He pulled himself up and took two hopping steps, trying to catch some air.

Priscilla? he called, but his voice was no more than a wheeze caught in his throat. He heard some movement behind him. He wheeled instantly and sighted his daughter's face down the barrel of the gun.

Her mouth gaped, and her hands clutched at her temples. Her eyes rolled up, and she fell to her knees.

"Oh, Jesus, God, please, not my baby!" He took one step toward her before a second, burning stab in his chest choked off what air he had left, and he collapsed.

7.

Voices rose from the street like distant chimes ringing at the edge of her dreams. Her hands clutched the thin lump of a pillow about her face, its musty smell and sweat-soaked cotton annoying her senses. If she didn't move, she thought, if she didn't open her eyes, maybe the nausea and the intense ache that circled from the base of her skull to the edge of her temples would go away. Another hour, another day, what would it matter? But above the voices she could hear her mother insisting in that maddeningly cheerful tone that she was just fine, that she was just imagining it all, that her stomach wasn't knotted and her heart wasn't racing and there was no pain pulsing behind her eyes, and if she would just keep a good thought, everything would be fine. *Hurry, Helen, or you'll be late for school.*

What day was it? Not Tuesday, she hoped. She hated Tuesdays and the underwear her mother would not let her throw away, the ones that said *Tuesday* on the frayed waistband, where the elastic poked through. She was much too old for underwear with the days of the week on the waistband.

Heavy wooden shutters rattled next door, and her eyes popped open. "What?"

A deep Germanic voice lifted her head from the pillow. *"Bei seben Uhr,"* the man barked.

She sat up quickly. Too quickly. A thumping dizziness caught her, and she took several deep breaths. The air scratched at her throat, and each part of her mouth, dry as sand, rasped against another. She braced her hands on the edge of the bed and squinted painfully at the sun filling the open doors to her balcony. The confusion ebbed slowly.

"Ja, ja, ja, einen Moment," the voice repeated, and a chill shook her. An ashtray filled with twisted cigarette butts stank at her feet and turned her stomach, and the sight of an empty bottle of Ruffino sitting on the sink only made it worse.

"Damn, damn, damn," she whispered. "Gotta get dressed, gotta go to school."

She stood slowly and steadied herself against the nightstand, pushing the fingers of one hand through her short dark hair, thickly matted with the remains of fevered dreams. She moved toward the balcony and took hold of the open shuttered doors, but did not close them.

On the neighboring balcony, the man to whom the Germanic voice apparently belonged stood in a thin cotton robe topped by a hairless head and bottomed by bare, hairless legs. He leaned stiffly against the balcony's railing, inspecting just how thoroughly the hotel's proprietress, Signora Tassara, was hosing down the terrace below. He turned suddenly, as if he sensed her presence, and when he saw that she was naked, he did not look away. Nor did she look away, but stood there motionless and numb, watching him watching her. *"Guten Morgen,"* he said finally, his eyes still on her. Helen nodded weakly and stepped back into the room without closing the shutters. "Jesus Christ," she mumbled.

A sudden urgent pressure on her bladder and bowels bent her at the waist, and she grabbed for the old iron key on the sink and a soiled chambray shirt she barely pulled around her as she raced down the hall for the *gabinetto*, pleading with whichever gods decided such matters that it be vacant. It was, and the quick, explosive relief was almost exciting, almost sensual, leaving her muscles weak and her knees shaking. "I can't do this anymore," she murmured. "I've got to stop this."

She had been in Santa Margherita more than a month, and the sameness of the days was beginning to wear on her. Each morning she arose to step out on her balcony and squint at the bright sun reflected off the water lapping ashore just across the street. She'd then shower and dress and shuffle down to the terrace, where Signora Tassara's son brought her a pitcher of dark coffee, a pitcher of warm milk, and a basket of rolls, each sealed in its own cellophane. She would squeeze a roll until the cellophane popped, and spread jam on the roll, and wait for the eggs she had not ordered. She had ordered eggs once, but only once, and with some difficulty, given her stumbling, tourist's Italian. Thereafter—out of kindness, she supposed, or, equally, to save them all the trouble of another halting, hand-signaled conversation—Signora Tassara prepared her eggs each morning, sometimes mixed with *pancetta*, sometimes with *salsiccia*, and she would smile gratefully and eat the eggs she really did not want. After breakfast she would go to the newsstand and buy a local paper and, if it was in, the *Herald Tribune*, or whatever English-language paperback she could find that she had not already read two or three times. And then she would go to the park and sit under the statue of Christopher Columbus and read until the sun was high, and she would go to the beach. Often, too, she would hike into the hills beyond the cemetery, beyond the abandoned palazzo, beyond the touring Germans and Brits and Americans, up where the wisteria vined through the trees and the grass was tall and the ground soft and she could lie there quietly and watch the *aliscafi* trace long white lines across the flat blue surface of the Golfo Tigullio. There she would stay throughout the long afternoon, alone and mostly napping, trying to catch up from the night before, which in turn would lead her to another sleepless night.

Nighttime was the worst time, particularly after the occasional concert in the park had ended, after the movie theatre had closed and the men in the bars along Via Pescino or by the marina and customs house had stopped trying for conversation and left her alone. Then and only then would she wander back to her room and numb the solitude and the fear with wine or whiskey or whatever it took. Every day and every night, it was the same.

Enough of this, she thought. It was time for a change, and

maybe this was the day to make it. There was, of course, nothing compelling about this day, except for the sudden thought that it just might be that one day too many that turned her complacent, that one night too many when the booze numbed her caution along with the boredom, and turned her careless or just plain stupid. Maybe it was time.

She stood and flushed and saw that someone had left a bottle of shampoo on the floor of the shower. She had no towel, but she did not care. She stepped into the shower and shampooed her hair and shampooed her body and rinsed her mouth with the hot water and felt the pain ease. Yes, she was certain it was time to go, but moving on meant she had someplace to go. Where? Chamonix? Perhaps. She could use the money, but Chamonix had its own risks. She had to choose carefully. She had to think ahead, to take each step in turn, just as she had been taught, just as she had planned. But, then, too, planning wasn't everything. Survival, she had learned, depended less on a plan than it did on instinct and the ability and willingness to bend and shift with an ever-changing reality. If recent events had taught her nothing else, it was that she could depend only on herself.

There had been no contact at all, no hint of an approach, not a single request to see her passport, not a single call filled with confused questions followed by an apology for having reached a wrong number. No odd messages had been left at the desk, no inquiries from Signora Tassara about how long she would stay or when she would leave. No stranger's face had repeated itself in town or at the hotel, except for the barmen and restaurateurs and the old woman at the newsstand who always smiled but never spoke.

Each morning she arranged her things carefully, and noted how and where she positioned various items in the drawers—a bra snap next to the zipper of her jeans, the corner of a postcard under a shirt button, the cap on the toothpaste set on top of a map and at the precise intersection of Via Dogali and the Piazza Mazzini. Every morning she had positioned different items in different positions, and every night, when she returned to her room, they had remained in place. Nothing had been disturbed. No one had gone through her things. They had not found her. Perhaps they had stopped looking. Perhaps they had never been looking in the first place.

She reconsidered a moment. There was no reason to rush. Why not wait a day or two? Why not spend a few days thinking about where to go next? Not Chamonix. Soon, maybe, but not yet. Maybe south and away from the coast and its high-season tourist rates, someplace where she could stretch her dwindling reserves of cash. But she had to plan. Yes, why not spend the next few days on the beach planning. No more bars, no more wine in her room, just a few days on the beach, thinking. For now that was plan enough.

She stepped out of the shower and slipped on the shirt, feeling it stick to her wetness. She poked her head out the bathroom door and, seeing no one in the hall, padded quickly to her room, where she grabbed a towel and began to dry herself. The simple fact that she had made some decision, however tentative, left her feeling better.

She opened the top drawer and reached for the toothpaste, but stopped. The momentary sense of relief quickly drained from her as she stared at the contents of the drawer. The toothpaste. It wasn't at the Piazza Mazzini. It was nowhere near the Piazza Mazzini. It wasn't even on the map. Even if the map had extended that far, which it did not, the toothpaste would be halfway to Genova. A shiver ran through her.

Wait! Just wait. Take your time. Think. Last night . . . when you got home, did you check? Of course you would have checked before you brushed your teeth. But did you even brush your teeth? Or were you too drunk? Too drunk to brush your teeth? Think! You must have checked. You always check. Think!

She opened the second drawer. The bra snap wasn't next to the zipper of her jeans, and the postcard, where was the postcard? There? In the back of the drawer?

Wait. Calm down. Which day are you thinking of? The postcard, was that yesterday? You had to have checked last night. You wouldn't have just gone to bed if things had been moved. Of course not, unless . . . Unless you just crashed.

She took a deep breath and moved quickly to the sink in the corner of the room. She turned the faucet on full and scooped cold water to her face.

Think, goddamn it! . . . No, don't think. What did they always say? When your instincts signal trouble, consider it a message from God and go for cover?

She stood up straight and shivered again.

Drunken fool! You don't know. You can't be sure. Damn it!

She had no choice.

"*Bei seben Uhr,*" the German had said. Almost seven. She could pack and breakfast and pay her bill by eight. Nothing rushed, nothing unusual. No sign of panic. She would be back, she'd say. Just going to meet some friends at Viareggio. A week, she'd tell Signora Tassara, ten days, no more.

Another ten minutes' walk to the iron shop just down the street from the cemetery, where she would recover her car from the back of the garage. She would thank Signor Bianchi and pay him well and promise to return soon. A week, ten days, no more. Just going to visit some friends at Viareggio.

She should make Chamonix easily. It had to be Chamonix. She had no choice. If they had found her, or were even close, she would need the money. She would spend the night in Chamonix, where she would recover the bag and codes she would need. Then? . . . Altdorf? Yes, she had always done well in Altdorf. She would stay in the old hotel, in the large room at the top of the stairs with the tattered Oriental rug and the huge four-poster bed. From the train station at the bottom of the hill, she would phone in the necessary account inquiries, and if she heard no unexpected signals, she would then walk into the offices of the banker with the one bad eye, unannounced as always. And for his customary fee, the banker would arrange the transfer of funds from the brokerage house in Geneva and, upon their receipt, convert those funds to bearer bonds. Then the trip over the mountains to Thun, where she would discount the bonds to a broker, take back some cash, and wire the rest through the West Caribbean Bank in Tortola to the several foreign currency accounts in Anguilla and the Caymans. Just as she had been taught. Just as she had planned. Simple!

He had always said it didn't have to be complicated: like knotting a monkey's fist, he had said, like wrapping a single strand in and around itself, over and over, in and out, until the eye can't follow its course, until the strand is multiplied by its sections, first by two, then by four, then by six, then more, until each section looks like its own strand, and each strand looks like another, and none leads anywhere but back to itself. Just keep wrapping the strand, he had said. Step by step by step. It had all been thought out. It had all been planned. Everything. Everything, that is, but the timing. Everything, that is, but where she would go and what she would do after Chamonix, after Altdorf, after Thun.

PART
TWO

8.

One foot, wide and rough-soled with gnarled, knobby toes like beached driftwood, poked out from under the covers. A familiar foot in a familiar pose. Every night, winter and summer, he would open the bedroom window wide to let in the fresh air, and every night, after he had settled in, she would lower the window to barely a slit to keep the heat in or the heat out, depending on the season. He had never actually voiced an objection, only a sigh of resignation, while his feet, like trapped animals, squirmed to escape the bed covers. Night after night, year after year, it had been the same.

Megs was angry; not as angry as she wanted to be, or even as angry as she felt she had a right to be, but, still, she was angry. She had spent a thousand nights imagining this scene and fearing it. The day tours that ran deep into the night without his calling. The night tours that ran into days without his coming home. The cuts, the bruises, the torn clothes, the foul odors brought home from the morgue, the gruesome answers to questions she wished she had never asked. It was just the job, he'd say. He never admitted to the fear and only rarely to the frustration. It was just the job, he'd say, and nothing more.

Now, years after the divorce, years after it had all stopped being part of her life, just when she had truly started over, here she was, sitting at the foot of his bed watching fluids drip through a tube stuck in his arm and oxygen forced through a tube stuck in his nose. They were alone, and her eyes never left him, and what she saw was a man twenty years younger and forty pounds lighter, a man who struggled through his shyness to tell her of dreams no one thought he had, a man whose gentle touch had not yet been lost to the back streets that were to become so much a part of him. So many years had passed, and so many things had changed, but, watching him lie there, she could see the man she remembered loving just as clearly as she saw that big ugly foot sticking out of the covers.

Eddie's eyelids fluttered open, and with drugged curiosity he followed her stare at his foot.

"You really should trim those toenails," Megs said.

He looked up and started to laugh, but a spasm of coughing stopped him. She jumped up and moved quickly to his side. "I'm sorry, this is no time for jokes." Her half-laugh mixed with sudden and unexpected tears. She took his hand in hers and felt his grip tighten as the coughing subsided, and he took a few deep breaths. "God, Eddie, what happened? What have you gotten yourself into?"

"Priscilla?" His voice was weak and gravelly.

"She's all right."

Eddie frowned.

"She's okay, really. She wasn't hurt. At least not physically. She's . . ." Megs looked away and shook her head.

He tightened his grip on her hand. "You're sure?"

"Yes, really. A bruise or two from when she fainted. Otherwise she wasn't injured. But she's a wreck emotionally."

"She here?"

"No. She wanted to be, but I had Martin take her to the farm. The detectives just kept badgering her, asking all these questions she couldn't answer. They wouldn't leave her alone. It was making things worse, upsetting her more and more, so I told Martin to take her home. To the farm up in Bucks County. I didn't ask if it was all right. I just did it."

He nodded. "Keep them away from her," he whispered. "Keep everyone away from her."

"What happened? What's going on?"

He shook his head.

"Oh, please, Eddie, don't give me that I-don't-want-to-know routine. Not this time. Please."

Eddie turned his head and for several moments stared out the window, until a slight shiver ran through his body.

"Do you want the window open?" Megs asked, and he nodded.

She searched for a latch or a pull that wasn't there. "I don't think they want these windows open. I'll go ask the nurse."

"It's all right," Eddie said. "Come here." He patted the bed for her to come close.

"You're going to be all right," she said, settling next to him on the side of the bed. "It's going to be a few weeks before you can rejoin the boys at the O.K. Corral, but you're going to be all right. The doctor says you'll be able to go home in a few days. You were damn lucky. Apparently the one bullet nicked your lung and did some muscle damage, but otherwise it missed doing anything major. The bullet in your leg missed the bone. You'll be limping around on a cane for a while, but—"

"Stop," he whispered.

"No, I won't stop. You listen to me for a change. You may be able to go home, but you're going to have to take it easy for a few weeks. I've talked with Martin, and I'm going to stay—"

Eddie raised his hand to stop her. "Please."

"Damn it, Eddie!"

"Please. It's hard to talk, so just listen." He reached for her hand, but she held back. "I don't want you to stay."

"But—"

"I don't want you to stay. I don't know what this is all about . . . really. I was hired to find a man. That's all. I did that. And then . . . then these guys I've never seen tried to kill me because of what I found. I don't know the reasons, but . . ." He took another deep breath. "Megs, I'm . . ." He stopped.

Megs waited for him to finish the thought she was imagining, but he just stared at her. "Scared?" she said finally, and he looked away. "Oh, Jesus, Eddie." She laid her hand on his.

"Listen to me, please. I'll be all right. But I want you with Priscilla. Don't let anyone talk to her, none of these bastards, no police, nobody. Understand?"

She nodded. "There's an FBI agent waiting out in the hall. He's been out there all morning waiting for you to wake up."

"FBI?"

"Yes. He says he needs to talk to you."

"There's just one?"

"One what?"

"Just one agent?"

"You're disappointed? You want more?"

"No . . ." He frowned in thought, then said, "It's just that they usually travel in pairs."

"Well, he's been pretty insistent that he talk to you as soon as you woke up. You want me to get him?"

"No, not now. Later . . . have you said anything to him?"

Megs nodded. "We talked some. He seems real interested in some woman named Helen. I'm not sure I caught the last name. Graham or Grim, I think."

Eddie's eyes narrowed. "Really?"

"Yes. He wanted to know if I knew her or ever heard you speak of her. What's that all about?"

Eddie shook his head slowly. "I don't know. She's . . . She was murdered over a month ago. The man I was hired to find ended up finding her wallet, but . . . I don't know, there's something real wrong about all this. It doesn't make sense."

"What?" asked Megs. "What doesn't make sense?"

Eddie took a quick, deep breath that caused another spasm of coughing, and Megs leaned closer and put her hand on his cheek until it stopped. "I'm not sure we should be talking like this," she said. "You need to rest."

Eddie nodded, then said in a near whisper, "Just listen a minute. Please. Don't say anything when you leave. All right?"

"What do you mean?"

"Don't tell the agent you're leaving. Just do it. Tell him I'm awake or whatever, and then just leave."

Megs stared at him with a deep frown.

"Don't give them your address. You haven't given them your address, have you? Your new address?"

"No . . . Well, yes, the address at our old house, but I told them I was moving."

"Did you tell them where?"

"They asked me to let them know where I'd be . . . and where Priscilla would be when they needed to talk to us. The detectives—

the FBI agent, too—they said they want to talk to her as soon as she has a chance to, you know, get herself together. I didn't say anything about sending her up to the farm. Was that all right?"

"Yes. But they don't have your new address, right?"

"No . . . I don't think so. God, I don't know, I don't think so, I wasn't really thinking about things like that."

"Just leave, Megs. Don't say anything to anybody. Give me some time to find out what's going on before you talk to anyone or let anyone talk to Pris. Act like this never happened. I'll keep in touch with you, but don't you call me. Priscilla either."

"Eddie, please, what's this about? You've got to tell me."

"I don't know." He stopped, wincing a bit with some pain. "I don't know, and that's the truth. I can't explain what happened. It's not that I don't want to, I just don't know. That's why I don't want you to take any chances. Okay?"

"But what are you going to do?"

"I don't know yet. But I'll be all right." She watched his eyes lower. "Okay?"

"But you won't be able to—"

He waved his hand to stop her. "Just tell me that you'll do what I ask. Just one last time. Please."

She turned toward the window, and several moments passed before she spoke, without looking back at him. "You are the most difficult man I have ever known. Why can't you just be . . ." She stopped and shook her head quickly. "Oh, hell, I don't know what I want you to be."

"But you'll do this for me, won't you?"

She let go a long sigh and nodded.

"I'm sorry, Megs. I'm sorry I screwed up again."

She turned to force a smile on him. "The boys are here."

"Tommy?"

She nodded. "And Carl. They went down to get some coffee. They should be back in a few minutes."

Eddie blinked slowly and took a deep breath, and she could feel his hand again squeeze hers. "Carl, too?" he asked.

"Yes, Carl, too." She felt his hand relax and watched his expression soften to a smile.

Damn this man, she thought. Damn his hold on her.

9.

On a promontory overlooking the Potomac River and the Lincoln Memorial, in a complex guarded by a gatehouse and an insignificant sign reading "Navy Department, Bureau of Medicine and Surgery," on the top floor of a building mostly hidden by trees, the drill was the same. The seven members of the Joint Operations Committee sat still and silent in seven chairs set in a circle while two security technicians packed up their forty-pound spectrum analyzer. No luminous green arcs or spikes had appeared on the screen, and one of the technicians gave a silent nod that the windowless room had been cleared. The committee's chair gave an approving nod in return, and the technicians then left without a word.

There were no telephones in the room, no fax machines, no intercoms, no radios or televisions, no recorders of any kind, no electrical outlets, no pictures on the wall, no briefcases, no pads of paper, no pens or pencils; only seven chairs in which sat the seven committee members, separated by seven side tables, on which sat seven glasses filled with each individual member's individual choice of refreshment. Several battery-powered floor lamps, each carefully checked and cleared by the now retired technicians, bathed the room in a soft yellow light.

There was an unusual tension in the air because of the unusual method by which the meeting had been called. Usually, each member of the committee would be hand-delivered a plain buff-colored envelope containing a plain buff-colored card on which was engraved an invitation to some dinner party or reception. From whatever date and time listed on the invitation the member would—depending on whether it was an odd- or even-numbered day—add or subtract his personal code to decipher the date and time of the meeting. RSVPs were not required unless a member found it impossible to attend, which occurred only on the rarest of occasions, for the meetings themselves were rare, usually called only to approve or disapprove an operation requiring the full committee's consent. Usually, agendas were neither announced nor discussed among the members prior to a meeting, the rule being that any questions, concerns, or background information necessary for a decision was to be aired only before the committee as a whole. But this meeting was different.

All through the morning, cryptic conversations over secure telephone lines had passed between the members. Questions and opinions normally reserved for their clandestine gatherings had been asked and offered, until finally the meeting was arranged and an agenda set. Such deviance from established procedures had not occurred since early 1989, when there had been delivered to a safe house in Amburg, Germany, near the Czech border, the body of a man who had been their most important source within the Hauptverwaltung Aufklärung—the "enlightenment" headquarters of former East Germany's Ministry of State Security—along with photocopied records of an account held in Menatep, one of Moscow's most successful commercial banks. Not even the recent murders of Trevor and Helen Grehm had occasioned such a hastily convened gathering as this. It was now clear to the committee, however, and to each of its members, that danger loomed on their collective horizon.

Like the other committee members present, Philo Machus, chief of the Special Projects Directorate, sat stoically, waiting for the proceedings to begin. But, unlike his fellow members, Machus understood that both he personally and his directorate, which had been specifically created by the committee to serve only the committee and its interests, were on the firing line.

The committee's chair, who was his own agency's director of covert operations, spoke first, the bulbous wattle beneath his nonexistent chin vibrating with his question. "Gentlemen, is there anyone here who is not fully aware of the events in Annapolis or the purpose of this meeting?"

Heads shook synchronously all around, heads representing the most clandestine units within their clandestine agencies, units carrying such acronymic titles as COINTEL and INSEC and JICSOG and POLOPS and SPECPRO and TECSERV.

"All right, Phil, what do we know so far?"

Philo Machus—"Phil" to those very few people familiar enough to so address him—did not move a muscle except to say, "Well, Amos's people got the first alert, so, if you don't mind, I'd like to start with the details from his perspective to make sure we're all dealing with the same background."

The chair nodded. "Amos?"

Amos Bone, who was his agency's deputy director in charge of counterintelligence, leaned forward and placed both elbows on his knees, rubbing his palms together slowly. "Well, I think we all know the outline, but let me go through it again. About four this morning one of my men got a call from a detective with the Anne Arundel County Police, a peripheral source, an old army friend who used to be a QC at the antenna in Augsburg. Said he had an unidentified body that had taken two shots in the back of the head. A third severed his spine. He was a John Doe: no identification at all, no driver's license or other ID. The coroner on the scene, however, noted that the man's dental work looked pretty unusual, not like anything you'd see in this country. He told the detective it looked more like what you'd find in Eastern Europe or Russia. Apparently, the coroner had interned in Brooklyn and seen examples of the same thing among the Russian-immigrant community. Also, the body was heavily tattooed on the upper arms and chest, which is typical of what we've seen on men who've spent time in Soviet prisons. The detective gave our man a pretty detailed description of the tattoos, and my people say at least one of the designs would indicate the man probably had done time at Novosibirsk. According to our victim—"

"His name again?" the Chairman interrupted.

"Nickles. J. Edward Nickles. A retired homicide detective."

"Where from?"

"Here in D.C. Just retired, maybe two, three months ago. Anyway, Nickles was hit twice, once in the right thigh, the second shot nicked his left lung. According to Nickles, there was a second shooter, who escaped. We don't have any clear description of the second man other than that he was tall, or at least taller than the tattoo. We don't know if he was hit—the second shooter, that is— but probably not. There were no blood trails leading out of the house. The county detective wasn't able to get much out of Nickles before he was rushed into the operating room. I understand Phil has arranged to have one of his people get in to see Nickles under . . . what is it, an FBI cover?"

Philo Machus nodded.

Bone continued; "So we'll see what comes of that. But right now all we have is that Nickles was hired to find the man in the bank photo, the one with Helen Grehm's ATM card."

All heads but that of Philo Machus nodded knowledgeably.

Bone went on. "We don't know if Nickles found the man or the ATM card or what, but it seems clear that the attack was somehow related to this Grehm business."

"Who hired Nickles?" asked the chairman.

"We have a name. Bolles. That's B-O-L-L-E-S. Garland Bolles, and an address on Fifteenth Street here in town. Anne Arundel asked D.C. Homicide to check it out. We have sources reporting on whatever progress the police make, but for obvious reasons we have not sent out our own people. All we know so far is that the address Bolles listed is one of those cooperative suites, you know, where they rent out an office and receptionist and answering services. No one in the suite ever saw this fellow Bolles, so again we don't have a description. Bolles—or whatever his name is—didn't actually rent an office, just the answering service. All contact was over the phone. So far Bolles remains a phantom."

"No description at all from Nickles?"

"No. Like I said, the detective was barely able to get that much out of him. We're waiting to hear if Phil's man has better luck."

"What's his prognosis?"

"Nickles? He'll live."

"Hmmm," the chair murmured, almost as if he were disappointed. "Can your people count on these police sources to keep us informed?"

"Anne Arundel County, yes. D.C.'s not so reliable, but even there I'd advise not sending out our people. There's too great a risk of exposure with so many agencies running around asking questions."

The members of the committee all nodded their agreement.

"And this man Bolles?" asked the chairman. "Everyone's checking the indices?"

"Yes," Bone said, "as far as I know, unless someone has anything new?" He stopped and looked to the others, each of whom shook his head. "No? Well, like I said, as far as we know now, Bolles doesn't exist, at least not by that name. No listing anywhere."

"No other witnesses?"

"Just one. Nickles's daughter. She's eighteen, and apparently had just gotten home from the beach when she walked into the middle of it. She wasn't hit, but the detective said she was hysterical and had to be sedated. He's sure she doesn't know anything. Just walked into the middle of a firefight. Never saw the second man, who escaped, just the tattoo and her father with the tattoo's brains all over his face, and she fainted."

"I see," the chairman said. "Phil?"

"I don't know," said Philo Machus, scanning the six other members, all of whose eyes were upon him. "We haven't made any connection here, other than what Amos has reported."

"What about Brecht?" asked the member to Machus's left, a thin, pasty man who was his agency's director of internal security, and whose coal-black eyes peered out from thick, rimless glasses.

"What about him?" Machus answered.

"Well, the Grehms were his people; does he have any ideas?"

Philo Machus shook his head. "No. I talked to Arlis a few hours ago. He's as baffled by this as we are. You know Arlis."

"I've never been all that confident that any of us really knows Arlis Brecht. God knows I've been voicing this same reservation for years. The man's too damn independent. We should have tightened the reins on him years ago."

Machus scowled. "I've never heard any reservations about the funds he's generated or, for that matter, the intelligence that's come out of the Iberia operation."

"Perhaps," sniffed the internal-security director, "except for that little matter of Treshkov and the ten kilos of uranium."

Philo Machus stiffened at the mention of Arkady Treshkov, the man who was both his greatest triumph and his worst embarrassment.

It was in the mid-1980s, and Treshkov, then head of the KGB's West European Operations, had made a cautious but determined pass at Arlis Brecht and the Iberia Trading Company, headquartered in Lisbon. Treshkov's pose had been that of representing a number of Eastern Europe's unrevealed entrepreneurs who were in search of a discreet means of trading off portions of their various countries' vast natural resources—to which they had access by virtue of their high-level positions within government ministries—and reinvesting their profits in the West. For his services and the use of Iberia Trading as a cover for their dealings, Arlis Brecht was to be rewarded with generous commissions.

Brecht, of course, had reported the approach to Philo Machus, who in turn reported the approach to the committee. After months of speculation and planning, the Joint Operations Committee decided to encourage the seduction. Whether Treshkov represented an approved KGB operation—perhaps devised for much the same reasons as had been the Special Projects Directorate—or whether Treshkov and his partners were simply hedging their bets against the ever more obvious stress fractures in the Soviet monolith, the Joint Committee did not know. Nor did they care. Either way, by allowing Iberia Trading Company to become a conduit for some part of the opposition's investments and funding, the committee would have both a unique window on its operations and, if they so chose, as an exercise in one-upmanship, the opportunity to divert some of the opposition's funds to their own purposes.

Over time it became abundantly clear that Moscow Center was no more aware of Treshkov's operation than were the Washington bureaucracy and its various oversight committees aware of the Special Projects Directorate. Still, the committee decided, there was every reason to continue and encourage the relationship. It was, of course, just as vital to monitor the activities of Treshkov and his band of outlaw apparatchiks as it had been to monitor his KGB-approved operations.

It was late 1991, as the Soviet empire was coming apart and after Treshkov and his associates had "retired" from Russian State Security, when Philo Machus suffered his worst defeat. Only after the transaction had been completed and it was far too late to do anything about it did the Special Projects Directorate learn that Arkady Treshkov and his associates had negotiated through a French lawyer in Fribourg, Switzerland, to sell ten kilos of weapons-grade uranium to the North Koreans, and that nearly six million dollars in net profits had been washed through several accounts opened in the name of Iberia Trading and two of its subsidiaries. The Joint Committee had expressed its "deep concern" that Philo Machus and Arlis Brecht had been used without their knowledge, and, worse, that the discovery of the uranium trade had come not through their own sources but through civilians in the Department of Energy's Office of Threat Assessment and the Z Division at Lawrence Livermore. Philo Machus vowed to avenge his embarrassment, and since then had been planning and waiting only for the right opportunity to do so.

"Gentlemen," the chair interjected, "please, let's not rehash old business. We have more immediate problems to resolve."

"I agree," said Machus.

"As do I," said the director of internal security. "My point is that we cannot afford this cautious wait-and-see attitude. I don't presume to speak for everyone, but I doubt any of us ever believed that the Grehm murders were the result of some random burglary, and, given this latest incident in Annapolis, we have to assume that there's a serious virus coming out of Iberia and we have to make damn certain it doesn't spread to us. Correct?"

"Well, no question this Grehm business is a problem," said Machus, "but I'm not so sure that means that Iberia is infected."

"Don't you think," posed the member to Machus's right, "that for security purposes we must consider Iberia and the Grehms one and the same? First, this business of Helen Grehm's ATM card, for which there are apparently people out there willing to kill, certainly tells me that there is at least the possibility, if not the probability, that this Helen Grehm was not simply an unfortunate innocent caught at the wrong place at the wrong time. Second, she worked directly for Brecht, which leads me to ask whether it's possible Brecht has a problem he'd rather we not know about, and he's out there trying to clean up his own garbage?"

"No," said Machus without hesitation. "He's never been involved with operations. He's an accountant, for God's sake. He doesn't have the people and wouldn't know what to do with them if he did. Besides, let's not confuse the relationships here. Helen Grehm was a courier and nothing more. She never knew the business beyond following very explicit and limited instructions. Opening accounts and making transfers, that sort of thing. Also, let's not forget Trevor Grehm. To say he was one of Brecht's people is really stretching the point. Certainly, he used Iberia for cover, but he still ran his own weapons trades. That was the whole idea, if you recall. We let him run his own business and make whatever profits he could. In exchange he kept us informed of who was selling and who was buying. Plus, we know Trevor was dealing more and more with the Chechens and the Russian mobs, right? Hell, we encouraged him to, isn't that right?"

Several members nodded.

"I mean, the arms trade's not exactly a Sunday picnic in any case, but dealing with the Chechens? Talk about wrestling with snakes!"

"So, what are you saying, Phil?" asked the chairman.

"I don't know, but maybe Grehm got a little greedy. Maybe he wasn't playing by the rules. How many times did we warn him about getting too cute playing customers off one another? Remember a few years back? The Israelis? How much dancing did we have to do to convince them that the Syrians weren't part of that same deal? Grehm was good, but he could be reckless, too. Maybe he short-changed his supplier or broker, and someone simply picked up the phone and called a cousin in Brighton Beach."

"Possible," the chairman said, nodding that he understood what everyone else in the room understood as well, that Russia's highly active and aggressive *Organizatsiya* had long since reached out and touched America, principally through its contacts among the more than forty thousand former Soviet émigrés in Brooklyn's Brighton Beach section. "But that doesn't explain Grehm's wife, and what appears to be an inordinate interest in her ATM card."

Machus shook his head. "I still believe she was just in the wrong place at the wrong time. She was never involved in her husband's business. We've checked every move she made, every contact, every account she's touched over the past five years. There's nothing there. She was a courier, like every other courier. She delivered messages, she didn't read them. Now, her husband's a different story. Maybe he was using her old credit cards to encrypt information—remember, the ATM card that went into the machine was expired."

"Yes," intoned the chairman gravely, "and we can all imagine just how much information one could encrypt on one of those magnetic strips."

"Agreed," said Machus, "but my point is that it has been well over a month and we have seen no evidence at all of any connection between the Grehms and a problem within Iberia."

"Don't take this the wrong way," pressed the member to Machus's right, "but I hope this isn't just wishful thinking on your part."

"Yes," chimed in another member, who sat opposite Machus and to the chairman's left, "I'm concerned that we're so concentrated on theories that we're overlooking the obvious. Whatever the reason they were killed, they are . . . they were connected to Iberia. However you cut it, that's a serious problem. And, given last night, it's a problem that's not going away."

"Look," argued Machus, "I'm not suggesting there's not a problem here, obvious or otherwise. I'm only saying that we haven't found any evidence of a breach in Iberia. We've tightened every screw we can find. Double- and triple-checked everything. Brecht's personally run a complete audit on every account."

"Yes, Brecht!" said the director of internal security.

"Yes, Brecht," Machus fired back, "and two of our own people. I sent Michaels in from London and Ousby from my own shop. They looked through everything themselves. I'm telling you, there's nothing there. They found nothing. We're still looking, but it seems to us the problem must be external."

"But why this business with Nickles, and the ATM card?"

"I don't know, but obviously that's a problem that has to be addressed. Whatever happened, whatever Grehm was into, it's a given that someone wants that card badly, which means that we want that card even more."

"That's right."

"But," asked the chairman, "has anyone figured out how the hell this bank card ended up on the street?"

"No," said Machus, "but somehow it did, and right now this fellow Nickles is our key. We need to know from him who this Bolles is, and whether he actually found the card or gave it to Bolles or whoever, and why they tried to kill him. And we have to do that without raising any more flags. We have to quiet this whole business in a big hurry."

"Are we still discounting the possibility of SVR involvement?" asked the chairman, referring to Russia's Foreign Intelligence Service, which had replaced the KGB.

"Not entirely," said Machus, "but it doesn't smell like them. Too sloppy. But don't get me wrong, that doesn't mean we're not looking, and looking hard. It's just that it smells more like a private deal gone bad."

"And your suggestion is?" the chair asked Machus.

"First, like I said, we need to muffle all the noise on this business in Annapolis. The last thing we need is another investigation and more scrutiny into the Grehms and their connections. Meaning, we need to step in with our friends—perhaps through the FBI—to cool down the police inquiries, to pull this out of the hands of any local authorities."

"Gentlemen?" the chair asked.

"Agreed," came several voices from around the circle.

"Amos," the chair asked, "can your contacts handle that?"

"I think so," said Amos Bone.

"Second," said Philo Machus, "I think it's time for us to deal more aggressively in finding the man with the ATM card, and with this man Nickles. We need both the information and to make sure whatever's out there goes no farther."

"Agreed," came the voice of the chair, and those of COINTEL and INSEC and JICSOG and POLOPS and TECSERV.

"And," added the chairman, "we need to look far more closely at this Helen Grehm's history. I don't care what we've done so far, it needs to be done again, and even more thoroughly. We have to assume she backfired on us and proceed accordingly."

"I agree," said Machus. "My people have already started."

"Good," said the chairman, "and are you also taking the lead on the rest of what needs to be done?"

"Unless there's any objection?" Philo Machus said.

"Gentlemen?"

The committee members nodded their assent.

"With joint support as needed?" asked Machus.

Everyone nodded.

Philo Machus paused, his eyes making the circle of the entire committee. "And what," he asked, "is our approved level of response if the problem is isolated? As determined in the field?"

No one moved, no one spoke for a long moment. Finally, the chair stood and arched his back in a stretch. "Whatever or whoever this problem turns out to be, I would suggest that it be neutralized as quickly and as quietly as possible—including the peripherals like Nickles, if that proves necessary."

Again there was a moment of silence before everyone nodded.

"Having settled our objective," the chair said, "let's talk about methods."

10.

Turning from the Fraumunster, Arkady Treshkov began the long climb through a web of medieval alleyways, laboring up the hill to a small apartment building, then up the stairs to the top floor, then down the hall to a window overlooking the Lindenhoff and the Limmat River beyond. He was a large man with the girth of one who enjoyed living well and the shallow, uneven breath of one who was paying a heavy price for it. He stopped before knocking on the door, taking gulps of air and patting his brow with a neatly folded handkerchief. "Ah," he thought to himself as he looked down upon the small park and the old men stepping across the checkered stone boards to move their knee-high chess pieces, "one day soon I will join you."

Suddenly the door to his right opened. "You are late, Arkady Sergeevich; where have you been?"

Yury Khavkin, whose partnership of former Soviet factory managers, military-supply officers, and high-level ministry officials supplied Treshkov and his customers with everything from Soviet-manufactured small arms to weapons-grade plutonium 239 smuggled out of the factory Krasnoyarsk-26, stood rigidly in the doorway, his face, as always, stiffened by an anxious scowl. Despite his fifty-two years, Yury Khavkin looked like what he had once been, his earlier years as a colonel in the Soviet Special Forces still apparent in his compact, muscular physique. His ruddy, weathered skin may have wrinkled about his eyes and gathered in a thin loose fold above his starched collar, but to Arkady Treshkov he was still unmistakably *Spetsney*, Special Forces.

"Yury Ivanovich," Arkady wheezed, stepping through the doorway, "why don't you simply put a bullet through my brain? Be merciful and do it quickly. Quit toying with me like one of your awful cats. But, please, a vodka before I die." He shuffled to a table and sat heavily in a straight-backed wooden chair.

"I have tea," Yury Khavkin offered.

"Tea? You have tea?" Treshkov said, loosening his collar and mopping the perspiration from his neck. "Of course you would have tea. And perhaps a watercress sandwich. Forgive me, I must have interrupted your calisthenics. You were probably in the midst of a hundred pushups while I crawled up that last flight of stairs on my hands and knees. Perhaps, while I catch my breath, you could mount some field artillery on your back and double-time it to the store for a bloody bottle of vodka!"

"Arkady Sergeevich, you will be dead within the year if you do not—"

"Stop! I will be dead within the hour if you do not give me a proper drink. Have you no decency?" Treshkov sighed deeply. "Do you understand, my friend, that we are in Zurich? This is not some forgotten village out on the Anadyr Plateau. There are actually restaurants here. Restaurants, Yury Ivanovich. Do you know what they are? They are places where one can go without a mountain guide and fifty pounds of rope and tackle. They are places where civilized people can meet and be served a meal that will make your heart sing and your spirits soar. We could be comfortably seated at the Kronenhalle, enjoying a fine steak with mustard sauce, surrounded by the genius of Chagall and Klee and Matisse and Miró."

"It is not safe."

"Safe? What a joke! I know you miss the old days, Yury, but everything has changed. We must adjust. Even if there are dozens of little spies following our every move, what do you think might raise their suspicions? Two ex-Soviets turned businessmen meeting in a fine restaurant, enjoying a glass or two of vodka and a raspberry mousse, or the two of us ferreting our way through back alleys to meet in this barren apartment rented to a Slav who gives himself an Irish or Italian name—or whatever it is you've chosen this time. And you! No, why would anyone be suspicious of you? You rent an apartment where you show up—what?—once a month, maybe? And for what? To entertain someone like me, who needs a bloody heart-lung machine after climbing those stupid stairs! Yes, very clever."

"I don't find you amusing."

"I am not trying to amuse you, Yury. I am trying to pry open that narrow military mind of yours and let in a little common sense."

Yury Khavkin maintained his stare a moment and then started for the kitchen. "I have a bottle, if you insist."

"I do insist," Treshkov said, "with what may be my dying breath if you do not hurry."

Khavkin brought out a bottle of vodka, a single glass, and some black bread before returning to the kitchen, where he spent the next few minutes preparing a pot of black tea.

"So," Treshkov called over his shoulder, "I take it that there is suspicion among the partners."

Khavkin did not respond until he returned to the table carrying a tray loaded with a teapot, a single cup and saucer, and several small cubes of sugar. He poured his tea, placed a single cube between his teeth, and then took a long sip. "Concerned, Arkady Sergeevich. We are concerned. Do we have reason to be suspicious as well?"

"Ah, well, we are always suspicious of one another, aren't we? It's essential to our trade."

"And who do you suspect?"

"Everyone. Even you."

"But not your friend Brecht?"

"Oh, yes, I suspect Brecht," Treshkov corrected. "Certainly I suspect Brecht. But what does it matter who we suspect? It's a different world than we are used to, and as I keep telling you, we must adjust. What matters, as the Americans love to say, is the bottom line."

"And what is the bottom line here?"

"You are referring to this matter of the scandium?"

"Yes, of course."

"Well," said Treshkov, "the bottom line is that we still don't know what Trevor Grehm was up to, but the trades were definitely not approved by Brecht."

"And?"

"And, well, if it turns out the problem is his, and by that I mean within Iberia, then Brecht will see to it that the partnership gets its normal commission. On the other hand, he wonders whether it's more reasonable to suspect that the problem is with your people."

"What does he mean, a problem with my people?"

"What he means is, are you sure the problem is on the American side? Could some of your people in Pskov have gotten greedy? Grehm obviously had to have help in Pskov, and certainly in arranging the original shipment from the mine in Oskemen. That scandium didn't take a taxicab to Kaliningrad," Treshkov said, referring to a small Russian enclave sandwiched between Lithuania and Poland that was one of the main transit points for smuggled Russian goods. "And who else better to have helped him but one of your own people? Maybe whoever it was has decided to help himself to a bigger piece of the pie." Treshkov tore off a piece of black bread, popped it into his mouth, and followed it by draining his glass. He turned to his host with a curious frown. "Yury Ivanovich, really, with your budget, I would think you could find something decent to offer your guests, not this very mediocre vodka."

"I think you are wrong, Arkady," Khavkin said, ignoring Treshkov's comment. "It would make no sense to steal from us and then let the whole business come to our attention. No, not even as a cover would that make sense. It would have been too easy for one of our own people to carry out the trade without any of the other partners' knowing of it."

"But that much scandium?" Treshkov questioned. "What was it, fifty kilos?"

"Almost sixty," Khavkin said. "Yes, even that much."

Treshkov shrugged. "Well, perhaps." He smiled mischievously and raised one eyebrow. "Had I known it was all that easy for you to deal in such volume, I would have been out finding even more customers. But, still, given what you've told me was the source and route of the material, it certainly makes sense for Brecht to suspect someone within your group was part of the deal."

"Maybe," Yury Khavkin murmured.

"Have you determined who the buyers were?"

"No."

"And how much money was involved? What is the market these days?"

"For a kilo?" asked Khavkin. "Depending on the buyer, sixty-five to seventy thousand."

"American?"

"Yes."

"So—what?—we are talking around four million U.S.?"

"Yes, and too much for one of our people to hide without our knowing about it."

"But who, then? Where'd the money go?"

"That's your job to find out."

"And the shipment itself?"

"I don't know."

Treshkov took a moment to pour himself another portion of vodka before asking, "But how does that much scandium just disappear?"

"In small half-kilo packages? It can disappear very easily. That's why we have moved so aggressively into that market. But trust me, sooner or later I will find the principals."

"Yes, I am sure you will."

"And you, Arkady Sergeevich, what are you going to do?"

"Me? What do you mean, what am I going to do?"

"Please, none of your games. The partners are very concerned. All these years, everything we've invested in Iberia and Arlis Brecht. We helped you build that operation from the ground, and you sit there as if we were only in danger of losing a few rubles trading coffee beans. These investigations in the States—what if all that causes someone to make the connection between Brecht and us? Even a hint of a problem. You know that pack of neo-democrats in the Interior Ministry would love to show our scalps to the Americans."

"The records have all been purged."

"As a State Security operation, yes, but, still—"

"I understand," said Treshkov. "I am not ignoring the problem. But I keep telling you, it's up to your people to track down whoever Trevor Grehm's contacts were. You have to track it back through Kaliningrad and Pskov, all the way back to Oskemen, if you have to. You can't just let that hang in the air as you have been."

"I understand, we are doing exactly that, but what about you? What is your next step?"

"I'm meeting Brecht in Lisbon. We'll rerun the traces. Maybe something will show up."

"And Brecht's people?"

"In Iberia?"

"No. I mean American intelligence. His handlers in Special Projects."

"They don't know anything about the trades. They suspect Grehm might have been dealing with the Chechens."

"So you are told."

"Yes, so I am told."

"You are certain that they haven't seen through the mirrors?"

"Can we ever be sure?"

"Has it occurred to you that Brecht may have backfired on us?"

"Yes, of course it has occurred to me."

"And so?"

"Listen to me, Yury Ivanovich. If you are truly worried that this is some devious American plot, your course is clear. Simply walk away from it. So the partners lose their commission on a shipment of scandium? So what? It is pocket change by comparison. Walk away if you are frightened."

Khavkin smiled a thin, sardonic smile. "It is not the money, Arkady Sergeevich, and fear can be a useful thing, if properly channeled. Remember, it is you who convinced us to invest in Iberia and Brecht—"

"And you have profited handsomely," Treshkov quickly interjected.

"True enough," said Khavkin, "but never before has so much attention been focused on any matter even remotely connected to us. We have trusted you, relied on you to keep the walls intact, but the partners are beginning to wonder if you may have lost some control, wondering even if your access to Brecht and Iberia is being turned against you by American intelligence. And if you are in jeopardy, so are we all. This is not a matter that any of us take lightly."

Treshkov leaned forward, his dark and close-set eyes narrowing with the sudden intensity of his concern. "Exactly," he said, then paused to emphasize the precision with which he expected Khavkin to answer. "Exactly what is it that concerns you most?"

Khavkin met Treshkov's stare. "It is these murders, these damned investigations! All it takes is a single crack in the wall. Remember the lessons of that fool Gorbachev. You allow the door to open just a crack and suddenly you are buried in infidels. Our business, our entire organization, our very lives are at stake here. Everything!" Yury Khavkin slumped in his chair and shook his head slowly. "And this incident with the man in . . . where was it?"

"Annapolis. It's about fifty kilometers—"

"Yes, yes, I know Annapolis. But this detective who was shot?"

"Yes?"

"He was looking for the same information as you?"

"Yes."

"A local detective?"

"So I'm told."

"And you believe that?"

"I have no reason not to believe it."

"Have you considered the possibility that he was connected to Special Projects or the Joint Committee? FBI, perhaps?"

"Yes, of course I have considered that possibility, but all evidence is that he was not."

"But you will find out for certain?"

"Of course, if I can."

"And then?"

Treshkov sat back, tossed down the last of his vodka, and emphatically snapped his glass down on the table. His expression was not threatening, but, like his voice, it was confident and unequivocal. "Listen to me, Yury Ivanovich, and listen well. And tell your partners. If and when I find the source of the problem, no matter who or what it is, no matter on which side I find it, I will eliminate it, and I will do so quickly and quietly and without mercy. Do we understand one another?"

Khavkin nodded, and for the first time allowed himself a brief smile. "Yes, we understand one another." He sat back and drained his teacup, then poured himself some vodka. "Fortunately, we have always understood one another. I admit that there are times when I worry that your taste for Western luxuries has made you soft, but I remind myself of the lesson you have always preached—the lesson our leaders never learned, which is why they so grossly underestimated the Americans—that it most often takes a hard man to earn and keep the soft life."

Treshkov returned the smile and raised his glass. "Another vodka, then. To the soft life!"

11.

Eddie sat on the back porch, his face lifted to the morning sun, his mind drifting with the flow of his pain medication. Five days before, his sons had brought him home to find that the kitchen had been scrubbed clean and cleared of all reminders of the shooting except the random scars of bullets the police had dug out of the ceiling, floor, and walls. The refrigerator had been stuffed with pre-prepared meals, and on the table were fresh flowers, a basket of fruit, and a note:

"There's gruel in the fridge and Jack Daniel's in the larder. Housekeeping will be here tomorrow & will come weekdays until you're settled. Her name's Lennie Mapes. Try not to scare her away. Pris fine but can't stop worrying. Call when you can. Brush your teeth and say your prayers. Be careful!!! Megs."

It had taken little more than an hour that first night home for Eddie and his sons to exhaust their stores of catch-up conversation and for a certain edginess to come over them, a thin but building cloud of old tensions and imagined injuries. By midafternoon the next day, the boys—with Eddie's encouragement—were making plans to drive to Bucks County to see their mother and sister before flying home. The following morning, Carl's rental car had been packed, and the three men stood in the driveway stumbling through the awkward lies that everything was fine and no one should worry and maybe one day soon Eddie would visit Tom in the Florida Keys and do some fishing, or Carl would take some time off so he and his father could travel the great Northwest, which Eddie had never seen—"or maybe, you know, whatever." And then they were gone.

Eddie was again thinking of all the things he could have said, and perhaps should have said, to his sons when Lennie Mapes stepped out on the porch. "Mr. Nickles, you want your coffee now?"

"Ms. Mapes, please, you don't have to—" Eddie stopped himself. "Oh, never mind, yes, I'll have some coffee. Thanks."

Eddie was more resigned than grateful. Ms. Mapes was a short, trim woman in her mid-fifties, whose coffee-colored skin was highlighted by a little too much rouge, and whose approach was always announced by a little too much perfume. Several times he had tried to explain that he neither needed nor was comfortable with someone hovering over him and constantly asking whether he wanted anything. Her second morning on the job, he had stumbled through an embarrassing effort to say that she wasn't needed at all, but she quickly let him know the rules by which they were operating.

"Mr. Nickles, you didn't hire me, so you can't fire me. Your ex-wife has already paid me a month's wages, and I will do a month's work. That's all there is to it. Now, you can throw me out the house if you want, but I will still come every morning at nine and I will leave every evening at four. If you want to embarrass me and yourself by having me set all day on your front steps waiting to do my job, you go right ahead. But seems to me you'd be better off showing a little gratitude and the good manners to accept what help people that love you want to give."

"I'm sorry," Eddie had said. "I didn't mean to insult you."

"None taken. Now, where'd you hide your dirty clothes, so I can get some washing done around here?"

The issue was thus settled.

Ms. Mapes returned to the porch with a steaming cup of coffee and an announcement. "The gentleman you were expecting is here."

"Jimmy? Already?"

"Detective Legget, his card says."

"You didn't leave him standing at the door, did you?"

"I figured, with all that's happened, you'd want your guests announced."

Ms. Mapes had been briefed by Eddie as to what had happened in the house. He had hoped it might discourage her from staying on. "I figure like they say," she had replied. "Lightning doesn't strike the same place twice. 'Sides, I've got a living to earn."

Eddie started to get up. "Now, you set still," she ordered. "I'll bring the gentleman in." She cocked her head. "Is he married?"

"Yes, he's married."

"Hmm. And here I was thinking I might have my daughter over to help out a bit. He sure is one fine-looking gentleman."

Eddie grinned as Ms. Mapes turned and started for the door. He had seen the reaction before. James W. Legget was indeed a handsome man. Tall, trim, and always immaculately dressed, Jimmy never seemed to sweat, never appeared rattled. Detective Legget had been new to Homicide when he and Eddie first met, and to Eddie, Jimmy looked to be everything he wanted to distrust in the new breed of detectives: too clean, someone afraid to get his hands dirty, too much by the book, and not enough of the street in him. But circumstances had later thrown them together in a case that had tested the limits of their individual and complementary skills. Moles in the police department, moles in the DA's office, snitches working both sides of the fence, and a drug-based financial empire that controlled City Hall and virtually all the heroin that came into the city. Eddie worked by instinct and experience, Jimmy by intelligence and analysis, and by the end of the case they had learned to trust one another like they could no one else.

Against all odds, and even against their own expectations, they had won, closing down the organization and making the single largest seizure of heroin in the city's history. There had been loose ends, plenty of them, and long discussions, even arguments, about the one loose end they could never settle between them: that of Michael Holden, once Eddie's closest friend and the DA who ran the investigation and then retired under circumstances they had since agreed not to talk about. The two men had not worked a case together since, Eddie having spent the last five years before his retirement working alone. But each knew that, if needed, the other would be there.

Eddie stood and clasped Jimmy's hand. "Man, I wasn't expecting you till later. Take your jacket off. Relax." Jimmy set down a briefcase and slid off the crisply pressed tan suit jacket and draped it over the back of one chair. "Ms. Mapes?" Eddie called.

"I've got the gentleman's coffee right here," Ms. Mapes said, coming onto the porch carrying a tray loaded with a pot of coffee, cup and saucer, and a creamer and sugar bowl. "Anything else you require, Detective Legget?"

"No thank you."

"Some eggs and bacon, maybe? Or some pancakes? I've got all the fixin's."

"Thank you, ma'am, but I'm just fine. I had some breakfast on the way down."

"Some juice? I've got some fresh-squeezed orange juice."

"No, ma'am, really, this coffee is all I need. 'Preciate it, though."

"Well," Ms. Mapes sighed, "all right, then," and she retired.

Jimmy looked over his shoulder quizzically, and Eddie said, "She wants you to marry her daughter."

Jimmy smiled. "So, how're you feeling?"

"Not bad. Still stiff as hell, and I run out of breath just climbing a flight of stairs, but I figure most of that is just from sitting on my ass all day. Otherwise I'm okay."

"That's good," Jimmy said, but without much enthusiasm. He then took a sip of coffee, frowning.

"What's wrong?" Eddie asked. "How come you're here so early?"

Since first visiting Eddie in the hospital, and after several phone calls between them, Detective Legget had been trying to piece together whatever information he could to unravel the reasons and people behind the attack on his friend. He reached into his briefcase and took out a thick file of photocopied documents, which he tossed on the table between them. "That's the entire homicide jacket. I copied everything."

"Was there a problem?"

"A little. Carlos told me the Grehm case had been held open, but they weren't really working it. They had run out of leads, and the word was, the front office was looking to close it as a murder-suicide. Which, for reasons I'll get to in a minute, even Carlos thought strange. But anyway, when this thing with you happened, the captain pulled the file back to his office. Said the case belonged to the feds now."

"The feds? You mean FBI?"

"Yep."

"What the hell does the FBI have to do with this?"

"I don't know. Carlos doesn't know. I even asked the captain. He doesn't know. He just said that a message came down from the chief's office to segregate the file. 'Inquiry from the feds.' That's all he said. It took some talking, but he finally let me make a copy."

Eddie looked at the stack of papers. "Anything interesting in there?"

"A few things, and a few things interesting that aren't in the file."

"Like?"

"You know this guy who hired you—Bolles, or whatever his name is—you understand that he doesn't exist, right? County police can't find him, I can't find him. Just that office on Fifteenth Street. No trace of him otherwise." Eddie nodded. He had heard the same thing from the county police. "Yeah, well," Jimmy continued, "what strikes me as strange is that even Carlos never heard of him. He said no one named Bolles—or anyone else, for that matter—ever came around representing the family."

"What?"

"That's right. Except this fella Arlis Brecht. You know, Trevor Grehm's boss? But all he did was identify the bodies and handle the arrangements for shipping the remains back to the family. According to Carlos, he never asked any questions or made any complaint. I called Brecht over in Lisbon. Apparently that's where the head office is. Anyway, Brecht says he never heard of Bolles and doesn't know anyone who even remotely fits your description of him. And as far as he knows, the family never made any inquiries, at least not through him. He assumed the case had been closed out as a murder-suicide. 'Course, he told the family what they wanted to hear—you know, that the police suspected it was a burglary or whatever and they were still working the case."

"So how'd this guy Bolles get all this information about the autopsies and the running résumé and all that?"

"I don't know."

"This is getting a little weird."

"Man, I haven't even started."

Eddie frowned. "How weird does it get?"

"Very. Let me ask you something. The FBI man who came to see you in the hospital. You sure you got the name right?"

Eddie's eyes narrowed. "Why?"

"What was the name? Wychek?"

"Yeah. At least I thought so. I was a little groggy at the time."

"Well, I talked to our old friend Dennis Curran. He's working out of bureau headquarters now. He tells me there is no Wychek, at least none assigned to either the Washington or Baltimore field office or in headquarters." Jimmy paused a moment. "I gotta admit I thought you were being a little hardheaded—maybe even a bit paranoid—you know, pretending you were too doped up to tell him anything—but maybe your instincts were right. Unless maybe you got the name wrong, he doesn't exist."

"I don't know," Eddie said quietly, "I could've got the spelling wrong, but I'm sure he said Wychek or something like it."

"Well, Curran checked. Tried every spelling he could think of, but nothing. No listing locally."

"Like I told you," Eddie said, "he didn't seem right, and when was the last time you heard of the bureau doing an interview alone and without taking notes? Plus, all he wanted to know was about Helen Grehm's credit cards."

"And you told him you didn't have them?"

"No, not really. I just mumbled some shit. I don't know what I said exactly. I just tried to avoid the question."

"And so no one knows you've actually got the cards?"

"No. Except this character Bolles, or whatever his name is, and my man LeRoi."

"Well, not LeRoi, not anymore."

"Whaddaya mean? You found him?"

"In a manner of speaking."

"Meaning?"

"Meaning he didn't split after all. He'd been in the morgue since about noon on the day after you were shot."

"You're not serious."

"Absolutely. Body was found in an alley. Shot once in the side of the head. He'd been carried as a John Doe. No one reported him missing, no one reported him killed, no one claimed him. Just another anonymous body, that's all. A number with a bad tooth. I just tracked him down yesterday afternoon."

Eddie stood up and moved to the porch rail, his back to Jimmy, leaning on the black wooden cane he held next to his wounded leg.

"There's something else," Jimmy continued. "I sent a crew out to scour the alley where LeRoi was found." He hesitated.

"And?"

"And they found the gun."

"The gun?"

"Your gun," said Jimmy. "Your Beretta. It was in the middle of a trash pile about fifty feet from where LeRoi's body was found." Jimmy attempted a smile. "Doesn't say much for the team that did the scene in the first place, does it?"

"My gun?"

"They matched the serial numbers last night."

Eddie turned back to face Jimmy. "Jesus, man, you're not telling me they matched the slug in LeRoi to my Beretta?" There was a long silence until Eddie asked again. "You're not gonna tell me that, are you?"

"Firearms made the match this morning."

"Jesus, Jimmy . . . you don't believe I did LeRoi, do you?"

"No, I don't. I don't want to believe it, but I gotta ask, straight up."

"No, no way, man. I didn't kill LeRoi. Jesus, man, like I said, the tall guy took that gun before all hell broke loose, before I got shot."

Jimmy nodded. "I had to ask. You understand, right?"

"Yeah, I understand. . . . Jesus Christ!"

Jimmy sat back and rubbed his temples with the tips of his fingers. "Look, the problem is there's gonna be cops all over you about this. The captain's making arrangements with Anne Arundel County now to send out a team to question you."

"Do they know you're here?"

"No." Eddie nodded appreciatively before Jimmy continued. "Anyway, the fact that LeRoi came in as a John Doe and sat in the morgue for more than a week is gonna make it difficult, if not impossible, to establish a precise time of death."

"Meaning I probably won't be able to prove he got shot after I did."

"Probably."

Eddie shook his head. "Christ, it just keeps getting deeper, doesn't it?"

"And a lot stranger, too."

"There's more?"

"Lots."

"Like?"

"Okay. First, the nine-millimeter found on Trevor Grehm, the same one that killed his wife and supposedly he used on himself? That was a P-64."

"A what?"

"Something called a P-64. It's a Polish-manufactured version of the Soviet Makarov PM. It had been stripped clean of any serial numbers or other traceable markings." Jimmy answered Eddie's deep frown. "Yeah, man, a pretty strange weapon for some British commodities trader to be carrying. Second, you'll see in the reports there that in the house where his wife was killed they found another slug, buried in the wall just outside her bedroom. No way of telling when that shot was fired, obviously, but it sure made Carlos suspect that this Helen lady might have fired off a round herself before she was killed."

"Then how the hell was anyone thinking of closing this out as a murder-suicide?"

"That's what Carlos wanted to know. But, like he told me, since they had run dry of any leads, there were hints from the front office to just let it die and go on to better cases. Anyway, what's really interesting is that the slug they found in the wall turns out to match the nine-millimeter you took off the man who caught it in your kitchen. And as you know, that gun's clean, too. Can't be traced."

"Wait a minute, wait a minute, this doesn't make sense," Eddie started, but Jimmy stopped him.

"Well, just hold on. There's something else weird that shows up in the reports that your Mr. Bolles never told you, or maybe he didn't know. The toxicology on Trevor Grehm came back showing he had a pretty heavy load of something called midazolam hydro-

chloride. It's a water-soluble benzodiazepine, which, to the unin-
formed, is one helluva serious goofball, a central-nervous-system
depressant. Doc Crowell says, if nothing else, the man probably
died with a smile on his face. He wouldn't have felt a thing."

Eddie paused a long moment, his eyes squinting. "I'm not sure
I get it. You mean he was on the stuff?"

"No, it's not one of your fashionable cocktails."

"Then what?"

"Well, other than knocking someone out for an operation or
whatever, it could also be used to loosen someone's tongue. Properly administered, Doc says under the influence a man would happily tell you whatever you wanted to know."

"Meaning?"

"Meaning, if this guy Grehm was shot full of some kind of dope
to open him up, what is it these people wanted to know, and what
does that have to do with Helen Grehm getting killed, and what's
this other bullet in the wall tell us, and how'd that gun end up in
your kitchen?"

Eddie smiled. "And you've got a theory?"

"Yeah, I got a theory," Jimmy said. "Let's say Helen and her old
man are up to some shit we don't know about. Let's say drugs.
That seems to be the crime of choice these days. Doesn't matter,
could be anything. But, whatever it is, it's enough for them to keep
a nine-millimeter around. She hears the black hats in the house,
maybe gets off the first shot, but misses. Then they plug her. Our
hit man's no dope. He says to himself, he says, 'Why not use the
gun I just whacked the lady with to do the old man and leave it behind?' He's thinking fast—maybe the cops'll buy murder-suicide.
Besides, his piece can't be traced, and he's got an instant replace-
ment: the nine-millimeter he takes off the lady and ends up wav-
ing in your face."

"But what's that got to do with her husband being loaded up on
some goofball?"

"I don't know, but maybe it was something about those credit
cards, or something in Helen Grehm's wallet they were after. A
bank-account number, a safe-deposit key—who knows? Maybe
that's why everyone's so interested in these credit cards, that's
what they came after Helen Grehm for in the first place."

"But that wouldn't make sense, would it? I mean, if that's what they were after, why toss the wallet on the street and then turn around and go through all this trouble to get it back?"

"I know, it doesn't make sense *unless*"—Jimmy stopped and raised one finger in emphasis—"unless they didn't realize the credit cards were the key until afterward. Maybe they tossed the wallet on the street figuring it'd end up with some dirt bag like LeRoi who'd might get caught with it, and the whole thing would look like a burglary. Then, later, they find the husband, and that's when they learned that whatever they were looking for was in the wallet."

"Maybe," Eddie said slowly. "And maybe LeRoi was lying. Maybe he really was on the scene."

"Maybe," Jimmy said, "but you don't believe that any more than I do. I mean, how does some wasted doper like LeRoi end up in business like this unless it happened just like he said."

"Yeah," Eddie said, "maybe you're right. He sounded straight at the time, but . . . shit, I don't know." Eddie scratched at his unshaven chin, his eyes darting from point to point as thoughts flashed through his head.

"Next," Jimmy said, "I talked to the detective in charge here in Anne Arundel."

Eddie smiled. "Man, you have been digging."

"Anyway, the detective tells me that the man who got whacked in your kitchen probably spent some time in a Russian prison. Something about the tattoos he had and the kind of dental work they saw during the post."

"Russian?"

"Maybe—they don't have an ID yet. The bureau's still running prints."

"And the captain says the feds have called for the file?"

"Yep."

A queer, twisted smile came over Eddie's face. "Man, all I wanted to do was buy my daughter a graduation present."

Jimmy nodded. "I know. But somehow you've been pulled into some real deep shit."

"Meaning?"

"Whaddaya mean, 'meaning'? Man, you're hired by someone who doesn't exist to find some credit cards of a lady who gets killed in a shootout by an untraceable nine-millimeter manufactured in Poland that's used to whack her old man, who just happens to be overloaded on some exotic nerve depressant. Then some local doper tells you he found the cards on the street, gives them to you, and then gets whacked with your gun. Next we have your standard hired gun who may have spent time in a Russian prison and who carries not one item of identification trying to kill you over these same credit cards, and with another nine-millimeter, which the original victim probably fired at him. And then, all of a sudden, the case files are pulled because of some unexplained inquiry from the feds, and an FBI agent no one's heard of comes to visit you in the hospital. Yeah, you're right. Doesn't mean a thing. Just your run-of-the-mill gumshoe case."

Eddie turned back to the water, his right hand nervously stabbing the rubber tip of the cane on the decking. "Jesus Christ," he mumbled, "should've known the money was too good. So much for not lookin' a gift horse in the mouth."

Jimmy spoke quietly. "These credit cards. You're sure no one else knows you have them, right?"

"Like I said, no one but Bolles and whoever the second man in the kitchen is."

"You don't have them here, I hope."

"No, they're in a safe-deposit box. Why?"

"Well, seems to me an awful lot of people're going to an awful lot of trouble to find them. You've gotta watch your back, man."

"Meaning?"

"Will you quit saying that? It's driving me crazy. What the hell do you think I mean? Man, this shit isn't over. You know that. Forget that the Department may very well try to tag you with LeRoi's murder. That's one. Two, you don't really think the people who came after you have lost interest, do you? You don't think they might come looking again? I think it's time for you to call in a few favors."

"Like?"

"Like maybe someone in the bureau. Like Dennis Curran, maybe. Like maybe we can find some technical people to look over these cards and maybe find out why everyone's so damn interested in them. Like maybe you're gonna need some friends looking out for you. You know what I'm saying?" Jimmy took a breath, and his voice lowered with his chin. "Like maybe you ought to take a vacation somewhere. Let things cool down, and give us a chance to find out what the hell is going on before the cards get stacked too high."

"You mean run?"

"No, I mean be smart for a change. Take a vacation while it's still your choice. Keep your options open. You know as well as I do that the minute they start coming around and asking all kinds of questions your options get limited."

"You don't think they're going for a warrant, do you?"

"I don't think so. At least not yet. But the point is, whatever's going on here, whatever this case is about, it's not being played by the rules, at least not by any of the rules you and I know. So, like I say, why not keep your options open? Take a little vacation while you can. Give us some time to work things out."

Eddie looked back over his shoulder. "What time is it?"

"Ten-fifteen. Why?"

"I think maybe it's time to break out that bottle of Jack Daniel's Megs left."

Jimmy paused, then cocked his head skeptically. "You think that's a good idea, with all that medication you're on?" Jimmy tried but he could not match Eddie's stare. "I'll get the bottle and a couple of glasses," he said.

office, where the air-conditioning was too cool, to dine outdoors, where the day was too hot.

"It's something new from our kitchen," Machus said. "A chicken salad, but with all sorts of nuts and grapes and curry and such. Miss Berksmere suggested the recipe. I think you'll like it."

"Yes, I'm sure," Brecht agreed. "Our Miss Berksmere is quite a gourmet. Or is it gourmand?"

"Whichever," Machus said, his eyes lowering. "Yes, isn't she, though. A woman of many talents."

Indeed, thought Brecht. Miss Berksmere. The woman he was certain had called for this meeting, although it was equally certain that she would not join them. Except for her annual dinner party in honor of Guy Fawkes Day—an intimate but terribly elegant affair for no more than a dozen of the directorate's top people—Miss Berksmere, like the chief, always dined alone, unless, of course, some business of theirs required a lighter, more personal touch.

Oh, yes, thought Brecht, it was Miss Berksmere who had directed that this lunch take place. Her presence was palpable, her spirit hovering. The Valkyrian Miss Berksmere, the chief's own sorceress, watching over the field of battle, choosing who was to be slain and who was not, and who was worthy of passage to Valhalla. Miss Berksmere, "the virgin virago," the boys on the third floor snickered. But Brecht knew better. Oh, he certainly knew better. Like his Helen, she was no virgin, she was no innocent. No, not Miss Berksmere, not Odin's sorceress and seducer. He had seen it in the sharp and unforgiving eyes Philo Machus suddenly lowered at the mention of her name, his slight but inevitable bow to her presence, the hint of shyness, the bit of stammer and throat-clearing as they'd meet in the halls like surreptitious lovers. He had seen it all, as if they shared some dirty little secret. He wondered again, as he had so many times, whether she used him in private as she seemed to use him in public. He imagined himself in the room with them, in *her* room, crouching at the end of *her* bed. It would be a large bed, he thought, with thick carved posts mounted by griffins and draped with blood-red velvet and black satin sheets. He imagined watching them along with Miss Berksmere's companion, the diminutive and reclusive Miss Alice Whiting with her dark, Keane eyes; both of them, he and Alice,

watching as Miss Berksmere took the chief's short, spare body and
mounted it upon her, clutching him in those powerful hands,
holding him like a tiny toy while his arms and legs flailed help-
lessly, using him like some autoerotic device until he was all but
spent, and still forcing him on, driving him until he pleaded with
her, gasping and choking as he begged, and she'd demand more,
commanding him, sucking out the last of his energy, wringing
him dry, taking him to the very edge of his life, while Miss Alice
writhed in the corner maenadlike, muttering oaths and squealing
encouragement. *More! More!*

"... Arlis?"

"What?"

"Are you all right?"

"What? Oh, yes, certainly. I'm sorry, you were saying?"

"I was only commenting on the chicken salad. Are you sure
you're okay? Is there something wrong with the salad?"

"No, no. I was only thinking of things I need to do when I get
back to Lisbon."

"You're returning to Lisbon? Already?"

"Yes, I think I should."

"When are you planning to leave?"

"Tomorrow. Unless ... well, unless there's some reason to
delay?"

"You tell me. Is there?"

"You mean because of this Grehm business and whatever happened out ... Where was it? Annapolis?"

The chief touched the thin scar line along his cheek. A light, un-
conscious touch. "Yes, Annapolis." He cocked his head slightly.
"Anyway, I'm told you were called by the police on this matter."

"Yes, a few days ago."

"And?"

Brecht shrugged. "It was nothing. A detective by the name of
Legget. James, I think. He asked a lot of questions about Trevor.
What was his job, what did I know of his background, had we had
any trouble with him. That sort of thing. He asked me about identifying the bodies, which brought back very unpleasant memories,
I must say. He wanted to know if the body was in fact Trevor's. Of
course I said it was."

"And Helen?"

"Yes, well, he asked much the same about her. He seemed a bit curious why I was the one to identify her body, and Trevor's, but of course I explained that Trevor's family was in London, elderly parents and all that, and how Helen had no family of her own here in the States. And, too, he was most interested in whoever this fellow Bolles was."

"And you said?"

"What else could I say? I have no idea."

"Did this Legget fellow seem satisfied?"

"I suppose." Brecht hesitated. Arlis Brecht was a tall man, just over six feet, and his every feature seemed clean and fair and constant, as if the messiness of life did not touch him. His thinning blond hair was always combed in the same style, his long fingers always ended in well-rounded and polished nails, and, despite his forty-six years, his physique remained trim and seemingly unaffected by any of the normal aging processes. His face, fair-skinned and smooth, rarely changed expression, but was on occasion given to reddening—as it did at that moment—at the first sign of anxiety. "I admit," he said, "that I may have sounded a bit uncomfortable talking about going to the morgue and all. I told you at the time it was a mistake having me identify the bodies. I can't be so detached as your people in such matters."

"Well, it was the only choice we had, Arlis. There was simply no time for alternatives. We could not have the curiosity of the police piqued by an unidentified body, now, could we?"

"Perhaps. I just wish it could have been someone other than myself."

"Yes, well, in any event, do you think they'll be doing any follow-up with you?"

"The police?"

"Yes. Did you say anything about your coming to Washington?"

"No."

"So, again, do you think this detective was satisfied? Is there any reason to think he might want to talk to you further?"

"I don't know. He didn't say anything along those lines, but I think my returning to Lisbon might be the cautious thing to do."

"And that's why you're going?"

"Well, yes, but also it makes more sense for the business. I need to keep a closer eye on things. I've been spending too much time away."

The chief speared a grape on the end of his fork, then stopped. He frowned ever so slightly. "It was Helen, wasn't it, Arlis? You were certain, weren't you? I mean, given the state the body was in and all?"

Brecht's face flushed a bit deeper, and he took his time, nodding slowly, before saying, "Yes, of course I'm certain. Please, let's not talk about that. I've never seen anything quite so grotesque. It still makes me sick to think of it."

"I'm sure. But, well, we all have our cross to bear, now, don't we?"

"Yes, I suppose we do," Brecht said, looking away.

The chief raised a glass pitcher and offered, "More iced tea?"

"No thank you."

The chief poured himself another glass. "And the business? All seals still in place? You've not discovered any problems or evidence that might give us some hint of what Trevor and his wife were up to?"

"No, nothing. But as an additional precaution I've had all our trading and financial accounts recoded. I've given the boys on the third floor a new listing. All fresh codes and access procedures."

"Good, good," Machus said.

"And you?"

"Me?" Machus inquired, sounding surprised.

"Yes. You've got your own seals in place? This Annapolis business isn't going to be a problem?"

"No. In some ways, messy as it was, it may have been a blessing in disguise. Gave us an excuse to step in, as it were. Our friends in the bureau have called in the investigative files. They've taken over the case as far as the official records are concerned. There will be no further involvement of the local authorities. Everything seems to have quieted down."

"Yet this Detective Legget calls me and, I understand, has talked to a number of people here in the Washington office."

"Well, it seems Detective Legget is a personal friend of this fellow Nickles, the one who was shot. Just some snooping on his own, I suspect. It won't get out of hand."

"And if it does?"

"We'll take care of it. You should consider the matter closed."

"Are you certain?"

Machus sat back and patted his napkin to his lips. "Yes, Arlis, I am certain. Do you have any reason to think me wrong?"

"No, it's just that this business has been more than a little unsettling for me."

"Yes, for all of us." Machus then leaned forward and took another bite of salad. "There is one other thing, however."

Brecht looked up sharply and lowered the forkful of chicken he had just raised to his lips. "Yes?"

"I am curious about our friend Treshkov. Nothing from him?"

"Treshkov?"

"Yes, Treshkov . . . Arlis, are you sure you're all right? You seem a bit distracted."

"No, I'm fine. Perhaps it's the heat, and a little jet lag. I seem to be spending all my time on planes lately. Anyway," Brecht said, taking a deep breath, "you were saying?"

"I asked whether you've been contacted by Treshkov."

"No, not since we last spoke."

"Well, ours was only a brief telephone conversation, Arlis. Do you mind if we go over the details again?"

"I'm not sure there are any 'details,' as you call them."

"No questions about this Annapolis business?"

"Yes, of course. I'm sorry, I thought we'd gone over that. He wanted to know the same thing he wanted to know after the Grehms were killed, whether there was any danger to them, whether there was any way these police investigations into the Grehms might open up a wider investigation into Iberia and all that."

"And you said?"

"I told him everything was under control."

"And he believed you?"

"He seemed to."

"He didn't say how he had heard of the shooting in Annapolis?"

Brecht smiled. "No, no more than you ever tell me how you come about your information."

"Yes, I see. He hasn't expressed any further concern?"

"Just for his accounts. Like us, he wonders what the Grehms

were up to, and whether there's any danger of their being compromised. It's all in the report I gave to the boys on the third floor."

"You're certain you still have his confidence?"

Brecht hesitated a moment, then said, "As much as I have yours."

Machus did not answer.

Brecht cocked his head. "Well?"

"You seem upset, Arlis."

"Should I be?"

Again, Machus said nothing.

Arlis dropped his fork on his plate and sat back, turning his chair a bit to the side. "Of course I'm upset. This isn't my line. I was hired to run a business, not to scurry around back alleys in trench coats and false mustaches."

Machus laughed.

"This isn't funny. Not to me. I know I'm responsible for Trevor Grehm. I brought him in originally, and the sonofabitch obviously involved himself in some side business that's created a serious security problem. I understand that. But I've done all I can, traced through every damn account, sealed every possible hole I could find. What else he knew, or if he was working with someone besides Helen, if in fact she was ever really involved, I don't know. That's for you and all your gumshoes to find out. Just let me get back to the business. That's all I want."

"Listen to me, Arlis—"

"No, wait a minute. Another thing, another thing while I have your attention. I don't appreciate that little band of green eyeshades up there on the fourth floor questioning me about my business trips."

"What do you mean?"

"This last trip to Grenada, for example. Asking me to justify it on national-security grounds or whatever."

"Who said that?"

"Well, that's an overstatement, perhaps, but you know what I'm talking about."

"Arlis, I'm sorry. Sometimes they get a little overzealous. But after all, you can imagine, sitting up there all day just keeping track of expenses and all. They're just trying to do their job. I'll have a talk with Miss Berksmere. I'm sure she'll set them straight."

Brecht took a deep breath and turned back to the table, pushing his fork through the remains of his salad. His head drooped, and his eyes lifted with a very quiet question. "You think Grehm might have been dealing with Treshkov?"

Philo Machus did not blink or change expression. He paused a moment. "That's a very interesting question, Arlis. What do you think?"

"I think it's possible."

"And how do we find out?"

"I don't know. Not yet, at least."

"But you are thinking along that line?"

"Yes, I am. I have been."

"Is there anything I can do to help?"

"I don't know. I think I just have to keep looking. If there is an answer, I suspect I'll find it in Lisbon, not here."

"Yes, I believe you're right. Well, whatever I can do, you'll let me know."

"Of course."

"And in the meantime, I think we have managed to lower the noise level over all this. I suspect our only problems are internal, if indeed there is any remaining problem."

"Yes, *if* there is a problem."

Both men looked at one another for a moment. Brecht broke the impasse with a weak smile and said, "We never seem able to stop asking about all the ifs, do we?"

"It's how we stay alive, Arlis. It's how we stay alive."

r

The sun-splashed square on the Rua Bacalhoeiros was cooled by currents of sea air drifting in from the harbor, but Arlis Brecht seemed not at all relieved. He leaned back from the table and lifted his chin as if something unpleasant had just passed under his nose.

"What?" asked Arkady Treshkov, looking up from his *lulinhas*. "You don't like squid?"

"Not quite so much of it, no," Brecht said disdainfully.

Treshkov shook his head. "*Zanuda,*" he grumbled.

"I beg your pardon?"

"*Zanuda!*" Treshkov emphasized. "*Zanuda!*" He stabbed the last few bits of squid onto his fork and waved them under Brecht's nose. "What is it you Americans say? Tight-ass? Yes, that's it. Tight-ass. That's you, Arlis. A tight-ass. Always worried about what might happen tomorrow, or next year, or what might never happen. Don't you understand? You are going to die, Arlis. Any minute now you will be dead. Maybe some of us will go to your funeral, but, on the other hand, maybe we won't. Maybe we will plan to go, but find that we have something more important to do, and we will do no more than make a phone call to send some flowers and go on with our lives. And what will all of your worry have gotten you?"

Brecht said nothing.

"Well, I'll tell you what it won't have gotten you. It won't have gotten you a decent meal. Look at you sitting there, looking down your nose. That fish died for you and you won't even show it the courtesy of eating it. You might as well relax, my friend, because I have no intention of leaving without a dessert. That custard, the caramel? What's it called?"

"Pudim flan."

"Yes, that. I have no intention of leaving before enjoying some *pudim flan.*" Arkady reared back in his chair, his hands braced on the table, satisfied and drawing in a deep breath of salt air. "You know," he said, his head cocked like that of a curious puppy, "I never much appreciated Lisbon, but that's because I relied on the likes of you to show me around. Every time I'd come here, you managed to find some awful Portuguese imitation of some awful English or American restaurant imitating awful Portuguese food. I used to think it was a tragic failure of Portuguese genetics, a curse endemic to the culture. I thought no one in this country knew how to cook anything. But all the while it was you, you and that tongue of yours, as sensitive as the sole of your shoe. And now it is I introducing you to the true delights of this city."

"Can we just get back to business here?" Brecht complained.

Zanuda, Arkady thought. It was both Brecht's strength and his weakness, part of what had first drawn Treshkov to him. For years Arkady Treshkov, then in charge of the KGB's West European Operations, suspected Iberia Trading was at least accommodating, if not a captive of, American intelligence. The simple fact that Treshkov and his minions had found it so difficult to find any information about Iberia's internal structure and operations, together with Iberia's reluctance to take on any new business offered it by several of Treshkov's fronts, had encouraged his curiosity but tested his patience. It was just at the point when Treshkov was on the verge of deciding that the prize was not worth the effort that he got his break.

Her name was Mireille Bujold, an elegant and very expensive whore in her mid-thirties who had worked the rich and famous from Marbella to Portofino. The generous stipend she received from Treshkov at the first of each quarter had long since proved a wise investment. For Mireille, her client's secrets were equally as marketable as were her sexual favors.

Arlis Brecht was then in the midst of his second divorce and looking for solace. As ordered and meticulous as he was in his accounts and business affairs, Brecht was reckless with his emotional attachments and unforgiving in his disappointments, which seemed to be many. It was not long before the dark and sensual Mireille—which was only one of a half-dozen or more aliases she used, depending upon her mood and location or the wishes of whoever happened to be her employer at the time—began seeking investment advice from Brecht, first for herself, and then for a friend, and then for friends of friends.

When Brecht began to complain about the time he was spending on Mireille and her friends' investments and started questioning where the funds, which by that time had reached well into six figures, were coming from, Treshkov began his approach. Mireille introduced Brecht to a man called Destino, and when Brecht told the man called Destino that he would no longer handle their investments, the man called Destino introduced him to Arkady Treshkov.

Their meeting was a quiet one, Treshkov's demeanor and expression evidencing nothing but confidence and calm. He made clear his understanding and sympathy for Brecht's attitude, but, he said, he was not altogether certain that Brecht understood fully his own position. First, as delightful and accommodating a woman as Mireille was, her friends were not of the same sort. They, unfortunately, were not people who would take lightly any decision on his part to abandon their investments. Aside from whatever these people might choose to do in their disappointment, Arkady was certain Brecht might find himself in an uncomfortable position with his "employers" should it become known that Iberia Trading was being used to shelter funds for his lover and her friends.

"Besides," Arkady offered after an hour or more of conversation, "it's not as if your people have been particularly straight with you."

"What do you mean, my people?" Brecht came back irritably. "What are you talking about?"

Arkady Treshkov had done his homework. Armed with the name of the man Brecht had the year before come home to find inside his house and inside his second wife, Treshkov had developed his wedge. Appropriate photos were taken and doctored, records searched and documents forged, and soon his wife's lover—in truth a sometime real-estate agent, at other times an antique dealer from Takoma Park, Maryland—was transformed into and presented to Brecht as an internal-security specialist detailed from NSA to the Special Projects Directorate. "I don't suppose you ever asked yourself why the directorate would have allowed one of their own to be . . . well, *involved* with your wife? Perhaps something more than an affair of the heart?"

It had been a full minute or more before Brecht spoke. "But he was in real estate or something. He . . . Did she know? Did she?"

"Well, I leave it to you to draw your own conclusions."

And so Brecht then knew that Treshkov knew, and Treshkov knew that Brecht knew. And for Treshkov, best of all was that Brecht assumed that he had been cuckolded not only by his wife, but by his other family, the Special Projects Directorate. Within a month, Arlis Brecht and Arkady Treshkov began their journey together. It was the biggest coup of Treshkov's career, turning to mole the financial wizard behind the Special Projects Directorate. Treshkov was a hero, but one few knew, for, to ensure the continuing success of the operation, it was quickly determined that this operation should mirror the methods of their American counterpart, and only a select few at Moscow Center were ever informed of its existence. And to ensure his own future—and that of Brecht as well—Treshkov embarked with Brecht on an investment plan of their own, siphoning off excess funds from both their American and Soviet masters, which funds were invested into a series of well-concealed and quite profitable ventures.

The dark and sensual Mireille disappeared, and for a while Brecht was distraught. Treshkov found him another woman, and when that failed, another woman, and then another. As tiresome and expensive as the process was for Treshkov, it kept Brecht calm and kept Treshkov informed of Brecht's mercurial moods. All in all, the operation was a complete success. Everyone was happy, at least until the unfortunate business of the Grehms. But that business, Treshkov hoped, would soon be resolved, if only he could assure himself that Brecht was still in the fold.

"Get back to business?" Treshkov asked. "What business is there left? We've gone through everything twice. The hole is plugged. Your Special Projects and Joint Committee people seem to consider the problem closed, except perhaps for this Nickles fellow, who knows nothing."

"He knows you."

"No," Treshkov said slowly, "he knows someone named Garland Bolles, and Garland Bolles, as far as anyone else knows, is nothing more than a figment of this man's imagination. And I don't think my friend Mr. Nickles is the sort to go looking for trouble. A clever fellow and all that, but his range is a limited one, purely a local man. Plus, he struck me as an eminently practical man. He survived his little scare and got his ten thousand dollars as well. It seems to me his only interest at this point would be to stay as far away from this business as possible."

"But he still has Helen Grehm's wallet and the credit cards, doesn't he?"

"Perhaps."

"What do you mean, 'perhaps'?"

"Well, perhaps he turned them over to the police or whoever."

"Do you think?"

"I don't know."

"That doesn't worry you?"

"Why should I worry? If he gave the cards to the police, what are the chances that the police would start looking for encrypted messages? If somehow the cards have ended up with your people, and the encryptions contain anything threatening to us, we are already dead. So why should I worry? There's little I can do. Besides, as I've said, I suspect our Mr. Nickles is simply thankful to be alive and will be quite satisfied to leave well enough alone."

"You plan to leave Nickles alone?"

"Temporarily, yes."

"What do you mean, temporarily?"

"Just that. Temporarily. He will be dealt with, but not now. Not while there is so much attention on him. Once again, Arlis, you spend far too much time worrying about things that don't concern you. Mr. Nickles and the cards are my responsibility. You needn't bother yourself with that. You need only concentrate on those issues that are your concern."

"Such as?"

"Such as the one loose end you cannot seem to resolve. Who assisted the Grehms with the scandium trade, and who is moving the money now? You and I both know he wasn't working alone, and I suspect that even you suspect that the trades might not even have been his idea. Correct?"

Brecht let go a long sigh. "I don't know what I believe anymore. I don't know what else I can tell you, what else I can do. I don't know what else I can check."

"But you must have some idea what or who might have caused people as dependable as you said the Grehms were to have suddenly turned thieves."

"How many times do we have to go over this? I don't know, and I never will know. And for that matter, neither will you, since you and your goons killed him . . . and her!"

"Yes, well, that was unfortunate. A simple problem of trusting an assignment to the wrong people. It happens in the best of families."

"Yes, well, we seem to be having our own communication failures, don't we?"

"Yes?"

"Yes, like your refusal to address the most immediate problem. You keep asking me about the Grehms when you damn well know that whoever facilitated these trades had to have been on your side of the fence. That's where the answers to all your questions are, and only you or your people can resolve that. I'm finished with this matter. I have a business to run, and I am not going to waste any more of my time on this. Do you understand?" Brecht turned and looked out toward the square, not waiting for an answer.

Treshkov turned and signaled their waiter. *"Pudim flan,"* he called across the room. *"Dois."*

"Really," Brecht protested, "I don't want—"

Treshkov quickly raised his hand in protest. "Please, just to make me happy. Join me in a dessert."

Brecht sighed deeply, like a petulant child who would not be excused from the dinner table, and again Treshkov called to the waiter. *"E eu quero dois cafes."* And to Arlis Brecht he said, "Yes, I understand your impatience with this business. Of course, it's an annoyance for all of us, but we can't let some temporary annoyance result in permanent damage, now, can we?"

Brecht leaned forward, and his tone turned angry. "Listen to me, Arkady Sergeevich. My point is simple. Cloak and dagger are not my business. Business is my business. I've done all I can to find out whatever I can. Now, if you have some brilliant idea what else I can do besides your rather silly orders to do 'something,' then fine. Otherwise, I do not expect you to run the business, and you cannot expect me to play your little spy games. Do we understand one another?"

Treshkov, too, leaned forward. "Of course!" He then sat back and smiled broadly while dabbing his napkin at the perspiration on his cheek. "There, you see? Our business is finished. You've made your point, as I have mine, and now we can go on to enjoy our dessert. Yes, I am coming to really appreciate Lisbon. Perhaps I shall visit here more often. I do so enjoy our little chats."

Treshkov looked directly into Brecht's stare, maintaining a look of pleasant equanimity. He was not the least insulted that Arlis Brecht did not return the look in kind.

13.

Eddie Nickles did not like the notion of running, or even the appearance that he was running, which of course he was not, at least not technically, not as a matter of law. He had, after all, done nothing wrong. He had not been charged, no accusations had been leveled. Still, it just did not feel right.

But it had been hard to quarrel with the logic of Jimmy Legget's argument. "There's a real bad odor to this," Jimmy warned when Eddie resisted. "Someone other than the police seems to be calling the shots here, and the problem is that neither you nor I nor anyone we can count on knows who that is, or why. You don't know whether it's already been decided to lock you up for no other reason than that just may be an easy way to clean up some untidy business. True or not, you can't afford to take that gamble. They charge you, lock you up, the whole system turns. You know that. They stop looking for answers, and start looking to make a case. And they're not gonna have to look real hard, given they got your gun and a slug to match from LeRoi's brain. And this guy Bolles? You don't think his people will be back and a lot more prepared the next time?"

It was all too much for Eddie to think about, far too much, far too fast. But he trusted Jimmy like he trusted no one else. Jimmy's advice counted, and so Eddie followed it.

He took his time packing a few necessities in a small duffle, and told Ms. Mapes that he had decided to visit some old friends at Dewey Beach. He'd be gone just a few days, he said, or maybe more. He'd just have to see how things went and go from there. Ms. Mapes argued the wisdom of Eddie's traveling in his condition, but ultimately she supposed he might rest just as well at the beach with friends as there at home. She would see to it that everything was well looked after while he was gone. Eddie insisted that she didn't have to do that, and Ms. Mapes insisted just as vehemently that she would at least come by the house once a day until he called to tell her that he was coming home. Fair enough, Eddie agreed finally.

Eddie did not call Jack Kelly to ask permission to use the hunting cabin nestled high in the West Virginia hills, nor did he stop by the Jiffy Lube to pick up Jack's key. He took his time and the old roads, stopping once for gas and a second time for groceries: just the basics, just enough to get him through a day or two, bread and milk, eggs and bacon, peanut butter and jelly, a few cans of soup and a bottle of sour-mash whiskey. Just the basics.

It took him almost six hours to make the two-hundred-mile drive, and by the time he turned onto the long-abandoned logging trail, night and a thick cloud bank creeping in from the west swallowed even the beams of his headlights. The sharp mixture of stone and slate rubble that covered the roadbed flattened one tire several hundred yards before he reached the narrow dirt drive leading to the hunting camp where he and Jack and Jack's cousin, Johnny Patchett—who several years before had lost the lower half of one ear to a wounded badger—had spent many a weekend staying warm with whiskey and a well-banked fire after a deer hunt. He knew that it was far too dark and that he was far too tired to change the tire, so he left the car and limped the rest of the way carrying nothing but a vial of pain pills, his cane, and his old six-shot Smith & Wesson. A flashlight was the one necessity he had forgotten to bring along.

Once he reached the cabin, he shouldered his way through the rear door, causing a sharp pain in his chest that nearly stopped his breath and turned him dizzy as he felt his way along the walls to find the main junction box to turn on the electricity. There was no food in the cabin, only a few fingers of truly bad blended whiskey which he found in a cupboard above the sink. Jack never had developed a taste for the good stuff. But neither hunger nor his taste for a proper sour mash could compete with the throbbing pain in his leg and the sharp spike in his chest that seemed to come with every breath, and he abandoned all thoughts of returning to his car before morning. He settled on the broken wooden steps to the weathered wooden porch and numbed himself with a double dose of pain pills and the last few swallows of the bad blended whiskey, staring into a starless night and listening to the stillness of the air and the secret rustlings of creatures he could not see.

Suddenly his thoughts began to fill with the names and faces of the pimps and thieves and contract killers that had so overpopulated his career. And just as suddenly it occurred to him that they all had one thing in common. Like him, they all knew what it was like to be chased down a hole, and sooner or later, like him, they all just wanted to go home.

He had always chalked it up to plain stupidity, and to that special arrogance that came with stupidity, the fugitive's belief that he was too clever and too fast and the authorities too stupid and too slow. Petty street dealers and first-degree murderers, they were all the same. A few days on the run, even a few weeks or months, and eventually they all came home—or nearly all, for it was truly the rare and special breed of fugitive that ever managed to disappear completely. Most simply could not stay away, but inevitably crawled back to their old haunts, back even to sitting on their own front steps just waiting for "the man."

Eddie, however, was beginning to question his assumptions, to think perhaps there was more to it, that something more than simple stupidity drove them. He was beginning to view the phenomenon from a different perspective. He had gone into hiding only hours before, and already the sense of forced separation and of being alone seemed overwhelming. Eddie Nickles was coming to an understanding. Less than a day on the run, and already he wanted to go home. But what separated him from the others, Eddie hoped, was that he could hold on to the knowledge that going home would be stupid.

14.

Like a commuter's journey home at the end of a too-long day at the end of a too-long career, the drive north to Aosta and then west over the mountains was a blur of highways and bypasses and narrow two-lane roads so familiar as to pass unnoticed. Her thoughts wound around the lives of old friends, envying their imagined routine of grocery shopping and Little League baseball, the juggled careers in real estate and industrial piping and the worrying whether the living room would be painted before the carpet arrived and if the kids would get into college and if they would ever have the time or the money for a winter in the Caribbean or a summer in Europe. She wondered, too, if they might envy her—if they even remembered her, it had been so long—and if they thought of her at all, whether what she imagined as their life was any closer to reality than what they might imagine as hers.

It was nearly nine o'clock when her Alfa Milano emerged from the long tunnel at the northern base of Mont Blanc, and the air all at once seemed sweeter and the stars brighter as she turned toward the center of Chamonix. It was not home, but it was as close as any place she had known since leaving college. She relaxed her grip on the steering wheel and felt the tension ease from her back and neck.

She turned left at the Place Balmat and headed toward the edge of town, where, at the end of a gravel drive at the end of a narrow street, L'Auberge Allevard nestled warm and welcoming in an aspen grove. The stone terrace glowed with the candle-lit faces of couples dining, and she could hear the murmurs of quiet conversation and the tinkling of glass and dinnerware and the aspen leaves trembling in a soft and intermittent breeze.

She switched off her headlights and followed the drive to the back of the inn, where she parked behind a storage shed and locked the car. Gaillard, who had been with Madame for nearly twenty years, was serving drinks to a couple in the garden, and she waited for him to retire before making her way along the garden's edge to the back door, leading to a hallway by the kitchen. She waited a moment, and when the hallway was empty, she slipped quietly to Madame's office, where she closed the door and sat heavily on the couch. She kicked off her shoes, curled her feet on the couch, and let her head sink softly onto a down-filled cushion. Her eyelids turned leaden, and her mind emptied, and she fell instantly asleep.

Minutes later—or perhaps it was hours, she had no sense of the time—she was barely awakened by a commotion in the room. With difficulty, she opened her eyes to see Madame kneeling next to her and insisting, "Hélène, Hélène, *Dieu merci! Réveillez!* Wake up."

With all the awkwardness of one just coming out of a deep sleep, Helen struggled to sit up and wordlessly wrapped her arms around Madame Allevard. The two women embraced while tears fell from each.

"Oh, *chérie, mon dieu,* where have you been? Why didn't you call? I thought you were dead. They said you were dead. Oh, *ma chérie,* tell me, what happened to you?"

She kissed Madame on both cheeks and smiled. "I'm so tired . . . and so hungry. Is there anything left in the kitchen?" She looked up and saw Gaillard standing by the door, wringing his hands nervously. "How are you, Gaillard?"

Madame took Helen's face in her hands and shook her a bit. "Gaillard is fine. But you, *chérie*, why did they tell me you were dead? What has happened? Tell me!"

Helen hugged the old woman again. "We'll talk. But, first, if I could just freshen up a bit and maybe get something to eat. Do you have room for me tonight? Are you full?"

"Oh, child, don't be foolish." She turned to Gaillard and directed him to speak to the young couple from Bonn just finishing their dinner on the terrace. "Tell them there has been a mix-up in the reservations," she said. "Tell them we will move their things to the large room in front. Give them their dinner and a bottle of wine with my compliments, for the inconvenience."

"You don't have to do that," Helen protested, but Madame would have none of it. Helen would stay in *her* room, the room in which she always stayed, the one overlooking the garden, with a private bath, and a fireplace in the corner.

While Gaillard negotiated the switching of rooms and retrieved Helen's suitcase from her car, Madame rattled on about how thin Helen was, and how she might as well be dead from the look of her, and she complained angrily of Helen's not calling ahead or otherwise contacting her.

With Helen's things finally settled in her room, Madame took her by the arm and led her to the room, where she drew a hot bath and told Gaillard to bring a tray of fruit and pâté and bread and a pot of tea.

"Now," Madame said, "have your bath, and then we'll talk."

A half-hour passed, and Helen was sitting on the edge of her bed drying her hair when Madame returned to the room with a black leather valise; this she set by the door, and told Gaillard to place the bottle of brandy and two glasses he was carrying on the small table next to the balcony. "We'll have dinner later," Madame said, "in the garden."

"Roast duck, as usual?" Gaillard asked.

Helen smiled. "Yes, thank you, Gaillard. That would be wonderful."

Madame shook her head. "Duck. Always the duck. You would think my kitchen prepared nothing else."

Gaillard bowed and left the two women alone.

"Now," Madame said, "tell me why you aren't dead." Again she hugged Helen close, then abruptly pushed her away. She slipped a handkerchief from her sleeve, and wiped fresh tears from her eyes. "I'm so angry at you. I thought I had lost you. I was not even told in time to go to your funeral. Oh, *chérie* . . ." One hand covered her mouth, and tears again fell.

Helen touched the old woman's cheek. "Please, I am all right."

"You are not all right. You are killing me, I am so angry with you, and so happy, too."

Helen moved to the small table where she sat down and poured two glasses of brandy. She took a sip from one while holding the other glass out to Madame. "Who told you?"

"That you were dead? Your husband's parents, Monsieur Grehm—"

"Ex-husband," Helen interrupted.

Again, Madame dabbed at her eyes and at her nose, then wagged one finger at Helen as she moved to the table herself and sat down. "You are not divorced. He is still your husband. Or was . . ."

"Please, let's not have that argument again."

Madame sighed. "Your father-in-law. Monsieur Grehm called me. And his wife. I spoke to them both for a very long time. They were so upset. They wanted to know if I knew what had happened. Of course I didn't know. How could I know? Who was there to tell me? You? Oh, I will never forgive you. But the Grehms, Monsieur and Madame both, they were very kind. We talked—it seemed like hours. They said that both you and Trevor had been murdered in Washington. My heart. I could not catch my breath. It was just like the night we heard about your parents and Janine."

Helen winced slightly, and she lowered her eyes. "I'm sorry," she whispered.

"A thief," Madame went on. "They said it was a thief, but they didn't understand why you were there. They wanted to know if you had said anything to me about going to America. They thought maybe you and Trevor were thinking of getting back together. Oh, Hélène, they love you. I could hear it in their voices. They were so upset. But what could I say? What did my Hélène ever tell me? Do they know you are alive?"

"No, I don't think so."

"And Trevor, he is alive, too?"

Helen shook her head and looked away. "No, he's dead. At least I think so. I don't really know."

"*Mon dieu!* What do you mean, you don't know? How could you not know? You were not there? Please, *chérie*, what is going on? What have you gotten yourself into?"

"When did they call?"

"It's this work of yours, isn't it? Tourist consultant. Bah! I know you are no tourist consultant. What are you up to?"

She looked back at Madame, then again lowered her eyes and spoke very softly. "Please, tell me, when did the Grehms call?"

"Oh, I don't know, months ago. April? No, May, I think. A week, maybe more, after your Monsieur Brecht was here."

"What? Arlis was here? When was this? What did he say?"

Madame's brow furrowed. "Yes, he was here. Sometime after your last visit. When you left that!" She gestured toward the valise by the door. "I don't remember the exact day."

"What did he want? What did he say?"

"He wanted to know if I knew where you were, if you had been here. He said that the two of you had argued and that he had not heard from you. He said he was worried. He talked like an embarrassed lover, wanting to know if I had heard from you, and if I would call him if I heard anything. And then he gave me this." The old woman pulled an envelope from her smock and laid it on the table. "A thousand dollars American, in cash. He said it was for you if you came here. That's what he said, but I knew what he wanted."

Helen did not move. She stared at the envelope. "Did he say anything else? Did he ask you anything? Did he ask if I had left anything here with you?"

"No, just that he had not heard from you and that he was worried. But his voice, it wasn't the voice of a worried lover. It was something else. And a lover does not leave a thousand dollars American for me to spy."

Again, Helen looked away. "You never liked him, did you?"

"I thought it was a mistake. You were still married."

"But you didn't like him?"

"I didn't know him. But I could see your face when you were with him. You never really smiled."

"Really?" Helen paused, then nodded weakly. "Maybe you're

right. It's funny. Suddenly it seems so long ago. I hardly remember what I felt." She released a long sigh. "No, you're right. It was a mistake, as big a mistake as Toddy." She smiled and shook her head. "Toddy! I should have known. A grown man they still called Toddy. It always sounded . . . I don't know, strange, I guess. It always made me uncomfortable somehow. Toddy." She paused again. "God, what a mistake!"

"But you loved him, no?"

"Toddy? No . . . Oh, I don't know, I thought so once, but I didn't even know him. I loved who I thought he was, like everyone else who ever met him. Somehow I feel like I should be excused for him. I wasn't the only one he fooled. Toddy collected admirers like he collected those Russian icons of his, lining them up one after another. I was just something else he had collected and put on display."

"Oh, no, *chérie.*"

"Oh, no, it's true. What a good show he put on. My life with him was like one long improvisation. Every place, every person, a different role, whatever anyone wanted him to be—anyone but me, that is. Remember? Remember that night he had your entire dining room convinced he was the crown prince of whatever? Do you remember?"

"Yes. He was charming."

Helen turned back, her expression twisting to a frown. "Charming? Oh, yes, he was charming. But *un cochon!*"

Madame shrugged. "Ah, but, *chérie,* aren't they all?" She leaned over and poured them both another glass of brandy while staring intently at Helen. "Still," she said, "I know that you loved him. You may not have liked him, but, deep down where no one else can see, I know you loved him. Yes?"

Helen smiled shyly. "Yes, if it will make you feel better for me to say it."

"Ah, child, it is not me you need to please." Madame stopped, then lowered her chin and lifted her eyebrows. "And your Monsieur Brecht?"

Helen looked away. "No, I did not love him. I wasn't looking for love. I was lonely. I was looking for something to get me through the night. And he was so . . . I don't know, different. So romantic. So unlike Toddy. So attentive. It was flattering, and I was ready for a little flattery. I needed a little flattery. But then it just got out of hand. He turned into something else. Maybe that's who he always was and I just didn't see it, or maybe I just didn't want to see it, I don't know. But it was never serious, not for me anyway."

"The Grehms, Trevor's parents, they said your Monsieur Brecht was very kind. He made all the arrangements in America, with the police and whoever. He arranged everything for them, they said."

"Yes, I'm sure he did," Helen said, looking away.

Madame's eyes narrowed with questions unspoken, while she took a sip of brandy. She asked quietly, "So tell me, now, what has all of this to do with Trevor being killed, and why does everyone think you are dead?"

"It's better that we don't talk about it. For you, I mean. You just have to trust me about this."

Madame reached across the table and took Helen's hands in hers, squeezing them. "*Chérie*, listen to me. How long have I known you? Since you were a little girl, yes? Since your parents first brought you here and you fell out of that tree in the back of the garden. Do you remember?"

"Yes, of course I remember."

"Oh, we were all so worried, but then you came back the next summer, and the summer after that, and all those summers. You and your sister—she was still so young then, Janine—the two of you came to stay with us when your parents were having their own problems. You have been part of my family, all of you. And after Henri died, God rest his soul, and we almost lost this place to the bankers, your father and mother were there for us. They helped us through some very bad times. And then the accident, and your parents died, and then Janine . . . Oh, what a terrible year that was. But you came to us, to your family. This is your home. I am your family. My sons are your family. All of us. Always. How can you tell me we cannot talk of things, you and I?"

Helen bowed her head and fresh tears fell. "I know, I know. But . . . You don't understand. It's not safe for you to know. Please."

"But who else can you talk to? How can I help you if you don't tell me? It's this work of yours, isn't it? What kind of trouble are you in?"

She shook her head. "I honestly don't know. Maybe none, maybe more than you or I could ever imagine, I don't know. That's why I have to be so careful."

"But this makes no sense."

"You're right, it doesn't make sense. It's just . . . well, I just didn't understand what I was doing or who I was doing it for until it was too late. I should have seen this coming, but I didn't. I thought I was just a courier. That's what I thought."

"A courier? What do you mean, a courier?"

"For the government."

"The government!" Madame sat back and made the sign of the cross.

"Well, I thought it was. It doesn't really matter. It just turned bad, that's all. And now I have to go away. I don't know for how long. But I have to go away until I can find some way of resolving this problem for myself."

"But can't you go to someone? Explain things?"

"No, I can't. I can't trust the people I was working for. I'm not even sure anymore who they are . . . or were. Not Toddy, not Brecht, none of them."

"Your Trevor, he worked for the government, too?"

"Well, he had his own business. But he did things for the government."

"Things? What kind of things?"

"Please don't ask. I'm not completely sure myself. He told me most of the same stories he was telling everybody else. I knew what he was doing, but not how, not the extent of his involvement. I still don't know. I know it sounds crazy. It *is* crazy, but that's the way it is. I got so I couldn't distinguish the cover from the reality, at least not until the very last, just before Toddy went to Washington. Even now, I can't be sure what the truth is. I only know that I was used."

"And your Monsieur Brecht!"

"Trust me. Even if I could explain it all, it is better for me that you not know. I was used. It's as simple as that, but I don't know anymore who was on whose side. I don't know who I can go to. Not yet. Can you understand? I just need to go away for a while."

"But you will be back."

"Yes, of course, someday."

A long silence followed before Madame said in a near whisper, "You are scaring me, *chérie*."

Helen quickly reached across the table for the old woman's hands. "Oh, please, don't be scared. I'm sorry. I had to come for the valise. That's all. I couldn't call you, because there was no way for me to explain things over the phone, and . . . you know."

"No, I don't. Tell me."

"It's nothing. I'm probably just imagining things, but you never know who might be listening."

"To my phone?" Helen could feel the old woman's fingers tightening on hers. "These people are listening to my phone? And so you can't even call me to say you are alive? You have to come sneaking home in the middle of the night, and you tell me not to be frightened for you?"

"No, I just don't want you bothered. I don't want anyone coming around to bother you just because they might be looking for me. That's all. I'm sorry I had to come here, but I need what's in the valise."

Madame took her hands away and raised a scolding finger. "Don't you ever be sorry to come here. You come whenever you want, for any reason. Understand?"

Helen lowered her eyes.

"Do you understand?" Madame repeated.

"Yes, I understand."

"You need money?"

"No. Thank you, but I don't need money. I only need that," she said nodding toward the black leather bag.

"How can I help you? Please."

Helen again took the old woman's hands. "You already have, more than you'll ever know."

Madame closed her eyes a moment, then looked up. "How long can you stay with us? You need to rest. Maybe you should go up to the meadow. No one is at the lodge, and it is all fixed up. No one will even know you are there. You can rest as long as you like, and we can just talk and laugh as if none of this ever happened."

"Oh, I would like that. But I can't. I just can't stay here. Too many people know this is where I might come . . . if they're still looking for me. Like Brecht knew to come here. Too many people. It's not safe for you."

"Bah! What can these people do to me? This is still France! We bow to no one!"

Helen smiled. "Please, understand. Don't make what I have to do more difficult. All right?"

"You are such a stubborn child." Madame sat back with a long sigh. "When will you go?"

"In the morning."

Madame pursed her lips and shook her head with disapproval. "No, you need to rest. A few days at least. We'll go up to the meadow, you and I."

"Maybe," Helen said. "We'll talk about it."

"And so, what if they do come here looking for you? What can they do?"

Helen sat still for a long moment, her silent stare fixed on Madame, but her thoughts traveling on to possibilities once but no longer beyond her imagination. Madame again reached out and took Helen's hands in hers. "Tell me, what if they do come here for you?"

"Tell them the truth," Helen said. "Tell them I came here and then left, that's all."

"I spit on them. I will tell them nothing."

"No, believe me it is better if you just tell them the truth. Tell them I was here, but then I left, and you have no idea where I went."

"And do I tell them about that?" the old woman asked, cocking her head toward the valise.

"Only if you have to."

"Will you call me? Will you let me know that you are all right?"

"Yes, whenever I can. But not here."

"Father Bouchard, then. You remember him?"

"Yes, of course."

"You call him. I will get you the number. He owes me more favors than I can count. You can leave messages with him."

"Yes, all right."

"You promise me that?"

"Yes, I promise."

Madame nodded. "Then, all right, I will do as you ask. Now take this," she said, pushing the envelope stuffed with Brecht's money across the table.

"No, you keep it. Spend it on something foolish. I don't want his money."

"Good!" Madame said briskly, then stood and took the envelope to the small fireplace in the corner. She took a long wooden match from the mantel and lit it. She held the flame to the corner of the envelope. "*Cochon!*" she muttered under her breath, as she turned the envelope over and over to make sure it was fully ignited before tossing it in the fireplace. "Now let us take our brandy to the garden and have some dinner and talk of happier times to come."

"Yes, let's do that . . . You have fresh strawberries and *crème anglaise?*"

Madame took Helen's face in her hands and smiled. "Yes, of course I have your strawberries and *crème anglaise.* You are home now and safe. Stay a while. Let me put some meat back on those bones."

Helen hugged the old woman. "We'll talk," she said through fresh tears.

PART
THREE

had given way to *pirozhki* and *blini*, where the coffee was black and bitter and the vodka flavored with pepper and lemon, where Hasidic Jews and Russian émigrés squeezed together in clapboard houses and high-rise apartments, in back-street tenements and oceanfront condominiums.

"Little Odessa," some called it, and Eddie had come down from the West Virginia hills to wander its streets and drink in its bars and stroll the boardwalk: getting a feel for the place, he thought, scoping out the ground where he hoped to find some answers. But limping about on his cane and having to repeat himself each time he'd order a beer had only advertised himself as a stranger in a foreign land. Sitting now in this Park Avenue lounge seemed to make no more sense than wandering about Brighton Beach. But this was where he had been told to be, where he might find help: and so he had come, and so he would wait, and if nothing else, he was enjoying the comforting sound of his own language.

Jimmy Legget had been right. He needed favors, and together they had called in a few. It had taken some time and a seemingly endless series of phone calls and repeated assurances that the confidential favors would forever remain so. Ultimately, however, small pieces of the puzzle began to appear. Fingerprints taken from the man who had died in Eddie's kitchen were matched to those on file with the FBI under the name Vladimir Lyubarsky, also known as "Mad Willy." It was not known how Mad Willy—a Chechen from the Caucasus region, east of the Black Sea—had entered the country, but according to information Jimmy Legget had gathered from a friend in FBI headquarters, who in turn had gathered his information from a colleague who once worked counterintelligence out of New York, it did not really matter. In the midst of the warm and fuzzy politics that accompanied the disintegration of the Soviet bloc, immigration restrictions—at least as they applied to oppressed minorities—had been "adjusted," a euphemism for all but abandoned. Mad Willy may have been oppressed, but if his several arrests for assault and weapon offenses—none of which had resulted in a conviction—were any indication, his oppression most likely had little or nothing to do with his ethnic heritage or spiritual values, whatever they might have been. But that was history, and a sketchy one at that. About all that could be said was that Mad Willy was "known" but never charged or proved to be a hit man for one element of the *Organizatsiya* working out of Brighton Beach. And so Eddie had come.

Eddie was still being sought for questioning. The authorities wanted to know more about Garland Bolles, more about his search for and talk with LeRoi, more about the shooting in his kitchen, its prelude and aftermath. Anne Arundel County Police wanted to question him, as did the Maryland State and District of Columbia Police and the FBI. They had all questioned Jimmy Legget and asked for his help in finding Eddie so they could "settle" the matter. Their questions were framed with skepticism or confusion or sympathy, depending on which they thought might be most effective. But Jimmy could only repeat that he did not know where Eddie had gone—other than to the beach, as his housekeeper, Mrs. Mapes had said.

There was talk of issuing a warrant, and debate whether the warrant should be for Eddie's arrest as a suspect or merely as a material witness. But that discussion was tabled—at least temporarily—when ballistics and firearms examinations established that the nine-millimeter rounds that had shattered Mad Willy's skull and severed his spine had been fired from a weapon that was neither Eddie's Beretta nor the nine-millimeter he had wrestled from Mad Willy's hand. It was not enough to clear him, but it was enough to corroborate Eddie's story of a second shooter in his kitchen, and to cause the police to stop and think. But they did not think long, apparently, before turning their respective investigations over to the FBI, for reasons that were never fully explained beyond a few catchwords like "interstate" and "organized crime" and "foreign nationals" and "counterintelligence," this last term seeming to Eddie the most apt. There were two FBI agents originally assigned to the matter, who, like the police officers before them, had sought through Jimmy to contact Eddie for questioning. But almost as quickly as they had been assigned, they were relieved of the case, again for reasons that were not explained even to them. Through intermediaries, they sent word to Jimmy that the case file had been sent on to yet another section, and they had no idea where the case had landed or who, if anyone, might be working it.

Ten days after receiving this last message, Jimmy Legget met

Eddie at a pancake house near Harpers Ferry and wondered aloud if Eddie shouldn't just let the whole matter drop.

"You're not even curious?"

"More than curious," Jimmy answered. "But it seems to me that everyone might be happy just to let the thing die. Maybe it's time to come home from your little vacation and answer their questions—if anyone's even gonna ask—and hope the whole thing goes away."

"You're not serious?"

"I don't know. Maybe. Aren't you the one who's always told me to let sleeping dogs lie?"

"Tell me," Eddie asked, "how do I know this dog's really asleep? Yeah, maybe the locals are just as happy to let the feds take over, and maybe the feds have gotten the word to let the case die a quiet death, but what does that tell ya? Doesn't that raise more questions than answers? Forget the locals and the feds, the question is, who's on the other side? You said it yourself, it's not over yet. Whatever this is, it's serious business involving serious folks. Serious people don't like loose ends. They didn't get what they wanted. They didn't get Helen Grehm's wallet. Plus, I'm still alive. I'm one of those loose ends they need to take care of. Worse still, maybe Priscilla's on their list of loose ends. How do they know she can't identify anybody? How do I let that go? When do I tell my own daughter it's okay for her to come home?"

Jimmy had no answers except to express his concern that Eddie use his head and not his heart in taking the next step. "I'll do whatever I can," he promised, "but just be careful you don't let this thing get away from you."

Eddie nodded his understanding and agreement. What he did not say, however, and what motivated him more than any other factor, was the image he could not drive from his mind: the image of Priscilla, her expression contorted with horror as he wheeled around and pointed that nine-millimeter semi-automatic directly to the center of her face. He could never let that pass.

"Nickles, right?"

Eddie looked up, startled by the sudden apparition of a man who hovered over him like a thin column of smoke, a gray, nearly translucent figure whose presence seemed marked only by the coal-black eyes that peered from under heavy and swollen lids. "Thin guy, mid-fifties, with white hair, what little he's got left," was the description Eddie had been given over the phone.

"Sit over here," the man ordered, nodding to a seat on the opposite side of the small round table.

"What?"

"Here!" The man stabbed his finger at the other chair. "I want your back to the room."

Eddie sat still. "Yalich?"

The man again nodded his insistence that Eddie move, and when Eddie did, he quickly took Eddie's seat. "That's better," he said. "Much better."

It had been clear from the start that whatever help Eddie might need would not—could not—come through official channels. It was clear, too, that those who wanted to help, particularly friends within the FBI, did not want to know any plans or intentions that might have been on Eddie's mind. Indeed, they much preferred indulging the fiction that whatever information they imparted through Jimmy Legget was going to law-enforcement personnel for background only. There were no memoranda or faxes or airtels or contact notes, simply a series of phone calls from one detective bureau in Brooklyn to the FBI office in Manhattan, from the FBI office in Manhattan to the field office in Fairfax, Virginia, from the field office in Fairfax to the Homicide Squad in Washington, from Jimmy Legget's home in Bowie, Maryland, to a pay phone nearly twelve miles from the West Virginia cabin, and then, finally, to Eddie's hotel room in midtown Manhattan.

Sid Yalich was the name Eddie had been given—a former New York City detective involuntarily retired on disability. The nature of the disability was suspected but never detailed. "They say he's more than a little strange," Jimmy had said, "but if you can get past it, he probably knows the players better than anyone. There's a bar at Fifty-sixth and Park Avenue. The Drake. If he decides to help, he'll be there tomorrow night. No later than six. If not, don't even bother trying to track him down."

"So, Nickles," the man said while his eyes ignored Eddie and scanned the room, "what the fuck is that? Irish? I told 'em. I told 'em straight off I didn't need to know what you looked like. I'd spot you in a heartbeat. An Irish cop outta D.C. trying to work the Beach. A fuckin' turd in a punch bowl, man. That's what you are. A turd in a punch bowl." He leaned forward and lowered his voice to a whisper. "You carrying?"

Eddie paused before leaning forward himself, very slowly. "Who's asking?"

The man sat back and shook his head. "That's good, Irish. That's real good. And who the fuck're you? Bogart?"

Eddie did not respond. "Strange" did not quite capture the full measure of this man.

"So, what do we do here, Irish? Flash badges? They tell me you haven't got one, and I suspect they told you I haven't got one either. Isn't that right?"

Eddie nodded.

"That's right. So it doesn't matter, does it? You knew right off. Soon's you looked up, you knew. 'Sid Yalich,' you said to yourself. Just like I spotted you five seconds into the room. Irish cop from D.C."

"Well, you got D.C. right."

"Not Irish?"

"Never laid eyes on the place."

"Haw! That's good. I like that. So, tell me, what do you do if you're not an Irish cop from D.C.?"

"A little of this, a little of that."

Yalich turned quickly to a passing waitress. "Let me have a double vodka with lemon." He pointed to Eddie's nearly full glass, and Eddie shook his head. "Not yet," he said.

"Bourbon?"

"Yeah, but I'm fine for now."

"That's right, keep your wits about you. You're gonna need 'em." He turned back to the waitress. "Just the double vodka, and don't forget the lemon. Please." The waitress nodded and left.

"This and that, hey?" Yalich continued. "This and that. Like wandering around the Beach? You put an ad in the paper telling them you were coming? Maybe handed out some leaflets saying you're an Irish cop from D.C. looking for Mad Willy's friends? Might as well have, you know."

Eddie leaned forward again. "I take it you're not inclined to chitchat, so let me lay it out plain. This may not be my town, and

I may not know the players, but I'm not exactly a virgin, you know what I'm saying?"

"Retired?"

Eddie nodded. "Twenty-five years."

"Homicide, right?"

"Yeah, and you?"

"Twenty-seven. The last ten working organized crime."

"What happened?"

"Whaddaya mean?"

"The disability retirement."

Sid Yalich started beating a quick rhythm with his fingertips on the edge of the table, and his head bobbed in time. He stopped suddenly and pressed his body forward. "I had a partner once. Dumbest fuck I ever worked with. Had to keep reminding him which shoe went on which foot. Just as dumb as a dog. 'Bout all he was good for was typing. A twenty-page report and you wouldn't find a single typo. Not one. But ask him what was in the report and there'd be nothing there. No lights on at all. Nothing, I'm telling ya, 'cept that big stupid grin. You might as well have asked him to compute the specific gravity of subatomic particles. I told him . . . I must've told him a thousand times. Never go alone. I told him never, never go alone. Never go without backup or letting someone know. I told him a thousand times. He took one in the back of the head and then they stuffed him in a trash can. Not in some dumpster out on the island, not someplace like maybe they didn't want him found. No, they stuffed him headfirst in a trash can. Right there by the racquet club at Brighton Beach and Coney Island Avenue. His legs were sticking up outta the can like some dress mannequin they couldn't use anymore. And you know what?"

Eddie shook his head. He didn't have a clue.

"I'll tell ya what. People just kept walking by. That was it. That's what got me. They just kept walking by. No one stopped. No one said a word until the trash man came. It took the trash man to call the cops. Dumbest fuck I ever worked with."

Eddie took a long swallow of bourbon, staring into the black holes of Yalich's eyes.

"What'd they tell ya?" Yalich asked after a long pause.

"Who?"

The man's eyes narrowed angrily. "Them, they, the ones who put you and I together. Don't fuck with me. They told you I was dangerous, didn't they?"

"No," Eddie said quietly. "No, I think the word was 'strange.' "

"Hah!" Yalich laughed. "I must be recovering. For a while there the word was 'crazy.' Then they added 'dangerous.' The lawyers kept saying I was 'dangerous.' They told the department I had to go 'cause I was dangerous. 'Course, there was this one day they might've been right. I was sitting there, see, with my captain and one of the shrinks." He sat back, his head bobbing and his eyes rolling toward the ceiling. "Oh, man, there were bunches of shrinks. But only one of them was there, and this little pissant lawyer 'bout twenty minutes outta Fordham her old man had paid for, and to tell the truth, if I had my weapon I just might have blown her away. It really would have made me feel better. You know what I'm saying? It would have made up for everything. I would've done the time smiling, you know? It really would have felt that good. But they already had my badge and gun, so I couldn't shoot the bitch, and I couldn't get my hands on her with everyone else in the room, so I just did what they said. Took the disability retirement and shut my mouth. Twenty-seven years, man. Twenty-seven! Jesus, I would have loved to pop her." He looked away, and a curious frown came over him. " 'Strange,' huh? Shit, I think I'd rather be crazy. What do you think?"

Eddie paused with a sigh. "You ever make the case?"

"What case?"

"Your partner's—"

Yalich interrupted with an impatient wave of his hand. "You don't get it, do you? I don't have a partner. You must be talking about the man in the trash can. Is that what you're asking?"

"Yeah."

"What about it?"

"The case! Did you make the case?"

"Oh, no, no. Aren't you listening? Didn't I just tell you I was too dangerous to make cases? I thought we just went through that. Remember? Disabled? I was disabled, man. I was retired. How could I make a case?"

"Did anyone?"

"Did anyone what?"

"Make the case?"

"Well, that's an interesting concept, isn't it? Making the case. Sorta leads us to a problem of definitions. I mean, is the case *made* if you identify the culprit? Or is it *made* only if there's an arrest, or maybe if there's a conviction? Or maybe it means when *the case* is taken from the board. Let's define our terms here. Exactly what do you mean by *making the case?*"

"I take it *the case*," Eddie said, mimicking Yalich's emphasis, "is still open."

"Well, you take it wrong Mr. Irish cop from D.C. The case is closed. Done. Finished. Buried and forgotten. Of course no one was ever arrested, no one was ever charged. But the case . . . ah, *the case! That* was closed."

Eddie's chin lowered and his eyes closed for an instant. He was beginning to understand; not the man, perhaps, but maybe the cause.

Sid Yalich's eyes opened wide, and he broke into a wide, almost mocking smile. "Yes, I see you've had a lesson or two. You're not unfamiliar with the half-life syndrome."

"Half-life?"

"Yes, the half-life. The natural forces of decomposition, like nuclear waste no one wants to touch. Much like an untidy case. It has its own half-life. Leave it alone and someday it'll just go away. Bit by bit, day by day, it breaks down into its individual elements, until one day it's gone. Poof! It just disappears. It's not what it was, it's something else. And then, well, if it's something else now, can we really be sure of what it was in the first place, if there ever was a first place? I mean, if it's not here now, how do we know it ever was?"

Eddie drained his glass.

"It's a Zen kind of thing. And besides, if it ever was, you know, a thing, a case, an event, well, what was it, really? Nothing, man. Just a cop, and a dumb-fuck cop at that. You need another?" Yalich asked and signaled for the waitress without waiting for a response.

They ordered another round and sat in silence while Sid Yalich scanned the room, his eyes stopping here and there, then moving on. Eddie turned his head, trying to follow Yalich's search.

"Don't!" Yalich ordered.

Eddie turned back quickly. "What?"

"Just don't. It's not time." Yalich looked at his watch. "You've got plenty of time."

"For what?"

"You don't have time?"

"I've got nothing but time, but that doesn't mean I like wasting it."

Yalich smiled. "You think you're wasting time? . . . Ah, our waitress. Thank you, my dear. No, no, please," he said, stopping the waitress from retrieving his empty glass. He poured the lemon wedge from his first glass into the second and took a deep swallow of fresh vodka. "So, tell me, Mr. Irish cop from D.C.," he said, as he watched the waitress move to the next table, "you think I'm crazy?"

Eddie thought a moment. That possibility was looming ever larger on his mind, but he thought he'd reserve judgment, at least for the moment. "I think you're pissed."

"Pissed? That's an interesting word. Pissed. Ever been to England?"

"No."

"I was there once. Actually got paid to go. Hands across the sea and all that. I was chasing a man. Irish chap like yourself. Blew the top two floors off a house in Brooklyn. One of the victims— well, at least a few pieces of him—actually landed in Green-Wood Cemetery. Anyway, the whole time I was in London—never did find the man, by the way—the boys in the Yard kept insisting he was still in Brooklyn. But what the hell, I'd never been to England. A strange place, I'll tell you. Anyway, Scotland Yard boys were always talking about getting pissed. Drunk. They meant getting drunk. So what is it? You think I'm drunk, or crazy, or both?"

"You may be drunk, you may be crazy. Maybe you're both, I don't really care. But, drunk or crazy, you're still pissed."

Yalich sat back, and the tightness in his expression seemed to drain a bit. "You're not Irish?"

Eddie smiled a bit himself. "I don't know. Never paid much attention to all that bullshit. Pure mongrel, as far as I can tell."

"So what do they call a mongrel dog like you?"

"Eddie'll do."

Yalich reached his hand across the table. "Sid Yalich, Eddie."

"Eddie Nickles, Sid."

"So, Eddie, are you pissed?"

Eddie did not answer.

"Right. But I gotta know, Eddie, is this a job or is this personal? I heard all about Mad Willy. Not a happy night for you. Okay, but that means nothing to me. I gotta know. I gotta know is this a job or is this personal."

"It matters?"

"Oh, Eddie from D.C., it matters. It's everything. What a man'll do for a job is one thing, but when it's personal? Well, that's something else entirely."

Eddie considered this man, and wondered about himself. He did not like talking about that night, and even less was he comfortable talking about his motives. But he needed help, and the only direct help on his horizon seemed to be this "strange" man running from his own set of ghosts. The urge came suddenly and he followed it. Without thinking, Eddie took his cane in his hand and began tapping it at the floor as he spoke. "They shot up my house." *Tap.* "The two of them. This guy Mad Willy and the tall man. The one running the game. I ended up with Mad Willy's face all over mine." *Tap.* "The tall one was firing at me, but a couple of rounds blew Willy's face apart. It was all over me, man." *Tap, tap.* "I took one shot in the leg, and now I walk around with this thing and can't go a block without hurting like hell." *Tap.* "I took another one in the lung, and now I can't smoke. And, man, I dearly loved my smokes." *Tap, tap.* "But that's the job. Understand?"

Yalich didn't answer, nor did he change expression. He simply sat there, still and unmoving, maybe moved, maybe not.

"But, see, my daughter was there." *Tap, tap, tap.* "She walked in the house, man. Just before the shooting started. She'd been to the beach. Just graduated from high school. She's going to college, see? Not like me. She's going to college, see? And she'd been to the beach, and she comes home to her ol' man, and she calls to me from the front of the house, and I can tell she's happy. You know what I'm saying? I can hear it. I can hear her voice, and I can tell she's happy. And I know as sure as I'm standing there, scared shitless—these two motherfuckers standing there with nine-millimeters in my face, just waiting to make sure they got whatever it was they came for before they pop me, and I know—man,

I know she's gonna die." *Tap, tap, tap.* "So I don't even think about it. I just do what I gotta do, and the place lights up, and alla sudden I got this piece of rat shit on top of me and his face is all over me and I got his gun and I'm firing. And then . . . and then I'm up and I don't see the tall man. I don't see him. And then I hear something." *Tap.* "I hear something behind me. And I turn. I mean, I just turn. And I'm gonna fire. . . . You know? I'm gonna fire." *Tap, tap, tap, tap.* "And I see her. I see her face covered in my sight. My own daughter!" *THUMP!*

He stopped himself, then took a deep breath, and his voice calmed. "I'll never know why I didn't fire. Maybe it was me. Maybe it was luck. Maybe it was God or some of your Zen shit or the fucking position of the moon. I'll never know. I'll never know anything except that I came within a hair's breadth of killing my own daughter."

Eddie leaned forward, and his eyes narrowed, and his voice turned low and mean. "And there ain't no fucking half-life for that!"

A very long silence followed, broken finally by Sid Yalich hailing the waitress once more. The two men said nothing until the drinks were brought and the waitress retired.

"Listen to me," Yalich said finally. "The fact of the matter is, I am crazy. I spend three afternoons a week with a shrink and he keeps me on more drugs than I can count. Understand?"

Eddie nodded.

"The good news is that I'm just sane enough to know I'm crazy. But you, my mongrel friend from D.C., I don't think you're crazy. And that's a liability here."

"Meaning?'

"Meaning you've got no idea what you're into. With respect— and I mean that—this isn't D.C. These people aren't your cocaine-whacked street niggers in gold chains and smoked-glass BMWs. They're not LCN, not anything like the Italians. They're smarter than the Italians and meaner than the Jamaicans. They don't think twice about going after a cop's family, if that's what it takes.

"You gotta understand the basics here. The Russian mob isn't just a bunch of dope peddlers and pimps and meathead bone-breakers. They came out of a different system. They're Soviets, you see, and with the Soviets, corruption and bribery and extortion and whatever else, that wasn't something outside the system. You understand? It *was* the system. It was the only thing that kept any semblance of a real economy going, and for the last seventy years they were party mobsters. They ran the store and the collective farms and the factories and whatever else there was to make money and keep them in power. They were government-sponsored racketeers. They know how it works. Hell, they're not afraid of governments: they're used to being the government. They know how to use the government for whatever they want.

"These people run games that matter. They run scams that affect the marketplace, everything from welfare systems to the commodities markets, credit systems, insurance, fuel tax, and bootleg gasoline. No small-time bullshit. I'm talking entire markets. One man, for example—just one man running one organization pulling down hundreds of millions of dollars on the fuel-tax scam alone. They're a different breed. The Italians, you see, they play boccie ball. The Russians, they play chess. That's what I'm talking about.

"Now they're here and they're big, and nobody wants to touch them. The poor, oppressed former Soviets just hungering for freedom. The persecuted and oppressed, that's what they claim. It's all bullshit. The names won't mean anything to you, but one of the biggest locally is a Russian Jew. Came here, his visa application said, to escape religious persecution. Bullshit! The man ran with the party bosses, managed one of the largest state co-ops. He came here 'cause the money was better and there was something to spend it on.

"But, no, we don't want to talk about any of that. Might upset Russian emigration, might upset the political balance, might upset the flow of money to the fuckin' whores in Washington. You beginning to get my drift?"

"You call that a drift?"

"Yeah, 'cause I haven't even scratched the surface. Bottom line, there are people who actually know about these things and have the balls to say it, who will tell you that the Russian mob is on the verge of becoming the largest criminal organization in the world. Not New York, man. Not the U.S. or Europe. The fucking world!"

"And?"

"And so maybe it's time you go home and forget it ever happened. Like maybe you count yourself lucky just because your daughter's alive, and that's enough. Like maybe you count yourself lucky you can still hobble around on that cane of yours."

"And if I don't?"

"Then you'll be dead soon. And if you live, you'll end up with nothing more than your dick in your hands and a perpetual prescription for shit you can't even pronounce. Trust me!"

"And the bad news?"

Yalich's eyes wandered again. "What?" he asked after a moment.

"Look, Sid, I—"

"Quiet." Yalich held his hand up, his stare focused on some other part of the room. "Just a minute."

Eddie shook his head with his diminishing patience, and he had started to speak when Yalich turned back with an almost frightened expression. "This is weird, man," he said.

"What?"

"I'm tellin' ya. This is more than weird. This is . . . I don't know, fate. Karma. Man, this is your destiny." He broke into a giggle. "Hee hee hee."

Jesus! Eddie thought. The drugs, the booze. The man seemed to be unraveling. "What is it? You all right? You're not gonna, you know, flip out here, are ya?"

"It's perfect. It's fucking perfect. It's . . . I don't know, but whatever it is . . ."

"What are you talking about?"

"Whatever you do, do not turn around. Do you understand?"

"Yes."

"Okay, see, this wasn't supposed to happen. No, no. Not this way. But someone wants you to win or someone wants you to die. Either way, it's outta my hands. You understand?"

"No."

"See, I'm not responsible for this. I didn't do this. It just happened. So now what choice do I have? None, right? Absolutely!"

"What—"

"No, no, listen." Yalich's face flushed deeply, and his excitement was palpable. "See, I couldn't have planned this if I had wanted to, but it's absolutely perfect. Remember. Listen to me and remember. Two things. *Ya nechevo ne znayu.* Say it."

"Say what?"

"*Ya nechevo ne znayu.* Let me hear you say it."

"Man, I think it's time to retire that vodka."

"No, no, no, just humor me. Say *ya nechevo ne znayu.*"

"Ya neet cha vo nu sigh you."

Yalich rolled his eyes. "Doesn't matter, doesn't matter. A fucking black-Irish mongrel, for Christ's sake. Doesn't matter. Just remember, *ya nechevo ne znayu.* It means 'I don't know anything.' Got it?"

Eddie nodded, but his expression clearly expressed that he had no idea what was racing through Sid Yalich's brain.

"And *ya ne govoryu po-angliijskii.* Okay? *Ya ne govoryu po-angiliiskii.* I don't speak English. That's what he's gonna say to you. That's what you'll hear. If nothing else, just remember the two key words. *Nechevo,* means 'nothing.' I don't know nothing. *Angliiskii.* English, right? That's easy. *Ya ne govoryu po-angliiskii.* I don't speak English. That's what he'll say to you."

"Who?"

"The man you're looking for."

"How do you know who I'm looking for?"

"Mad Willy. Vladimir Lyubarsky. That's the man who got his brains spread all over your kitchen, right?"

"Yeah."

"The second man. Tall, thin, straight black hair, thirty-five to forty, low smooth voice, no hint of an accent, right? That's what they told me. Is that right?"

"Yes."

"His name is Viktor. That's Viktor with a 'k.' Viktor Samoilov. He's thirty-six years old, and he's never worked a straight job in his life. He was born here. His parents are Russian, from Kaliningrad. Ever hear of it?"

Eddie shook his head.

"A little pocket of Russia stuck between Lithuania and Poland. It's a main transit point for running shit out of Russia to the West. Doesn't matter. But that's Viktor's connection. That's how he made his connection. But he's not made, if you know what I mean. Grew up in Brighton Beach, a punk from day one. Too much of a punk, and a little too flashy for the boys that count. And trust me, too flashy for the Russian mob is really saying something. Anyway, Viktor's connected but not made. Understand?"

"Yeah, I know the difference."

"But Viktor likes the high life, and so he learned what he had to do to get it. Now, what's a guy that's connected but not made do?"

"Hit man?"

"Hit man. But a step above. When the occasion calls for it, he can actually dress and act and speak like a gentleman. Still, he's a weasely little shit. You wouldn't go to him for something neat, something that took long planning and a high degree of care. But if you want someone whacked quickly and you don't care for a little mess, well, then, Viktor's your man. His biggest attraction is reliability. He's had his chances and lots of incentive, but he's never rolled. No *stukatch*, he."

"*Stukatch?* You mean snitch?"

"Snitch. Good, you learn fast. You'll need it. So just listen. There's no time."

"Why, what the—"

"Just listen!" Yalich blurted angrily, then softened his voice. "Just listen. Mad Willy was a moron. He's the man you throw in the sewer for shit work. Viktor used him for backup. Kept him on retainer, as it were. If it was Mad Willy in your kitchen, it had to be Viktor who took the job. It fits."

"If you know all this, why not the feds?"

"They probably do."

"And so?"

"And so?"

Eddie nodded his understanding of the obvious. "Yeah, okay, and so there's something else, some reason I'm never gonna hear about, why the feds don't want my fingers—or anyone else's, for that matter—stuck in this pie."

"An odd metaphor, but precisely to the point."

"You got any photos of this man Viktor?"

"Don't need them."

"Oh, really?"

"That's right. You see, Viktor is also a man of certain habits. He may have been born in Brighton Beach, and Brighton Beach may be the source of his sustenance, but Viktor really thinks Brighton Beach is a stinking shithole. I must say that, on this one point, Viktor and I see eye to eye. Viktor yearns for the real America. He wants to play with the real Americans, the ones with no accents, the people who spend more on a suit than his family spends on rent and food combined. Park Avenue, for example. Viktor really likes it *uptown.*"

"Are you telling me the man hangs here?"

"He does indeed. Well, it's one of several such places he frequents."

Eddie was stunned. "You mean to tell me you called for a meet where the man hangs? Are you fucking crazy?"

"So I'm told."

"You're telling me this creep might walk in here any minute?"

"Well, no, I'm not gonna tell you that."

"What are you gonna tell me?"

"Well, I thought I might tell you that your creep walked in here just a few minutes ago."

"What?"

"Just over there—don't look!—by the front window, in the blue suit, talking with the young woman in black and a very handsome sapphire ring."

A quick chill crawled down Eddie's spine, and he wondered suddenly who was the more dangerous, the man said to be standing and talking by the front window or the man seated at the table across from him. His jaw dropped a bit and he took several breaths before addressing Sid Yalich with the most obvious question.

"Have you completely lost your mind?"

"Well, not completely," Yalich answered equably, then cocked his head as if considering the matter further. "But a good part of it, they say."

16.

"Rats."

"Where?" Eddie asked, the tone of his voice clearly signaling more patience than interest.

"Where? Well, just about everywhere."

Eddie looked over to the passenger seat, where Sid Yalich slouched, his head resting on the back of the seat, his eyes fixed on the wide alley running between two rows of darkened warehouses leading to the waterfront. There was a long silence before Eddie said, "Somehow I should know better than to ask, but what about them?"

"The rats?"

"Yeah, the rats."

"Much maligned, the rats. And unfairly so, don't you think?"

"I dunno. Never gave 'em much thought."

"I do. I think about them all the time."

"Why, they bother you?"

"No, quite the opposite. I appreciate the rat. Even more, I respect the rat."

"Oh?"

"I do. I really do. I have a theory, you know?"

Eddie turned toward Yalich with a look one might reserve for a tiresome in-law. "I was afraid you might," he said.

"Consider for just a moment," Yalich said, suddenly sitting up, his eyes narrowing in thought. "I mean, why is it that we hate the rat?"

"I don't know, Sid. Why do we hate the rat?"

"I'll tell you why. It's because the rat is one of those rare species we can't conquer or even control. One of the true survivors. I mean, mankind's been trying to annihilate them, wipe them from the face of the earth, for hundreds—hell—maybe thousands of years. But with all our genius, with all our science and technology, developing all sorts of traps and poisons and whatever, still we haven't fazed them. They're still here, in numbers we can't even imagine. You have to respect that, don't you?"

"Like I said, I haven't given it much thought."

"Well, think about it. If survival is the ultimate objective, they've got us beat hands down. I mean, we like to think of ourselves as so evolved, so superior, but all our advances are really regressions. Do you know that we can actually measure the expansion of the universe and predict with reasonable accuracy when the sun will cool and the earth will turn to just another barren stone floating in the void? So what's our response? What does this highly evolved human animal do in the face of its potential annihilation? Well, we come up with the means to speed up the process. The neutron bomb, for example. We've developed the means to push a few buttons and kill every human on earth and still leave our cities and towns intact. Isn't that amazing? Truly. I mean, we've advanced so far that we've taken to figuring out how to wipe ourselves from the face of the earth without disturbing the monuments to our insanity. It's like we're bent on living out some grand Ozymandian nightmare. But, still, the geniuses that figured all that out also figure that, if any mammal could survive such an event, the rat would be right up there at the top of the list. We can't get rid of them. The rat just gets stronger and stronger. You gotta respect that."

"Hmm."

"But we don't respect them, do we? No, we don't, and do you know why?"

"Because they're nasty, dirty little buggers?"

"No, we don't respect them because, somewhere deep in our evolutionary souls, we understand that the rat is better than we are, and we just can't stand it. True survivors scare the hell out of us. We're embarrassed by strength, we're constantly apologizing for it, as if it were something to be ashamed of. We've turned ourselves into a freak show, just so the halt and the lame will feel better about themselves. I mean, for all our history of struggling against the odds, you'd think we'd come to admire the strongest and the brightest and the least dependent. But, no, we're evolved to the point of exalting weakness. We're constantly searching for the lowest common denominator so no one will feel left out. If one of our brothers is a freak, then we should glorify the special attributes of the freak so the freaks won't feel left out. Freaks and fuckups, the more dysfunctional the better. Any day now, Congress will probably pass a bill to establish National Freak Week, only they won't call it that. They'll come up with something *sensitive*, something like the *evolutionarily impaired*. National Evolutionarily Impaired Week. The glitterati will all wear little gold lapel pins in the shape of a bib to honor those who drool all over themselves." Yalich stopped and frowned at Eddie's expression. "What? You think I'm crazy?"

Eddie did not respond.

"I'm telling you, man. We've stood Darwinism on its head, for God's sake."

"Well, I—"

"No, wait! Just ask yourself. Who do we hate? Who do we fear? I'll tell you who. The survivors, man. We hate and fear the true survivors, those species smart enough to tell mankind to go fuck itself, the ones who stay pure, the ones who won't cuddle up to us. Like the shark, man, and the rats. God, I love rats. Don't you?"

Eddie turned toward Sid Yalich and cocked his head curiously. "You got a girlfriend?"

"What?"

"A girlfriend. I mean, do you ever talk to anyone besides your shrink?"

"What's that mean?"

"Nothing. I just think you could use a girlfriend, that's all."

It was their fourth night together. Eddie understood that Yalich was measuring him and wondering whether Eddie was worthy of his assistance, whatever form that assistance would ultimately take, which Yalich never said. But more and more Eddie wondered, too, whether he was simply filling the void in which this man seemed to be drifting.

The first night, after Eddie eluded Viktor Samoilov by quickly slipping out the rear entrance to the Drake Bar dragging a grinning Sid Yalich behind him, the two had wandered—it seemed to Eddie quite aimlessly—about Brooklyn. Throughout the night and long into the morning, Eddie drove his battered Oldsmobile in and out of neighborhoods as varied as Sid Yalich's moods, from the quiet and well-kept to the dark and dangerous and depressing. Yalich never said where they were going or why, he simply directed a turn here, a turn there, while telling tales of the Russian mob and rattling on about vivisection and the racist paternalism of the liberal left, and what he thought the "curious debate" over the Black Talon bullet. "I mean, what the hell do these people think a bullet's for? Marking someone for a party favor at the end of the game?"

The second night was the same, as was the third. They wandered from the Green-Wood Cemetery and Sunset Park to Bay Ridge and Bensonhurst, from Red Hook and Park Slope to Owls Head and Borough Park. Hour after hour they drove, while Yalich talked about everything but why they were there and what they were doing. But each night, three or four times Yalich would direct Eddie back to the dock and rail yards and warehouses along the edge of Gowanus Bay. He was obviously orienting Eddie to the area, but refused Eddie's questions beyond, "Look and learn, Irish. Just look and learn."

That morning, sometime just before dawn, Eddie's patience had run dry. "You just like spending your nights on the street, or do you actually have something in mind here?"

"You mean a plan?" Yalich asked.

"Yeah, well, the thought had crossed my mind. You know, it might be nice if I had some clue what the fuck we're doing out here."

"You want to talk to Viktor?"

"Yes."

"Do you know what you want to talk to him about?"

"Yes."

"Then you've actually got a plan, don't you?"

Eddie shook his head. "Yeah, well, Sid, you've got me there."

"So, I assume, since your plan is all worked out, you don't really care what anyone else might have in mind as long as it furthers your objectives, correct?"

"I suppose you're right."

"You're a quick learner, Irish. I like that. I think you'll do just fine."

"That's a real comfort, Sid. Yes, sir, a real comfort."

This, the fourth night, Sid Yalich had changed the routine. He had not met Eddie at his hotel as usual, but called and told Eddie to pick him up in Greenwich Village, at the corner of Waverly and Sixth Avenue at ten o'clock, several hours later than they had started out the nights before. "Remember Red Hook?" Yalich had asked as he jumped in Eddie's car.

"Yeah."

"Go there," he said. It was not an order. Yalich's tone was serious but soft, almost too calm, and Eddie suspected that this was the night.

It was now nearly midnight, and they had been sitting at one corner of the alley for more than an hour. *God, I love rats. Don't you?* The question seemed no more odd to Eddie than did any of the questions that randomly popped from Yalich's brain, but the tone was different, as if Yalich's question, like his earlier rant, was little more than noise to cover other, more immediate thoughts.

Yalich turned to Eddie with a queer, pinched smile. "A girlfriend, huh? Maybe you're right. Anyway, it's time," he said, holding up his watch.

"Time?"

"Yeah, let's go." Yalich started to open his door and then stopped, looking back with a frown. "You are carrying, aren't you?"

Eddie nodded.

"Okay, let's go."

As they started down the alley, Yalich stopped and looked back at Eddie's Oldsmobile with its rusted fender and capless wheels and cracked windshield. He smiled. "I was gonna say that, given the neighborhood, I wouldn't count on your car being here when you get back, but . . . well, nothing personal, you understand, but

I suppose the one thing certain about what will or will not happen tonight is that that old heap will be here when you return."

Eddie smiled. "There's a method to my own madness," he said.

"I hope so," Yalich said and walked on.

Eddie followed Yalich until they neared the water, then turned down another row of warehouses to the end. Of the half-dozen doorways they passed, only two had lights over the entrances. Several spotlights positioned high on the corners of buildings cast the wide alley in separate cones of soft blue light. There were no cars in the alley, and no sign of life in any of the buildings. Yalich stopped and gently pulled Eddie into one of the darkened doorways and pointed to the five-story building opposite them. "Over there," he said. "The street door will be open. Here's the key to the office, third floor, front of the building. It's the door on the left. When you're finished, toss the key in the harbor. Wait by the window. You'll see the package delivered, but it'll just be dumped on the street. You'll have to drag it in yourself. But don't show yourself until the delivery man leaves. Understand?"

Eddie nodded.

"Understand, Irish, once the package is delivered, you're on your own. No one will come back for you, no one will check on you or provide cover. Understand?"

"I understand."

"If it doesn't happen tonight, it's not gonna happen ever. You understand that."

"Yeah."

Yalich stared a moment, then smiled and offered his hand. "I hope it works out so I never have to hear from you again."

Eddie paused, then shook Sid's hand. "I hope so, too. And thanks—"

Yalich stopped him with a quick shake of his head. He turned and started up the alley, then stopped and looked back. "Irish?"

"Yeah?" Eddie answered.

"Remember, the whole point of this exercise is survival. To stay alive."

"I'll keep that in mind."

"You do that, Irish. You do that."

The office was a single room with two windows overlooking the alley. An old desk with one broken leg sat tilted in the corner. Two straight-backed wooden chairs and a third, metal swivel chair were thrown together in another corner. Papers and trash covered the floor. A single desk lamp with a bent metal shade lay on the floor. Its frayed wire led to a socket, but it was not plugged in. Eddie didn't bother with the lamp. There was no need. The windows were barren, and just enough light filtered through the grime-covered glass so that after a minute or two of his eyes' adjusting, he could see all that he needed to see.

He pulled one of the wooden chairs up next to a window, sat down, leaning his cane against the sill, and removed the pair of latex surgical gloves he had donned to open the door and make his way up the darkened staircase. The gloves had made his hands sweat, and he wiped them on his pants legs. He pulled his old Smith & Wesson from the small of his back and checked the cylinder. Each chamber was loaded. He checked one coat pocket for the twelve extra rounds, and the other pocket for a length of thin nylon cord and a black-handled knife with a single spring-loaded four-inch blade. He then checked the tape recorder in the breast pocket of his coat.

He was ready, or as ready as he would ever be, and he would wait as long as he had to wait to get this business over. To finish it. To stay alive, like Yalich had said.

Waiting was nothing new to Eddie. It seemed as if he had spent half his life doing nothing but: waiting in observation posts for the drugs to change hands; waiting day after day for the mindless drivel of a wire intercept to turn to that one minute of useful conversation; waiting in cars with cold coffee and stale sandwiches; waiting in alleys and abandoned basements for snitches and suspects—working the sewers, he called it, just waiting for the right turd to float by; coming off midnights to catch snatches of sleep on the floor of some DA's office, waiting to paper a case; waiting for the witnesses to show up or not; waiting for the grand jury; waiting for the judge; waiting to testify. Just waiting.

But this was different. This wasn't the job. There would be no arrest, no case to paper, no grand jury or trial, and if it all turned bad, no one to appreciate or applaud his reasons for coming here, his reasons for doing what he was about to do. Not any of the ones who counted, at least. They would just shake their heads like they had so many times over so many years—Megs and the boys: never Priscilla, but Megs and the boys, and his father—all of them, like tired parents grown accustomed to being disappointed.

He knew the look well, a look of confusion as much as disappointment. It was his father's look the night after they buried his mother. They had all moved to the back porch, looking out to water, he and Megs and his two younger sisters and their husbands who had flown in from San Diego and Bozeman, and his father, who was ruminating over the auto accident that had killed his wife of forty-nine years.

"Sarah Evelyn was just out trying to do a good thing," his father had said. "Like always. All those things in the attic, all those clothes and such you girls never seemed to find time to clear out. And you, Edward, living so close 'n' all, she never could figure why you couldn't've found a Saturday to help her clear out all that stuff. Always thought someone should get the use of it. I don't know how many times she must've asked you, but, well, y'all're so busy. She just decided to take it all down to the Goodwill. Just a mile down the road she was when it happened. Well, I suppose such things happen. No telling what might've been if you'd done as she asked. Well, never mind, what's past is past. You children go on to bed. I know you're tired. You just go on. I'm gonna sit here a while. I'll be fine. You all go on."

Eddie thought of his father now, curled and comatose and waiting to die. If he knew, and if he could, Eddie supposed, his father would be shaking his head at what his son was up to. Eddie didn't have to be here. None of this had to happen. If only he had gone into the business like his father had planned. If only he had done what had been expected of him.

There was a rustling sound among some papers in the corner, and Eddie looked over to a pair of tiny eyes reflecting what little light there was. He tapped his cane on the floor and the rat disappeared. Eddie smiled and turned back to the window.

An hour passed, maybe more, before he saw a car turn into the alley with its lights off. It was an unmarked squad car moving quickly before it made a sudden U-turn and stopped in front of the building. Eddie watched as the trunk lid popped open and Sid Yalich jumped from the passenger side to move to the rear of the car. The driver, a tall, heavy-set man in a dark suit, got out, and the two men dragged a limp body from the trunk of the car. Its head was covered by a black sack, and its hands were bound behind its back. He watched them drag the body to the front of the building, and heard it thump against the door.

Eddie put his surgical gloves back on, left his cane propped against the sill, and quickly descended the two flights of stairs to the front door, which he opened slowly. The body didn't move or make any sound but for its quick and panicked breathing. The squad car was gone.

Eddie dragged the package inside and closed the door. He knelt down and put the barrel of his gun under the hood and pressed it hard against the throat just under the chin. "You listen to me carefully," he said. "You do anything—and I mean *anything!*—that doesn't please me, and I swear to God you will wish with every fiber of your being that I had just blown your fucking head off right here and now. Understand?"

There was no response and no movement.

"And the first thing that will not please me is your trying to run some fucking game that you don't speak the *angleeski* or you don't know *neechavo*. Do we understand one another?"

Again there was no response, and Eddie pushed the gun barrel even harder up under the chin.

"Yes, yes," a man's voice hissed through clenched teeth, and he tried to nod against the pressure of the barrel.

Eddie backed away. "Good. Now you're gonna stand up and the two of us are going up a coupla flights of stairs. But first let me tell you the plan. See, the plan is that you're gonna end up back on the street and someone is gonna find you. The question is how many of your body parts are still gonna be with you when you're found. Understand?"

"Aaaaah, Christ."

"I take it that your answer is yes, that you understand. Good. Now understand that every bullshit move you make, every bullshit answer you give is gonna cost you a body part. Understand?"

"No," the man's voice quavered. "I don't understand. This is a mistake, man. I'm telling you, man, whatever you want, it's not me. The others, the police or whoever they were, they wouldn't listen. They made a mistake. I'm telling you, they got the wrong man."

"Viktor Samoilov."

The man stopped squirming. Even the sound of his breathing stopped.

"That's right, Viktor. We got the right man."

"No. This is wrong. You've made a mistake, I'm telling you. We can talk about whatever this is, but I'm telling you, man, you've made a mistake. For real, man, a big mistake."

"See, Viktor? Now that's an example of a bullshit answer. I'll give you that one, 'cause you're just learning the game. But now that you know, you get no more passes. The next wrong answer is gonna cost you a body part. Understand?"

Viktor took a deep breath that drew the cloth of the hood to his mouth, and he coughed several times. "Yes, okay, I understand."

"Good!"

Eddie grabbed the back of Viktor's coat collar and pulled him struggling to his feet. Viktor stumbled a few times as they climbed the stairs, but he made no move to resist. In the office, Eddie sat him in one of the straight-backed wooden chairs and tied his already bound hands to the chair back. He then tied Viktor's ankles to the legs of the chair, and ran cord from the man's knees around the sides of the chair and pulled them tight, spreading his legs painfully, if Viktor's groan was any indication. He reached into his jacket pocket and turned on the tape recorder. Then he removed the hood. Viktor struggled to focus his eyes for a moment, but there was no sign of recognition.

Eddie rolled the metal swivel chair across the floor and sat down directly in front of the man. "So, Viktor, I figure you for a man who's got a well-developed sense of the practical. Am I right?"

Viktor said nothing and did not move.

"What I'm saying here is that you're more practical than loyal. I mean, you never even bothered to have someone come and pick up Mad Willy's remains. Seems to me that's the least you coulda done after spreading his brains all over my kitchen."

Viktor Samoilov's jaw dropped slowly, and his eyes widened, but again he said nothing.

"Oh, well, just business, right? . . . Viktor, I asked you a question."

He shook his head, his expression frozen as if he had no idea what his answer should be.

"Oh, Viktor, you're such a slow learner," Eddie said, and took the tip of Viktor's right ear in one hand, the other hand holding up the bright steel blade of his knife.

"Yes, yes! Whatever. Just business, yes."

"You see, Viktor, you came in a little late with that answer, so it doesn't count. The object here is that whenever I ask a question you answer it immediately. Don't even think about it. Just answer the question. Now, maybe you didn't fully understand the time requirements of our little game, so I won't take the whole ear. But, like I already told you, the rule is that if you fuck up I gotta take something. We gotta play by the rules, don't we? So I'll just take a little bit. You know, just so you sorta get the hang of things here." Eddie pulled the earlobe taut and quickly sliced off its tip.

Viktor's howl shook the room, and Eddie stepped back and tossed the small bit of flesh at Viktor's feet. Eddie waited a few moments until Viktor's expression of pain lowered to a series of quick, gasping moans. "You know, Viktor, the last time I heard someone howl like that was Mad Willy, just before you blew his head off. And as I saw things, it looked like it was my head you were going for. Is that right? Were you aiming for me?"

Viktor just shook his head, trying to catch his breath until he saw Eddie move forward again and raise the knife blade.

"Yes!" he cried. "Yes, yes, Jesus, yes."

"Ah, see? You're getting the hang of it, already. You're not as stupid as everyone says."

"Aaaah," Viktor wailed as his eyes rolled back and he took heavy gulps of air against the pain.

Eddie wiped the blood on the knife blade onto Viktor's pant leg, and then he smiled. "So, Viktor, shall we get down to business?"

"Yes. I mean no! This is a mistake. You're making a big mistake. You have no idea who you're dealing with."

"The boys on Brighton Beach Avenue? That little office above the nightclub?"

"What?"

"Beep! There goes the buzzer, Viktor. Fucked up again." Eddie took the bloodied remains of Viktor's one earlobe and made another slice.

"Ahhhhhh, fuck!" Viktor screamed, and he thrashed about until he and the chair tumbled to the floor.

Eddie left Viktor writhing until the wails of pain subsided to his breath hissing through clenched teeth, and he sat him upright once more.

"Now, where were we?" Eddie asked. "Oh, yes, the boys on Brighton Beach Avenue."

"What?"

Eddie shrugged and again raised his knife.

"*No!* Please . . . no, no, please, I didn't. I don't know what you're asking, for Christ's sake."

"Viktor, what can I do? Those are the rules."

"No, no, no. Really, I didn't mean to fuck up. Really, I just didn't understand the question. For Christ's sake, this isn't fair!"

Eddie burst into a laugh. "Fair? Hah! That's good, Viktor." He leaned over and sliced through Viktor's leather belt. "That's really good. Not fair, you say. Yeah, well, what's fair or unfair depends on the rules. You know, when you play an away game, you gotta play by local rules. Home-field advantage and all that." He then grabbed the waistband of Viktor's pants and began cutting through the material, opening his pants over his lap.

"Oh, God, oh, God, no, no, please, for God's sake, don't do this."

"Oh, Viktor, quit whining. They say all you need is one, and unless you fuck up again that's what you'll have."

"Ah, Jesus, please, please, don't do this. Anything you want, just ask me anything. Anything you want."

"Anything?" Eddie said as he exposed Viktor and began moving the knife blade around the scrotum, separating the testicles.

"*Anything!*"

"Anything? You're sure?"

"Anything, for Christ's sake."

"Well, Viktor, you know, I really would like a chocolate milkshake."

"What?"

"Yes, a chocolate milkshake."

"A milkshake?"

"Yes, a milkshake. Chocolate. Can you handle that?"

"Aaah . . . yeah, sure, yeah, anything, you mean now?"

"Yeah, now."

"Well . . . what? I don't understand. I'm trying, man. I swear to God I am. Whatever you want. I mean, I don't understand. Just tell me what to do here. Don't get crazy, please. Whatever you want."

"So you don't have a chocolate milkshake for me?"

"I mean, Jesus Christ, man, you know, like, I gotta go someplace . . . you know, to get it. I mean, whaddaya talking about milkshakes?"

"You see, Viktor? That's what I'm talking about. You'll say just about anything whether you mean it or not. That's a fuckup, which means you lose another body part. Those are the rules."

Eddie again moved the knife blade over Viktor's scrotum.

"No, no, that's not the rules. That's not what you said."

"I don't know, Viktor. I think it's another fuckup, so now we got two fuckups to deal with."

"Ah, man, don't do this. Swear to God, man, swear to God. That's not the rules. You didn't tell me about any milkshakes. I mean, nothing about milkshakes. I remember what you said and that wasn't part of the rules."

"Okay, let's say I give you this one."

"Yeah, okay," Viktor said, his breathing quick and heavy. "That's fair, man. Yeah, that's okay."

"So we only have one fuckup, is that right?"

"That's right, just one fuckup . . ."

"So, Viktor," Eddie smiled, pressing the knife blade on the soft flesh now shriveled into a small, tight ball, "you got a preference here? I mean, you right- or left-handed, or something? I mean, you got a strong preference for which one I cut out?"

"No! God, no. Wait! Really, it wasn't a fuckup. I didn't say . . . I mean, I didn't do anything. . . . You didn't ask me a question. . . . I don't know what you want. . . . I didn't understand. . . ." He was weeping now. "I didn't understand. . . . Oh, Jesus, Jesus, Jesus, don't do this."

Eddie took the point of the blade and pinned a bit of flesh against the wooden seat of the chair. A soft whimper escaped Viktor as his body went rigid and he winced in anticipation. "Do you understand the rules now?"

Viktor nodded quickly.

"Garland Bolles—his real name and where I'll find him."

Viktor's mouth gaped as if he was caught suddenly between two opposing forces of paralyzing fear, one immediate, the other future if he broke the code of silence. Eddie waited only a second or two before stabbing the knife point through the flesh and into the wooden seat. *"Aowwwwwwaaa!"*

"Garland Bolles—his real name and where I can find him."

ɼ

Viktor Samoilov didn't know Garland Bolles by any other name. The original contract had come through a man named Semyon Birshstein, a local mob leader for whom Viktor had worked in the past. In vouching for Bolles, Birshstein had made it clear that Bolles was a man of considerable importance. *"Rukovodstvo,"* Viktor said, a made man, "what you might call a godfather." Birshstein made it clear, too, that Viktor was to treat any instruction from Bolles as if it had come from the head of the mob itself.

Viktor first met Bolles in Manhattan, at a restaurant on Columbus Avenue near Lincoln Center. It was late, and Bolles had come from the ballet, and for a long time Viktor thought that there must have been some mistake, that perhaps this Bolles had no real business to contract. They sat for more than an hour, while Bolles talked of the ballet and ordered and ate course after course. Viktor drank only coffee and ate only a dessert—Black Forest cake, if he remembered correctly—to keep the man company. They spoke mostly in English, but occasionally Bolles would slip into Russian, as if to test Viktor's *bona fides*. When finally they did get down to business, the details were sketchy. Viktor's assignment was to assist Bolles in getting certain information from and then eliminating a man named Trevor Grehm.

Grehm was reported to be in Washington at the time, but it was said that he would not be there long, and so the job had to be done quickly, within the next day or two. The job paid fifty thousand dollars, twenty-five up front and twenty-five on satisfactory completion. It was up to Viktor to hire and pay for whatever backup or assistance he required.

The talk was brief, but ultimately Viktor agreed to the job, and the two shook hands. Bolles gave Viktor an attaché case containing twenty-five thousand dollars in one-hundred-dollar bills. Also in the case was an envelope containing a key to an apartment located in Washington, on Eighteenth Street near Dupont Circle. "Your final instructions, how to contact me, and everything you will need will be in that apartment by noon tomorrow," Bolles had said.

Vladimir "Mad Willy" Lyubarsky was Viktor's first choice for backup. Willy may have been none too bright, but, as Viktor told Eddie, Willy did what he was told, asked no questions, and if ever approached by the authorities would not provide them answers. Viktor went to Willy's apartment near the corner of Brighton Four and Neptune Avenue early the morning after his meeting with Bolles. He gave Willy twenty-five hundred dollars in cash and told him to be ready in an hour. Viktor then rented a car in the name of one of his many aliases, which one he didn't remember, and by ten o'clock that morning, they were on the road to Washington.

Viktor's job was simple. Trevor Grehm worked out of London, for some company that had offices in Washington. He wasn't told any more than that. Grehm had a wife, but Viktor could not remember her name. It had not mattered at the time. It was not expected that she or anyone else would be with Grehm. His and Willy's assignment was to snatch Grehm and bring him to Bolles for questioning, after which they were to kill him. It was made clear as well that anyone found with Trevor Grehm was expendable. No one was to stand in the way of their assignment. It was Viktor's understanding that Grehm had stolen a lot of money— "coupla million or more. I don't know anything about how or where he stole it from, but Bolles said it belonged to the *Organizatsiya*."

"The what?"

"The mob."

"This Grehm worked for the Russian mob."

"I don't know. And that's the truth, 'cause when we finally got to the guy he was talking about things I didn't understand. Besides, I wasn't paying all that much attention. It wasn't my business. Bolles did all the talking."

"How'd Bolles get this Grehm fella to talk?"

"Some kinda drug. I don't know what it was, man. Bolles had a little leather case with him and there was a syringe filled with the shit. We had the guy tied up, and Bolles shot him up. I mean, he didn't even bother to see if the man would talk first, he just shot him up. Like he knew beforehand the man wouldn't say anything without it, and he didn't want to waste time."

"Seem to you like Bolles and Grehm might've known one another?"

"Yeah, maybe, but I can't say. It was like neither one did anything but stare at one another when me and Willy brought them together. Bolles just said something like, Let's not waste time, and got out the syringe."

"So tell me what the man said."

"You mean, Grehm?"

"Yes."

"I don't know."

Eddie positioned the knife tip again.

"No bullshit, really, honest to God. Like I said, it wasn't my business and Bolles was doing all the talking. Besides, what little the man said didn't make much sense, and he wasn't conscious all that long. The drugs must've been too much. He was talking all this stuff, and he had this weird smile at the same time, like he was really out in space somewhere. The load in the syringe must've been too much, or else he must've had a bad reaction to it. He went out, pretty quickly. I mean Bolles managed some questions, but the answers sounded all garbled to me. I think even Bolles was surprised, like he hadn't figured the right dosage or whatever. About all I can remember is the man was saying that something called Iberia, whatever that is, he was talking like it had to do with American intelligence. Bolles kept pressing him about something called the Special Projects Directorate, but this Grehm guy kept talking about Iberia and slurring some names I didn't get. The only reason I remember any of it at all was because . . . well, to tell the truth, soon as I figured out we might've been screwing around with the government or whatever, I started getting a little nervous."

"You hear any names mentioned?"

"Yeah, some. There were some Russian names, but, like I said, I wasn't paying attention, and he was just mumbling and stuff. Some woman's name came up a couple of times, but I couldn't understand what they were saying. It didn't make any sense."

"Did you hear the name?"

"I mean, I heard it, but it didn't mean anything to me."

Eddie nodded. "And what about the lady?"

"You mean the wife?"

"Yeah, her. How'd she get into it?"

"Like I said, she wasn't supposed to be there."

"So what happened?"

"Okay, that first night we went to the house, this guy Grehm's house. Bolles had given us the address along with some other places we might find him. So we went to the house first. It was early, not much past dark, and there were no lights on. We were gonna wait for him inside. We went in through a window on the side of the house. Broke the window and went in. I mean, you know, like we were ready, you know, in case someone was inside or whatever. I mean, Bolles had said to be ready, 'cause Grehm was known to carry, you know, like he was no choir boy."

"So what happened."

"Well, after we got in, we started looking around. Didn't seem like anybody was home, but, still, you know. Anyway, Willy was ahead of me. He was checking out the back of the house. So, anyway, the noise must've woken her up, the wife. She was in the back bedroom. I don't know, maybe she heard us, but we didn't hear a peep. Nothing at all, man. Not until Willy got to the bedroom and opened the door, and, man, she just opened fire. Just like that, man, almost like she was waiting for us, you know? But she missed. One shot, and Willy fired back. Caught her right away. Damn lucky shot. Willy wasn't that good, he was just lucky. But he caught her in the chest and that was it."

"The husband wasn't there?"

"No. We didn't find him until the next night. Actually, he found us. We spent more time looking around the places Bolles said, but then I figured the guy'd show up eventually, so we just sat on the house until he came to us. It was the next afternoon, pretty late, actually. Again, it was almost dark. We just took him to see Bolles and that was that."

"Where?"

"Where what?"

"Where'd you take him to meet with Bolles?"

"I can't tell you the name of it. This place out on the east side of town. Bolles showed us how to find it first. It was out where there were a lot of old warehouses. I remember you went out New York Avenue for a while and then turned down a couple of streets. There was nobody there, man. We stuffed Grehm in the trunk of his car, and I drove. Willy followed in our rental. That was it."

"What about the wallet and the credit cards?"

"What about them?"

"How'd they end up with LeRoi?"

"Who? . . . Oh, you mean the black guy?"

"Yeah."

"Well . . . you know."

"No, I don't know. Tell me."

"Well, after Willy shot the lady in the house, I called Bolles and he said to make it look like a burglary. You know, tear the place up a bit and take something to drop on the street, you know, like a wallet or whatever, so some credit cards or whatever might get into circulation, and it'd just look like a burglar shot her."

"And so?"

"So that's what we did. Took some stuff, including the wallet and spread it around *chërnyi* town."

"Chorney? Whaddaya mean, chorney town?"

"Black, you know."

"So?"

"So me and Willy drove downtown and looked around for one of those neighborhoods and just tossed the stuff, you know, bit by bit. We didn't take much. Figured the wallet would do the trick. Figured it'd take about twenty seconds for some nigger—"

"For what?" Eddie interrupted.

Viktor hesitated, seemingly confused, then started to speak a bit more cautiously. "Well . . . you know, for some black guy to pick it up and try to pass the credit cards or whatever. Make it look like a regular burglary or whatever. We didn't find out until later, you know, after we snatched the man, the husband, that there were some codes or whatever on the credit cards. That's what the guy Grehm was saying to Bolles, that the codes were on the cards."

"What kind of codes."

"Man, I don't know. Like I say, the guy was babbling by that time, but whatever he was talking about sure had Bolles upset. I can't say what it was about."

"Bolles was not happy?"

"No, man, he was upset. I don't think he really understood what was on the cards either, but all of a sudden he was real worried about it. You know, what might be on those cards. That's all I know. Then he started talking like *we* fucked up, which started getting me worried. You know, like he might tell Birshstein we fucked up. And, man, I didn't want that."

"So what'd you do?"

"Well, you know . . ."

Eddie leaned forward. "Viktor, you're on the edge of another fuckup."

"Man, you know how it is. We made him happy. Me and Willy."

"How?" Eddie asked, but Victor just looked at him. "How?" he repeated as he moved the tip of the knife blade toward Viktor's bloodied scrotum.

"Well, I didn't ask for the second twenty-five thousand and we . . . you know, we did you for free."

Eddie shook his head. "I'm insulted, man."

"Yeah, well, it was just business."

"And me?"

"What about you?"

"Why did Bolles hire me?"

"Shit, man, you knew the territory. We didn't. He . . . You know, Bolles, he wanted to find this black guy bad. When he found out the guy had tried to pass the credit cards or whatever, he wanted him found real bad. We tried, but there was no way guys like me were gonna be able to work that ground. So he hired you. I don't know how he came up with your name."

"And?"

"And so we tried following you around. I mean, we tried the first night you went out—you know, after Bolles hired you. But we lost you 'bout a half-hour after you hit town. The way you disappeared on us, we figured you had made us or something. Anyway, Bolles said to just lay low and wait for you to report in. And once you found the guy who had the wallet, well, that's when he sent us down to get it from you."

"You stayed in town the whole time?"

"Just after he hired you. We owed him, you know, so we came

back to D.C., Willy and me, and waited for you to turn up something."

"Where'd you stay?"

"That same apartment off Dupont Circle."

"And?"

"And, well, you know what happened then."

"You do LeRoi before or after our little meeting?"

"Right after. Bolles figured we didn't have much time. I called him from the road and told him what happened in your kitchen and, you know, that Willy was dead and that I had your gun. It took him about five seconds to figure I should whack the nigger"— Eddie leaned forward and Viktor leaned back quickly—"the black fella. You know. So, anyway, Bolles said to use your gun and leave it behind. He said to do it right away, that night, and get out of town. Bolles told me where to find him. I guess he got the information from you. So I found him. Wasn't hard spotting him with that tooth. So I did him, tossed your gun down like Bolles said, and split. That's it."

"What number did you call? For Bolles, that is, after you left my place?"

"Man, I swear to God I don't remember. It was an answering service. A local Washington number, that's all I remember. Probably the same number he gave you, I don't know. It's been some time, you know."

"Hold it. Just a moment," Eddie said, reaching into the breast pocket of his jacket and pulling out the small recorder and turning over the tape.

"Ah, man," Viktor groaned.

"Oh, yeah, I think the boys in your little club there on Brighton Beach Avenue are gonna love listening to this tape, don't you?"

"Man, why don't you just cut my throat here? Get it over with, for Christ's sake."

"Nah, I don't think so. I got lots of things in store for you."

"Meaning what?"

"It's like ice cream, you know. See, creeps like you will bite off big chunks of an ice-cream cone, 'cause you've got no patience. Me, I enjoy the long haul. I like to lick my ice cream. I like to take my time, enjoy the taste. Like killing a piece of shit like you. No fun just popping you. Not when it's personal like this. I wanna take my time, cut you down piece by fucking piece."

"Man, I'm telling you all I know."

"Ah, well, maybe, maybe not. But, see, the point is, I'd kinda like seeing what your own boys might do if they got a hold of this tape. Might be interesting, you know? Yes, I think I'll save you like an ice-cream cone. I haven't decided how much of you I'm gonna cut tonight, but I think I just might leave enough behind for me to come back another time. Maybe tomorrow, maybe next week, I'll have some more questions for you. Maybe not, but rest assured, Viktor, I will be back. I'm going to see to it that slowly, bit by bit, you get reduced to that little gob of spit that you are. 'Course, in the meantime, you'll have a chance to come after me. A second chance, so to speak. The problem for you, however, is the copies of this tape. Anything happens to me, you gotta deal with that. Whaddaya s'pose, Viktor? What would someone like your Mr. Birshstein do if he heard you calling his name in the middle of your confession, and him knowing this same tape was going to the feds? Think you'll be spending much time up there on Park Avenue after that? Or do you think maybe Mr. Birshstein might have ways of dealing with situations like this that even I couldn't imagine?"

Viktor's mouth opened slowly, but he said nothing, sitting absolutely still.

"See, the point is, you fucked up. Business is business. I understand a man just trying to make a living. But you, you brought your business into my house. You made it personal. Understand?"

Viktor did not answer.

"Worse, you really upset my daughter. Remember her?"

"No, man, I don't remember anybody."

"Oh, Viktor, now you're lying again." Eddie raised the tip of the knife blade and Viktor blurted out, "Yes, yes, I remember. I didn't see her, man, I only heard her come in."

"Yes, now, that's better. Anyway, you and Mad Willy really upset her. Understand?"

"How was I to know someone would walk in?"

"You pay your dues and you take your chances. So, anyway, when you upset my family you upset me. Understand?"

Viktor nodded quickly.

"So you gotta pay. Big-time."

"Jesus, man, if you're gonna do it, just do it."

"Ah, no, Viktor, I keep telling you, I like to drag my pleasures out. Trust me, I haven't even started what I have in mind for you."

Viktor was breathing heavily and his eyes closed tight, tears weeping from each corner.

"And in the end, whether it's me that cuts you down or your boys in Brighton Beach—or, hell, maybe both of us—either way, I figure you're gonna die as slow and as hard and as scared as a man can die. And, Viktor, it gives me no end of pleasure to think of you that way. Yes, sir, Viktor, no end of pleasure."

*

It had been many long weeks since Eddie had been home in the house on the river, and he thought the chances of either side's running a prolonged surveillance were slim—slim enough that he could return for a few days before deciding what to do next. A few days stretched into a week and no one tried to call, no strangers were seen lurking about, and there were no signs that the house had been disturbed. He had almost started to relax when he pulled from his mailbox a small envelope postmarked Manhattan but containing no return address. Inside, folded in a plain piece of white paper, was a short article cut from an unidentified newspaper. The article reported that the body of Viktor Samoilov, age thirty-six, of Brooklyn, had been found stuffed headfirst in a trash can at the corner of Brighton Beach and Coney Island Avenues. Beyond the statement that Viktor had been murdered, no specific cause of death was indicated. There was no note attached to the article.

Eddie's stomach tightened, and a slight wave of dizziness swept over him. He took several deep breaths, staring at the article, then lit the stove and held the article and the envelope in which it had come over the flame. He dropped the burning remains in the sink and washed all evidence of them down the drain.

"Rest easy, Sid," he said, then turned his thoughts to where he might go next.

17.

Hans Talpa was a collection of nonspecifics. He was neither young nor old, neither tall nor short nor thin nor fat nor dark nor light; a quiet man easily overlooked, a man one might meet a dozen times over and still not remember his name. He was, in a word, an anonym, a man perfectly suited to his work with the National Security Agency, the largest and, at least among those that were publicly acknowledged, the most secret of America's intelligence agencies. Within this most secretive agency, Hans was a specialist in one of its most secretive sections, his particular specialty being the offensive penetration of computer-security systems to steal information from the enemy, however loosely that term was applied, and the development of defensive systems to prevent penetration by his counterparts on the other side.

But, however well suited he may have been to the netherworld of "black ops," Hans Talpa was not well suited for murder, at least not of the kind that had ended the life of Letitia Bernay. Hans Talpa had particularly thin wrists and delicate fingers not well suited to holding down and manually strangling while anally sodomizing a five-foot-seven-inch, 155-pound, and reasonably well-muscled whore struggling for her life.

The moment they first met, Eddie Nickles knew that Hans had not killed Letitia Bernay. It wasn't that Hans was incapable of murder—no, Eddie knew all too well that, given the proper incentive and circumstance, murder resided in even the meekest of souls—it was just that, if called upon to kill, Hans would have used a weapon, not his hands.

Eddie had never shared this insight with Hans—not at their first meeting or at any of the half-dozen subsequent interviews. He wanted Hans to worry and to wonder. It had given Eddie the edge he required, for, though he was certain that Hans had not committed the murder, he was equally certain that Hans had witnessed it.

It was a sorry and sordid little case, not one that raised any public eyebrows or excited any departmental concern: just another whore dead at the hands of her john. But at the time it was just the type of case Eddie needed. He had recently come off the biggest case of his career, the one in which he and Jimmy Legget and the now vanished DA, Michael Holden, had uncovered corruption within the police department, the United States Attorney's Office, and City Hall, and at the same time closed down an international cartel of drug dealers with the single largest heroin seizure in the city's history. Eddie hated the spotlight that case had focused on him, and he had happily escaped into this insignificant killing of this insignificant woman. It was a case he could work quietly and alone, a case that had excited no one's interest but his own.

Eddie found Hans Talpa through a notebook Letitia Bernay had kept, one in which she catalogued her steady customers by nicknames and telephone numbers and their individual and sometimes unique sexual peccadilloes. Hans was a watcher, not a doer, and the Rose Tattoo, a small, three-room massage parlor above a Mexican restaurant in Tenleytown, was Hans's favorite venue, a place where he could huddle in a closet and peer through a two-way mirror while Letitia collected double fees for single services. Hans's telephone number was the only entry Letitia had made on her schedule of appointments for the night she died.

But Hans had an alibi, albeit an alibi that he could not publicly claim, and which he was deathly afraid anyone—and particularly Eddie Nickles—might try to corroborate. He claimed he was "in the field" that night, although "national security" prevented his revealing where he was or what he was doing. Hans begged Eddie for understanding. Even the most neutral of inquiries at NSA, even to ask nothing more than whether he was working on the day and at the time of Letitia's death, Hans claimed would have ended his career. NSA was notoriously unforgiving when it came to even a hint that one of its covert employees might be publicly compromised. Therein lay Hans Talpa's problem and Eddie Nickles's opportunity.

The problem, unlike the murder, was ultimately resolved by a simple agreement. Eddie would trust Hans's claim that at the time in question he was indeed on the job and had no knowledge of who might have murdered the object of his passive lust, and that his clandestine activities, both official and otherwise, would remain their secret. In return, of course, it was agreed that, should the occasion ever arise, Eddie could count on Hans to return the favor.

Nearly five years had passed since their last contact, and Hans was obviously shaken by Eddie's call. Throughout their first meeting, Hans squirmed like a worm suddenly unearthed, but ultimately, although with much wringing of hands and anxious sighs, Hans agreed to try to gather what information he could. It was another ten days and several calls from Eddie before Hans agreed to a second meeting.

It was a Saturday, the middle of the morning, and the two men sat at a small table outside a French café in Arlington, Virginia, drinking coffee from paper cups and eating almond croissants. Eddie had asked for a donut, but a croissant was as close as the establishment could come, and he was annoyed at the flakes of crust that kept clinging to his chin and falling to his lap.

"Detective," Hans began—Eddie had not mentioned that he was no longer with the police department—"before I say anything more, there are some things I have to make clear."

"What's that?"

Hans looked down at his fingertips constantly moving back and forth along the edge of the plastic tabletop as if he were smoothing the wrinkles from an imaginary cloth. "Well, first, I suppose it may have been obvious to you that I was a little . . . well, shall we say *unsettled?*—I guess that's the word—by the information you asked me to gather for you. I didn't say so at the time, because I was not at all sure how to deal with this situation. In any event, this group you asked about, this Special Projects Directorate . . . Well, the point is that I am aware that such a group exists. But what you have to understand is that, as far as anyone outside our little community is concerned, there is no such thing as Special Projects Directorate. You understand?"

"I think so, but why don't you explain it to me anyway."

Hans lifted his eyes, but only for a instant before returning his stare to his fingers tracing the edge of the table and tapping the rim of his cup and twirling his plastic spoon. Several women passed by the table to enter the café, and Hans waited for the clips of conversation about day care and soccer practice to fade before starting up again. "What I am trying to tell you, Detective, is that I—that is, my group—have had occasion to do work for this directorate. I can also tell you that I don't know a thing about their mission or what they're involved in, but there have been occasions—very rare, I might add, only two or three that I am aware of—when we have been assigned to do some special work for them. We were never told who we were working for, but one can't help picking up bits and pieces. My first contact was some years ago, back in the eighties, when it was suspected that they might have had a security problem, an internal-security problem, that was thought to require our special expertise. A problem within their headquarters, or at least I assume it was their headquarters. And, please, don't even ask where that was. I wouldn't tell you no matter how many people you might tell of my past."

Eddie shook his head. "Hans, relax, man. It's just you 'n' me. I didn't come here to hang you up. I only came to you for a favor. Actually, the return of a favor. That's all."

Hans took a deep breath, while his eyes squeezed shut and his fingers massaged his temples. "Yes," he expelled, as his eyes opened wide and he looked out toward the traffic on Lee Highway, "you're right. I'm looking at this all wrong, aren't I? You did. You went out of your way to do me a great favor. I suppose you had to bend a few of your own rules to do that. I must remember that. Yes, I must. And, like me," he said more to himself than to Eddie, "you have found yourself caught up in trouble not of your own making. My God, at least I didn't have people shooting at me, did I? No, I need to keep this all in perspective. It's only right that I try to help you. It's the least I can do."

"Listen—" Eddie started, but Hans cut him off.

"But!" Hans exclaimed, then paused before repeating more

softly, "But, Detective, you have to understand something. I can't go back to the well on this one. I can only tell you what I have found so far. I can't do any follow-up. All right?"

"I don't know. You tell me."

"Yes. All right, all right. Okay, how shall I put this? You see, the Special Projects Directorate doesn't exist. All right?"

Eddie frowned and shook his head slightly.

"It has a headquarters that doesn't exist. It has a director who doesn't exist, and a whole staff and field operatives who don't exist. Not on personnel lists, not on organizational charts. Nowhere. Understand?"

"Except in the intelligence community, right?"

"Not even there."

"Come again?"

"It's a special group. I honestly don't know where they fit in, who they belong to, who runs it, or what they do. Nothing. I only know that it exists because several of us have done some work for them, but even on those few occasions we were assigned off the books and using all sorts of cut-outs. We were loaned out on special orders from our headquarters. Not even our supervisor was told what we were doing or for whom. The director's office would simply call down for two or three of our top technicians, ones who had special expertise in special areas, and then we'd be detailed. We reported only to one man. We'd meet him in an office in one of these complexes outside the beltway. No names were ever used, and we were not allowed to tell anyone, not even anyone in the agency, what we were doing or where. We were put on annual leave for each of these details, and told that if anyone asked, even our own people, we were going on vacation. They gave us hotel brochures where we were supposed to be, and restaurant menus and canceled airline tickets and receipts, so if ever asked we could talk like we had really been to these places. And then we'd get cash bonuses to make up for the loss of annual leave." Hans smiled for the first time. "I can tell you that I've had some perfectly lovely vacations in places I've never seen. Once they even had us spend time in a tanning booth as part of the charade. Are you beginning to understand?"

"Yeah, I think so."

"Well, the whole point is this. Any inquiry from any source about the Special Projects Directorate causes concern. Okay?"

"Okay."

"Particularly if there is any inquiry specific to the people or work of the directorate. Okay?"

"Yeah. But are you trying to tell me—"

"I'm not trying," Hans interrupted. "I *am* telling you, Detective. You are treading on very sensitive ground here."

"In other words, there is no information but what you've already told me."

Hans took a moment, again lowering his eyes. "No. I'm telling you that I could only go to the well once. If what I have to tell you is not enough, I'm sorry, but I can't go back for more."

Eddie said nothing and waited while Hans's eyes lifted to scan the horizon and he took a deep breath.

"Look," he said, "the Achilles' heel of any intelligence operation is the need to store information. Information stored is information that can be retrieved. Security over that information obviously comes from special lock-out and access codes and all sorts of elaborate procedures designed to protect the integrity of those codes. Now, no matter how sophisticated such codes and procedures are, there are always ways to override them, particularly if the one attempting the override is the one who helped develop the lock-out system in the first place."

"Someone like yourself?" Eddie asked.

Hans ignored the question. "The secret is to override in a way that can't be traced, which is no mean feat, I can tell you, since part of the system is to have in place the means to automatically source-trace any inquiry or attempted override."

"In other words, you can get in but they'll know you got in. Right?"

Hans smiled again. "Well, that's the way it's suppose to work, but there are ways to make an inquiry or entry look like a glitch, some strange computer anomaly that may raise an eyebrow but can't be traced. Now, one such event, like I say, may raise an eyebrow or two, but without a tracing there's no real way to establish that it's anything but a glitch. But a second event? No, a second event will definitely set off alarms, and it wouldn't take long before we, or in this case they, will figure out that the event wasn't a glitch. Once they figure that out, the rest is a simple process of elimination. There are only a few people or groups who would have the expertise to run such an override. Understand?"

"Understood."

"Okay, so here's everything I can tell you, which is all I could find out before the entry would no longer look like a glitch. Okay? I can't go back in. You understand that."

"Understood."

"Okay. First, the Grehms, Trevor and his wife, were both coded as family."

"Meaning?"

"Meaning they both worked for the directorate. In what capacity, I don't know. But in whatever capacity, they were definitely government, definitely directorate. Next, Iberia Trading. Also government, also directorate. Whether a captive independent—you know, a legitimate business doing favors—or whether it's pure directorate, I can't tell you. I could only scratch the surface."

"What about Garland Bolles?"

"An infidel. It would appear that the agency is equally interested in who he is or who he works for. He's definitely not family."

Eddie waited a moment, then asked, "That's it?"

"Well, to tell the truth, it's more than I expected to be able to get without overextending my welcome, so to speak, but it was made easier by the fact that all this information was grouped in one subfile, which obviously means it's all connected. I assume that comes as no surprise to you. But there was no way I could get past the character list to any narrative without ringing alarms." Hans looked at Eddie and, for a moment, held his stare.

"There's something else?" Eddie asked.

"Well, yes. You're listed with a watch code."

"A what?"

"A watch code. It means they're interested in you."

"What's that mean?"

"It could mean anything. There's nothing specific listed, but anytime there's a watch code you can bet they've checked you out, your background, who you are, and all that, and they may well be keeping an eye on you. How extensively, there's no way to tell."

Eddie looked around suddenly, and Hans smiled. "No, don't worry. I've had some experience at this. Well, you can imagine—you know, given my former habits, I learned to be careful. I followed you coming here, and I'm certain no one was behind you or me."

Eddie sat back and released a long sigh.

"I'm sorry," Hans said. "That's all I can tell you."

Eddie nodded, then leaned forward. "Look, I appreciate this." Hans looked down shyly, and Eddie asked, "Are you okay with all this?"

"Yeah, sure," Hans whispered, then looked up. "You scared the hell out of me when you called, but, I don't know, I feel better about it now. Really. In some ways I'm glad you needed a favor. I feel like we've finally settled things between us."

Eddie nodded and reached into his pocket and laid some money on the table to cover his coffee and half-eaten croissant. "I don't expect we'll be seeing one another again."

"No," Hans said, "I expect not. Particularly since you've retired from the police force."

Eddie started to speak, but Hans cut him off. "No, that's all right. I figured I owed you."

Eddie stood up slowly. "It was never a debt, Hans, it was a favor."

Hans nodded and looked down. "Did you ever find out who killed her? You know, Letitia?"

"Nope, never did."

"I didn't do it," Hans said, his stare fixed on the table top.

"I know."

Hans looked up quickly. "I didn't see it either. I swear to God I didn't. I've thought about it a lot since then. I really have. I don't know what I would have done if I had seen it, you know, if I had seen whoever it was that killed her. I hope I would have done the right thing. I don't delude myself by thinking I would have had the courage to try to stop it, but I hope I would have at least had the courage to help you identify whoever did it. But I'll never know, because the fact is I didn't see it. I really wasn't there, at least not that night. I hope you believe that."

Eddie nodded. "Forget it, Hans. It's ancient history."

Hans's eyes again dropped toward the table. "I hope so," he said.

"Take care," said Eddie, reaching out his hand.

"You, too, Detective," Hans replied, shaking it.

18.

The offices of the Special Projects Directorate were all but empty late that Saturday afternoon, and deathly quiet but for the slow creaking steps of the three security officers separately making their rounds and the jabber in the fourth-floor communications center, where the two men assigned to monitor the phones and cable traffic were quibbling over who was cheating whom in their game of piquet. Only in the second-floor office of Miss Wendy Berksmere was any business of note being conducted, and that business was being noted only by Miss Berksmere and the man upon whom she most often relied when an assignment called for a "unilateral," an agent having no connection to any other agents.

"You're certain of this?" Miss Berksmere asked.

"Yes, ma'am," the man answered. "There's no doubt. He's level-seven. Covert work only."

"And this was his second meeting with Nickles?"

"The second that I've witnessed."

"And the first?"

"Ten days ago, in a bar up on Capitol Hill. Talpa arrived and left on foot, so all I got was a photograph. But this time he came in his car. I traced him off the license plate."

"You have the original photograph?"

"Yes, it's there in the file."

Miss Berksmere fingered through the papers in the manila folder to retrieve an eight-by-ten-inch glossy photograph taken through a telephoto lens. "Did you get any photos this morning?"

"Yes, but I haven't had time to develop them. You want the film?"

Miss Berksmere nodded, and the man took a roll of film from his pocket and placed it on her desk. "Hmmm," Miss Berksmere pondered. "A less suspicious person than yourself might well think this nothing more than two old friends meeting for drink or brunch or whatever, yes?"

"Perhaps. But a less suspicious person would be wrong. Talpa lives in Laurel. Nickles lives down near Annapolis. Why wouldn't they meet somewhere near there? Why would they both come all the way across town and out to Arlington just to chat over a cup of coffee?"

"Yes, why indeed?" Miss Berksmere pulled her sweater a bit tighter about her shoulders. "Well," she said, "it seems our Mr. Nickles is proving to be a worthy adversary. We might well have underestimated his resourcefulness . . . and his cool, I might add. I'm more than a little surprised that he's back in the area."

"Well, like I told you before, the police and the FBI have all but buried the case. As far as I can tell, there's no one out there but us keeping an eye on him."

"But there's a warrant still outstanding?"

"Yes, but it's only a material-witness warrant, and no one's pursuing it, at least not actively."

"Do you suppose he knows that?"

"I'm certain he does. His friend Legget would keep him informed."

"And you still think a tap is a waste of time."

"Yes, I do. Nickles is no fool. There's been no traffic at all. Obviously they're using pay phones or whatever. If it hadn't been for that lead out of the FBI in New York that let us pick up the surveillance there, I doubt we would have found him."

"Well, he's certainly been busy."

"Yeah, too busy, I'd say."

"You're certain the murder of Samoilov is connected."

"Yes. We don't know where Nickles was beforehand or how long he was in New York, but by the time we picked up on him he was already in contact with this character Sid Yalich. I gave you Yalich's background. He spent years working the Brighton Beach crowd. That is, till he went round the bend and they gave him the equivalent of a section eight. He may be nuts, but word is no one knows the local Russian mob better. Second, we know the man killed in Nickles's kitchen was this Mad Willy character. And Mad Willy was known to work backup for Viktor Samoilov, who mainly pulled contracts from Birshstein's crowd. It makes sense that Samoilov would've been the second man in Nickles's kitchen. The description fits, everything. Finally, the same morning Nickles left New York, or at least the morning we think he left, they found Samoilov's body in a trash can in Brighton Beach. You do the math."

"And where is he now?"

"You mean where is he staying?"

"Yes."

"He's got a cottage down near St. Michaels."

"Really? You mean down on the Eastern Shore?"

"Yeah, the owner's an ex-cop from D.C. We don't know if he's renting or they're just letting him use it or what."

"How interesting. Well, he certainly does get around, doesn't he?" Miss Berksmere sat forward and folded her hands together on her highly polished desk. "Tell me, how many people have you had working on this?"

"Three in New York, and two here, besides myself."

"All independents?"

"Yes, except for my contact at NSA."

"And how did you code the inquiry about Talpa?"

"Routine security. No alarms. I included him with a list of a half-dozen others."

"Good. And your other people? You trust them?"

"Oh, yes. Plus, I kept their work separated as you asked. None of them know what the others are doing."

"Very good. Very good indeed." Miss Berksmere sat back in thought. "I take it that we don't know how Nickles might have come upon this man Talpa, what the connection is."

"Not yet. I can find out, but how much time it'll take will depend on how much dust you want me to raise. If you need the information quickly, I'd suggest you let me go to Talpa directly. I'm certain he'd want to . . . well, shall we say, cooperate?"

Miss Berksmere considered a moment, then shook her head. "Perhaps, but I need to do some backtracking before we go ahead. We're treading on very sensitive ground here."

"What about Nickles? Maybe it's time to have a talk with him."

"No, not yet. We may need to make an approach soon, but not right now, not until we know a bit more about this fellow Talpa. We may be able to use him. Anyway, I have all I need for now." Miss Berksmere sat back and took a deep breath. "Yes, I think this is all I need. Now, about this woman in New York."

"Martina Wolecki?"

"Yes. What have you found?"

"Well, it seems as if she's just disappeared."

"What do you mean, 'disappeared'?"

"No one seems to know where she is. Like I told you before, when you first asked me to check her out, her contact said she was out of the city."

"And her contact is?"

"Henry Bergman."

"Ah, yes, the clothing manufacturer."

"Right."

"But you think she's missing?"

"Well, I don't want to jump the gun here, but you said to follow up, so I checked with Henry again yesterday and had my man in New York go by her apartment. Seems like no one's seen her since April."

Miss Berksmere's eyes narrowed and she slowly leaned forward over the edge of her desk. "April?"

"That's right. Latter part of April."

"And Mr. Bergman, he wasn't concerned?"

"Well, he's used to her being out of town for long periods. She travels a lot, only works on commission, as far as he's concerned.

He keeps her on the books for cover, but basically she comes and goes pretty much as she pleases. Plus, he's a blind cover. He doesn't ask questions. He just launders her pay for us."

"But since April? What about her paychecks? And her rent?"

"Her pay is electronically transferred to her checking account. I don't know about the rent, but maybe it's handled the same way."

"I see."

The man frowned slightly. "Do you want me to start a trace?"

Miss Berksmere did not move, did not gesture or say a word for what seemed minutes before she said, "No, I think it's better if I look into this internally. If this woman is on assignment, we wouldn't want anything drawing attention to her."

"Whatever you say."

Miss Berksmere reached for a pad of plain white paper and wrote a note to herself in small block letters. She then sat back and turned in her chair to peer out her window. Without looking back, she said, "As I recall, you are long overdue for a vacation. Is that right?"

The man hesitated. "Well, yes, I suppose."

"Do you have any pressing business that requires that you stay in town?"

"No, nothing pressing. How long a vacation did you have in mind?"

She swiveled back to face her informer. "As long as necessary. At least a month, probably more. Will that be a problem?"

"No, it shouldn't be. When would you like me to start?"

Miss Berksmere leaned down and opened the bottom drawer of her desk. She retrieved a thick manila envelope and handed it across the desk. "As I recall, you are well known to have a particular affection for the Italian Riviera. There's a flight leaving Dulles for Rome tomorrow morning at nine. I've booked a first-class ticket in your name. You've arranged for a prepaid rental car that you'll pick up at the airport and drive to Rapallo, where hotel reservations have already been made. You've been planning this trip for some time."

The man smiled. "Why do I get the feeling that I'm not going to enjoy the fruits of all this planning?"

Miss Berksmere smiled in return. "I need you underground. Do you mind?"

He shrugged. "My wife will. Are we having marital problems again?"

"I'm afraid so, but you can tell her that, once this business is over, the two of you will enjoy a first-class holiday for as long as you want to wherever you want, on the company."

"Very generous."

"Trust me, you'll have earned it. This is serious business we're about."

"I understand."

Miss Berksmere nodded. "All the information about your trip to Rapallo is there in the packet. Your wife can reach you through the switchboard there. In the meantime, I've taken the liberty of arranging a place for you nearby. I think you'll find the accommodations to your liking."

"I'm sure," the man said.

"Also, you'll find in the envelope a generous cash advance and two corporate credit cards. Use them for whatever you want. A little reward for going out of your way on this one."

The man took the envelope hesitantly, then nodded with a smile. "Again, very generous. Just how serious is this?"

Miss Berksmere paused, and her expression darkened a bit as she turned and looked out the window. "I really don't know," she said in a near whisper, "but until we prove differently, I think we must assume it's as serious as it gets."

The man sat still for a long moment, until he broke the silence by asking, "Do you want the same check-in schedule, or should I just wait to hear?"

"No, check in. Same schedule, same codes."

"All right. Anything else?"

"Just one thing more," Miss Berksmere said. "All your people have been pulled back, correct? There's no one still out there following Nickles or Talpa, is there? No one doing any more checks on Martina Wolecki?"

"No. They're waiting for instructions. I'll make sure they all understand the job is over. There won't be anyone out there tripping over you."

Miss Berksmere smiled. "Good. Now, as to this Wolecki woman, should the issue ever arise, you do routinely check on your contractors, isn't that right? Make sure the family's all safe and tucked in at night?"

The man nodded. "Yes, ma'am. Every few weeks or so."

"And that's how this situation came to your attention?"

"Yes, ma'am, just part of the routine."

"Yes, I thought so. Very good. I'd appreciate your discretion, should that ever come up."

"Understood. Just part of the routine."

"And our meeting today?"

"You had questions about the Miami group, right?"

"Yes."

"And I reported that nothing new had cropped up. Things have been quiet there for months now, correct?"

"Yes, that's right."

"Plus, I wanted to see you personally to ask for some time off."

"Yes, and you certainly deserve it. You've done excellent work."

"Thank you, Miss Berksmere," the man said, as he stood and stretched his back.

"No," said Miss Berksmere. "Thank you!"

ɾ

Saturday night. Late. A single large pewter lamp hung from the cedar-board ceiling of the Sequoia Club's front porch, and a single moth struggled to free itself from an ornate spiderweb stretching from the center chain that held the lamp's weight to one of the four looping chains that kept it centered and mostly motionless. Two cut-glass ovals in the double oak doors looked down on the street like jaundiced cat's eyes, and Miss Berksmere, more out of habit than concern, halted at the bottom of the steps to take one last look along the street before mounting the steps and approaching the front door, where she rang the bell.

A moment or two passed before an old man in butler's livery opened the door and inquired, "Miss Berksmere?"

"Yes," she answered.

The old man bowed, ever so slightly. "Yes, do come in. The gentleman is expecting you. If you'll follow me, please."

She followed the old man's slow, even pace through the foyer and past a small Victorian table where a large leather-bound guest book sat under the yellow light of a library lamp. They traveled down a long hallway covered by threadbare Oriental carpets, past an empty parlor to her right and an empty dining room to her left, past a wide staircase rising to the second-floor landing, where a single lamp glowed weakly against the dark mahogany wainscot, past two closed doors, each adorned with a small brass plaque— "Earlingham," said one; "Westlaake," said the other—to the far end, where a door opened to a library. The old man stopped and again bowed. "Would you care for anything, madame? A brandy, perhaps?"

"Thank you," she replied. "A sherry would be nice."

"Any particular sherry?"

"Whatever you have that's not too sweet."

"Yes, ma'am. A nice dry sherry. I'm sure I have one that will please you." He smiled and with one hand motioned for her to enter the library.

She stepped in front of the old man and entered the room, then hesitated to allow him to catch up and lead her to one corner, where the chairman of the Joint Operations Committee sat in one of the two high-backed leather chairs set on either side of a low round table. A cup of coffee and a large snifter with several fingers of dark brandy sat on the table. The chairman smiled and motioned for Miss Berksmere to have a seat. "Do forgive me for not standing," the chairman pleaded, "but I'm afraid my arthritis has been kicking up again."

Before Miss Berksmere could offer her sympathy, the butler said, "I'll be bringing our guest a sherry, sir. Is there anything else you'd like?"

"Thank you, Robert. But that will be all. I'll ring if we need you."

"Very good," said Robert, retiring.

The chairman strained to sit a bit taller in his chair, the effort seeming to have little effect but to stretch his narrow shoulders and chest from the static bulk of his midsection. The substantial wattle beneath his chin shook ever so slightly as he spoke. "Thank you for coming, Miss Berksmere. You have been here before, haven't you?"

"Yes, sir, several times, as your guest."

"Yes, of course. I know it's a dull old place with all the ambiance of a funeral parlor, but I do enjoy it here. One of the last havens of calm in a world that seems to define culture as anything that makes a great deal of noise or a great deal of money."

Miss Berksmere smiled. "You're living here now?"

"Yes, when I'm in town. Ever since my wife died. Oh, I still keep the place in St. Marys, but whenever I'm there, it seems, my daughter and her family all think I can't get along without them. I know they mean well, but sometimes it's a bit too much of a good thing, if you know what I mean."

"Yes, I do. I find it rather odd myself that so many people cannot imagine how one might prefer being left alone."

"Indeed. I've often wondered, Miss Berksmere, is it really the work that isolates us, or are we drawn to the work because we prefer isolation?"

"I don't know, and, to be quite honest, I avoid asking myself such questions. I find I have enough to worry about just doing the job without concerning myself with why I do it."

"Yes, I see your point. . . . And are we worried tonight?"

"Yes, sir, I think we are."

Both sets of eyes shifted to the front of the room, where Robert entered carrying a tray with a small decanter of sherry and a single glass. He set the tray down on the table between them, then poured a sip of the sherry into the glass. Miss Berksmere took the required taste and nodded. "Yes, very good," she said, and Robert poured a full measure before setting the decanter down.

"Thank you," the chairman said, and with a nod, Robert turned and left the room, closing the door behind him.

The chairman leaned forward with a soft groan and poured a bit of brandy into his coffee, then held up his cup as if to toast. Miss Berksmere returned the gesture with her sherry. "So," the chairman said, "how worried are we?"

"I'll leave that to you," she said. "I've confirmed that our friend Mr. Nickles has had two meetings with a level-seven code-and-computer technician at NSA."

"Level-seven?" he asked with obvious surprise.

"That's right. He's one of only a half-dozen or so who have ever done work for the directorate."

"My, my. I take it these meetings were not purely social."

"It would appear not."

"I see. And is there any evidence of a breach? Any files accessed?"

"I'm having a check run now. It may be fruitless, however. If anyone could access without leaving a footprint, it would be someone out of level seven."

"Yes, I see. Well, the obvious question is, how might a local police detective, and retired, manage to make contact with and possibly compromise one of our top security technicians?"

"My question exactly."

"Well, this is an interesting development, isn't it? This, on top of that business in New York and his running down one of Birshstein's thugs, tells us what?"

"That either we have seriously underestimated the range of investigative skills one might find in a local homicide detective, or . . ." Miss Berksmere stopped.

"Or?"

Miss Berksmere took another sip of sherry, staring at the chairman over the rim of her glass.

The chairman raised his eyebrows. "You suspect our Mr. Nickles might be a false flag?"

"I have considered the possibility."

"And who, in your opinion, might be running him?"

"I don't know."

"But you suspect?"

"Before we get into what we suspect, let's talk about what we know."

"There's something else?"

"Yes. I've just learned today that one of our contractors has gone missing."

"Oh?"

"Yes. Her name is Wolecki. Martina Wolecki. An independent working under a nonofficial cover out of New York?"

"When you say 'ours,' you mean . . ."

"The directorate."

"I see. And you think there's a connection?"

"Yes, I do."

"Her background?"

"A Polish émigrée. She came over here with her parents when

she was just a child. Joined the army out of high school and was sent to DLI," Miss Berksmere said, referring to the Defense Language Institute in Monterey, California, where her own career in intelligence had begun. "She spent five years with Army Intelligence in Berlin before she was recruited by your people for counterintelligence."

"She was a spider?"

"Yes, black widow."

The chairman, about to take another sip of his coffee, stopped at the reference to the small cadre of specially trained assassins. "I see," he said. "But she turned independent?"

"In '89. Our files show she had to be pulled out of Germany after our friends in Stasi uncovered Peter Rabbit and dumped his body on our doorstep in Amburg. Remember?"

"Yes, certainly. How could I forget? A messy business, that."

"Anyway, Operations decided she had been soiled, so she was given a handsome retirement and cut loose. That's when we picked her up as a contractor."

"For?"

"Whatever necessary, but mostly surveillance."

"Wolecki, Martina Wolecki. Worked out of Berlin, you say?"

"Yes."

"Hmm, I don't recall the name. It seems as if I should, but I don't. Well, no matter. And now she's gone missing?"

"Yes. Her cover in New York hasn't seen or heard from her since April. She hasn't been seen at her apartment either, not since April."

"April?"

"Yes, the latter part of April."

"April?" the chairman repeated. "Was she on assignment?"

"Not according to our files."

"And the connection?"

Miss Berksmere reached into her oversized purse and retrieved a plain white envelope. From the envelope she took two sheets of paper, each a photocopy of a personnel cover sheet containing the employee's photograph and other relevant information. She handed the papers to the chairman.

For a full minute the chairman studed the documents, his eyes switching back and forth as he compared the two line by line. He

returned the papers to Miss Berksmere, added the remains of his
brandy to his coffee cup, and took a long swallow. He then sat
back, closing his eyes for a moment and joining the fingers of both
hands on the shelf of his belly. "My, my, my. The similarities are
quite remarkable."

"Yes, sir."

"And in an advanced state of decomposition, and with no fingerprint or dental records, one might easily mistake one for the
other."

"Yes, sir."

"And who was Miss Wolecki's control officer?"

"One of my people. We hadn't called on her for some time. He
was running a periodic bed check but couldn't make contact.
He brought it to my attention, and I asked him to check again.
That's when he determined that no one has seen or heard from her
since April."

"And?"

"Sir?"

"Come, come, Miss Berksmere, surely there is more to this little
puzzle, something that causes you to connect the missing Miss
Wolecki with this Grehm business."

Miss Berksmere cocked her head and narrowed her eyes, as if
the question required a carefully considered answer. "Well . . . I
don't want to overstate the case."

"Miss Berksmere. I appreciate your caution, but I need to hear
your thoughts. Allow me to draw my own conclusions."

"Yes, sir. Well, our operations files show that this woman was
only used for three assignments over the past two years, and her
assignment bonuses were paid in the regular manner. However, I
have found two other occasions, once in October '91 and this past
April, on the twentieth, when noncoded draws were forwarded to
the woman's cover in New York."

"What do you mean, noncoded draws?"

"Monies drawn on funds not coded for any specific operation.
Slush funds, if you will."

"And the authorization?"

"Not recorded."

"I see. And who within the directorate might be able to issue
such noncoded payments? A greedy clerk, perhaps?"

"No, sir. The clerks have limited access codes only."

"Who, then?"

"Well, I could certainly do it, and I have on occasion. For example, on special request from someone like yourself, or one of the other members of the Joint Committee."

"But the authorization still comes from inside, correct?"

"Yes, sir."

"I see." The chairman took a slow, deep breath. "October '91? That was just about the time that we got that rather embarrassing bit of news about Treshkov and the North Koreans, wasn't it?"

Miss Berksmere's eyes lowered, and she did not answer.

"Yes, of course. Caused quite a flap, what with Treshkov selling off that uranium and using Iberia to wash his profits right under our noses. Quite a flap, indeed." The chairman began massaging his temples with the tips of his fingers. "And what about Philo Machus?"

"Sir?"

"I assume that, besides yourself, Philo Machus would have the ability to issue noncoded payments."

"Yes, sir."

The chairman dropped his hands and sat forward. "April, you say?"

"Sir?"

"The last noncoded payment you discovered?"

"Yes, sir, on the twentieth."

"What, about a week or so before this Grehm business blew up in our face?"

"Yes, sir."

"I see. And it was Arlis Brecht who identified the bodies of both Trevor Grehm and his wife, ah . . . ?"

"Helen; yes, sir."

"And whose idea was that? Having Brecht go down to identify the bodies?"

"Philo . . ." Miss Berksmere stopped herself. "The chief's, sir."

"And we never called for the morgue prints for comparison?"

"No, sir. The thought was to keep as low a profile as possible. And we did have Arlis Brecht's identification."

"Yes, we did, didn't we. And there was no discussion about double-checking?"

Miss Berksmere did not answer.

"I see. My, my, my," the chairman said, laying his head back and closing his eyes. "It's quite remarkable. The similarities, I mean, between this Helen Grehm and Miss Wolecki. Close in age, their height, weight, hair color. Quite remarkable, indeed." He took a moment before leaning forward and looking at her with an almost sleepy stare. "Tell me, Miss Berksmere, why have you brought this to me?"

She met his gaze over another sip of sherry, then said, "Well, it seems to me that I have either stumbled upon what might be a serious internal problem, or I have stumbled upon an operation which I have no business knowing about. If it's the latter, I imagine that you will tell me to cease my little inquiry and go about my business as if none of this had ever come up."

"And if it's the former?"

"Then you should be aware of it."

"Yes, quite. And which are we dealing with here, Miss Berksmere, the former or the latter?"

"I don't know, but unless I'm told differently, I think we must assume it is the former."

"Yes, I quite agree." The chairman sat back with a sigh and again closed his eyes for a moment. "Now," he said finally, "tell me something else. Just how much do we really know about this Detective Nickles, who keeps popping up in the most unlikely places and under the most unlikely circumstances?"

"In my opinion, sir, we don't know nearly enough."

"Yes, I would agree. That's certainly a situation that needs correcting, doesn't it?"

"Yes, sir."

"Perhaps we have been just a bit too passive in this matter. Do you agree?"

"Yes, sir, I do."

"Yes, Miss Berksmere, I think it is time we assert some control, starting with this Mr. Nickles."

"Yes, sir."

"And let me assure you that I understand what a difficult position you are in. But I am equally certain that we share the same concerns. Am I right? The mission comes first?"

"Yes, sir."

"And you would agree that, if we have a virus among us, it must be stamped out."

"Yes, sir."

"And quickly."

"Yes, sir."

The chairman sat forward and took a last, long swallow of his brandied coffee. "Well, dear lady, it would appear that you have your work cut out for you."

She nodded. "I have your authority, then?"

"Yes, my full authority, and whatever backup support I can provide."

"By any means available?"

"Yes, Miss Berksmere, by any means available."

*

On the western edge of Georgetown, on a high bluff overlooking the C & O Canal and the Potomac River, in a loft atop a narrow, clapboard-sided townhouse, Philo Machus sat perfectly still, the index finger of his right hand still on the button which had just disconnected the telephone line over which his longtime informant, an old butler named Robert, had just completed his latest betrayal, for which he would receive his usual reward. "Thanks," Machus mumbled a few seconds after the line had gone dead.

He removed the telephone headset and sat back and closed his eyes. The room was dark except for the light of two gooseneck lamps at either end of a long workbench crowded with computers, keyboards, telephones and their scramblers and decoders, and a bank of radio equipment. A single window at one end of the room had long since been boarded up with the same sound-insulating material that composed the single, solid door, which had no handle but only a case-hardened dead bolt. A row of steel safe file cabinets lined one wall, and between the safes and workbench an old couch sat piled with books and papers and The Cat, which napped among them. It was here that Philo Machus did his best work.

A hint of music hung in the air as he considered Robert's revelations, and his neck and shoulders squirmed to take full advantage of the soft leather cushioning of his high-backed chair. He was not surprised by the information. Concerned? Yes. Disappointed? Perhaps, but not terribly so. Loyalty was the one thing he truly appreciated but never expected. Not in this business. No, in this business, in this world, betrayal was not so much a cause for surprise or alarm as it was a signal to go to Plan B.

Fact: Miss Wendy Berksmere, without his prior knowledge or approval, had met with the chairman of the Joint Operations Committee, which meeting in and of itself violated the established protocols of both the directorate and the committee.

Fact: the meeting had followed directly on the heels of a bed check run on Martina Wolecki, a bed check run by a unilateral hired by and reporting directly and only to Miss Wendy Berksmere.

Conclusion: it was not coincidence; a connection had been made.

Questions remained, however.

First, what had put Miss Berksmere on the scent of Martina Wolecki in the first place, and, perhaps more important, why would she have been so sloppy in carrying out the bed check? After all, Martina Wolecki had been his own hand-picked agent, and her unofficial cover had been established by him personally. Surely Miss Berksmere knew, or should have known, that any bed check on such an agent through such a cover would certainly be brought to his attention. Sloppy, or was it by design?

Second, the meeting with the chairman. Why had it not been disguised by any one of a dozen or more reasons which could have easily been put forth to explain their need to meet alone? More to the point, why not conceal the meeting entirely? Why invite attention by an almost too obvious meeting late on a Saturday night, and at the Sequoia Club? Did they want to draw attention to themselves, and if so, why? Ineptitude? No. They each suffered their weaknesses, but such an obvious lapse was inconsistent with their methods and experience. He had to assume that they had purposely let their slip show. The question was why. Were they following a live trail, or had they only caught a whiff of something untoward? Were they looking for a response to confirm or to identify? Either way, his course was clear.

First, Helen Grehm moved to the top of the list. Priority one: she had to be taken—alive, if possible, but otherwise at all costs and in any condition. All stops had to be removed. Time was of the essence.

Second, this fellow Nickles. A bit trickier, perhaps, given the noise level his disposal might create. He had to be located, contacted, and assessed before his final disposition could be decided.

Third, all other business was assigned a nonpriority status.

Philo Machus rubbed his temples with the tips of his fingers and worked his jaw in hopes of loosening the already tense and tightening muscles to stave off the piercing headache which threatened to creep from the base of his skull to the backs of his eyes. It was not as if he hadn't considered such a turn possible and planned accordingly. It was just that he had hoped that the passage of time and the lack of any new or apparent crisis would have lowered the level of interest, would have sufficiently closed the wound so that he could have avoided the unpleasantries that now seemed inevitable. But in this business, unpleasantries were intrinsic, and it was a foolish man who did not anticipate them.

He reached for a remote control that both switched selections on his compact disc and turn up the volume, and he took a deep and relaxing breath as the room was filled with the sounds of Highland harps and Scottish voices singing their lament for the harvest of death on Culloden Moor. Ah, yes, he thought, a proper battle among proper warriors. He could almost picture himself there, a bone-weary and poorly supplied Jacobite standing in that raw April rain watching the Duke of Cumberland and his well-armed Hanoverians steadily advancing with their superior numbers and heavy cannon. And stand there he would, had it been two centuries before, side by side with men of equal purpose and resolve who knew their cause and looked their enemy in the eye, men who knew the taste of blood and the sound of bones breaking and the tensile strength of human flesh under sword or knife.

But, alas, his wars were of a different sort, and if he had tasted the blood and heard the bone and felt the flesh, the cause had never been particularly clear, or the resolve any more steady than the latest polls of the president's popularity. His were the wars fought with sniper scopes and piano wire, with hired whores both sexual and political, with funneled funds and fulsome praise and fulminating mercury; the secret wars seeking subtle victories over subversive forces whose identities varied with the phases of the moon, wars wherein there were no battle lines, where former

friends were sudden enemies who would be friends again when the check cleared and the election was won.

In the end, Machus understood, the only purpose was the game itself, the object of the game was survival, and survival meant winning, and winning meant at all costs and by whatever means available. Therein lay his advantage.

Unlike others who pretended at the game—unlike Miss Wendy Berksmere, who read the books that others wrote and studied the maps that others drew, who memorized the codes and mimicked the language and practiced the politics—he knew firsthand what it meant to win when the only alternative was to die. He knew the sound of the last chopper disappearing over the horizon and leaving him alone more than a hundred kilometers from the nearest friendly. He knew the taste of staying alive by sucking condensation off the stone walls of a basement in Prague, and the sight of a friend left to rot on an electric fence along the Czech border. He knew how it felt to promise the only woman he had ever loved that he would be back, knowing full well that she knew full well that it wasn't true.

But not Miss Wendy Berksmere. To her and her kind, there was no such thing as an absolute. Survival was an abstraction, a plastic concept defined as getting by in a world of endless alternatives. Miss Berksmere played by the Washington Rules, which held that there was no principle so sacred that it could not be sacrificed to advantage, and that, when it came to the competition, it was not nearly so important to win as it was to make certain that the other fellow lost. Losers' rules, Machus thought. The game then on the board was his game, and he would play it by his rules. Object: to win at all costs. Method: by whatever means available.

The Cat suddenly awoke and stretched out of its nap to begin clawing rhythmically at the already tattered material covering the arm of the couch. Machus looked over with a hard stare and The Cat stopped and hunkered down with a soft hiss of protest. Machus then turned back and learned forward, picking up the telephone headset and carefully adjusting its earphone and mike. He dialed the first of his many preplanned calls and, while he waited for an answer, simultaneously booted up two separate but interlinked computers, and then a third computer attached to a special modem coded to a line that the level-seven technician from NSA guaranteed was impenetrable. He then reached for a notebook thick with names and codes and contact points, and he smiled.

The threatened headache was fading. It was good to be back in the game.

19.

In the main square of Altdorf, in front of the town hall and tower dating from the Middle Ages, stood a statue of the legendary archer William Tell. Helen Grehm stopped for a moment and stared at the statue, wondering not so much about the archer as about what must his son have been thinking, standing there with the apple on his head, watching his father play out the game ordered by some petty Austrian bureaucrat. "Stay cool," she muttered to herself, "and you might just dodge the arrow and get to keep the apple."

It took her only a minute or two to make her way across the square and down a narrow cobbled street to the small bank she had visited a dozen times or more over the years. Inside the bank, she went directly to the rear of the open lobby, and smiled at the plump and graying woman who sat at a desk just outside the manager's office. "Frau Niedermeyer," she said. "How nice to see you again."

The woman looked up, apparently confused for an instant, then she sat back with a wide smile and raised her hands and her voice in recognition. "Ah, *ja*, goot morning. Frau Gerbling, *ja?*" the woman said referring to the alias Helen Grehm had long used when conducting business at this particular bank. "How long we have not seen you. Herr Kessler knows you are coming?"

"No, I'm afraid I didn't have time to make an appointment. Do you think he might have a few minutes?"

If there was anything about which Helen Grehm was certain, it was that the banker with one bad eye would make time for her. Otto Kessler had always been a perfect gentleman, never a word or gesture out of place, never a suggestion that was not entirely professional, even if at times his solicitousness did carry with it the obvious and hesitant shyness of a schoolboy's crush. She had once thought it cute and shamelessly played the coquette to amuse herself—and to amuse him, she was sure. But then it was easy to play that game. Nothing serious was at stake then, at least nothing of which she had been aware. It was all different now. It was not a game anymore.

"Frau Gerbling" was announced, and almost immediately Herr Kessler emerged from his office to bow slightly and shake Helen's hand before leading her into his office and shutting the door. "How good to see you again," the banker with one bad eye said, as he quickly shuffled papers to the sides of his desk to clear a space. He folded his hands and asked what if anything he might do for her. Helen stated her business, which took several minutes, while Herr Kessler sat still, nodding occasionally but ever more slowly as the full nature of her request became clear. "Yes, I see," he said finally. "Do you have the account list and codes?"

"Yes, I have them written out," she said and pulled from a thin, soft leather attaché case several sheets of paper containing the information required.

Herr Kessler took a moment to look over the listings and then said, "Excuse me, please." He went to the corner of his office, where he opened the cabinet door she had watched him open so many times before, and he began twirling the dials of the combination safe inside. From the safe he retrieved a dark-blue file folder, then returned to his desk. He sat down and looked at Helen with a weak smile that appeared now more concerned than shy.

"Please forgive the formality," said Herr Kessler, "but you understand. Could I have your pass code as well?"

Helen nodded. "Yes, of course. The monkey's fist."

Herr Kessler looked to his account folder and nodded in return. "Yes, thank you. Well, it will take a little time to arrange the transfers and prepare the bonds. Perhaps you would like to do a little shopping or see the town? It is such a beautiful day for a walk."

"No thank you—"

"Or take the time for something to eat, and I will call you when they are ready. You are staying at the Schwarzer Ritter, as before?"

"Thank you, Herr Kessler, but I'll wait. I'm afraid I'm on a rather tight schedule today, and you know how my people like for us to abide by established procedures."

Herr Kessler smiled, again barely. "Yes, of course. Could I offer you some coffee at least? Some tea?"

It took more than forty minutes, with Helen Grehm sitting quietly on the other side of his desk, for Herr Kessler to arrange the wire transfers from Geneva, calculate the exchange and discount rates, prepare, log in, and then sign over to her bearer bonds valued at just over $3 million U.S. He then personally went back into the main vault to collect in cash, which he counted out and handed to Helen, forty-two thousand Swiss francs, approximately thirty thousand U.S. dollars.

Their business concluded, Herr Kessler stood and bowed and offered his hand, which Helen Grehm took with just the tips of her fingers.

"Perhaps, the next time you're in Altdorf, you'll do me the honor of having lunch," Herr Kessler said, indulging the fiction that she might one day return, though that it was a fiction was no doubt as clear to him as it was to her.

"Why, thank you, Herr Kessler," Helen said with a smile. "I look forward to it."

"Until next time, then." He bowed again, not quite so deeply, his one good eye fixing upon her a deposit of sympathy against which this pleasant and most attractive woman might draw in the future, while his other eye twitched and wandered, trying to keep her in focus. "Do take care, madam," he said.

She hesitated for just a moment, then smiled. "Thank you, Herr Kessler—"

"Please, call me Otto."

"Otto, then. Thank you, I will do just that." She smiled a smile that made him blush suddenly, and there was a brief and awkward silence before she felt the color rise in her own cheeks, and she turned quickly and left.

Herr Kessler returned to his desk and sat down. He started to reach for the phone, then stopped himself and sat back to consider his options. He let forty-five minutes of busywork engage him before he again reached for the phone and dialed.

"Herr Brecht? Otto Kessler here . . .

"Yes, you asked me to call. . . .

"Yes, she was just here. She left not two minutes ago. . . .

"No, she didn't say. . . .

"Yes, I have it all right here," and he repeated the amount of the transfer, the name of the bank in Geneva and the account numbers from which the transfers had been made. He repeated, too, the amounts of the bearer bonds and cash handed over to the woman who over the years had conducted dozens of similar transactions on behalf of Arlis Brecht, the Iberia Trading Company, and its many subsidiaries.

"I understand that, Herr Brecht, but I had no choice. . . .

"Yes, I understand, but remember, too, your instructions were very clear on this point. . . .

"No, no, I could not. She was right here with me the whole time, as always, precisely according to the procedures you yourself had established. There was no other choice but to complete the transaction. . . .

"Yes, of course I will, but understand these are bearer bonds. Like cash, not easily traced, as you well know . . .

"Yes, if I hear, but I strongly suspect that will not be the case. You understand. . . .

"No, that is all . . . except one other thing. I think it is time that we sever our relationship. I do hope you understand. . . .

"No, not at all. However, I think for the foreseeable future our business interests are not compatible. . . .

"No, no. Quite the contrary. I rather like the young lady. It has always been a pleasure dealing with her, but, frankly, this whole business, the fact that I even have to make this phone call, it makes me quite uncomfortable. I have the bank to think of, you understand. . . .

"Most certainly. Such a course would be in neither of our interests. . . .

"Well, yes, perhaps, if you're ever in Altdorf . . .

"Yes, we understand one another. . . .

"Well, then, Herr Brecht, *auf Wiedersehen.*"

20.

It was Eddie Nickles's turn to be nervous, and he was; and his discomfort was only heightened by Hans Talpa's apparent calm, as if Hans was enjoying the serenity of one already passed to his grave.

"Fear's only useful when you're on the run," Hans said, "when you're hiding. Like yourself, for example."

"Who says I'm hiding?"

"Well, denial's one approach, of course, but my point is, once you're caught, once you're standing in front of the firing squad, why not relax and just let it happen?"

Hans Talpa had first contacted Jimmy Legget at home and brushed aside Jimmy's insistence that he had no knowledge of Eddie's whereabouts or how to reach him. "Do your best, Detective," Hans said. "This is not a matter that can be put off or ignored. Trust me when I tell you that it is in your friend's best interest that we meet as soon as possible, alone and not in a public place. We can meet at his house, if he wants. I doubt at this point anyone expects to find him there, but wherever he wants, I don't care. However you do it, let him know how important it is that we meet tonight. Tell him, too, that we know he's not so far away as to make this an unreasonable request." Hans's words were far more insistent than his tone, which made even Jimmy Legget nervous.

Eddie was not about to allow any meeting at his house, the memory of Garland Bolles's call and its consequences being all too fresh in his mind. If they were to meet at all, Eddie insisted through Jimmy Legget, it would be in a public place. Hans relented, and Eddie suggested a pool hall only a mile or two from his house, but still more than an hour's drive from the small cottage near St. Michaels, the waterfront town on Maryland's Eastern Shore where Eddie had been staying.

"Man, I'm sorry I ever got you in the middle of all this," he told Jimmy over the phone.

"Me, too, to tell you the truth, but the hand's dealt, so let's just play it."

"Yeah, well, so, anyway, I'm thinking maybe it's time for you to just back away. You know what I'm sayin'?"

"It's a nice gesture, but not a smart one."

"Yeah, but—"

"Look," Jimmy interrupted. "You can't walk in without some kind of backup. This is no time to turn stupid. Now, tell me again, where's this pool hall you're talking about?"

"Scardina's. It's out on General's Highway, just past the golf course. It'll be on your left coming out of Annapolis."

"Okay, I'll find it."

There was a brief silence before Eddie said, "I gotta tell ya, Jimmy, this business is making me jumpy as hell. You know, it's beginning to feel like everything's getting out of hand. It's definitely not what I had in mind for my retirement."

"Whatever. Listen, the meet's set for ten, right?"

"Yeah."

"All right, get there a few minutes after ten. I'll be there ahead of you, around nine-thirty or so. It'll give me a chance to look things over. All right?"

"Okay."

"There's a bar, right?"

"Yeah, and maybe a dozen tables in the back."

"Okay. Now, assuming I don't have any hassle from the

rednecks, I'll be at the bar. I'll try to get a seat nearest the tables. Pick a spot where you and I can keep an eye on one another. You do your thing with Hans, and we'll talk afterward."

"Okay. Thanks. And tell Kitty I'm sorry, you know, for calling you out like this."

"Relax, man. Kitty's okay with this."

"Does she even know?"

"She's used to the job."

"Look, really, maybe it's better I do this alone."

"Will you relax, for Christ's sake? Nothing's gonna happen. I'll be there."

"Yeah, okay."

"I'll see you at ten. Not before, understand?"

Eddie understood, but he couldn't shake his nerves. He paced the floor for several minutes, then called Priscilla, who was still with her mother and her mother's new husband at the farm in Bucks County. Once, several weeks after the firefight in Eddie's kitchen, Megs had accompanied Priscilla back to Annapolis, where she was interviewed by Anne Arundel County detectives, who were ultimately convinced that she knew nothing that would be of any assistance to their or anyone else's investigation. That opinion was passed along the line, and no one had tried to contact her since. However, with matters still unsettled, Eddie suggested to Megs that Priscilla delay her start for a semester and remain at the farm. Megs agreed and made the appropriate arrangements with the university. This decision both angered and frightened Priscilla, her parents' repeated insistence that everything was fine being so transparent a lie.

"You all right?" Priscilla asked. "You sound kinda funny."

"No, I'm fine. Feeling a lot better. How 'bout you? Everything going okay?"

"Yeah, I guess. But I'm bored as hell. It's getting so bad I'm talking to the stupid ducks."

Eddie laughed.

"Really, Daddy, I'm going nuts up here. Can't I come home? You keep saying everything's okay. Right?"

"Well, I still got some traveling to do, you know, with this job."

"Daddy, I can take care of myself. God, I'm eighteen years old."

"That old, are ya?" A long silence followed. "Okay, look, I'm sorry. I know you can take care of yourself, but, still . . ."

"Still what?"

"Just give me a little more time. Let me finish this job. It won't be much longer. Okay? It'll make me feel better."

"Why do you keep lying to me? Do you really think I'm that stupid? Nothing's even close to being okay, is it?"

Eddie squeezed his eyes shut and hesitated. "No, baby, everything's fine. I'd just feel better if I didn't have to travel while you were here. I'm just a little gun-shy, okay?"

"An interesting choice of words."

"I didn't mean it that way."

"How did you mean it?"

"Listen, I'm still your father."

"Oh, really?" She stopped, and Eddie listened to the both of them hold their breath a moment. "I'm sorry," she whispered.

"No, no, that's all right. It's my fault. I know this has really screwed up everything, your summer, school, everything."

"Daddy?"

"Yeah?"

"Are the police still looking for you?"

"Pris, please."

"Why don't you just let me come home? Why don't we both sit down and talk to the police? I mean, those men came after you. I don't understand—"

"Please, baby. It's not the police. That's all been settled. No one's looking for me, really. The police understand what happened."

"Then why—"

"Because!" Eddie interrupted, almost angrily.

Another silence followed.

"Look," Eddie said, "I don't mean to bark at you, it's just that you don't understand."

"Then explain it to me."

"The fact is . . . Okay, there are a bunch of loose ends, that's all. I'm fine, you don't have to worry. I'm trying to help the police wrap up their work, okay? I'm just doing what I always did when I was on the force, okay? That's all it is. But I have to travel around, and I don't like the idea of your being alone at the house. That's all."

"Why don't I believe you?"

" 'Cause you're stubborn."

"Maybe, but I'm not stupid."

"I know. Just give me a little more time. Okay?"

Another silence.

"Okay?" Eddie again asked.

"Yeah, all right."

"Okay, well, we'll talk soon, and say hello to your mother."

"Daddy?"

"Yeah?"

"You sure everything's all right?"

"Absolutely," Eddie said. "Look, as soon as I finish this job, maybe we'll take a trip somewhere. A real vacation before you start college in January. Wherever you want. Just you 'n' me. Okay?"

"I don't want to take a trip. I just want to come home."

"Soon, Pris. Real soon."

It was now a few minutes past ten, and Jimmy Legget was nursing a beer at one corner of the bar, facing the rear of the pool hall, where Eddie sat with his back to the wall. Hans Talpa sat opposite him, leaning low over the table, passing on his message.

"Look, all I can say is that they know about us, about our meeting. They know I passed information to you about the directorate and the Grehms and that you're listed with a watch code. We don't need to know any more than that, you and I."

"Who are these people?"

"What do you want me to tell you? Some James Bond, maybe? Well, this is not James Bond. They're very ordinary people of very ordinary intelligence and very ordinary talents. That's what makes them so dangerous."

"What do you mean?"

"Look, you take a very ordinary person of very ordinary intelligence and give him extraordinary power and what do you get?"

Eddie nodded. "A very dangerous person."

"Exactly. Now, imagine this very dangerous person with extraordinary power being in a position where he is accountable only to himself?"

"I see your point."

"I hope so, Detective. I truly hope you understand our position here. These people are not to be taken lightly, particularly not when they feel threatened."

"Who's threatening them?"

"You, for one."

"Me?"

"Of course you. Your mucking around in their business threatens them with the one thing they can't afford."

"Whaddaya talking about?"

"Exposure. They cannot operate in the light. Exposure means loss of power. To them you're a loose cannon, a spark, if you will, creeping too close to the powder and threatening to send all that power up in smoke. Such thoughts can make otherwise reasonable men most unreasonable and extraordinarily dangerous."

"Exactly what is it I'm threatening to expose?"

"One can only imagine. I certainly have no idea, nor do I care to know. No, I care only to do what I'm told and ask no questions. It's quite a relief, actually. No more secrets of my own. No more anguishing over whether they know, whether they don't know. No more messy questions about right and wrong and duty and honor. Yes, sir, it's quite a relief, I must say."

"Really?"

"Oh, absolutely! Beyond running this little errand for them, it's over for me. Maybe they'll let me live, and maybe they won't. At best I'll be detailed to a forgotten little laboratory out in the midlands somewhere. Or maybe I'll just be retired. Perhaps I'll open up a little TV-repair shop, or maybe I'll work with home computers or develop little games that'll make Nintendo green with envy. Yes, I can see it all. I'll find a little cottage at the edge of a little town, and all the neighbors will talk among themselves." Hans smiled, almost wistfully. " 'A strange little man,' they'll whisper. 'Keeps to himself, mostly. Just him and his cat in that little house. But he does keep his lawn well groomed. Yes, indeed, an odd little man, but he seems friendly enough.' " Hans chuckled. "Yes, Detective, I'll wait my turn doing regular work in regular hours. No more of the night-soil circuit. I'll simply wait for someone else to decide whether I'll die of old age and on a government pension, or whether national security will require a more expedient end. Suicide, perhaps. 'How sad,' the neighbors will say. 'Do you suppose he had some illness? He never said a word. Has anyone seen his cat?' "

Eddie sat motionless for a long moment, his stare fixed on Hans Talpa. He leaned forward, finally, and said, "Man, there's gotta be other choices."

"Oh, really?"

"Yeah, really. I mean, if exposure is what they fear . . ."

Hans shook his head. "Ah, Detective. You and I, we're talking on entirely different planes. You're thinking perhaps of the press, the news media?"

"Well?"

Hans smiled sympathetically. "No, Detective, that alternative only works among Hollywood scriptwriters. Get a firm grip on reality here. This is the real world. It's not the press or the public they fear. The legends have already been prepared, the covers are in place, I assure you. By the time you finish telling some eager young reporter your fractured tale of unprovable conspiracies among unnamed conspirators in nonexistent agencies, the whole world will be suggesting that you line your cap with tinfoil to deflect the signals from UFOs."

Eddie cracked a smile. "I see. Who, then? Who's afraid of being exposed to who?"

"Whom, who's afraid of being exposed to whom?"

"Whatever. Who's afraid of *whom?*"

"It's simple, really. You see, there are sides here, but neither you nor I will ever know who is on whose side, or even how many sides there really are. But the point is, if one side is exposed to another, somebody loses. But, whoever they are and however many they are, I suspect that you represent a threat. Understand?"

"No."

"Look, somehow you've managed to land in the middle of the game. That's what it's all about. War games, if you will. The need to top the other side, the ultimate exercise in ego, all in the name of national security. Black ops and blinds and double-blinds and false flags and backfires, real and simulated. It's all quite fascinating, actually, unless of course you somehow become a personal threat."

"But to who . . . or whom?"

"Why do you keep asking the unanswerable? Who knows?

Side one may be afraid that your meddling will expose them to side number two, or side two may be afraid that you will expose side number one to side number four, which may threaten their relations to side number three. Understand?"

Eddie shook his head. "I don't know."

"Try harder. For your own sake, try to comprehend the simple face that you will never understand it all. It's not a game based on logic. Nobody ever truly understands it. They just do it."

"So why am I sitting here with you?"

"Only you can answer that. I'm just passing on the message."

Eddie slumped back in his chair, as Hans Talpa shrugged and said, "Now, if we can get on with the business at hand?"

Eddie sat up. "Okay, shoot."

Hans smiled. "I do wish you had chosen a different expression, but, in any event, here it is. My assignment, which I have chosen to accept, is to pass this envelope on to you." Hans took a manila envelope he had been holding, its sides marked with the prints of his perspiration, and pushed it across the table. "There are two file sets of fingerprints in there. One belongs to Helen Grehm. It's marked with the letters 'ML.' "

"What's 'ML' mean?"

"I don't know. Does it really matter?"

"All right, all right, go on."

"As I said, the fingerprint cards marked 'ML' contain the known fingerprints of Helen Grehm. The second, unmarked set of finger-prints belong to someone else."

"Who?"

Hans squeezed his eyes shut for an instant. "Please, Detective, just listen. I can only tell you what I know, and for our purposes here, I only know what I have been told I know, which is really all I know, if you know what I mean."

"Look, man, I'm just trying to get a grip on things here. This is all beginning to sound just a little nuts, you know?"

"Oh, yes, indeed, I know." Hans chuckled again. "Perhaps we should both order a sheet of tinfoil for our caps. All those rays beaming down from the cosmos, hey?"

"Just get to the point."

"I'm trying to, if you'll just listen. Now, where was I?"

"The first set of prints . . ."

"Yes, yes, of course. The first set of prints, as I said, belong to Helen Grehm. The second set of prints belong to someone unknown. At least to me. Of course, since it's quite obvious that this second set of prints came out of some file somewhere, you and I must assume that the people who sent me know to whom the prints belong. But that's of no significance to me. I assume that it will be of some significance to you—otherwise, what would be the point of this exercise? Correct?"

"Go on."

"The message I am to pass on with these fingerprint exemplars was very explicit. I am told to tell you that you should check both sets of prints against the morgue prints taken off Helen Grehm. But!" Hans emphasized, then stopped.

"But what?"

"But! They suggest in the strongest possible terms that you go through private sources to compare the prints. It is assumed, of course, given your background and apparent contacts, that you will know how to do that."

"Why the hell don't they check it out themselves?"

"Because, Detective, it should be quite obvious that they are trying to pass the information on to you, for what reasons I don't know, and I am not about to ask. But I would suggest that you do what they ask. It would seem, at least on the surface of things, that they are placing some trust in you, given that this information is being passed on and they're leaving you to your own devices, as it were."

Eddie shrugged. "And if I get a comparison done, then what?"

"Then, if as a result of whatever comparisons you make you are interested in meeting with whoever it is who passed this information to you, you are to contact me, and I will arrange for a meeting whenever, wherever, and however you choose. Again, not to overstate the obvious, but they who have sent me on this little mission clearly assume that the results of the comparison will both pique your interest and establish in some way their *bona fides*. You are being recruited, Detective. You should be flattered."

"Not hardly. And what if I just take these prints and turn them over to the police or the bureau or whoever? Let the chips fall where they may?"

"Well, of course, that's one choice you could make. In fact, I raised that possibility myself. I admit my doing so was motivated by my own self-interest. I certainly did not want to be held responsible if you chose a different course than that suggested. I did, however, offer them a warning. I told them it was my impression that following orders and standard operating procedures may not have been the hallmark of your career. I hope you don't find that insulting."

Eddie shook his head, but said nothing.

"I will tell you, however, that they suggested you not choose such a course. Apparently they believe that, over the past few months or whatever, you may have become involved in matters about which they are aware, and about which you might not want others to become aware. The matter in your kitchen and the unfortunate death of some drug addict and what I understand is an outstanding warrant for you were suggested to be a minor problem for you compared to an incident in Brighton Beach."

"They said that? They said Brighton Beach?"

"Yes. Specifically Brighton Beach. They feel that whatever that matter involved might be of some concern to you."

"And they told you to tell me that?"

"Yes, but they did emphasize that you were not to take it as any form of threat. Simply as one issue to be considered in the context of your own self-interest."

"Sounds like a fucking threat to me."

"Well, I'm only the messenger here. You'll have to take that up with them. If you so choose, that is."

"Who *are* these people?"

Hans Talpa leaned forward with a thin smile. "I thought we had already gone over this, Detective. They are nothing more than ordinary people of ordinary intelligence with extraordinary power who are accountable only to themselves. They are more dangerous than you could ever imagine. Trust me."

r

Both men stood leaning against the trunk of Eddie's car at the edge of the Eisenhower Golf Course parking lot.

"So, whaddaya think?" Eddie asked.

"Like the man says, you're being recruited." Jimmy Legget held the two sets of fingerprint exemplars up to get a better look in the moonlight. "Yep, you're definitely being recruited."

"For what?"

"I have no idea."

"So, what do I do?"

"First you put these print cards in your safe-deposit box. I'll get a copy of the morgue prints. Then the two of us are gonna take a ride down to Chesapeake Beach and get Barry to do a comparison."

"Is he sober these days?"

"Hell no, but he can still do a comparison for us, and he won't ask any questions."

"And then?"

"And then we'll see. Let's just take it one step at a time. All right?"

Eddie nodded. "Just like the old days, huh?"

"Not quite," Jimmy said, "but close enough."

21.

It seemed only yesterday that it had all started, right here, in this very room, with the same doors opened to the same balcony and the same sea air so thick and hot he could taste its salt and feel it swell his fingers. She had stood there, naked and motionless in the near darkness, a pastel form haloed by the reflected lights of Lisbon. He had stood back from her and said nothing for a very long time, studying her, studying every shape and shade and shadow of her, his breath caught in his throat. He remembered the sudden, self-conscious lowering of her eyes and the slow, awkward movement of her hands to guard herself, as if she was certain that he was judging her.

But how could she think he was judging her? Couldn't she see that he worshipped her? Helen, daughter of Zeus, the source of his strength, his only passion. He had come to recapture her, to lay siege for her, to slay Paris and burn Troy for her; and he had told her this, and she had laughed and said he was drunk. He laughed, too, but only so that he would not frighten her, only so that he could move close to her, so he could touch her, so he could run the tips of his fingers down the sides of her neck and over her shoulders and down her arms slick with heat, so he could feel the rise of her breasts and the swell of her hips, so he could drop to his knees and touch the backs of hers, so he could lay his face against her belly and drink in the scent of her skin, so his hands could travel the smooth round of her ass and the backs of her thighs and the curves of her calves, so he could lay her down on the warm, knotted rug over the cool, hard tiles, so he could bury his face and feel her fingers in his hair, so he could listen to her breath turn deep and quick, so he could taste her excitement, so he could feel her shudder. . . .

"*Arlis!*"

Brecht twitched and looked up.

Arkady Treshkov leaned forward, his impatience apparent in the very small features of his very large face. "Have you heard a bloody word I've said?"

Brecht reached over and switched off the lamp.

"What are you doing?"

"It's much too hot with the lamp," Brecht said. "Do you want another drink?" Brecht stood and staggered a bit as he went to the kitchen, not waiting for Treshkov's answer. For the third time that evening—or was it the fourth?—he filled his glass with fresh ice, mixed vodka with just a splash of tonic, squeezed a wedge of lime around the rim of the glass, and dropped it in his drink. He then moved to the balcony, where he leaned against the wrought-iron railing, staring past the city to the sea.

Treshkov moved to the open doorway but did not step onto the balcony. "Arlis, I have neither the time nor the patience for another one of your black moods."

"It's all bullshit," Brecht said without turning back.

"What?"

"I said that it's all bullshit. Do you know what that means? It means . . . well, if you must know, it means the shit of the bull. That's what it means."

"Listen to me, Arlis, and listen carefully."

"No, I don't want to listen. I don't want to hear any more. I've listened far too much for far too long. I'm tired of it, I'm telling you. What's the point?"

"The point is—and I'd suggest that you pay careful attention to what I am saying—the point is that Yury Khavkin is beginning to

ask some very disturbing questions. Apparently, he has determined that Trevor Grehm used the same line of brokers for the
scandium that we used for that uranium sale in '91, and I doubt
he thinks this is pure coincidence. Are you getting the point?"

"We? I don't remember any we in the uranium deal. I remember
you. I don't remember there being any we."

"You handled the financing, if you'll recall."

"Perhaps, but not for the sale of fucking nuclear weapons,
which was just another one of those minor details you so conve-
niently failed to share with me."

"They weren't nuclear weapons, only base materials. What our
customers choose to do with them is their own business. Much
like your own government, by the way."

Brecht started to argue but stopped himself and shook his head.
"So, what is your point?"

"The point, Arlis, is that Khavkin and his group may well suspect that you and I were behind the scandium trade; that perhaps
Grehm was fronting for us."

"He said that?"

"No, he didn't have to. The point, if you are not too drunk to understand the obvious, is that Khavkin's group will not take it
kindly if they come to the opinion that you and I were dealing on
their territory and behind their backs. And they are beginning to
ask questions about their own accounts with Iberia. Now do you
understand?"

Brecht took a long swallow of his drink and turned back to face
Treshkov with a twisted grin. "Khavkin isn't nearly as dangerous
as he is greedy. He and his band of Chechen thugs. So we pay
them off. What do they care who's stealing from whom?"

"Pay them off?"

"Yes, we pay them off. What's it going to take? A million? Two?
Who cares? So I engineer a few market losses with offsetting accounts to make up the difference. A little here, a little there, isn't
that what I'm so good at? Stealing from people who have no way
of knowing what's going on with their money? Hell, maybe I'll
even steal a little from you."

"Be careful what you say, Arlis."

"What do you care, Arkady? You have more money stashed

away than you could ever spend decently. And how do you know I haven't been stealing from you all along?"

"This is not amusing."

"I'm not trying to amuse you. I'm trying to tell you that you are worried over peanuts. I am trying to tell you that I could have been stealing from you just as you have had me stealing from everyone else and you wouldn't have a prayer of figuring it all out. That's why you seduced me into working your dirty little games in the first place, wasn't it? Turned me against my government to help you turn against your government. What's the point?"

"The point—"

"No!" Brecht interrupted, gesturing with his glass and slopping his drink all over his hand. "No, I'll tell you what the point is." He paused a moment, trying to remember his point. "The point . . . the point is that there is no point. That's the point. My government hires me to screw your government. Your government hires you to screw my government. So what? That's what governments do. But we fooled them, didn't we, Arkady Sergeevich, my pimp, my seducer, my *friend!* Yes, we fooled them all. Hah! He screwed them both. So what does it matter any more? It's just money. There is no problem that can't be solved by money. Isn't that the point?"

"You are talking the fool, Arlis. I can forgive your drunkenness, but fools are dangerous, so I warn you—"

"You warn me? You warn me of what?"

Treshkov's jaw tightened. "I warn you that you cannot take Khavkin and his people for just another group of investors. There is far more to this than money. I warn you that money will not save you or me if Khavkin believes we have turned against him."

Brecht leaned back against the balcony's railing. He shook his head. "Tell me something, Arkady. Can Yury Khavkin really be so stupid to think that *I'd* be so stupid to run the scandium trades in his own back yard, and be so obvious to use the same brokers and investment houses you used with him before? Can he be so stupid to think that *I'd* be so stupid to follow the same trail and leave the same footprints? What would be the point?" Brecht stopped and cocked his head, then mumbled to himself, "What would be the point . . . unless . . . ?"

"Unless what?"

Brecht's glass slipped from his fingers, and there was a second or two before they heard it smash on the intricate stone mosaic bordering the courtyard below. Brecht leaned over the railing. "Shit," he mumbled long after the glass had reached the stones.

Treshkov did not move. "What do you mean, 'unless'? Unless what?"

"I need another drink."

"I asked you a question! Unless what?"

"I can't think without a drink," Arlis said petulantly, turning away from the railing.

"No!" Treshkov ordered. "You stay there. I'll fix your damned drink."

"Oh, no," Brecht said, staggering a bit as he reached out to stop Treshkov. "Oh, no, no. You will not get my drink. You will not touch my lime or pour my vodka or splash my tonic. You have the curse, Arkady Sergeevich. There's the scent of death about you. Everything you touch, every breath you breathe, like Rappaccini's daughter."

Treshkov looked down at Brecht's hand on his shirtsleeve, and Brecht let go. "What are you talking about?" Treshkov asked.

Brecht turned away. "Nothing," he mumbled.

Treshkov moved a bit closer, and his already narrow eyes narrowed further. "You're babbling, Arlis. And you are more than trying my patience with this nonsense."

"Nonsense?" Brecht paused, leaning back against the rail. "Jesus, you really believe that don't you? You really think all those bodies you trail behind you are nothing more than bits of nonsense. That pathetic little man in Bonn, and that courier in Rome, and Trevor Grehm, and your goons in Nickles's kitchen, it's all just nonsense to you? Even that wasted wreck of a dope addict in Washington, who probably couldn't even remember where he slept the night before, much less tell tales he would not have even known. No, no, Arkady Sergeevich, I'll get my own drink, thank you very much. . . . Can I get you anything?"

Treshkov took a handkerchief from his pocket and mopped his brow. "Get your drink, Arlis," he said through clenched teeth.

Several moments passed before Brecht returned with a fresh drink, only to be stopped at the balcony door. "Sit down,"

Treshkov ordered, nodding to an upholstered chair in the living room.

"I don't care for your tone," Brecht complained, his look turning suddenly hard.

Treshkov stood his ground. "Let us both be careful," he said slowly. "Neither one of us can afford to let this get out of hand."

Brecht stood silent for a moment, then nodded and sat down. He winced as Treshkov reached over and turned on the lamp. "Please, Arlis," he said, his voice controlled and even, "just answer my question. Unless what?"

"What are you talking about?"

"You said there would be no point in running the scandium trades through the same brokers using the same methods, 'unless.' What did you mean? Unless what?"

"I don't know—"

"Answer me!" Treshkov barked. "I am through coddling you like a damned child. Now answer me!"

Brecht sat back and stared at Treshkov, taking an exaggerated moment and a slow sip of his drink before asking, "Or what? You'll kill me?"

Treshkov said nothing.

"Do it, Arkady Sergeevich. Right now! Go into your pocket or into your bag or wherever you need to go for your gun or your knife or your lethal injections or whatever. It's a beautiful night, and you're right, I am quite drunk. I won't feel a thing. It's a good night to die."

Treshkov leaned forward and braced himself on the arms of Brecht's chair, his face coming close enough for Brecht to turn away from his foul breath. "Don't fool yourself, Arlis. You know if I must I will. Don't make it a choice between you and me. The game, as you have too long thought of it, has turned serious. For both of us. Like it or not, we are joined at the hip in this business, and I will not let you drag me down with you. Now, please, answer my question. What did you mean, 'unless'?"

Brecht shrugged. "Well, unless maybe we were being set up. Or more likely that you were being set up."

"Me?" Treshkov straightened up and stepped back, a twisted frown forming over his face. "And who do you suppose might want to do that?"

"Who? My God, think about it. Gentlemen, the line forms at the rear." Brecht rolled his eyes.

"Be specific, Arlis. Give me your candidates."

"Well, me for one."

"You?"

"Certainly me. Why not me? Maybe I want to cut you out? Maybe I've decided to turn Khavkin and the partners against you while I walk away with the profits?"

Treshkov raised his eyebrows, and a curious smile crossed his face as he took a seat opposite Brecht. "But you wouldn't do that, would you?"

"Why? Because you and I are such close personal friends? Wake up, Arkady Sergeevich. You've used me for more than ten years. You pushed all the right buttons and turned me for your own purposes. Games and countergames, just so we could both profit handsomely from our respective governments' trying to screw each other. You don't think I'm tired of it all? Can't you imagine my devising a little plan to make it look like you're stealing from the partnership, and while you and Khavkin fight it out among yourselves, I simply resign from the directorate, divert all the account funds they never knew about, and walk away? It's not a bad plan, and who better to carry it out? No one, that's who. You've said so yourself, I run financial games that could baffle a computer. Who else better to devise a plan to screw you?"

Treshkov sat down opposite Brecht. "The problem with that plan," he said quietly, "is you."

"Me?"

"Yes, you. It's too obvious. You'd be the first one I'd suspect."

"Which means I'd be the last one you'd suspect."

Treshkov frowned.

"Think of it," Brecht said. "Aren't I right? I'd be the last one you'd suspect, simply because it is too obvious." Brecht snickered. "But if I'm the last one you'd suspect because it's too obvious, then I should be the first one you'd suspect; but, then, if I should be the first one to suspect, I'm really the last . . . which makes me first, or . . . Hell, now I'm confused." Brecht rested his head on the back of his chair and closed his eyes. "Maybe we should diagram this. Develop a formula or something. Yes, that's what we need, an algorithm of treachery."

Treshkov sat silently for several moments before he asked, "Tell me again, Arlis, who else besides you and me and Trevor Grehm knew that particular series of accounts?"

Brecht neither lifted his head nor opened his eyes. "Or Khavkin. What if Khavkin set this whole thing up as the ultimate end game? After all, I've said all along that Trevor Grehm had to make contact with someone on your side to carry out the trades. Do you really think he could have done it without Khavkin's knowledge, or help? Are you really so certain about your friend Yury? Is it so impossible for you to imagine him setting this up to take the money himself while turning the partners against you and me? I mean, not only might he turn a tidy little profit for himself, maybe he'd end up taking over the whole operation, while you and I scurry off to find some safe hole to hide in. . . . That's a preposition, isn't it? Sorry, some hole in which to hide." Brecht laughed. " 'This is the sort of English up with which I will not put.' Who said that? I can't remember."

Treshkov leaned forward. "Once more, Arlis. Who else besides you and me and Trevor Grehm were aware of that particular series of accounts."

"You got a pen and paper?"

"Don't!" Treshkov said sharply, then lowered his voice. "Please, no more of your joking. Tell me again. Who knew about those accounts?"

Brecht sat up. "Christ, Arkady. The list could go on and on. How many people on your side knew you ran the uranium deal? And on my side? Hell, you know we used those accounts for other deals all the time."

"Yes, but who knew the particular footprints, as you call them?"

"Grehm, obviously."

"And his wife?"

"No, not her."

Treshkov's frown turned deeper. "No? How can you be so sure?"

Brecht hesitated. "Because . . . well, because they never worked together. His business never overlapped ours, at least not in the accounts."

"Yes, but they were married."

"They were separated. They had been separated for more than a year. They didn't get along at all. They . . . No, they didn't overlap."

"But wasn't she one of your main couriers? Wasn't she the one who set up so many of your accounts?"

"Still . . ."

"And those particular accounts, didn't she set up most of them in the first place."

"No, you're wrong. I mean, yes . . . but you're getting things confused. She wasn't involved in transactions, don't you see? She was only a courier, for Christ's sake."

"And what makes you so sure she and her husband were so estranged? Couldn't they have been dealing together?"

"They weren't."

"How do you know?"

"I know, that's all."

"And what was she doing in Washington if she and her husband were so estranged?"

"I don't know."

"Maybe they weren't so estranged as you thought."

"No, that's not true."

"How do you know?"

"I . . . I just know."

"How?"

"All right, maybe I don't. I just don't believe it."

Treshkov leaned forward. "Tell me your reasons."

"Get off it, Arkady. What difference does it make? She's dead. You killed her, remember?"

"Did I?"

"You know you did."

"No, I don't. I wasn't there. I never saw her."

"She's dead. That's all there is to it."

"Is she?"

Brecht looked away. "I saw her. I saw what your goons did to her."

"You saw a corpse all bloated and turned black with rot."

"Stop!"

"Why?"

"Goddamn you! Why are you doing this to me? Why did you have to kill her?"

"Why do you care?"

Brecht shook his head slowly, while Treshkov stood and began pacing in front of Brecht's chair. "Were you seeing her, Arlis?"

Brecht did not answer.

"Answer me! Was she yet another woman you fancied the love of your life?"

"That's a shitty thing to say."

"You were seeing her, weren't you?"

Brecht looked away, shaking his head.

"My God, Arlis, you were fucking Helen Grehm, weren't you?"

Brecht looked up. "Jesus, you really are a pig."

"You were fucking her, weren't you?" Treshkov asked as his pace quickened.

Brecht, too, stood and moved toward the balcony, stopping at the door. "I thought I loved her," he said quietly and without turning back.

"Fool!" Treshkov exploded, and Brecht turned to see Treshkov's face swell and turn a deep red, and his fists were clenched and trembling as if it was all he could do to keep from striking Brecht. He turned away quickly and again began pacing. "Fool! I should have seen it right away. No wonder it was so easy for them. Grehm and his whore of a wife. She was fucking you. No wonder you've been so blind. You've always been blinded by tarts. How could I have missed it?" He stepped forward and raised his hand to strike, but stopped himself. "Damn you! You and your whores."

Brecht turned to face Treshkov. "What do you mean, my whores?"

"Be serious."

"No, I mean it. What are you saying?"

Treshkov shook his head and his lip curled in a sneer. "We have more important issues to deal with than your bloody ego."

Brecht took another step forward. "What do you mean, my whores?" he repeated in an even louder voice.

"Arlis, please, for all your genius with numbers and money, for all your good looks and charm and whatever, did you really believe that it was you? Did you really believe that you were all that irresistible? Surely you must have had even a single lucid moment when you wondered how it was that every time you'd drive one woman away with your obsessive fantasies, yet another one would just pop into your life."

"You mean Mireille?"

"Surely you suspected."

"Mireille? Yes, I thought . . . Her and her friends, and then you. But?"

"But what, Arlis? What did you think?"

"Nicole?"

"Of course Nicole, and Katya, and the others."

Brecht wheeled and threw his glass against the far wall. "You sonofabitch!"

Treshkov didn't move, but a slight smile came over him. "You see the difference, Arlis? Between you and me? You throw your drink against the wall in some grand but meaningless gesture. How very American of you. If you had told me such a thing, I would have either cut your throat or ignored the matter entirely. You see the difference? You see why it was so easy for them? You are a fool for whom face is everything. You sleep with the woman who not only steals from you, she may very well have put you—and me!—she may have put us both in front of a firing squad, and you call *me* the sonofabitch."

A long silence followed as Brecht stood stone still and staring, until finally he closed his eyes and took a deep breath, then moved to his chair and sat down.

"You're right. I am a fool." He let another long silence pass before he said, "But you're wrong about Helen. You're chasing ghosts. You just don't understand."

"Of course I understand, you idiot. She's still out there. Can't you see the obvious? It all makes sense. She's the one who raided the account after Trevor Grehm's body was found. She's the one who ran the money and left the footprints."

"Jesus, will you listen to me? I saw her. I'm telling you, she's dead. You're not thinking. Listen to me."

"I don't think so. What you saw was a corpse rotted beyond recognition. It could have been your mother, for all you knew. You saw what they wanted you to see. I should have seen it. Damn!"

Treshkov's pacing turned quicker, his voice following as he thought aloud. "The question is, why? Why would they steal that way? They had to know you'd run a trace. They had to know you would find it eventually. So why be so obvious?" Treshkov turned back, his expression turning even, almost pleasant. "Maybe you've hit upon something, Arlis. It wasn't the Grehms, was it? They didn't have the file access to pull something like this off. They were fronting, weren't they? They, or whoever put them out there, intended all long to leave footprints? But why?"

Brecht sat up, and he began to speak in a voice straining for calm. "All right. I should have told you about us. But it has nothing to do with this. Nothing. Listen to me. No, listen to yourself. You're not thinking clearly. You're beginning to sound like the analysts at Langley and Moscow Center. You're turning a wild theory into a self-fulfilling prophecy. She wasn't involved. There was no *they*. There was Trevor Grehm and whoever he dealt with on your side. That's it! Hell, Trevor Grehm didn't even need a conspirator, for that matter. He'd been in the business a long time. He had his own contacts."

"But washing the money through the same banks and trading houses?"

"A coincidence. It's not exactly a state secret which banks are cooperative in these matters."

"The same accounts? The withdrawals after Trevor died?"

"I don't know, I don't know. Jesus, how many times do we have to go through this? I'm telling you, you're wrong. Helen Grehm's dead. You're chasing ghosts. You're just not thinking!"

Treshkov gave no sign that he was listening, continuing to ask himself questions. "But who? Who was running them? They wouldn't step out like that unless they were certain they had protection, unless they were certain they had cover. Who would that be, Arlis?"

Brecht just closed his eyes and shook his head.

"Yes, Arlis, think. She's still out there. She's still running the game. The question is, for whom?"

"You're going off the deep end, Arkady. Really you are."

"I don't think so. Did you ever ask yourself why they sent you to identify Helen's body? You of all people. Why they would take such a chance to involve you?" Treshkov's eyes suddenly widened, and he stepped quickly to Brecht's side and lifted Brecht's chin in his hand. "Tell me, my horny little friend, how much did the directorate really know about the uranium deal in '91?"

Brecht brushed his hand aside. "I told you. How many times have I told you?"

"Tell me again."

"They knew about the sale. They knew your group was involved. They knew the uranium ended up with the North Koreans. That's all. We've been over this a million times."

"And they asked you to help find out where the money went, correct?"

"Yes. But it was covered. They never found out Iberia was used for the wash."

"Then why would they ask you to help trace the money?"

"Because of my bank contacts. Why do you think?"

"Tell me again who asked you to run the trace."

"Machus, of course."

"But why Philo Machus? Why was the directorate involved? This wasn't their area. Why not CIA, or better yet your so-called Z Division, or the Threat Assessment people? Why the directorate?"

"Jesus, how many times have we gone over this? They were trying to track the money. I don't know, maybe they thought they could queer the deal if they could find and stop the money transfers."

"And you don't think they ever suspected you?"

"And left me to keep running the company? Don't be a fool."

Treshkov smiled. "Only foolish, Arlis, but not yet a fool." He shook his head at Arlis. "Oh, how pathetic. And for a man who is such a genius with money."

"What do you mean?"

"He almost pulled it off, didn't he?"

"What are you talking about?"

"Machus, you idiot. Philo Machus. Of course, it's so simple. They know you're dealing with me, just like I know you're dealing with them. It's just that neither one of us is supposed to know that, which is why it's been so easy for us to run the game. Right? But Machus got burned. He was supposed to know everything about us, but somehow we manage to run ten kilos of uranium right under his nose. Imagine the heat he must have taken." Treshkov broke into a wide grin. "I can just see him sweating it out in front of the Joint Committee, trying to explain how he got taken."

"You don't understand," Brecht said. "You just don't understand how it works. If that were the case, you and I wouldn't be sitting here. Get it? At best, I'd be standing in some chow line at a maximum-security prison. At worst, I would have suffered some unfortunate accident."

"No, Arlis, it is you who do not understand. What would such a simple solution get him? More embarrassment, that's all. What, you think they would prosecute you for stealing from an organization that's not even supposed to exist? You'd be dead, but we'd go untouched. We'd have won. No, don't you see? He doesn't care about a few kilos of uranium or the money. Machus wants revenge. Machus set us both up. He wants to collapse the whole operation. He's used you to get to me to get to the whole network. That's why. He wants to win!"

Brecht again closed his eyes and let his head fall back against the chair. "How can I explain this? Why won't you listen? If for even a minute Machus or the Joint Committee thought I was involved . . . No, you just don't understand. You see, Americans don't think that way. They'd never let it go on. Never."

"Ah, my foolish friend, you're wrong. That's exactly what they'd do. You see, we Russians would not let it go on. We'd simply take you to the basement and put a bullet in your brain. We know how to cut our losses and move on. But you Americans, you live and die for your image, for your ego. It's what drives you. Ego. No sense of the practical. It's what will eventually drive you to your knees, this need to look good no matter the cost. And Machus, the ultimate American. He wants to look good, he wants to feel good. The sonofabitch wants revenge, and he used the Grehms to run the game."

Brecht looked at Treshkov with a vacant expression, his words hesitant, his voice weak. "You're wrong. She's dead. I saw her."

Treshkov turned away, shaking his head. "All that time wasted with Nickles and that stupid card and its codes. It was her; the whole time it was her out there running Philo's game." He stopped and turned back quickly, staring at Brecht. "Nickles? What about this detective? Do you think it's possible that he found her? Is it possible that Nickles somehow made contact with Helen Grehm, and that's why he suddenly turned so independent? If he did . . ." Treshkov stopped, then began to pace while he talked to himself. "If I'm Philo Machus and somehow this local detective type stumbles upon my agent who's supposed to be dead, what do I do? I turn him, of course. What else? Of course, I'd turn him to my own purpose. I'd use him to draw the other side out. How else would this local policeman manage to track down the contractor in New York? He had to have had help. He's just a cop after all. And at the same time, it maintains the fiction that Helen Grehm died. Very neatly done, Philo. Very neatly done."

Brecht pressed the heels of his hands against his temples. "Arkady, listen to me. Helen Grehm is dead. I saw her body. Who else do you think your goons killed?"

"Who cares? Maybe Grehm had a girlfriend, maybe it was another agent passing messages or debriefing him. Who knows? But what a stroke of good fortune for Machus. Think about it. He used your little whore against you, and then, suddenly, everyone thinks she's dead. Now she's able to run Machus's games with the perfect cover. It's so simple. We did him a favor."

"I need another drink."

"No. No more drinks. You and I are going to talk. You and I are going to find your whore. Helen Grehm is out there and you are going to help me find her. And my friend Mr. Nickles. Yes, I think it is time to revisit him as well."

Brecht watched as Arkady Treshkov looked west toward the sea, a smile of anticipation creeping across his face. "Ah, Philo," he mused, "it seems you have been too clever by half. Yes, I think it is time that we turned your game around."

22.

No matter how still she sat, the thick, humid heat drew beads of perspiration down the edges of her face and pasted her light cotton blouse to her chest. It felt good. It felt as if the old poisons were being flushed from her body, only to be replaced by the fresh gin and tonic that numbed her mind against thoughts of what had brought her here and how long she would stay and where or how the journey might end.

From Altdorf to Thun to the French coast at Riec-sur-Belon, to the small, tree-cloistered hotel in Ballsbridge, on the outskirts of Dublin, to the guest house high in the hills above Charlotte Amalie, Helen Grehm had wandered, alone but for a single suitcase stuffed with clothes, cash, a variety of passports, and, of course, the codes with which she had moved nearly three million dollars along trails so entwined that for a time she worried that even she might not be able to unravel them. Ultimately she had spread the funds among a dozen or more investment and foreign-currency accounts in the Bahamas, the Caymans, and the Lesser Antilles. She then retreated with what cash she needed to sustain herself in this forgotten village on this forgotten island off the southwestern coast of Florida. She had been on the island for nearly two weeks, and for the first time in a long time, she was starting to relax.

The screen door's spring strained behind her, and Helen barely cocked her head to the sound of the door banging shut and Marta's bare feet padding across the veranda. Marta wore an oversized man's workshirt, a loose pair of cotton pants, and smudges of oil paints that colored her hands and streaked her cheek and brow. She leaned back against the railing and finished rolling a joint of marijuana. "Want some?" she asked.

Helen shook her head. "No thanks. The gin is working just fine."

The two of them, best friends since childhood, were so comfortable with one another that neither felt the need to speak as they spent several minutes watching the last of the setting sun flash through the dripping tendrils of a banyan tree and sink below the horizon.

"I thought you had a date tonight," Helen said at last.

Marta took a deep hit on the joint and held it. Then, releasing her breath in a long sigh, she smiled. "A date? Sweetheart, women our age don't date twenty-six-year-old boat mechanics, particularly not twenty-six-year-old boat mechanics named Rod. We have sex with boat mechanics named Rod, we don't date them."

Helen chuckled. "Safe sex, I hope."

"Sex is never safe. That's half its allure, isn't it? That it's always dangerous? Isn't that what you always said?"

"Me?"

Marta lurched forward with a laugh. "Oh, please. Ninth grade, and I still believed I was going straight to Hell because I let Ricky Snyderman unsnap my bra while you were out *doing it* with that football player—or was it baseball?"

"Baseball, and it was eleventh grade. And I wasn't *doing it*. A little heavy petting, that's all. Besides, I thought we were talking about your sex life."

"Oh, no, you don't slide that easily. We've already done my sex life, what there is of it, and now that I have you talking, I want to hear about the ninth grade. Well, okay, maybe it was the tenth, 'cause I remember you had just gotten your driver's license. But you were definitely doing it. You told me so yourself."

Helen laughed. "Oh, please, I was just making it all up."

"No!"

"Of course I was. You knew it the whole time. You just loved listening to me talk dirty."

"I don't believe it. You're serious? You were lying?"

"Of course I was."

"God, how could you have done that to me? Your best friend. Really?"

Helen laughed again. "Seriously, you never believed all that stuff."

"Of course I did. The whole time, I was praying for your salvation and torn between going to Hell and being the last living virgin east of the Mississippi. What was his name?"

"Who?"

Marta scuttled the wicker rocker over next to Helen and sat down. "Mr. Baseball. What was his name? Something goofy, wasn't it?"

"No, it wasn't goofy. Ernest. Ernest Stampel."

"God, yes, Ernest." Marta laughed. "Not Ernie, or good ol' Ern, or Spud or Butch or whatever. Ernest. I remember everyone had to call him Ernest or he'd get all hot under the collar. And you! You went into such detail, and I believed every salacious word of it."

"No, you didn't."

"I did! You told such great stories. What *it* looked like, how big it was, and all the terrible things you'd do with it. And then I'd go racing home to pray for you and go to confession because I secretly wanted to be just like you, and the whole time you were lying! I don't believe it." Marta rolled her eyes, then sat up and looked directly at Helen. "So," she said. "Really, how big was it?"

Helen, in the midst of taking a sip of her drink, spewed gin down the front of her shirt, laughing between coughs. "Larger than his brain, I can tell you that," she said, recovering. "Poor Ernest. He was so sincerely stupid."

"Oh, come on, you loved it. You loved the way he followed you around like some dog on the scent."

"Yeah, well, maybe a little."

"Please."

"All right, so I loved it. I loved listening to him beg." She laughed again. "I was awful, I really was."

Marta sat back again and chuckled. "Hell, he probably deserved it." She sat silent for a moment, and her smile began to fade. "They all do, for that matter. My only regret was taking so long to figure that out."

Helen pressed her glass against her face, letting the condensation dripping from its sides cool one cheek and then the other. She took a deep breath and looked over at her friend suddenly silent and staring into the night. "Was it really that bad? Between you and Rick, I mean?"

Marta laid her head on the back of her chair and took another long drag on the joint. She then pinched off the burning tip and put the remains in her shirt pocket. "No," she said slowly. "It wasn't that it was so bad, it was more that it was never that good. You know what I mean?"

Helen did not answer.

"I don't know," Marta continued. "I thought I'd be happy just playing with my paints while he was off conquering the commodities market. We made a great team, he always said. 'A great team!' Just what a girl wants to hear . . . And then, when I got pregnant, I could see that look in his eyes. At least I thought I could. I mean, he never said anything, but I could see that look like he was wondering, Do I really want to spend the rest of my life with this person? Maybe it only looked so clear to me because I was wondering the same thing. Anyway, after . . . you know, after I lost the baby . . . I don't know, all the questions just seemed to answer themselves. Oh, he was very kind, and he gave it a respectable year before he said anything. By that time, I think I was actually relieved. He saved me from having to end it myself. And, God bless his greedy little heart, he had made just indecent amounts of money. Pork bellies or soy-bean futures, or whatever the hell he was trading. Left me quite well off, thank you very much." She looked over at Helen with a brief smile. "Now, every time I see a pig, I tip my hat out of respect."

Helen raised her glass. "Here's to the pigs."

"And to the divorce lawyers who butcher them," Marta said in return.

There was another long silence, interrupted only by the sound of crickets and tree frogs and the raccoons rummaging through the trash cans at the end of a dirt path. Helen, too, laid her head back, and asked, finally, "Do you ever miss the real world?"

"The real world? Where's that?"

"You know what I mean."

"No, I'm not sure I do. Seems like the last time I left the island the hot topics of conversation were President Billy Joe Bob discussing his skivvies on MTV and the social significance of the Bobbits and O.J., whose combined IQs probably wouldn't match your shoe size. If that's your real world, save me from it."

"You don't get restless?"

Marta shrugged. "Sure, once in a while, but if I ever feel the need to converse in complete sentences, I take a few days in Miami or New York or wherever. A few days is all I really need to remind me of the things I don't miss. Life here is just fine. For me, anyway. No one bothers anyone. Half the island fishes to eat or to stock the restaurants. The other half fleeces the tourists, because that's what tourists are for. Me, I sell a few paintings here and there, maybe drink a little too much at The Lost Dog, buy my dope from the sheriff's brother-in-law, and occasionally allow myself a minor indulgence with my randy boat mechanic. I haven't any complaints, and as far as I can tell, not many people around here do." She cocked her head thoughtfully. "You know, I'd bet that if Washington decided to cede this island to Guatemala, no one would much care one way or the other, except to ask whether the ferry would still make its regular run to the mainland. That's about as real as I need."

Helen nodded slowly, but said nothing. Marta waited a moment, then asked without looking over, "You trying to decide how long you can stand hiding out here?" She stopped and stood up quickly, turning her back to Helen and leaning out over the railing. "I'm sorry, I didn't mean for it to come out that way. I'm not asking. You know. Whatever you want to do."

Helen took a moment before saying, "No, that's all right. You're right. Listen, I . . . ah . . ."

"I'm sorry," Marta repeated, "you don't have to say anything."

"No, I do." She took a deep breath. "You've saved me, Marta. You really have. I don't know what I would have done if you hadn't been here. It had been so long since we had seen one another—hell, since we even talked—and I was worried, you know, that somehow things would have changed between us. That we would have changed."

Marta turned back to face her. She shook her head. "Don't say that. We go back too far. I would have been upset if I wasn't the one you came to. I know it's been hard, with Toddy gone and all."

Helen lowered her eyes a moment, then said, "Marta, listen, there's some things I ought to tell you."

Marta looked up hesitantly, then smiled. "You mean, what really happened that night after homecoming?"

Helen smiled, too, then looked away, her expression darkening. "No, I'm serious."

"Helen, listen to me," Marta said. "I like having you here. I really do. You stay as long as you want, no questions asked. We've got more room here than either one of us needs, and if it ever becomes a problem, I'll tell you. And if you want to talk about it, or not talk about it—whatever it is—either way, that's okay."

Helen drew her knees up to her chest and wrapped her arms around them. "The fact is, I need to tell you. It's more than just Toddy, you know, the whole thing about his being murdered." She lifted her eyes to meet Marta's. "You're right, I am hiding, or at least I was. I'm not really sure anymore."

"What do you mean?"

"It wasn't a burglary. It wasn't just some random thief or whatever. Toddy worked for the government."

Marta's eyes narrowed. "Toddy?"

"Yes."

"I don't understand. I mean, what does working for the government have to do with being murdered?"

"It's not the government you're thinking of, it's the government no one talks about. I mean he had his own business, and all that, but it wasn't exactly farm equipment. He was an arms trader. And he was . . . I guess you'd say he was *connected* with the government."

Marta paused for a moment. "You mean he was a spy?"

"Well, not exactly, but that's close enough."

"So . . . What? What are you trying to tell me?"

"Well, I'm pretty sure that's why he was murdered."

Marta leaned back against the railing. "Jesus. What do you mean, you're pretty sure? I mean I'm sorry. I mean you're sure? Did you know what he was doing?"

"Sort of. Not really, but, ah, I worked for the government, too."

"What?"

"At least I thought I did. . . ." Helen stopped and shook her head.

"What are you talking about?"

"It's too bizarre to explain, and you wouldn't want to know even if I could. It's just that we weren't what everyone thought we were. The point is, in different ways we worked for the government."

Marta reached into her shirt pocket and retrieved the short stub of marijuana. "Jesus, you mean all those time shares in Marbella, and the villas in the Algarve, that was all . . . I don't know . . . what, a front?"

"No, no, I did that. It's just that I did other things for the company, and the company did things for other people, you know?"

"Government people?"

"Yeah."

"Jesus. And Toddy?"

"Well, he was more involved than I was. I guess that's the best way to put it."

"Jesus," Marta said again, and she sat back down in her chair, lit the stub and took a deep drag.

"And after Toddy died, you know, I just needed to get away from it all."

"You're hiding? You really are?"

"I was, but I don't know anymore. It's been—what?—over five months, and I haven't seen or talked with anybody. I don't know if anyone's even looking anymore, if they ever were. It's just that I walked away without telling anybody anything, that's all."

"Damn, Helen, what were you doing?"

"Running errands, I thought. I was just running errands and collecting a paycheck. And I really don't know what Toddy had gotten into. I mean, we'd been separated for more than a year, and even before that we never worked together. We had completely different jobs. It's just that . . . I don't know, when he got killed I got scared, and . . . I just bolted. That's all."

"And you've been running since then?"

Helen nodded but said nothing.

Marta sat back and folded her feet under her, stubbing the final ash against the arm of the chair. "You think someone might try to find you here? I mean, what were you into? No, no, don't answer that. I'm just a little confused."

"Me, too."

"Wow," Marta said softly, starting to rock back and forth and wrapping her arms around herself. "This isn't another Ernest Stampel story, is it?" She shook her head quickly. "Shit, I'm sorry. I didn't mean that. I'm saying all the wrong things. I'm just, you know, a little weirded out, you know? I mean, what does all this mean?"

"I wish I knew myself. I'm sure it's over. I really don't think anyone's looking for me. Not anymore. If they ever were looking for me, they had plenty of chances to find me, so . . ." Her voice trailed off for a moment. "Besides, I was nothing but a small fish, and now they think I'm dead. There's no reason for them to be looking. So, like I say, I think it's all past me. It's just that I thought you should know why . . . well, why I've kept to myself so much. And, too, if I'm wrong and one morning you wake up and I'm gone, you'll know why."

"God, Helen, I'm not sure, but I think you're scaring me. I mean, are you trying to tell me some bloody terrorist or whatever is going to come creeping over the walls or something?"

"No—God, no. That's not their style. They don't like messes, not a lot of noise, if you know what I mean. If they come at all, they'll come and leave quietly. If there's going to be a problem it'll be my problem, not yours. I really believe that. Besides, if I know them at all, this would be one of the last places they'd look. I mean, who in their right mind would try to hide out in a place as obvious as with her best friend? I wouldn't have come here otherwise. At least I hope I wouldn't have. I just thought you should know, and, if I haven't said it already, I want to say thanks for letting me stay here, for just being here. I haven't felt able to relax like this for, I don't know, it feels like years."

Marta sat still and silent for a long time, her eyes focused on Helen, who was still sitting in a fetal ball, her stare fixed on the creeping darkness. She reached over and took Helen's glass and finished the last gulp of gin and tonic. "Well, honey, if you were looking to drop off the edge of the world, you came to the right place." She chuckled to herself. "Around here they think Fed Ex is an ointment for psoriasis."

Helen looked over and smiled. "You're sure?"

"I'm absolutely sure, for as long as you can stand it."

Helen reached over and squeezed Marta's hand. "Thanks."

Both women sat in silence for several long minutes before Marta drew a deep breath and said, "So, now that we're trading confessions. Senior year, after homecoming, and you went off with that bad boy from Thurmont, the one with all the hair and the Vincent Black Shadow."

"Billy? Billy Clewes?"

"Yes! That's the one. Bad Billy Clewes."

Helen sat back and ran her fingers through her hair, her expression turning to a sly grin. "Ah, yes, Bad Billy. Talk about the real world!"

23.

The old dirt road met the highway at a precise right angle and traveled east in a straight line for nearly a quarter-mile before it stopped just short of the water where Kent Point divided the Chesapeake and Eastern Bays. Countless generations of oyster shells had been dumped along its path and been pulverized and mixed with the dirt to form a hardpan that few weeds penetrated and from which little dust rose as the open Jeep approached. Flat, open fields extended a hundred yards or more to either side, and their wild grasses sat still and withering under an early October sun.

At the end of the road, an old shack leaned precariously, its tin roof torn and rusted, its board siding weathered to dried tinder; behind it, Eddie Nickles had parked his car under the shade of a single pin oak, where he sat with the driver's door open. He watched the Jeep stop midway along the drive and the driver take a moment or two to survey the scene before he again crept forward. Eddie took his revolver from the glove compartment and laid it on the seat beside him. He wiped his palms against his pant legs and mopped his brow with the sleeve of his shirt.

The Jeep came to the side of the shack and stopped. The driver stepped out slowly, holding his hands away from his body. He was tall, with the look of an athlete, with thick forearms and large sun-freckled hands reaching out from the partly rolled sleeves of an old workshirt. He smiled pleasantly and removed his sunglasses and mopped his face with one arm of his shirt. He looked back toward the shack and then out toward the water and called out, "Nice spot."

Eddie stepped out of his car but remained behind the open door and held his gun down at his side and out of sight.

The man took a few steps closer, then stopped. "How long you figure before the developers crowd this property with condominiums?" he asked.

"A long time, I expect," Eddie answered without moving. "There's still a few people left who value the land more than they do the money."

The man nodded. "I'd like to meet one of those people someday."

Eddie lifted his chin. "So, is there something I can do for you?"

"I hope so, Mr. Nickles, I surely hope so." The man paused, again looking toward the shack, before turning back to Eddie. "You mind if I share a little of that shade? I'm neither mad nor English, and this sun's a bitch. Should've had enough sense to take the wife's station wagon, but she doesn't much care for the Jeep. I'd suggest we go inside," he said, flipping his thumb toward the shack, "but that place looks like it's ready to lay down any minute."

"Yeah, kinda looks that way, doesn't it? Sorry, but I didn't catch your name or your business."

"Yeah, well, our mutual friend Hans told me to meet you here. As far as a name, might as well call me whatever you want. I could give you one—hell, I could give you a half-dozen or more—it's just that I can't remember which name goes with those license plates I stuck on the Jeep this morning, so why not just pick whatever you like."

" 'Preciate your honesty, but to tell the truth I don't much care for dealing with people who know my name but won't give me theirs."

"Can't say I blame you, but, given our situation here, we all need to bend a little, don't you think?"

"Depends on who's doing the bending and how much."

"Fair enough," the man said as he cocked his head toward the shack. "Why don't I start by suggesting that we invite your friend Detective Legget to join us. I suspect he's in that shack watching every move I make. I know he would be if I were in your position. But I suspect, too, that it's a mite cooler out here, and I doubt he's any more comfortable than I'd be wondering if and when that old roof'll come down on his head."

Eddie nodded with a hint of a smile. "You mind if I check you out?"

The man shrugged and raised his hands to the back of his head. "Help yourself."

Eddie slipped his revolver in his belt, then stepped away from his car and called out, "Jimmy? C'mon out."

Jimmy Legget stepped out to the middle of the open door holding his department-issued Glock down at his side.

The man smiled pleasantly. "You boys are kinda edgy this morning. Not that I blame you, I suppose. Like they say, once burned, twice cautious." He turned to face Jimmy while Eddie patted him down. "Howyadoin', Detective?"

Jimmy nodded but said nothing while Eddie removed the man's wallet and inspected several pieces of identification. "Harold Walmsley? Government Printing Office?"

The man nodded. "Yeah, well, close enough. Need any pamphlets? I hear we got pamphlets on just about anything you'd want to know."

Eddie tossed the man's wallet to Jimmy, who had stepped off the back porch and holstered his pistol. "Yeah," said Eddie, "you got any pamphlets explaining why I had a couple of Russian thugs try to kill me in my own kitchen?"

"Nope, no pamphlets, but . . . You mind if I drop my hands now?"

"No, go ahead."

"But under the driver's seat of that Jeep is a manila envelope filled with all sorts of things we need to talk about. You want me—"

"I'll get it," Jimmy said quickly and started toward the Jeep.

Eddie motioned to the back porch of the shack. "Okay, Harry from the Government Printing Office, why don't we sit down over there?"

Harry shook his head. "Why is it all the movie and TV guys get to run around places like the Bahamas and Monte Carlo, and I end up on the Eastern Shore waiting for some old crab shack to fall on my head?"

"Seniority?"

Harry laughed. "Yeah, that must be it."

Jimmy returned with the envelope, and all three settled on the floor of the porch, each taking his own cautious look at its sagging roof before picking a door frame or roof post to lean against.

"So," said Harry, "why don't we just get to it? Let me guess what you gentlemen discovered as a result of doing the fingerprint comparisons."

Eddie shook his head. "No, first let me ask what's gonna happen to Hans Talpa."

Harry frowned. "He's been reassigned."

"What's that mean?"

"It means he's been reassigned." A thin smile came over the man's lips and disappeared as quickly as it came. " 'Course, we'd sure like to know a few more details about how it was you managed to get to him, but I expect, too, you're not about to tell me, at least not till we get to know one another better. Is that about right?"

Eddie ignored the question. "So, why all of a sudden are you coming to us?"

"Well, the truth is, you gentlemen have presented us with a bit of a problem. Yes, indeed, quite a problem. And, although I hate to admit it, you seem to be doing a better job of running the rats out of their holes than we are."

"I'm flattered," Eddie deadpanned.

"You should be."

"Yeah, right, and so now you want us to join up?"

"Well, not exactly. You see, all your good work has a down side . . . for us, anyway. The point is, all this dust you've been stirring up might well settle on the wrong people, on the good guys, as it were."

"The good guys?"

"Well, we kinda like thinking of ourselves as the good guys."

"And who's we, exactly? This Special Projects Directorate?"

"Special Projects? Never heard of it. And, like your friend Hans probably told you, you'd be far better off if you never heard of it either, so why don't we just say 'American intelligence'?"

Jimmy Legget chuckled. "Gee, that narrows it down."

Harry smiled. "Yeah, sorta like saying 'law enforcement.' 'Course, these days seem like both are oxymorons, doesn't it? The point is, we're like you, just your everyday servants of the people. Truth, justice, and the American way."

"Well," Eddie said, "I'm certainly relieved. Why didn't you say so in the first place?"

"Humility. We like to keep our good deeds kinda quiet. Know what I mean?"

"So, what's the point of all this? Why are you reaching out?"

"Two reasons. First, we'd like you to confirm or deny a couple of suspicions that seem to be keeping our people awake at night, and, second, we'd like to encourage you to let us take it from here. You know, accept our congratulations for some remarkable detective work and maybe go about the rest of your lives with our thanks and maybe even a little bonus."

"A bonus?"

"Well, like all good masked avengers, we're a little shy about publicity, so we thought a trophy and a parade down Pennsylvania Avenue might not be in order. We thought maybe a cash bonus might help. You know, just enough to reimburse your expenses over the past few months. Travel, hotels, meals, medical, and whatever. And a little extra just to say 'Atta boy.'"

Eddie looked at Jimmy, who shook his head with a twisted grin.

"Please, gentlemen," Harry said, "don't misunderstand. I'm not trying to insult you."

"What if I just told you to go to Hell?" Eddie asked.

"Well, I'd certainly be disappointed. And, speaking personally, it would not look good when I came up for my annual performance rating."

"So why don't we get down to business? See just how well you do perform. Okay?"

"Okay." Harry nodded to the manila envelope lying on the porch next to Jimmy. "Like I said, that envelope contains a few things I suspect we'd both find interesting. But, first, I'm guessing that you did what Mr. Talpa suggested you do and ran a finger-print comparison. Am I right?"

Neither man responded.

"Yes, of course you did. And I suspect from that you found out that the woman known as Helen Grehm was not the woman murdered in the house on Q Place, correct? The print cards marked 'ML' did not match the victim's prints, am I right?"

"If you were so interested, why didn't you just check it out yourself?"

"Well, let's just say it was a judgment call. Not a particularly smart one, in my opinion, but, then, I'm just hired help, you know? It seems there were those who thought that calling for copies of the morgue prints might raise a question or two no one wanted to answer."

Eddie chuckled. "So now the field agent's gotta clean up some desk jockey's fuckup."

"There you go. Pick an agency, any agency, and it's always the same."

"So, who was the victim on Q Place?"

"Like myself, her name doesn't matter. Even if you had her name, you'd never find a trace of her. Not through Social Security or NCIC or the bureau and whatever other files you might search."

"Which means what?"

"Which means she was a contact agent, an independent. And now that she's dead, she never existed. Understand?"

Eddie nodded. "Whose side was she working?"

"Frankly, that's what we'd like to know. We thought she worked for us, but we're not so sure now. Plus, we're really trying to find out how many sides we're dealing with here."

"Meaning you got a bad seed."

"Meaning *maybe* we got a bad seed. Then again, maybe not. That's what we need to know."

"So, tell me," Eddie said, "this Helen Grehm. She still alive?"

"Precisely the question we've been asking ourselves. We were wondering if you might not be able to tell us."

Eddie glanced at Jimmy, who kept his eyes fixed on Harry. "Assuming I know, give me five reasons why I should tell you."

"Five?"

"At *least* five."

"I'll give you the reasons. You keep count. All right? First, I figure your stake in this has been satisfied. It started off as just a job, a little investigative work to supplement your retirement. But then it turned ugly, and it turned personal, just like it'd be with me if someone tried to kill me in my own house and in front of my daughter. I figure that's why you went to New York."

Eddie's eyes met Jimmy's, but neither spoke.

"That's right," Harry said. "We've been watching. Since sometime after that little incident at your house. I know you met up with an ex–New York cop named Sid Yalich, and I know Sid Yalich has had a hard-on for the Brighton Beach mob for years, and I know about Viktor Samoilov."

"What is it you think you know?"

"I think I know that somehow you hooked up with Yalich and I think Yalich helped you find Viktor. I don't know how the two of you put it together. . . ." Harry looked over to Jimmy.

"Jimmy had nothing to do with New York, understand? Nothing!"

"Fine. Let's assume this has nothing to do with Detective Legget except maybe he's done you a favor or two watching your back and maybe making some phone calls and computer inquiries that aren't so easy for you to make now that you're on the outside. I've done my own research, a little background on the two of you, and from what I've seen, you guys have been through a wringer or two yourselves. Am I right?"

Neither man reacted.

"Doesn't matter," Harry said. "Like I say, I don't know how you put it together that Samoilov was the second man in your kitchen, but however you did it, it was a nice piece of work. I wouldn't mind having a few men like you working for me. At any rate, Detective—"

"Just Eddie. I'm not a detective anymore."

"Well, Eddie, you may not be carrying the badge, but you're still a detective, and a damn good one, I'd say. But whatever, somehow you made the connection, and you went to New York looking for Viktor. And the truth of the matter is, our people couldn't keep up with you, so I can't say for sure, but I think you found Viktor."

Eddie first looked at Jimmy and then turned back to Harry and spoke softly. "I didn't kill him."

"I didn't say you did. And, frankly, I don't give a damn. Viktor was pond scum. Whoever killed him did the world a favor."

"I didn't kill him."

Jimmy shifted uneasily but said nothing.

"Trust me, Eddie, Viktor's not an issue. Whatever happened, I suspect that you may have had a little chat with Viktor before whoever it was stuffed him in a trash can, where he belonged."

Jimmy looked away and mopped his brow with his shirtsleeve. Harry continued without noticing.

"I suspect, too, that Viktor might have said something that led you to look up Hans Talpa. Obviously, I'd be real interested in hearing about that connection and what Viktor had to say."

"What's all this got to do with Helen Grehm?"

"Well, seems an awful lotta people were chasing after Helen Grehm's wallet or ATM card or whatever. Now, I'll tell ya, no one's got a clue—except maybe yourself—but no one's got a clue how or why that ATM card ended up with some street dude that no one can put together with anyone. All I know is what you told the police after you were shot, that you were hired to find him and the card. Now, I suspect—hell, why bullshit?—I know Hans Talpa told you that both Helen and Trevor Grehm were family. Isn't that right?"

"And?"

"So whoever hired you is mucking around in family business and more than likely killed Trevor Grehm, or had him killed, and probably thought this contract agent was Helen Grehm. We'd like to know who that was, and why they went after the Grehms, and why they're so interested in the ATM card. And, of course, if you might have that card."

"Like I told the police . . ." Eddie stopped.

"Yes?"

"I don't have the card."

Harry nodded. "I see. Well, that is a shame. We were hoping that we might be able to get a look at it. See what all the fuss is about. Oh, well, maybe it will turn up one day."

"Yeah, maybe it will. But, speaking of the police, let me ask you something. When I was in the hospital, some guy calling himself Wychek and claiming to be FBI came to see me."

Harry nodded. "And you since figured out he wasn't FBI, right?"

"Right."

"You guys are good, I must say. Yeah, okay, he was one of ours. Like you, we're just trying to find out what the hell is going on without dropping our drawers. Understand?"

"Yeah, I understand. But, like I said, I told the police the man who hired me called himself Garland Bolles."

"And, like the police probably told you, this Garland Bolles doesn't exist, correct?"

"Right."

"Okay, so let's go to the envelope." Harry nodded to the manila envelope, which Jimmy slid across the floor to Eddie. "There's a bunch of photographs in there. Mug shots, surveillance and file photos, and the like. Why don't you take a look, see if you recognize anyone."

Eddie removed a stack of photographs from the envelope. One by one, and very slowly, he went through them, some side-by-side heat shots, some full-face photos typically taken for identification or file cards, some five-by-seven glossy prints of subjects obviously unaware that they were being photographed. Eddie looked on the back of each photo, but none contained any name or other identifiers. After a moment or two, he flipped one side-by-side mug shot at Harry's feet. "Mad Willy," he said, and Jimmy Legget reached over to pick up and study the photograph. "Viktor Samoilov," Eddie said, flipping another mug shot. A moment passed before Eddie stopped and took a deep breath while holding up a single five-by-seven glossy. "That, gentlemen, is Garland Bolles."

Jimmy reached over and took the photograph from Eddie's hand, and Harry shook his head and smiled. "Well, well, well. Now, you see? That one small snippet of information makes this whole trip worthwhile."

"Whaddaya mean?"

"Well, you have just confirmed as fact what up to this point was only suspicion."

"So, who is he?"

"His real name is Arkady Treshkov. Arkady Sergeevich Treshkov. Former KGB, now in business for himself. He and his pals have seen the error of their Marxist-Leninist ways and turned capitalists. Big-time! They've taken advantage of their many contacts among the old apparatchiks to rip off Mother Russia for the many goodies she has to offer. Everything from oil and precious metals to shoulder-launched missiles to weapons-grade uranium and plutonium, whatever there's a market for. And believe me, gentlemen, there are plenty of markets out there. Mr. Treshkov and friends are true entrepreneurs. They don't much care who they sell to, as long as the money is right."

Eddie looked to Jimmy, and both shook their heads slowly.

"That's right. You boys have managed to land yourselves smack dab in the middle of some serious shit, which is why I would urge that you consider taking a step back. You've settled whatever business you had with the fellas in your kitchen, so why not relax and let us take over from here?"

"And if we don't . . ." Eddie stopped and looked at Jimmy Legget. "If I don't?"

"Well, I would think that you'd be making a big mistake, but, beyond that, there's nothing I can do. You make your own choices, understanding that we have a job to do, and if by some unfortunate turn of events you . . . well, you end up getting in the way of our doing our job, then at least we will have given you fair warning of the situation and how dangerous it might be. Fair enough?"

Eddie did not answer.

"Besides, Detective, wouldn't you rather spend your time fishing than chasing nasties that are nothing to you at this point. Maybe just putter around the house, plan a trip around parents' weekend at your daughter's college or whatever?"

Eddie stiffened visibly.

Harry frowned. "Listen to me, Detective. I'm not suggesting any threat here, but of course we've looked into you and know about your family. All I am saying is that you have more than enough reason to just walk away from this. Maybe let us in on what you've found, maybe not. But in the end, seems to me that your interests would be best served by backing off."

"Maybe, maybe not," Eddie said. "But the point is, how am I supposed to trust that? Even more, how am I suppose to trust that this Bolles . . . or Treshkov, or whatever his name is . . . hasn't done the same research? Are you gonna protect me? Are you gonna protect my family?"

"You're right. That's a problem. Officially, I can't do a thing for you, because, officially, I don't exist. But if you think you need it, there are things that can be done. Secondly, I can't speak for Treshkov or his crowd, but I suspect that enough time has passed since that incident in your kitchen and the fortunate demise of Viktor Samoilov up in New York, that, if Treshkov thought he needed to come after you, he already would have done so. No, it seems to me that you've proven to be more than a worthy adversary, and Treshkov would want to stay as far away from you as he can. I'm only suggesting that the smarter course would be to keep it that way. Let sleeping dogs lie, and all that. Don't you agree?"

Eddie stared at Harry for a long moment before he nodded once. "What about the outstanding warrant?"

"Well, I think I can assure you that, if you cooperate with us, we'll cooperate with you."

"Meaning what?"

"Meaning that whole business might just disappear from the records."

"And New York?"

"It never happened."

"And if I don't cooperate?"

"Well, then, I suppose the wheels of justice might have to grind on."

"I see."

"I hope so. I think you'll find us to be reasonable people. I'm sure you'll find us both willing and able to hold up our end of the bargain."

"And if you don't, who do I go to? The Government Printing Office?"

Harry laughed. "Yes, well, I understand how you might have a problem there, but the fact of the matter is we're both dealing with issues of trust here."

"Tell me, Harry from the Government Printing Office, if you were in my shoes and I came to you with the same deal, would you trust me?"

"That's a good question, Eddie. But, yeah, I think I'd trust you."

"And the desk jockeys behind the curtain? Would you trust them?"

Harry paused a long moment, staring straight into Eddie's eyes. Finally, he said, "That's a tough call, Eddie, a tough call. But my point is, I don't think you have a choice."

Eddie returned the stare for an equally long moment.

"Listen to me," said Harry. "All bullshit aside, it really could get messy if we found ourselves tripping over one another."

Eddie nodded, then asked, "So what is it exactly that you want from me?"

Harry relaxed and raised his arms in a wide, yawning stretch. "Well, I really need to know if you ever came in contact with Helen Grehm. We both know she was not the victim found in the house. Secondly, I need to know exactly what Garland Bolles—or Arkady Treshkov, if you will—exactly what he told you about the Grehms, what his approach was, as it were. And even though you don't have it, I really need to convince you to help us find that ATM card or whatever Treshkov was so intent on finding. If Treshkov was so intent on finding it, we'd sure like to know why. We are more than willing to reward you for any help along that line."

"And punish me if I don't?"

"Oh, I wouldn't care to put it that way, but you understand that we all have a job to do here."

"That's it?"

"That's it. Except, again, I'd be sure to get a few bonus points if you helped me out here. Maybe even employee of the month. Get to see my picture up on the lunchroom wall."

Eddie paused with a smile, and then his expression turned instantly serious. "What about this Helen Grehm?"

"You tell me, Eddie."

Eddie said nothing, and reacted not at all.

"Look," said Harry, "she's family, and her family would like her to come home. Now, I get the sense that, even if you know something, you don't want to say it. Understood, but let me say something to you. If by some remote possibility you know how to get in touch with her, please tell her to come home. She is in way over her head. Trust me. It's a mean world with lots of mean-spirited people out there. She'll be a lot better off with us than with them. There's nothing that can't be settled between us. That's what families are for, right?"

Eddie did not answer, and Jimmy looked away, shaking his head.

"But tell her that she has to come in. Nothing will ever get settled as long as she's out there. You'll tell her that for me, won't you?"

Eddie leaned forward and spoke in a voice as hard as his expression. "Now, you listen to me. I don't know where she is or if she is. Hell, I don't even know who she is. That's why I was asking. Now, you tell *the family*. You tell 'em that for me. All right?"

"And the ATM card?"

"I never saw it."

Harry returned Eddie's stare for a long moment before saying, "Right. And whoever does have it is probably thinking it might make a halfway decent piece of insurance if for any reason he might need it."

"Could be."

Harry smiled. "Right! Yes, well, be that as it may, the only other thing I wanted to accomplish is to say, Well done, thanks a lot, and I hope we never have to bother one another again. Unless, of course, there's anything else you'd like to share with me?"

Eddie shook his head. "No, we've done enough sharing for one day. I need a little time to think things over."

Harry stood up and put on his dark glasses. "Don't take too long, Eddie. You don't want events to overtake you, if you know what I mean."

"You see, Harry, there you go again. That sounds an awful lot like a threat."

"Not at all, Eddie, not at all. Simply laying out the facts as I know them, one professional to another. Remember, I'm just the messenger here. I'm not going to be making the decisions, I just carry out my instructions and report back on what I see and hear."

"And think?"

"Well, in my section we don't think an awful lot, you know? That's another division, the thinkers." Harry grinned. "Well, gentlemen, unless there's anything else, I guess I'll be on my way. I love meetings that are short and to the point. Gives me a chance to go poking around that bait-and-tackle shop I saw just over the bridge. 'Course, you understand my report will detail the hours and hours I took to artfully wheedle what little information I got from you."

Eddie nodded. "Of course."

Eddie stood and reached out his hand to lift Jimmy Legget to his feet.

Harry bent over to retrieve the manila envelope. "You don't

mind if I take my photos?" he said. He then reached into the envelope and took out another, smaller envelope, which he held out to Eddie. "Your bonus?"

Eddie shook his head.

"For your favorite charity. Whatever."

"Thanks," Eddie said, "but no thanks. Bonuses make me nervous."

Harry shrugged. "Whatever you say. Oh, yes, one last thing. I don't think you will, and I certainly hope you won't, either of you, but if for any reason you think you might need some help, call Mr. Talpa's number. He won't be there, of course, but . . ." He stopped and looked at his watch. "In about one hour there'll be an answering service covering that number. Twenty-four hours a day, seven days a week. All you need do is ask for Harry. That's all. Just ask for Harry and leave a telephone number or a location. You might be surprised how quickly we'll respond. All right?" He held out his hand.

Eddie nodded and shook his hand, and Harry turned to shake Jimmy Legget's hand as well. He then turned back to Eddie. "Give it some thought, Detective, but don't waste too much time. Do the right thing, the smart thing, get back to your life and your family and let us do our job. You've been in the business. You know what I'm saying is right."

"I'll give it some thought."

Harry smiled. "Yes, do that. . . . Well, gentlemen, it's been a pleasure. You all have a nice day."

"We'll try," Eddie said.

24.

Both men stood silently for the minute or two it took for Harry's Jeep to disappear down the long, straight road, and even then neither spoke for a long time, Eddie staring into the distance, Jimmy staring at his friend. "Please tell me," Jimmy said at long last, "that you are not going to do what I think you're thinking of doing."

Eddie turned to him. "What choice do I have?"

"Well, the most obvious choice is to just back off. Maybe, just maybe, Harry from the Government Printing Office really is trying to do you a favor."

"Yeah, and maybe pigs have wings," Eddie said, as he turned and walked over to his car, unloaded his gun, and tossed it into the trunk.

"Man," Jimmy called across the yard, "we're out of our league here. These people are playing by a whole 'nother set of rules."

"I know what the rules are," Eddie said, as Jimmy sat heavily on the edge of the porch and wiped the perspiration from his brow.

"Oh? You do?"

"Yeah." Eddie slammed his car door shut and walked over to where Jimmy was sitting and leaned close to him. "Yeah, I do.

Their rules, and I don't happen to like their rules. Maybe it's time to start playing by my rules."

"And what are your rules?"

"My rules are that I don't like hanging by my thumbs waiting to find out whether people with no names in jobs that don't exist might find it convenient to have me charged with a coupla murders I didn't commit. My rules are I don't like people threatening me through my family. I don't like sitting around wondering whether next week or next month or whenever someone just might decide to throw one of my kids into the soup, just to see what happens."

Jimmy looked away. "My point is that, if you keep pushing, you may just force their hand. Maybe the smart thing to do is give them the damn wallet and the credit cards or whatever, tell 'em what you know, and let them handle it."

"But who are *they*? I mean, who are we dealing with, and how do we know what side they're on? Plus, how many sides are we dealing with? Who do we check with? The Government Printing Office? The FBI? The department?"

"Yeah, maybe. Maybe it wouldn't be such a bad idea. Maybe we just oughta go back inside, go to someone we can trust and lay it out. Someone in the department maybe."

"Yeah, man, good idea. Why don't I just walk into the department and say, 'Hey, Captain, understand you're looking for me. Oh, and, by the way, here's the ATM card some guy hired me to find, 'cept he's not who I thought he was. He's some Russkie, or at least he might be, I'm not sure, 'cause all I know is what some guy named Harry from the Government Printing Office told me, only his name's not really Harry and he really doesn't work for the GPO, but he drives a Jeep, I think. 'Course, I'm not sure it's really his, but here's the tag number. 'Course, it's probably not registered to a Jeep, or for that matter to anything else you'll ever be able to trace, but if you want the real scoop, you ought to check out something called the Special Projects Directorate, which doesn't exist, but maybe you can check out this guy named Hans Talpa, who I once had as a target in a hooker murder. He was a peeper, and we all know how reliable peepers are. But, of course, you probably won't be able to find him, 'cause he's been 'reassigned.' But you can check out the old case file. Oops, sorry, I forgot. Can't do that,

'cause I didn't put him in the reports, 'cause at the time I kinda figured he didn't do it, and I might use him for a favor later. You following this?'

" 'Geez, Eddie, good to see ya,' says the captain. 'And, listen,
thanks for all this valuable information, but the fact is, what we
got here is a body with a bad tooth and a bullet from your gun in
his brain. So maybe you oughta just relax a while in D.C. Jail
while your lawyer and the shrinks at St. Elizabeths try to
straighten this all out. In the meantime, some folks up in Brooklyn say they'd sure like to talk to you about a guy got stuffed in a
trash can.'

" 'Oh,' says I, 'I can explain that. See, there's this guy up in New
York who got a disability retirement from the force 'cause he's one
serious head case, who they got on more psychotropic drugs than
you can count on both hands. He'll explain everything. 'Course,
maybe he won't, 'cause maybe he can't, 'cause maybe I really can't
say anything about him in the first place, 'cause the guy was doing
me a favor, see, and, as weird as he might be, I kinda liked him
and figure it's not up to me to bring any more shit down on his seriously bent brain. So, anyway, you know, just trust me on this. I
didn't kill the man in the trash can.'

" 'So, Eddie,' says the captain as they're putting on the cuffs and
hauling me off for an extended mental observation, 'how's the
family?' Which, by the way, is a question I can't answer, because
who knows what this Bolles character—or whatever the fuck his
name is—what he's got in mind. And who do I go to to make sure
no one touches my family? The Government Printing Office?"

Jimmy smiled. "That's what I like about you, Eddie, you've always had such faith in the good intentions of your fellow man."

"You ever been disappointed underestimating your friends in
the department?"

"Shit!" Jimmy stood up, and started pacing back and forth.
"Man, I am telling you. This shit is way out of our league."

"I've been told that before. So have you, for that matter. But we
haven't done so bad."

Jimmy stopped, his back to Eddie, his hands planted firmly on
his hips. "Goddamn it!" he muttered to himself. He turned back
quickly. "So all right. What do we do now?"

"*We* don't do anything."

"What do you mean?"

"I should never have let you get in this far. You've done more than anyone could've asked, and you know I appreciate it."

"You can't handle this alone."

"Maybe not. Maybe I'll come asking for another favor, and the same time tell you you're a damn fool if you do it, but for now there's nothing to do but what I can do on my own."

A long silence followed before Jimmy asked with a shake of his head, "You're really gonna do this, aren't you? You're gonna go looking for this woman."

"You see, that proves my point. We've been spending far too much time together. You're starting to read my mind."

"You're crazy."

"I've been told that before, too."

"You do understand, don't you, that she's one of *them*. And if they can't find her, what in hell makes you think you can?"

"Luck?"

"Oh, yeah, good choice. You 'n' luck have really been on a roll lately."

"I don't know, I figure a man's only due so much bad luck. Maybe it's time for things to turn around."

Jimmy chuckled. "Yeah, right. Well, like you say, maybe pigs have wings."

PART

FOUR

25.

From the southern tip of the island the small ferry could be seen creeping eastward toward the mainland, trailing a shallow wake and a gaggle of gulls gliding above the fantail begging for handouts that were not to come. High season was months away, and, like the few local islanders who rode the ferry to their second-shift jobs, the gulls would have to wait for the coming of the tourists before their meals came easily.

Late afternoon lowered toward evening, and at The Lost Dog Café, a bar and sometimes restaurant—at least on those days when Mirandella showed up sober and in the mood to cook—an already slow day had almost come to a halt. The old man who ran errands and swept the floors and mucked out the restroom sat on a narrow strip of beach in front of the bar, the plastic webbing of his chair sagging under his weight and resting on the sand. His head was bowed, and a tattered straw hat was pulled low over his eyes. A few feet away, a giant blue heron stood as still as the old man sat, and, like the old man, kept its eyes fixed on the fishing line reaching out in the water. Together they waited, as they did every day, for a fish to bite or a stray tourist to pay them a dollar or two to take their picture. Season after season, year after year, they worked this beach for what little it had to offer.

Earl Barkin, The Lost Dog's proprietor, stood nearly motionless himself, leaning over the bar and tallying figures from tattered slips of paper. One hand worked the stub of a pencil, while the other scratched idly at the thick gray stubble of his three-day beard. Empty beer glasses crusted with old foam gone dry sat on the bar, where customers had sat earlier waiting for the ferry. Somewhere in the background, a radio crackled with bits of music and bits of static, which Earl ignored as easily as he ignored the young couple sitting at the corner table made stable by several cardboard coasters, a young man with wet-combed hair and a black T-shirt reading "Hard Rock Café," and his bone-thin companion in jeans and a tight top that smelled of the fish she had spent the day cleaning. His only other customers, a middle-aged man and a younger woman sitting two stools apart at the open end of the bar, both stared at their drinks or at the beach or the disappearing ferry with equal indifference. Once, maybe twice, they had eyed one another cautiously, as if each might be wondering whether the other was up to the effort or even worthy of conversation.

Earl, too, had eyed the man cautiously, as he did all strangers, but over the past week the man had come close to establishing himself as someone Earl could ignore with comfort. He was a quiet man who spoke when spoken to but never asked any questions or forced unwanted conversation, a man who left a decent tip and went about his business without the need to know yours. He seemed to Earl to be someone who in time might fit in, but who in time would be gone, probably sooner than later. He didn't have that lost look.

The woman, of course, was used to being ignored, and seemed to prefer it that way. She was a regular, so regular as to be someone Earl might call a friend, if anyone were to inquire, which no one would, at least not on this end of the island. On this end of the island, down around the ferry ramp and repair yards and the commercial-fishing docks, folks didn't much cotton to questions about one another. On this end of the island, people understood that anyone asking too many questions most likely didn't deserve to know the answers.

And so Earl ignored her as well, as he did most all of his customers. They were adults, after all. They knew how to ask for whatever they needed, and if they did not, well, they didn't belong here in the first place. They belonged on the north end of the island, where the restaurants and bars were judged by how closely they matched the glossy images found in *Travel & Leisure,* where exotic ferns and flowers were imported from the mainland and waiters volunteered their names and chipper smiles and chipper talk about hometowns and careers and when, if ever, the island was going to get cable. Besides, Earl was too busy with his calculations: mathematics, even at its most elementary level, required his undivided attention, and even with that it was an effort.

Earl was close to figuring out that, if he took the chance that his generator would make it through one more season, if he managed to put the bank and his lawyer off for at least one more month, maybe even two, then he might just have enough cash to pull off this one last deal. Actually, now that he thought about it, his lawyer could wait till Hell froze over; unless of course the grand jury actually handed down an indictment before he could get delivery and collect on the resale. It wouldn't be a big deal, he thought, but, then, it didn't have to be. He only needed enough to get him out from under those first-priority debts, out from under those debts no lawyers or courts were needed to enforce. And if Raoul was being straight with him, there should be enough left over for him to buy that used Hinkley he had long had his eye on. Earl needed a fresh start. Some place down south. Turks and Caicos, maybe. Earl needed to move on.

"Excuse me?"

Earl turned toward the open end of the bar, where the stranger gestured for another drink and one for the woman sitting two stools away. Earl nodded. "Yeah, in a second," he said, and turned back to his figures. He could walk away from the bar. That was no problem. He probably owed more on it than the place was worth. The pickup and the runabout he'd leave for Mirandella and the old man to fight over. Once he paid off the folks in Miami, the rest would be easy. Screw the IRS. A plane ticket to Key West, pay cash for the Hinkley, and he was gone. Maybe not Turks and Caicos, maybe the Bay Islands, off Honduras. Just this one deal and it'd all be behind him. Easy street. He hoped Raoul wasn't bullshitting him.

"Yo, Earl," he heard his regular call, and he turned to see her smile at the stranger and say, "Earl sometimes requires a less genteel approach."

"Awright, awright," Earl said and began fixing a double bourbon with just a splash of soda, and a gin and tonic with two limes.

Just this one deal, Earl thought. That's all it'll take.

He set the bourbon down in front of the stranger and the gin in front of his regular. "So," said Earl, setting his arms down on the bar and leaning close to the woman with a smile, "where's your friend? I thought you were gonna put us together one of these nights."

"That's right, Earl, you keep on dreaming. That's what you do best." She turned to the stranger. "Earl's got a thing for my girlfriend. His only problem is that she happens to have good taste."

"Haw!" Earl laughed and turned to the stranger. "Don't listen to her," he said, "she's a hard case. One of these artist types, ya know?" He offered his hand. "Name's Earl, Earl Barkin."

"Eddie," the stranger said, shaking Earl's hand. "Nice to meet ja."

"And you know Marta?"

"Well," said Eddie, "we haven't been formally introduced." He extended his hand to the woman. "Marta, was it?"

She nodded and shook his hand. "Nice to meet you, Eddie."

"My pleasure, Marta. My pleasure."

26.

Eddie Nickles hesitated at the screen door and took a deep breath. "Well, here goes," he muttered to himself. He tapped lightly on the door frame and took one step back. He heard her bare feet hurrying down the hall. Then, through the screen, he saw her pause a moment before cracking the door open. Helen squinted at him, then offered a polite, if somewhat hesitant smile. "Oh . . . hi," she said, then paused again. "Ah, listen, Marta's not here. She's down at the gallery, or at least I think that's where she went."

Eddie took another step back and leaned against the porch railing. He affected as shy and innocent a pose as possible, stuffing his large, beefy hands in his pockets and looking down at the toe of one sneaker rubbing smooth the splintered edge of one deck plank. "Actually, I kinda wanted to talk to you."

"Me?" Helen stepped out onto the porch, but stayed by the screen door and kept one hand on its handle. Skepticism filled her expression.

Eddie kept his distance. "Yeah, well, look. I don't wanna step out of line here. Really. And I don't want to invite myself in or anything. I saw this little sandwich shop or whatever down by the beach there. I thought maybe if I could buy you a cup of coffee or something?"

"What's this about?"

"Well, I'm a little embarrassed, you know. But I thought maybe if you had a few minutes I might talk to you, you know, about this thing with Marta."

Helen frowned quizzically. "Thing? What thing?"

"Ah, well, yeah, you know, maybe I am outta line here. Look, if you're busy or somethin', I understand. I don't want to bother you."

Helen let the screen door close and took a step closer. "Well," she said, "you've certainly got my curiosity up. I wasn't aware there was a thing between you and Marta."

"I'm sorry, I'm feeling kinda stupid here. Maybe I oughta just forget it, you know?"

Helen smiled a genuine smile. "No, that's all right. Actually, I could use a cup of coffee. C'mon in while I throw on a clean shirt and get my sneakers."

"Nah, that's all right. If you don't mind, I'll just wait out here."

"Okay, whatever, I'll just be a minute."

Ten minutes later and a block away, they were seated on the open patio of the Ruptured Duck, a small and rather seedy restaurant overlooking the Gulf of Mexico. Helen kept her eyes on Eddie while she stirred milk and sugar into her coffee, then took a bite of her Danish. She smiled again. "So, Eddie. What about this *thing* between you and Marta?"

Eddie took a long swallow of his black coffee, then sat forward. "Look, I'm sorry I had to lie to you, but the fact is, it's not about Marta. There is no thing. It's about you."

Helen sat back, and the smile left her face. She looked around and began to move as if to leave.

"Wait," he said. "Before you jump up and go, just listen to me. First of all, last night, when you came down to the bar and had a drink with us—"

"I don't think I want to hear any more of this," she said, and again started to push her chair back.

"Mrs. Grehm, I think you not only want to hear this, you need to hear this."

She stopped, and her expression turned instantly cold and stiff. Eddie reached into his pocket and took out the ATM and credit cards he had recovered from LeRoi and laid them one by one on the table. Her breathing turned quick and audible.

"That's right, these are your cards. I know who you are. Your name's not Helen Parlan, or whatever alias you're using today. You're Helen Grehm, and before you start to panic, just listen. I'm here alone. I'm not carrying any weapons. No one else besides you and your friend Marta knows I'm here. I don't work for your old bosses—or anyone else, for that matter. I am here on my own. But the point is this, if I could find you—and let me tell you, it wasn't all that hard—eventually so can whoever else you got out there searching. And you gotta ask yourself one question. If I was your enemy, if I was one of that pack you got after your hide, don't you think I could've just snatched you up without going through all the charades?"

Helen began to shake as if chilled despite the bright sun and eighty-degree temperature. "Who are you?"

"Like I told you all last night, my name's Eddie Nickles. I'm a retired cop from D.C. Twenty-five years on the force. Nineteen in Homicide. That's who I am and that's all I am."

"Bullshit."

"Okay, you're right, there's more, but it's not what you're thinking."

"You have no idea what I'm thinking."

"I've got a notion."

"Who hired you?"

"Like I said, no one. Look, it's a long story."

"And, like I said, I don't think I want to hear it."

"I think you're wrong. I think you do want to hear it. More important, I think you need to hear it."

"Why?"

"Simple. Your name is Helen Scott Grehm. You are or were an agent, or at least worked for something called the Special Projects Directorate. Your deceased husband, God rest his soul, was murdered apparently because he got squeezed between some ex-KGB types and, I suspect, your people. Now, as far as I can tell, the black hats and the white hats—and let me tell ya, it's hard for me to tell the difference between the two—are all out looking for you because they've all figured out, first, that it wasn't you that got shot in the house on Q Place, and, second, besides whatever might be on the magnetic strips of these credit cards, you're in posses-sion of information that's making them all very nervous. Lady, you need a friend."

"And that's you, I suppose?"

"Just listen to what I have to say and make up your own mind."

Helen wrapped her arms around herself, still shaking. She took a long moment staring straight out to the water. Without looking back at him, she asked, "Tell me something. Why the little school-boy act? Why bring me down here? Why not back at the house?"

Eddie shrugged. "Well, to tell you the truth, you people make me nervous as hell. I've been burned myself. You probably noticed the limp?" She looked at him but showed no reaction. "For all I know, you got exploding coffee cups back there, or a toothbrush that converts to an M-16. I just thought it'd be safer out here in the open."

She didn't respond at all. She just sat there staring for several moments, then took a deep breath. "So. Eddie Nickles. Retired homicide cop from D.C. What is it you think I ought to hear?" She shook her head and looked away before he could answer. "That's a great act you got there, Eddie. The hesitant suitor. The little shrugs of the shoulders and the shuffling feet and the averted eyes. The shy schoolboy stammer. It's a killer. Does it always work with the ladies?"

"I dunno, never tried it before."

She again shook her head. "Yeah, right. Well, whatever, keep it in the repertoire. Don't change a thing. It's a bit of genius, 'cept for one problem."

"What's that?"

"When you drop it, when you show your true colors? Makes a lady feel like a damn fool. Not a real trust builder, you know?" A quick, violent shake ran through her body.

Eddie nodded. "I'll remember that."

Helen sat up and lifted her chin defiantly. "All right," she said. "You've won this round. Consider me snookered and seduced. So what now? You want to fuck me before you kill me?"

Eddie looked at this woman, who looked away, her dark-brown eyes framed by a fair complexion turned dark, and dark hair turned light by the sun, her thin features accented by a healthy fig-ure. And her hands, there was something about her hands. Long, thin fingers, and the strength of her handshake. And her smile, of which he had seen only hints, as if she smiled rarely, but when she did, she meant it. He could never kill her, but in another time and under other circumstances, he would most certainly consider . . . He shook his head. "No," he said quietly, "I just want you to listen."

It took some time and a second round of coffee and Danish for him, and a gin and tonic for her, for Eddie to explain. He left out little. He started with Arkady Treshkov's approach in the guise of Garland Bolles. He took her through the search for LeRoi and her ATM card, through the firefight in his kitchen, and he told her all about Priscilla, and about his sons and about his divorce. He told her about Brooklyn and his conversation with Viktor Samoilov, but spared her the details of his interrogation techniques. "I didn't kill him," he assured her, but she gave no hint that she either believed or disbelieved him or even cared. Leaving out nothing but their names, he told her about Hans Talpa and about his meeting with the pseudonymous Harold Walmsley of the Government Printing Office, and how he and Jimmy had confirmed through fingerprint analysis that someone other than herself had died in the house on Q Place.

He told her everything he could think of, and not once did she interrupt him, not once did she ask a question or answer his, or offer an opinion or even a gesture. She simply sat there, stone-faced, never taking her eyes off him but once, and for only the briefest of moments at that, when Eddie described how the president of Iberia Trading, a man named Arlis Brecht, had identified what was thought to be her body, and when Eddie asked about Brecht, she didn't answer him.

"That's it," he said finally.

Helen leaned forward and planted her elbows on the table. "Not quite," she said. "How did you find me?"

Eddie shrugged.

"Oh, please," she said. "Don't start running that 'I'm just a good ol' country boy' bullshit."

"No, really, like I told you before, it took some time and leg-work, but it wasn't all that hard. I just went back through whatever public records I could find, which included your marriage license and certificate on file in D.C., and I saw that your friend

Marta and her ex were listed as witnesses. I just figured maybe you'd need a friend, and maybe something that simple was the last thing all these super spooks'd think about. I figured, what the hell, give it a shot."

Helen leaned way back, her head lopping over the back of her chair, her fingers running through her hair, and she let go a laugh. "Hah! Jesus, you're absolutely right. They probably have every phone from Lisbon to the Arctic Circle tapped, doing computer runs on customs forms and entry and exit logs, black-bag jobs on banks and investment houses, and if somebody ever suggested, 'Say, fellas, how about we check out some of her friends,' they'd laugh and call him a fool." She dropped forward and leaned toward Eddie. "But how'd you find Marta?"

"Her ex. He's listed in the phone book."

"As simple as that?"

"As simple as that."

She shook her head, then paused a few moments, again turning her attention to the sea. "So now what?" she asked finally.

"Well, I don't know about you—I mean, what choices you have—but mine are limited."

"And they are?"

"One, use you as a chip with the bad guys, essentially turn you over in exchange for getting them and the outstanding warrants and whatever off my back."

"Not my first choice, obviously. Have you got an alternative?"

"Yeah, actually I do, but it's a bit of a gamble."

"For who?"

"Oh, for me, definitely. For you, I don't know."

"I'm listening."

"Well, somewhere along the way I started developing a theory that maybe you're not a black hat. 'Course, I could be wrong. Like I said before, it's kinda hard to tell the difference with you people. But the point is, from what I've seen and heard, and trying to put things together, I figure you and I, we're both being squeezed, so maybe together, you know, we might be able to do a little squeezing ourselves. You know what I mean?"

She did not answer.

"You know, last night, and sitting here, I've been watching and listening, I think maybe I'm not so far off. Now, just maybe you're snookering me like you thought I snookered you, who knows? But at some point you gotta take chances. So maybe I take a chance on you, and maybe I've got a plan to get us both out from under."

"And that plan is?"

Eddie smiled broadly. "Lady, I'm not *that* stupid. You want to hear the plan, you gotta, like you say, show your colors."

"You show me yours, I'll show you mine?"

"Exactly."

"You do like to keep things simple, don't you?"

"Exactly."

She laughed again. "Jesus, you must be driving them crazy."

Eddie said nothing, and again she ran her fingers through her hair, then clutched two thick locks in her fists and let go a long, low growl. "Errrrraaagh, shit! Okay, okay, okay. So, you're here. Obviously. So, okay, what choice do I have? None, right? So, okay, okay, okay. All right," she said finally, as if in those few seconds of jabber she had evaluated the possibilities, made whatever judgment calls were required, assessed the risks, and weighed the benefits. "What do you want to know?"

"Everything," Eddie answered, and so she told him.

Helen Scott Grehm suspected far more than she knew, but from what knowledge she did possess, he was not surprised that all sides were after her.

She had no idea how she had first come to the attention of "the company," as she called it, "but, looking back now, I certainly fit the profile."

Helen had wandered through life like she had wandered through school, like she had wandered through marriage and jobs and friendships, as if each was a hobby to distract her from the others. "By the time I hit the sixth grade, I think all the teachers and school counselors decided to save themselves a lot of time and just make up a rubber stamp. Every term, every semester, they'd get out that stamp and—WHOP!—there it'd be on the report. 'Helen's very bright and could accomplish great things if only she would learn to concentrate and apply herself.' "

In college she had majored in finance, not because she had any particular interest in the subject, but because it set her apart from the hordes of social apologists who spent the seventies herding into sensitive courses. "You know, the courses with titles like 'The Conflict in Vietnam, A Study in White Male Aggression Against Gay Afro-American Feminism,'" and Eddie laughed.

Fluent in French from her years in Chamonix with her second family, the Allevards, and conversant in German she had learned from her father as if it were their own private language, Helen ignored her advisers' urgings to switch majors. Although doing well enough in her classes, she showed an obvious lack of interest in the world of finance. "They kept pushing me to major in French or German." She laughed. "Anything but finance, apparently, but what was the point? I mean, why bother studying what you already know? For a degree?"

She quit college in the spring of her junior year to marry "an art-slash-philosophy major" who had dropped out the year before, convinced that organized education was a conspiracy against true intellectualism. "I was impressed. Tony could quote chapter and verse from all these philosophers I had never heard of. I'd actually go through his books when he was sleeping, or go to the library just to check out all those quotes he kept spouting. And he'd be right. Word for word. I was really impressed—for a while, anyway. It took me a little time to realize that he didn't have a clue what any of it meant. He just memorized the words, like an idiot savant. Sooner or later it became quite clear that the dominant element of the equation was idiot, and I bailed. It didn't even last six months; then I just left and never came back. I sent him a letter—I was living in Antibes, in the south of France, and waiting tables, and I just sent him a letter. I never saw him again, never heard another word. I don't know, but I assume somehow he managed to get a divorce or whatever."

She stopped a moment, staring at Eddie's curious frown. "Like I say, I fit the company profile."

Then her parents died in an automobile accident along with her younger sister, Janine, who hung on for three months in a coma before finally succumbing. After that, she spent several years traveling back and forth between Chamonix and a series of odd jobs and odd relationships, until she eventually landed a position with Regent's International. "I loved it. I mean, I really loved it. I was making good money with a healthy expense account just to travel around Europe and the Caribbean signing up elegant condos and homes and estates so the rich and restless could have a vacation they could brag about to the folks back home.

"And then, one day, I was approached. It was the president of the company, down from London, and he said how pleased he was with my work and my ability to deal with people and that he had looked into my résumé or whatever and saw that I had some background in finance.

"That's how it started. Just as simple as that. It wasn't long before I was spending most of my time dealing with banks all over Europe, setting up accounts in all sorts of corporate names, making transfers and whatever. Then, about a year later, I was in London, and here comes the president again. This time he asked me to lunch, and he introduced me to Arlis Brecht, and by the time lunch was over I was recruited. I didn't really understand much of what was going on, except that it was made clear that I'd really be working for the government. I mean, it wasn't as if I hadn't already figured out that was what I had been doing all along, but they made it official, you know? And, to tell the truth, I guess I was flattered. I thought it was kind of exciting, just like the movies. James Bond and all that. Plus, they doubled my pay and gave me an expense account they said was limited only by my personal sense of shame and embarrassment. I thought that was terribly clever of them."

"And your husband was part of this? Your second husband, I mean."

"Toddy? Oh, no, well, yes, but . . . it's kinda hard to explain. I didn't meet him until a few years later. He had his own business, but, still, he was part of the network. I never knew exactly how that all worked. We didn't mix business." She stopped, and cocked her head. "After a while we didn't mix much pleasure either, but that's another story."

"So what happened here? I mean, all these codes and accounts you mentioned before?"

She took a deep breath. "Toddy and I had been separated for almost a year. We kept talking about a divorce, but neither of us ever got around to doing anything about it. It wasn't as if we hated one another. We got along quite well, actually, and I was pretty close to his parents. Actually, I miss them more than I do him. Is that a terrible thing to say?"

He didn't answer.

"Anyway," she continued, "the point is, we still talked, we still . . . I don't know . . . *liked* each other. You know what I mean?"

Eddie nodded. "I know."

"So one day I got a call from him. I was in Brussels at the time, running errands, setting up accounts. Business as usual." She cocked her head again, a curious expression coming over her. "You ever heard of a monkey's fist?"

"You mean like the knot?"

"Yes," she said slowly, "exactly." She sat back with a genuine smile. "You surprise me, Eddie Nickles, but you're used to that, aren't you? I mean, people constantly underestimate you, don't they?"

"I grew up on the water. You learn a lot about knots growing up on the water."

She studied him a moment, then shook her head quickly as if dismissing a thought.

"So, anyway, what about the monkey's fist?" Eddie asked.

"Oh, nothing, it's just how Brecht once described what we were doing. I never heard of a monkey's fist, and he showed me. He showed me how to tie one. You know how you take one or two strands and start looping them in and around each other and by the time you're finished you can't tell one from the other or how many there really are or which strand leads where?"

"Yeah."

"That was my job. I took millions of dollars through hundreds of accounts in scores of business names, setting up accounts, transferring them back and forth and in and out, until no one could trace anything that we didn't want traced. That was my job. I mean, I didn't design the system or make any decisions. I was just a courier, if you will, following instructions, one transaction at a time. For me, it was simple."

"So you were in Brussels. . . ."

"Okay, so I was in Brussels, and Toddy called me at my hotel. I don't know how he knew I was there, he just did. He did that kind of thing all the time." She stopped and looked away, and her voice softened a bit. "It was creepy sometimes, how he'd just show up out of the blue, and we'd go through this little charade of ours. I'd never give him the satisfaction of acting surprised or asking him how he knew where I was, and he'd never give me the satisfaction of asking whether I was surprised or telling me how he had found me. We'd just go on as if it was all perfectly natural. It was all very, very strange, like two children playing spy, like it was all some silly game."

Eddie watched her eyes fix on the horizon and her brow wrinkled just a bit, as if she was suddenly confounded by a question never asked before. He waited a moment, and then asked, "And so?"

"What?"

"You were saying?"

"Oh, yes, I'm sorry. Where was I?"

"You were in Brussels, in the hotel, and . . ."

"Yeah, right, okay." She sighed deeply. "So . . . anyway, he called me at the hotel and he told me there was a problem. He said he had been doing a project for the home boys. Toddy loved American slang, and he had taken to calling the people in directorate headquarters 'home boys.' " She stopped again and shook her head. "Jesus, it was. It was just like we were playing some role in a spy movie. It was never real. Not up to then, anyway. And then everything changed. Everything turned too real."

"What do you mean?"

"That night, when he called me, it was as if suddenly it wasn't a game anymore. All of a sudden it sounded, I don't know . . . scary. It sounded real."

"Why, what did he say?"

"He told me he had begun to suspect he was being used by the home boys to ferret out a mole, meaning—"

"I know what it means. Did he say who?"

"No, he didn't. But he did say he was worried about me."

"You? Why?"

"Well, whatever he was doing, he had run across a series of accounts I had set up. He said he thought it was something more than coincidence that the setup for the mole was following my footprints, meaning using accounts that I had established. He also said that Arlis Brecht's footprints were everywhere. It was the only time I ever heard him sound really worried. He always had this cavalier attitude, as if nothing bothered him, nothing worried him. But this time he sounded different. He sounded really worried about me, as if I might get swept up in a witch hunt or whatever."

"Did he know about you and Arlis Brecht?"

"Yes. That was just another one of those things that didn't bother him. He had no idea how disappointing that stiff upper lip was, always the proper English gentlemen, always so civil no matter how much crap was being tossed at him. I wanted him to be bothered. Maybe if it had bothered him more we'd still be together. Maybe not, I don't know." She frowned deeply, then went on. "Anyway, okay, back to business." Another deep breath. "So he said he was going back to Washington. He didn't say why, just that he was going back. And then he said he was sending me a disc for safe keeping. He told me to hold on to it for him, and if anything happened . . . He said that, if anything happened, if I found myself in any trouble, the disc was my security. And then he said something which really made me worry. He said that the last two account numbers and pass codes listed on the disc were for accounts at Barzini's."

"What's Barzini's?"

"It's a trading house in Brussels. Commodities. We had used it almost like a bank for years, washing monies in and out. The great thing about commodities trading is that no one outside the business really has a clue what goes on, and it's remarkably easy to hide transfers of very large sums of money. Anyway, he told me if anything went wrong I should move the monies out of those accounts immediately and hold on to them and the account information as my insurance. I can tell you this was not like Toddy. It scared the hell out of me, but that's all he would say. He said he was going to take care of everything and not to worry and all that crap, but . . . I don't know, somehow I just knew that all of a sudden it wasn't a game anymore, and I got scared."

Eddie let a long silence pass before asking, "Did you ever get the disc?"

"About an hour later." She nodded, then smiled briefly. "Just that quick. A box of chocolates arrived." Her chin dropped, and several sudden tears fell to her cheeks. "My favorites. These special Belgian chocolates with mint-cherry fillings."

Eddie reached into his back pocket and produced a fresh linen handkerchief.

Helen took the handkerchief and wiped her eyes and nose, then smiled weakly. "Mrs. Nickles raised her boy to be a proper gentleman, I see."

"Yeah, well . . ." Eddie stumbled, then asked, "The disc was inside?"

She nodded.

"And then?"

Helen looked away. "And then I made a very big mistake."

"What was that?"

"I went to Arlis Brecht. I was scared. I wasn't thinking. I grabbed the first flight to Lisbon to meet with Arlis and I told him about Toddy's call and . . . God forgive me, I gave him the disc. I made a copy for myself first, and then, I don't know, just because of what Toddy had said, I deleted the Barzini account information and the following codes from the copy I gave Brecht. But I wanted him to look at what was there, to see if there was anything we really should be worried about. I just never thought Brecht was . . . I don't know, what he was."

"And what happened then?"

"I spent all night with him, with Arlis. I sat there watching him working his computer, taking information off the disc, and running all sorts of traces and comparisons. It was way over my head. It took the entire night, and by morning Arlis said he thought he understood what was happening but he needed to run more traces. He said the account codes only took him so far. I didn't tell him about the information I had deleted. I don't know if he suspected that or not, but he said he needed a few days, maybe more, to really figure out what was going on."

She stopped and sat back and again ran her fingers through her hair. "He said it was only a guess at that point, but he thought, if there was a mole operating, it was operating out of headquarters. I said that didn't make sense. I kept asking him, if that were true, how could it possibly be a danger to him or me? I didn't understand, but all he would say was that he needed a few more days. He told me to just stay calm and quiet and he'd work it out."

"Did he?"

"It was almost a week later that I heard that Toddy had been murdered. Just by chance I learned. I was in the airport, getting ready to fly back to Brussels, and someone just happened to leave a copy of the *Washington Times* behind. It was the strangest feeling. I mean, it was as if I was reading about someone else. It couldn't have been Toddy. I mean, the article said I had been killed along with him, and I knew that wasn't true. So maybe . . ." She shook her head.

"So you ran."

"So I ran."

"With the disc?"

"Yes, my copy, the one with the Barzini accounts, and the codes for some other accounts where the money was supposed to go. I raided the accounts and moved the money like Toddy said, and I've been running ever since."

"You think Brecht killed your husband or had him killed?"

"I don't know. I would never have thought him capable of that, but who knows what anybody is capable of, particularly in that business. Like you, Eddie Nickles, does anyone really know what you're capable of?"

"I know."

Each stared at the other for a long moment, until Helen broke the impasse by turning away. "Tell me," Eddie said finally, "what about these ATM and credit cards?"

Helen answered without looking back at him. "I don't know."

"Really?"

"Really," she said, turning to face him, and for the first time she reached over and picked up one of the cards. She looked at it for only a second or two, then dropped it and withdrew her hands as if she had just touched something unholy. "I have a guess, but I really don't know. I mean, you said the autopsy showed Toddy had been drugged before he was killed, right?"

"Right."

"And then suddenly everyone wants to get a hold of the cards?"

"Right."

"It makes sense. He gets drugged and tells them whatever they're looking for is on the cards. You know, on the magnetic strip. You know something about encryption methods, right? You know how much information just one of those strips can carry."

"You think that's what he did?"

"I don't know. Toddy never said much about his trade craft, if you will. But I can tell you he loved the toys and gadgets and codes and all that. He was like a little kid that way. He loved the business because he loved the games and the toys. I always worried that he liked the game too much—like the reality of what he was involved in, the dangers involved, was never part of the equation."

"But why your cards?"

"Look at them. They're all out of date, expired. If somehow they got lost, a thief or whoever picking them up would take a look and figure they were no good and just toss them. You know, it'd just lower the chance of them ending up in the wrong hands." She looked at him curiously. "I'm surprised you haven't already had them decoded. You must know someone who could do that, or someone who knows someone."

"No. The only people I know who might be able to do that are in the bureau, and I can't take that chance right now. What about you?"

"You mean, do I know anybody who could do it?"

"Yeah."

"Yes, but, like you, I'm not sure who I can trust."

"So what now?"

"Well, Eddie Nickles, good old country-boy cop from D.C., you seem to be holding all the cards, you tell me."

"Like I said, I got an idea."

"And now that we've inspected each other's laundry, do I get to hear this idea?"

"You sure you want to?"

"Yes, I think I do. Aside from the fact that I seem to have very few if any choices here, you certainly have piqued my curiosity."

Eddie sat back and raised his hand for another cup of coffee. "You want another?" he asked, pointing at her empty gin and tonic. She shook her head. "Okay, here it is."

It took only a minute or two for Eddie to explain his plan, and Helen sat back and laughed. "You really do like to keep things simple, don't you?"

"You don't think it'll work?"

She shook her head. "God, I don't know. It's so simple it just might work. The idea, anyway. But you do understand, don't you, that pulling off this real simple idea is going to be very complicated?"

"That's why I need you."

"See? There you go again."

"What?"

"Tell me you don't know every woman's a sucker for being *needed*."

"Damn, you are a cynic."

"With good reason, don't you think?"

"So? Whaddaya think, you ready to go to work?"

Helen took a deep breath and released it in a long, slow sigh. "Well, first of all, I think you're going to need a passport."

𝓻

Early the next morning, Eddie Nickles sat on the end of a short bench, leaning to one side, his ear cocked toward the open phone booth from which Helen Scott Grehm had placed a call to a small bank in the small Swiss town of Altdorf. There was some conversation in German, and then, after a pause, the conversation turned to English. "Herr Kessler, yes, it's Helen Gerbling, how are you?" Pleasantries were exchanged and there was talk of her being in Altdorf soon, and perhaps they could have that lunch they had promised one another. Until then, however, she wondered if Herr Kessler might do her one small favor.

Thus, the first step in Eddie Nickles's plan was set in motion. Arlis Brecht, president of Iberia Trading, S.A., and the financial genius behind the Special Projects Directorate, was to be contacted and a meeting arranged.

27.

Should a stranger ever have found himself wandering the interior halls of the Percy T. Unger Foundation—which to anyone's knowledge had never been allowed and never would be—said stranger might well think he had happened upon the main house of a proper New England prep school. The building's floors were out of level and its random-width planking was well worn but well cared for and covered by threadbare Orientals. Between the long runs of walnut wainscot and crown molding hung varnished frames with gilt edging around old portraits of old men in old suits and starched collars. Victorian gas lamps converted to electric sconces provided the halls with barely enough light, and at the end of each hall on each of the building's four levels, a marble-hearthed fireplace with carved wooden mantel centered an oversized room variously used for quiet receptions and quiet meetings, occasional lounging and regular lunching.

On this particular day, however, and at this particular time, a wandering stranger would have seen few such amenities, for most were hidden behind closed doors adorned by thick, raised panels and heavy brass fixtures. More and more the staff, too, were hiding behind closed doors. Fewer and fewer loitered in the halls or lounged in the lounge or lunched in the lunchroom. Less and less did one chat with his neighbor or consult with his cohorts or arrange for a drink or plan for a party or call for tickets, and no one knew quite why. No memoranda had been sent, no policy had been announced, no complaint had been voiced. No, it was more that a slow, viral mood had spread through the building, floor by floor, hall by hall, office by office: a mood that had infected seriatim each and every staff member with an undefined but certain understanding that for reasons unknown those profiles which were lowest were also the safest.

If the cause of the infection was not known or even suspected, certainly its source was. The titular head of the Percy T. Unger Foundation seemed unusually weighed down by the mantle of his responsibilities as chief of the Special Projects Directorate. If anyone were to have said, which no one, of course, did, the onset of the virus would have been pegged sometime between a week and ten days before. More and more, it was noted by all, Philo Machus spent his days sequestered in his office, refusing meetings and ignoring phone calls, barking at anyone who dared to interrupt whatever it was he was doing. And on those very few and very brief occasions on which he was seen hurriedly entering or leaving the offices, he barely acknowledged, if acknowledged at all, those greetings that were offered. What was neither seen nor noted by those outside the closed door of the chief's second-floor office was a small, tidy man pacing a large, disheveled room, a man who was managing on brief snatches of sleep between very long days, and even longer nights. Back and forth he paced, constantly squeezing his hard rubber ball until his forearms ached, keeping a constant watch on only one of his four phones, that phone which never rang but signaled incoming calls by a small red light, the special phone wired to a special scrambler on a special line specially ordered and fitted with a device designed to alert its user of any surreptitious monitoring.

The last few days had been particularly difficult for Philo Machus, for whom the old saw "No news is good news" was particularly inapt. Patience had never been his strength, and what little reserves of it he had were being sorely tested by the sudden silence of his sources. Success—indeed, survival—depended upon information, and information was the one thing he did not have. He had a plan. In fact, he had several. He had plans and contingencies to plans, and alternatives to contingencies to plans. Everything had been thought out, possibilities and probabilities and improbabilities. But not impossibilities. Philo Machus, after all, had been fighting and surviving wars both overt and covert his entire adult life, and to him nothing was impossible. All one needed was the will to win at whatever cost and information. He had the former, he needed the latter.

Machus looked at his watch, calculated the difference in time zones, and was about to leave his office for another and smaller office several miles away, where he could send and receive private messages, when the small red light on his special phone suddenly blinked. Should any enemy within or without the organization have accomplished the improbable and managed to defeat the scrambler-and-monitor-signaling devices, all he or she would have heard was a disappointed Philo Machus complaining about the unavailability of theatre tickets in New York.

"No," the caller said. "We've had no luck at all. We've contacted every friend we know, and the tickets are nowhere to be found."

Philo Machus, however, had one more suggestion.

"You know the producer, don't you?"

"No, not personally," answered the caller.

"But you do know how to get in contact with him."

"Yes, well, I can try."

"Yes, please do. I would certainly appreciate your giving him a call. I very much want to see this show. Whenever a ticket is available. Whatever night, or even a matinee. Would that be all right?"

"I'll do the best I can."

"I won't forget this," said the chief. "I can't tell you how much I have looked forward to this play."

Thus the conversation ended, and thus the first contingency action to Plan B was set in motion. Arkady Sergeevich Treshkov, former chief of the KGB's West European Operations, turned entrepreneur, was to be contacted and a meeting arranged.

r

Miss Wendy Berksmere sat up on the edge of the bed, rubbing her eyes and letting the phone ring several more times to see just how persistent the caller might be. On the sixth ring, she picked up the receiver.

"Sorry to bother you this late," said the caller, "but I think I have something you need to hear."

"You think?"

"I know."

"When?"

"Now."

"Where?"

"Wherever."

"It's that important?"

"It's more than that important."

"The bookstore?"

"The same one as before?"

"Yes."

"All right."

"When?"

"It'll take me about a half-hour to get there."

"It'll take me a bit longer. Have to put on my face, you know."

"Forget the face, put on your gloves. It's getting cold out here."

"Really?"

"Really."

"You'll order some coffee?"

"Cream and sugar?"

"Skim, and just a touch of sugar."

"See you in a bit." The caller hung up the phone.

Wendy Berksmere heard the click but did not put down the receiver. She held it a moment, letting her thoughts collect. She puffed her cheeks, then released her breath in a long slow sigh, hanging up the phone and switching on her lamp. "So," she said, but there was no one there to hear her, "it begins."

It was nearly 4:00 A.M. before Miss Berksmere finished listening to the tape recordings, reviewed the long list of phone and cable traces, and read and reread the surveillance reports. She put down her second cup of coffee and said, "Excuse me, where is the loo?"

"Upstairs on the right," answered the man sometimes known as

Harold Walmsley of the Government Printing Office. "Shall I freshen your coffee?"

"No, I'm fully awake now."

"Yes, I thought this might pique your interest."

She looked to her watch. "Nearly four, what's that in Zurich?"

The man thought a moment. "It's six hours, I think."

"Hmm, ten o'clock. Well, I think Karl's had enough sleep, don't you think?" Miss Berksmere asked, referring to one of Harry's contract agents, a longtime resident of Switzerland's largest city.

"Oh, I think so. Are we going to Plan B?"

"Yes, it's time," said Miss Berksmere. "Give Karl a call while I freshen up. I won't be but a moment."

It took several hours for Karl to get the message and return Harry's call. It was just about the time when Philo Machus was returning to his office to start a new day that Karl was receiving his instructions directly from Miss Berksmere.

"No, no," she cautioned, "it's important that you make the approach yourself. He needs to know we are serious, that this is not just a feeler. . . .

"Yes, as soon as possible . . .

"No, our meeting has to be face to face. And alone. Just him and me."

Thus Plan B was set in motion. Yury Ivanovich Khavkin, former colonel in the Soviet Special Forces turned black marketeer, was to be contacted and a meeting arranged.

28.

The weather was mild, as it seemed always to be in Montreux, where magnolias and walnuts and almonds and even palm trees flourished, a bit of the Riviera removed to this Edwardian town north of the Alps. To the top floor and the best room of Le Montreux Palace, overlooking Lake Geneva, two meals had been sent and set before two men who for nearly a generation had studied the most intimate details of each other's lives but who were meeting face to face for the very first time. Arkady Sergeevich Treshkov, former head of West European Operations for the KGB, made his priorities abundantly clear. Spread before him were several plates constituting several courses of an opulent meal befitting the opulent setting, no part of which was to be sacrificed to the conversation. From plate to plate his fork moved, spearing a morsel here and a morsel there, and doing so quickly and constantly, as if any delay between any bite was a direct insult to the art of good eating. His companion, however, displayed a far less hearty appetite.

Philo Machus, chief of the Special Projects Directorate, nibbled sparingly of his already spare meal. He did not want sauce, he had argued to the waiter, nor did he want spice. He did not want dressing, he did not want garnish. He wanted his chicken boiled, his salad simple, his coffee black, and he had not retreated when the waiter lifted his chin and furrowed his brow as if there had to have been some misunderstanding. "That's *all!*" Machus had barked, dismissing the waiter. "And call the room before you deliver the meal. Understand?"

"Well?" Machus asked, sitting straight-backed and clench-jawed like an ascetic missionary suffering at the sight of the unconverted.

Treshkov did not look up, concentrated as he was on sopping up just the right amount of curried cream sauce on a small new potato and stuffing it whole in his mouth. "Weh wha?" he barely managed to ask. He chewed twice and swallowed heavily, then reached for his wine.

"What?" Machus inquired.

Treshkov sat back and sighed heavily before taking a long swallow of Piesporter Michelsberg '89. "Not a grand grape, the Mosel, but I rather like it. The Coca-Cola of white wines, one of my more effete associates once remarked, but there's a reason why Coca-Cola is so popular, don't you see?"

"Can we get back to business here?"

Treshkov shook his head. "I am beginning to see where Arlis Brecht got his decided lack of good taste and bad humor. Part of your training, perhaps? Do you people all start your day with a cold shower and a thrashing with thorns?"

Machus did not answer.

"Perspective, my friend. You lack perspective."

"I am not here for perspective or friendship. I have all I need of both."

"Do you, now? How fortunate. I've never before met anyone who could not do with at least one more friend, if not a fresh perspective."

"Friendships require emotion, and emotions interfere with sound judgment, and survival requires the ultimate exercise in sound judgment. Make no mistake, what's at stake here is survival, and *that*, Comrade, is the only perspective relevant to our situation."

"Comrade?" Treshkov chuckled. "Really, Colonel," said Treshkov, more yielding to the habit of using the title under which Machus was carried in their intelligence files than paying respect to his former military rank, "there are no comrades anymore. The union is dissolved and the party is an irrelevance. Accept your grand victory over the evil empire and move on. It's a whole new world, my friend, a whole new world. And it's your world. It's the world you always wanted. Capitalism. No more war of principles, no more battles over theoretic politics and moral objectives, no more slogans appealing to the very large hearts and tiny little brains of the people. It's the real world, the world of competitive advantage, of free trade and economic Darwinism, natural selection and survival of the fittest. It's just business now. Isn't that what you people have always dreamed of? Well, rejoice! Now you have it. Put your old, stale grudges behind you and get on with it. We certainly have."

"I do not need a tutorial in realpolitik, and I certainly do not need your advice. I need only your answer, an answer without condition or equivocation. Are we agreed or not?"

"It is you who have equivocated, Colonel. I have already agreed that we find ourselves suddenly and most curiously bound together by mutual self-interest. I agree that your plan has a delightfully Machiavellian appeal to it, but I have not yet heard the limits of your commitment."

"Meaning what?"

"Meaning, for example, your Mr. Brecht."

"What about him?"

"Precisely my question."

Philo Machus leaned forward and spoke with deliberate force. "Expendable!"

"And Helen Grehm?"

"Expendable."

"You've found her?"

"I think we are close. I should be hearing anytime now."

"May I know where?"

"In your own back yard, actually." Machus smiled. "Not all that far from that condo of yours in Miami."

"Really?"

"Yes, we have confirmed that she passed through Miami customs under an old alias, and we have a lead on some friend of hers not too far away. I have people on the way there now. As I say, we should know soon."

"Well, that is good news, isn't it?"

"Not yet, but hopefully. And what about this Detective Nickles?"

"What about him?" Treshkov asked.

"Are your people looking for him?"

"Yes, but unfortunately he's proven to be more than I expected of him. And your people?"

"Yes, we're looking as well. Like you, we're finding him to be more of a nuisance than we had hoped."

Treshkov paused to spear the last of his potatoes. "Have you thought whether his family might be used to advantage?"

"Only as a last resort. This matter has already raised more dust than any of us can afford. To go after the family would only raise more. Besides, the closer we get to Helen Grehm, the less important Nickles becomes."

"Yes, perhaps, but he remains a problem, don't you think?"

"He does, but right now Helen Grehm is the priority. Once we have her, we will turn our attention to Nickles."

"And when you find him?"

"He will no longer be a problem. Have no doubt, Arkady Sergeevich, I am committed to success at all costs."

Treshkov smiled broadly. "There, you see? You address me as a friend, and so we are. And not so far apart philosophically as we might have thought. Yes, to answer your earlier question, I agree to your plan." Treshkov raised his wineglass in toast, and Philo Machus returned the gesture with his cup.

"To success at all costs," said Treshkov, and Machus nodded, taking a sip of cold coffee.

r

Considerably north and east of Montreux, where the Limmat River emptied into the Zürichsee, the air was considerably colder, and Miss Wendy Berksmere sat huddled in the back seat of a black Audi, while her agent and companion sat stiffly in the front seat nervously drumming his fingertips on the steering wheel.

Neither had spoken for several minutes, and Karl again looked at his watch and checked his cellular phone to assure himself that it was on and functioning. "Patience," said Miss Berksmere, quietly.

"Yes, ma'am."

It was nearly 3:00 A.M., and they had been waiting more than an hour, parked at the darkened end of a narrow street leading onto the Bahnhofplatz. Only an occasional car and an even less occasional pedestrian had passed by, and none had slowed or turned or looked or otherwise given any indication of having noticed the two people seated in the dark and silent car. Miss Berksmere closed the wide collar of her wool coat around her chin. "Would you mind starting the car for a few moments to get some heat?"

The phone rang, and Karl chose to answer it rather than turn on the ignition. "*Oui ... Oui, noir, et vous?. . . Oui, d'accord.*" He hung up and Miss Berksmere asked, "How long?"

"Right away," Karl answered. He started the car and turned on the heat.

Within moments, a dark-green Alfa Romeo passed slowly by, blinked its lights once, and continued on. Karl pulled away from the curb and followed the Alfa out onto the Bahnhofplatz, then around the train station and onto the bridge crossing the Limmat. They turned left at the end of the bridge and traveled some distance before turning right onto a narrow street lined with narrow buildings with wide, full-story-high doors. They were commercial buildings with small signs advertising carpenters and mechanics and metalworkers, and the Alfa Romeo pulled up next to one and turned off its lights. Karl stopped on the opposite side of the street and several car lengths behind. Without a word, he stepped out and walked over to the building's front, where the driver of the Alfa waited. The two men talked for a moment, and then Karl returned to the car. "They're ready," he said.

Miss Berksmere nodded and stepped from the car, to follow Karl into the building. The driver of the Alfa Romeo, a short stocky man in a long leather coat, stood by the door and bowed politely at Miss Berksmere's approach, but said nothing. She answered his bow with a nod, and then followed him and Karl as they led her through a darkened garage and up a barely lit staircase. At the end of a short hall, she entered a spare but not unpleasant office furnished with a desk and a single lamp, several wooden chairs, and a small kitchenette. There, by the stove, stood a man she recognized only by the dozen or more surveillance photographs maintained in directorate files.

"Miss Berksmere," he said.

"Colonel Khavkin," she said.

Neither moved toward the other or offered a hand, and Miss Berksmere turned toward Karl. "Thank you, Karl, I won't be long."

Yury Khavkin nodded to his man, and both attendants left the room.

"Would you like a drink? Some vodka, perhaps?"

"Is that tea you're brewing?" asked Miss Berksmere.

Khavkin smiled, but only slightly. "Yes, would you care for some?"

"Thank you, I would, if you don't mind."

Khavkin went about the business of preparing the tea and putting out several small cakes, while Miss Berksmere took a chair behind the desk and said nothing.

The offerings prepared and set on the desk, Khavkin asked, "Some cream?"

"No, thank you, just a cube of sugar if you will."

Khavkin watched Miss Berksmere place a small sugar cube in her mouth and take a sip of tea. He lifted his cup in toast, and said, "You know our customs."

"As you do ours, I am sure."

He nodded thoughtfully. "Yes, sometimes I wonder if it is such a good thing that we know so much about one another."

"Well, I think tonight it is a good thing. It will save us many hours wasted on games neither of us can afford to play right now."

"You are very direct."

"I think we must be. There is no time to be otherwise. Besides, I think our people have gone over the ground rules here, so there is little reason for pretense."

"You are right, but I must tell you there remain serious concerns among the principals of our organization."

"I can well imagine. Are you authorized to resolve them?"

"Yes. The point is we need guarantees."

"I am afraid that I can't give you guarantees, any more than you can guarantee anything to us. This is a tricky business we are about. Let's not fool ourselves that either one of us is here for any other reason than our own self-interest."

Khavkin smiled, a bit more broadly than before. "Yes, we find ourselves in a most unusual predicament, don't we? All these years playing against one another. And now, how do we assure ourselves that we can trust each other?"

"I'm not sure we can, except to say that we each know that the other wouldn't be here unless we saw some significant advantage in it. Am I right?"

"Yes."

"And so I suspect that neither one of us would want to do anything to throw away such an advantage, correct?"

"Yes, I agree."

"And, after all, we are no longer bothered by the old problems of politics and principle which had us all confused for so long. Am I right?"

Yury Khavkin bowed slightly, his expression breaking into an even broader smile. "Exactly!"

"So?"

"So!" said Khavkin. "Then let us move on. I was told you had evidence, as I am sure you were told I do as well."

She nodded. "I would suggest that, rather than try to examine each of our papers separately, we put them side by side. Make our comparisons together. I don't think it will take us long to find out whether we are following the same tracks."

"Yes, I agree. Shall we start with the last Barzini trades?"

It was not long, no more than twenty minutes, before each sat back and stared at the other.

"One question," Khavkin asked. "If we go forward with this plan of ours, after it is finished, what then?"

"In reference to what?"

"In reference to us, our two organizations. Rest assured that we have no more interest in joining your camp than you do ours. This is merely a temporary expedient to resolve a temporary problem, am I right?"

"You're correct."

"You understand, any hint of an association would greatly compromise our business interests."

"Understood, as I am sure you understand that, should anyone other than my people even learn of this approach, much less our agreement, far more than our business would be at risk." Khavkin nodded. "Once this project is finished," she continued, "we are finished. Agreed?"

"Agreed." Khavkin raised the plate of small cakes and offered one to Miss Berksmere. She shook her head, and he shrugged and took one for himself, and then a sip of tea. "One thing more," he said. "Your people, Philo Machus and Arlis Brecht?"

"Expendable," she said without hesitation.

"And the woman Grehm?"

"I am told we are close to tracking her down."

"And then?"

"Also, and most definitely expendable, as is the police detective, Nickles."

"Yes, I was not aware until recently what a nuisance he had proven to be. I received word from some people in New York. Did you know about that?"

"Samoilov, you mean?"

"Yes."

"Yes, we knew."

Khavkin hesitated, then nodded briefly. "I see. Yes, this man Nickles must be dealt with."

"And Treshkov?" Miss Berksmere asked.

Khavkin smiled a tight smile. " 'Expendable' does not quite capture the full measure of what my friend Arkady Sergeevich faces, but in the end it is the same."

"Then we are agreed?" Miss Berksmere asked, extending her hand.

"We are agreed," said Khavkin, shaking it.

29.

It was a small matter, to be sure; still, it made Eddie Nickles uneasy to be so dependent upon Helen Grehm, and in particular upon her language skills, which left him with nothing but to trust that her various telephone conversations and other talks with those necessary to their plan were being carried out as they had agreed. Totally isolated by his inability to comprehend even the most basic terms of the French and German she most often used with others, could he really be certain that no betrayals had been laid between the lines, that no hidden signals were being sent to the other side?

From many years of hard experience, Eddie Nickles understood all too well that trust had to be earned, and earning it required time. Time, however, was the one thing they did not have. What Eddie Nickles and Helen Grehm had was a simple pledge of allegiance. But it was all they had, and though he resisted drawing the obvious inferences, Eddie knew that Helen Grehm came from a different world, a world where loyalties were at best ephemeral and at worst something easily traded for short-term advantage. And, too, if he were honest with himself, he would have to admit that some measure of his discomfort came from his knowing that,

given the business in which he and Helen Grehm were now involved, he was inadequate without her, and that his inadequacy
was so obvious to her. For reasons he did not care to think about,
Helen Grehm's opinion of him mattered, and he worried that she
knew that as well.

For the moment, however, Eddie Nickles put such thoughts
aside. He strolled down the sun-filled but chilly streets of Interlaken, the tourist capital of Switzerland's Bernese Oberland,
allowing himself some satisfaction in his most recent accomplish-
ment. It was a small victory, perhaps, but a victory all the same.
He had just come from a wurst shop where the young clerk spoke
no English at all, and still he had managed, through hand signals
and pointing and pidgin English, to purchase a carryout order of
food. He wasn't all that certain what he had purchased, but it was
warm in the large paper sack that he carried and its odors made
his mouth water. He was in no hurry, and he stopped by the docks
where the tour boats to Thun sat idle. He took a moment to mar-
vel at the pristine cleanliness of his surroundings and at the
beauty of the mountains hovering high above and all around this
town between two lakes. He continued on and turned down a
footpath to a side street leading over a narrow bridge, at the end
of which sat a small hotel where, on the third floor, Helen Grehm
and Arlis Brecht awaited him. But he wasn't thinking of them.

Eddie was thinking of Megs and imagining how she would have
loved this place. He wondered, too, if she and her insurance-
executive husband might have already traveled here, or to some
place like it. He knew so little about Megs's life over the past few
years. They had talked so rarely, and Priscilla volunteered very little of what she and her mother talked about; and although he was
often tempted, Eddie was always too embarrassed to ask Priscilla
directly, too afraid of what her answers might be, too afraid to
learn that he and his life were no longer any part of their conversation. He stopped again, and again let his eyes take in a scene
quite unlike anything he had ever seen before, and he wondered
why year after year it had never occurred to him to do anything
other than rent that same cottage at the same beach for the same
two weeks every July. What the hell had he been thinking? "God,
she would have loved this place," he whispered to himself.

He entered the lobby, nodded to the desk clerk, who nodded in return, and saw that the small elevator was on another floor. He decided to take the stairs, despite the awkwardness of carrying his cane in one hand and the large bag of wurst and hot potato salad and sauerkraut and green pepper and rolls and a half-dozen bottles of clear fruit soda in the other. He stopped at each of the three landings to rest his leg and catch his breath. He did not want his newfound partners to think that he could not keep up.

They had been at it steadily and without a break for nineteen hours, Arlis Brecht huddled over a bank of three portable computers and a tangle of wires and cables joining them and a portable printer and a telephone he had dismantled and rewired to enable him to do whatever it was he was doing. Helen Grehm alternately paced or worked one of the computers, explaining to Brecht her own code system and the various banks and investment houses and accounts and trades she had worked. Eddie, asking questions far more often than answering them, spent most of his time lounging on one bed trying to make some sense of the endless sheets of computer runs Helen and Arlis Brecht produced.

They had started in London, where Helen began her seduction of Arlis Brecht in an East End pub while Eddie watched from a far corner. Against Helen's arguments to the contrary, Eddie insisted that his presence and part in the scheme not be revealed until Brecht had completed his first test, that of returning to Lisbon, where he was to gather what code and account information he needed and then follow Helen's instructions to their next meeting in Geneva. Over the next two days, before leaving for Geneva themselves, Helen made contact and ultimately met with an electronics and computer expert who was, as Helen put it, "in the trade." He was an old friend of Toddy's, the two having gone through the English public-school system together, and, like Toddy, an independent who applied his skills to the benefit of whoever's check cleared first. Putting aside the shock of learning that Helen was still alive and his reticence about the presence of Eddie Nickles—a hurdle they got over by the man's speaking to Helen only in German, which he insisted she do as well—the man ultimately agreed to lift the coded information from the magnetic strips of her expired credit and ATM cards, which he then deciphered, compiled, and formatted onto computer discs. He refused payment for his services, requiring only that Helen give him a hug and a promise that she would think long and hard about what it was she was up to.

"I promise," was all she said, as she took the computer discs.

They next flew to Geneva, where Helen had arranged to meet Brecht at a rental-car agency. Still unsure whether Brecht could be trusted, Eddie told Helen to leave a note at the agency desk instructing Brecht to pick up the prearranged rental car and drive to a hotel in town. Brecht, as he was directed, found his way to the rental lot and the prearranged Opel; here Eddie first introduced himself, by stepping quickly out of a car driven by Helen, snatching Brecht by the back of his collar, and tossing him and his single carry-on bag into the back seat of their car.

The drive to Interlaken did not take long, but it was long enough for Helen, speaking into the rearview mirror as she drove, to introduce Eddie more formally and to convince Brecht to put aside the insult of his rough treatment and join their plan. It was long enough, too, for Eddie to conclude that Brecht's hesitance and long periods of silence had little to do with any objection to their plan—although he repeatedly questioned the means of executing it—and everything to do with his fear that Helen truly believed he had betrayed her. From that point on, Eddie suspected that every word Brecht spoke, every gesture he made, from lowered chin to averted eyes to agreeing nods to pleading silence, was designed solely to change her mind.

Once settled in the hotel and set up with their locally purchased computers and equipment, Brecht barely moved, rarely stretched or stood or paced or even spoke, unless he asked for or gave out information important to the mission. Hour after hour he worked the computers and modems and phone lines, comparing and analyzing entries from his own banks of information with those taken from the discs both Helen and Eddie had supplied. He worked obsessively, as if each and every step toward completion of the task was a deposit in the bank of Helen's good will. Eddie wondered, however, if that account had not been closed forever. Though there were moments when he questioned whether there wasn't some residuum of affection on her part, at other times he convinced himself that it was simply the well-honed arts of her trade with which Helen kept Brecht's hopes alive.

Eddie tapped on the door, and Helen opened it and, seeing the large paper sack, exclaimed, "My God, what have you done? I thought you were just going out to get some air."

"Lunch."

She looked at her watch. "You realize, of course, it's only nine-thirty in the morning?"

He shrugged. "Breakfast, then . . . So, how's he doing?"

They both looked over at Brecht, whose back was to them, and whose blond hair poked out in all directions from his constant habit of grabbing locks of it in his sweaty hands when confused or frustrated. He could be a handsome man, Eddie thought, tall and thin and neat-featured, with clear blue eyes under narrow, nearly colorless brows. But the apparent effect of too many nights without sleep and too many days without eating had left him drawn and sallow, almost ghostlike.

"All right, I guess," Helen answered, and then suddenly Brecht sat back and both arms shot straight up in the air.

"There it is! Sonofabitch, there it is!" He wheeled around and looked almost shocked to see that Eddie was in the room.

"What?" asked Helen, and Eddie dumped his package on the bed and followed her to Brecht's side.

"There! Look at that," Brecht almost shouted, pointing to the computer screen's listing. "Right there." He looked around anxiously. "Get that last series of deposits," he told her.

"You mean Toddy's?"

"Yes, yes, the Barzini accounts." He poked at a few computer keys, and the printer started to churn out another list of numbers not unlike those that had been strewn in odd piles all over the floor and desk and bed.

Helen recovered a folded sheaf of papers and returned to Brecht's side. Together, they fingered down columns of numbers, until at last they looked at one another and smiled. Helen looked back at Eddie and said, "He's right. He's absolutely right."

"What?" Eddie asked.

Brecht took a deep breath, then stood up and stretched widely, releasing his breath in a long, audible sigh. "Machus."

"What about him?"

Brecht rubbed his scalp vigorously and yawned. "I smell food," he said. "Do we have anything to eat here? Suddenly I'm very hungry."

Helen raised her eyes toward the ceiling, and she whispered, "Thank you, Toddy."

Eddie understood little of what Helen and Brecht tried to explain, not the least because much of what Brecht said was muffled by the wurst and potato salad he began to wolf down, but the long and the short of it was that the profits Trevor Grehm had generated from the scandium trades had been funneled through a series of accounts directly traceable to Arkady Treshkov. To anyone following the tracks without the benefit of the encrypted information on the disc and ATM card, it would appear plain that Treshkov, with the probable if not certain assistance of Arlis Brecht, was double-dealing his own partners. With the encrypted information, however, it became clear that it had not been intended that the trail end there. What had been intended was that the monies would thereafter travel through a labyrinthine set of transactions before ending up in accounts which were under the personal and exclusive control of Philo Machus. It was thus that Machus had planned to exact his revenge for the ultimate insult of Treshkov's using Iberia Trading to wash the profits of his 1991 sale of weapons-grade uranium to North Korea. He intended to steal nearly four million dollars for himself and point every finger of evidence at Treshkov and, inferentially, at Brecht.

"But why you?" Eddie asked.

Brecht shrugged. "I'm sure he suspected that I helped Treshkov back in '91."

"Did you?"

"I helped him wash the money. At the time, I didn't know where it came from."

"And after you found out?"

"I had my own reasons for not blowing the whistle."

"But why Helen?"

Brecht looked at her, but said nothing. Helen answered for him. "Several reasons, I suspect. First, pure circumstance. Since I set up most of these accounts, it was unavoidable that my name came up. Second, I'm small fry and easily sacrificed to the cause. Third, he may have found out Arlis and I were seeing one another, and he started conjuring up all sorts of conspiracies in his mind. That's what people do in this business. Create conspiracies to justify screwing one another." She looked away for a moment and shook her head. "His only mistake was in using Toddy. On its face, it was a nice touch. It would make the connection to me and Arlis look even stronger. Maybe he thought that, even if Toddy put together what was really going on, he'd probably be just as happy exacting his own revenge for my leaving him and taking up with Arlis. A man like Machus can't imagine that two people could end up separating and still not want to hurt one another."

Eddie nodded. "All right, that may explain Machus. But it doesn't explain how this character Treshkov got into the chase, or who else may be out there. The real question is, who's really hunting us down and why?"

Brecht looked at Helen, then answered for her. "Everyone, I suspect. No one knows exactly what Helen has or what she knows, so they all see her as a threat. Treshkov's afraid his double-dealing will be exposed to Khavkin and his crowd. Khavkin's afraid his happy little band of thieves and thugs'll be exposed to the witch hunters in Moscow. Machus is afraid his own thievery will be exposed. The directorate and the Joint Committee are petrified that their very existence will be exposed. The money is meaningless. They'd all pay ten times that amount just to see this go away. The problem is, none of them can ever be assured that it'll go away permanently unless she's eliminated." Brecht stopped and raised his eyebrows at Eddie. "You, too, Detective. Treshkov may be the only one certain that you have the credit cards or whatever, but, for the others, even the possibility that you might have information that could hurt them makes you as much of a target as Helen." He paused to yawn, then shook it off, and suddenly his expression broke into a wide, if quizzical grin. "Which," he said, "now that I give it a little more thought, may be the one reason why this little idea of yours, as nutty as it appears on the surface, just might work. If you really pull it off, you give them a negative incentive. But make no mistake here, the game is survival, and it's survival at all costs, which is why everything has turned so dangerous. If everything goes just exactly as you hope, you win. But if you only come close, you die. Are you really ready for that?"

Eddie ignored the question. "Tell me something, this other woman, this contract agent or whatever, where does she fit in?"

Brecht looked hard at Eddie. "I'm serious, Detective, do you re-

ally have any idea what a long-shot this all is? And the consequences of not pulling it off?"

"I think I do," Eddie answered, "and I also think you worry too
much. Right now we need to put things together. We'll start worrying about the plan not working once we put it together. Now,
this contract agent, what do you know, or what's your guess?"

Brecht looked at Helen and shook his head, as if somehow she
were responsible for this man who just wouldn't listen. He then
turned back to Eddie. "All right. Understand it's just a guess, nothing more, but I suspect Machus probably brought her in to kill
Toddy." He looked at Helen as if to ask her permission to go on.
She said nothing and Brecht continued. "Toddy could sometimes
let his principles get in the way of common sense. If he challenged
Machus, or in some way threatened to expose him, well . . ."

Helen sat down on the edge of the bed and pulled her feet up
under her. "He's right," she said quietly. "Toddy had this odd notion that there was a gentleman's code of honor at work here. He
divided the entire world in two. There were gentlemen and there
were savages, and a gentlemen never let a savage upset the code.
It was that British thing, you know? A million wogs are overrun-
ning your camp but you'll be damned if you'll let that disturb high
tea. Well, he probably thought Machus was disturbing his tea.
Worse, he suspected Machus was threatening me. A gentleman
just wouldn't do such a thing, and it would be just like him to
think the only honorable thing to do would be to challenge
Machus face to face."

Eddie looked to Brecht who shrugged. "And," Brecht said,
"when this other woman died, Machus was just as happy to let everyone think it was Helen while he tried to track her down."

"Did you really believe it was Helen?" Eddie asked. "The body,
I mean?"

Brecht hesitated, then shook his head. "No, I never did." He
turned to Helen. "I knew it wasn't you. Somehow, I thought you
must have heard about Toddy and run. I wanted them to think
you were dead."

"Do you really think Machus believed you?" she asked.

Brecht looked away. "Yes. I don't know. I think so. God, who
knows? Does it really matter anymore?"

A long silence followed before Eddie broke in and said, "All right, next, this guy Harry, the one I told you about with the Government Printing Office ID?"

"Yeah?"

"You think he's Machus's man?"

Brecht paused a moment. "I don't know. But if you want me to take another wild guess, I'd say no."

Eddie turned to Helen, and she shook her head. "I don't think so either."

"Why not?"

Brecht smiled weakly. "It's not Philo's style. If one of his men found you, you'd be dead. Nothing personal, Detective, but you're nothing more than an annoying threat to Machus. No, my guess is that your friend Harry comes from another quarter."

"And what's that?"

Brecht and Helen both stared at one another, and said nearly in unison. "*Miss* Wendy Berksmere."

"I'm almost afraid to ask," said Eddie, "but who's Wendy Berksmere?"

Brecht sat down heavily and started massaging the back of his neck. "Look, it's a long story and I'm beat. Can't we do this later?"

"We're all tired," Eddie said, "but I need to know. Just give me the short version."

And so Brecht did, ending his brief in a low and ominous voice. "She is the dark force, the *éminence grise,* the wicked witch lusting after Dorothy's slippers. I suspect our Miss Berksmere may have smelled a rat. The fact that this Harry guy tracked you down, arranged a meeting, and left you alive means that they're still looking. They've caught a whiff, but that's all they have. What they want is the source of the odor. Wendy Berksmere likes to follow procedure. She'll actually wait to review the evidence before killing you. But make no mistake, that doesn't mean she's any less dangerous. If she decides that you or me or Machus, or anyone else for that matter, is a threat to her or the directorate—which in her mind is the same thing—she will do whatever it takes to eliminate that threat. Do you understand?" Eddie nodded. "Good. Now, like I said, I am tired. I need some sleep. A couple hours at least. You do what you want, but I've had it for now."

They agreed that they would all retire and meet back at Brecht's room in three hours. Eddie followed Helen out to the hall, where he stopped her. "So, what do you think?"

"About what?"

"About Brecht in there. Do I cuff him to the bed or what?"

Helen smiled. "Why, are you worried about my virtue?"

Eddie blushed and looked at her with equal parts annoyance and sudden self-consciousness. "No, my question is whether you have him under control."

She smiled again.

"You listen to me," Eddie grumbled. "He may seem like he's on-board, but I don't think he's convinced yet. Also, consistency doesn't seem to be his strong suit. It would not be a good thing if he suddenly wakes up and flips back to his 'this plan is nuts' mode, and decides to go south while we're sleeping."

"Everything's under control."

"You're sure?"

"Yes, I'm sure. Besides, Sheriff," she said, lowering the register of her voice, "if he tries to make a break for it, I'll fill 'im fulla lead."

"This isn't a joke."

She reached up and gently touched his cheek. "You worry too much. Everything's under control here. Trust me."

ɼ

Eddie awoke slowly, sat upon the edge of his bed, and squinted at his watch, which he could not read. The room was dark, as if storm clouds had rolled over the city. He turned on the bedside lamp. A few minutes before eleven, his watch said, and he wondered that he wasn't more tired after little more than an hour's sleep. The few minutes he took to decide whether to try for some more sleep only wakened him further, so he gave up and squeezed into the tiny bathroom, where he took a quick shower, brushed his teeth, then stepped back in the room to put on fresh but luggage-rumpled clothes. A strange duck, this Brecht, he thought over and over, trying to put together in his mind how a woman like Helen had ever gotten involved with him. She, too, was an odd one, the pendulum of his emotions constantly swinging between thoughts that everything was indeed "under control," as she had put it, and worry that she was playing him just as she seemed to be playing Brecht. Just the way she had touched his cheek. Was it the touch or the fact that he could still feel it that bothered him?

He began to feel, too, the pangs of serious hunger, and he wondered why he had not eaten the wurst and potato salad he had gone to so much trouble to buy. He wondered if there was any left over and how it might taste cold. He again looked at his watch, and it suddenly struck him. Nine-thirty? Was she talking local time? She must have been. It was clearly morning when he went to the wurst shop. He looked again at his watch and sudden and serious concern swept over him. Eleven-twenty. What was the time difference? Six hours? He rushed to the window and looked out. There were no storm clouds, it was simply dark. It was five-twenty in the evening. He had been asleep nearly seven hours. Those damn pain pills! He started to pace the room, his concern deepening with his thoughts. They were supposed to meet four hours ago. Why had they let him sleep through? A string of worst-case scenarios began scrolling through his mind, and he scrambled about the room searching the pockets of the pants and shirt and coat he had worn earlier for the spare key to Brecht's room, where all the computer work had been done. He found it finally, on the bedside table, and had started for the door when he saw a note that had been slipped under it.

"E, Couldn't bear to interrupt your beauty sleep, but we're starving. We'll be at the Barenstube, 2 blks south on Bernastrasse. In the small room behind the fireplace. It's almost 4:30 now. H."

Calm down, he thought, everything's under control.

Fifteen minutes later, Eddie found them sitting at a table in one corner of the restaurant, sipping hot mulled wine and nibbling from a large plate of hot hors d'oeuvres.

Helen looked up and smiled. "Feeling better?"

"You should've woke me. It's those pain pills, you know, for my leg."

Helen cocked her head. "You didn't think we skipped, did you?"

"Nah," Eddie said quickly, then looked at Helen. "Well, for a minute there I wondered. It took a few minutes before I saw your note."

"Sorry if you panicked," Helen said, "I should have woke you up. I guess trust is kinda in short supply these days."

Arlis Brecht sat still and silent, staring at his pewter mug. Eddie looked at him, and then back at Helen, and frowned. "So, where are we?"

Helen looked at Brecht, who looked back at her without expression. "We've been talking. We'd suggest that we all have a nice dinner, and then go."

"You mean leave town? Tonight?"

"Yes, tonight," said Brecht. "We're finished here. Everything we need is already in the car. We left our bags and clothes behind. If anyone checks, hopefully they'll think we're coming back. It'll give us a few more hours."

"A few more hours for what?"

"Who knows? But, with all the calls we've made, we have to consider the possibility that someone out there has picked up the trace. We have to stay ahead of that."

"You want me to go back and get my stuff?"

"You have anything you absolutely can't do without?"

"Nothing that can't be replaced."

"You have your passport with you?"

"Yes."

"And Helen's note?"

Helen screwed up her mouth with impatience. "Arlis thinks it was poor trade craft to leave you that note."

"We shouldn't have left you there sleeping in the first place," Brecht said.

"You're right," Eddie said, nodding at Arlis, and reaching into his jacket pocket to produce the note.

"Then we'll just leave from here," Helen said, brushing aside their sudden alliance. "Whatever you need we'll buy, okay?"

"Okay, but where now? What's the plan?"

"Your plan, Detective," Brecht said. "We're just the facilitators here."

He looked at Brecht. "Are you sure you're okay with that?"

Brecht sat up and nodded. "Yes, I am. If we can pull it off."

"You sound like you think that's a mighty big if."

"It is, trust me," said Brecht. "We're taking a big gamble based on pure guesswork."

"Meaning?"

"Alliances," said Helen. "If the wrong people decide to join forces, we're in serious trouble. If not . . . maybe, just maybe we'll all walk away alive."

"This guesswork?"

"Yes?"

"I mean, we're talking about educated guesswork, right?"

Brecht and Helen looked at each other. "We've been trying to figure that out ourselves," Helen said. "The bottom line is that we're counting on everyone biting off on their own self-interests."

Eddie chuckled. "From what I've seen, I expect that's a safe bet."

"Maybe, Detective. Then again, maybe not."

Eddie looked at Brecht, curious at the man's insistence upon keeping up the formality that set a distance between them.

"So tell me, Arlis," addressing him by his first name for the first time, "what's your guess?"

Brecht sat back and took a deep breath. "I don't have a guess. The basics are simple. First, there are no true loyalties here, at least not on any personal level. Treshkov and Khavkin are both pure pragmatists. If either one of them sees a clear advantage in doing so, he wouldn't hesitate to cut the other's throat. Otherwise, they're thick as fleas. Machus is a tough call. He's a firm believer that once an enemy always an enemy. It's hard for me to imagine his lining up with some old Sovs, particularly Treshkov. But having a gun at his head certainly might give him a whole new perspective. Berksmere? I don't know. We can't be sure she's even a player.

"My point is this. If these people start forming alliances with one another, if they even start talking to one another, we're probably dead. If not, it might just work."

"Who's the most dangerous here?" Eddie asked. "The biggest threat?"

Brecht leaned forward and spoke quietly. "You haven't been listening, Detective. I keep trying to tell you. They're all the same. There is no degree of danger, no partial victories, no draws on the horizon. We either win big or we lose big. That's it!"

Eddie sat back and pursed his lips. "Well," he said after a moment, "I feel much better now."

"Now, let me ask you something," said Brecht. "Are you sure you can pull off your end back home? I mean, if not, we're all wasting a hell of a lot of time that might be better spent looking for a hole to hide in."

Eddie cocked his head and scratched one ear. "Well, there's no way to know until we try."

"Well," said Brecht, lifting his mug of wine, "now that we've managed to instill so much confidence in one another, let's order. I always swore that I wouldn't die hungry."

Helen leaned forward. "So, Eddie Nickles, you all rested and refreshed?"

Eddie stared at Arlis Brecht for a long moment, then turned to Helen. "Sure, but where are we headed?"

"We're headed home, wherever that turns out to be. It's time to make the phone calls, but not from here. We have to stay ahead of the traces."

"Fine," said Eddie as Brecht signaled for a waitress. "But one more thing. We got time for me to pick up some souvenirs? You know, for the family?"

Helen smiled and turned to Brecht. "You see, Arlis? What did I tell you?"

30.

One by one the calls went out, and one by one the calls came in, from different people to different phones at different locations. Helen Grehm had been found, and the bidding for her hide began. Day after day, from country to country, from town to town, from offices to restaurants, from restaurants to motels, from motels to street-corner phone booths, offers and counteroffers passed back and forth. Hints were dropped and warnings were issued and threats were implied. Questions were asked while answers were avoided and truths were denied. Conditions were sent and deals were struck and meetings were arranged to seal the fate of Helen Grehm, who by then had been raised in the collective suspicion to the rank of keystone in the arch of survival.

Eight-fifteen and the night was cold, even for late November. Eddie Nickles sat behind the wheel of his rental car idling at the edge of a gas station in Anacostia, that far-removed and forgotten colony in Southeast Washington, D.C. He turned to Jimmy Legget, who sat in the passenger's seat staring back with an expression both curious and concerned. "You oughta see it, man," Eddie said, breaking an awkward silence that had fallen between them. "It's like something off a postcard. You know what I mean?

Everywhere you look the streets are clean. And not just the streets, I mean everything. It's like the whole country was expecting their in-laws for dinner."

Jimmy chuckled. "Yes, I know."

"You've been there? To Switzerland?"

"Yeah. Kitty and I went skiing a few years ago."

"No kidding? You never told me that."

Jimmy shrugged.

"Skiing, huh? When'd you start skiing?"

"Long time ago. When I was in college."

"No kidding? I never knew that." Eddie paused, wondering just how much he really knew about Jimmy's life beyond the badge. "Man, aren't those mountains something?"

"Uh huh."

"Look, I got a couple of sweaters for you and Kitty. The big thick kind, you know? With these collars that come way up under your chin?"

"Hey, man, that's nice. You didn't need to do that."

"Yeah, but you oughta see these sweaters. I mean, these are really something. I hope they fit. I hadda sort of guess at the sizes. 'Course, I didn't pick out the colors. Helen did that. She just laughed at the ones I picked out, so I let her choose. I hope you like 'em. I got 'em back at the hotel, y'know, where I'm staying."

Jimmy shook his head. "Like I say, I appreciate it, but the question still on the table is what the hell are you up to?"

Eddie looked away. "Yeah, well, you know, hard to say. Guess what I'm doing is playing for all the marbles."

"Meaning?"

"Meaning I don't think it's a good idea your getting involved beyond this one little favor." Eddie turned back and cocked his head toward the portable police radio and stack of blank fingerprint cards which Jimmy had placed on the seat between them. "You're sure nothing can be traced back to you?"

"I'm sure. What I'm not sure of is you."

"Whaddaya mean?"

"You got that look."

"How so?"

"I don't know," Jimmy said, "like you're worried. Like you're not sure how close to the edge you are. And your looking like you're not too sure how things are gonna go makes me want to ask a lotta questions."

Eddie looked over and scratched at his chin a moment. "It's not like I'm not sure, it's just that it's never been about me before. It was never personal, you know?"

"Are you over the edge?"

"Man, six months ago I could've answered that. Right now I don't know where the edge is. It's like you were saying before, we're playing by a different set of rules. All I'm doing is trying to end it once and for all."

"You trust this woman?"

Again, Eddie looked away. "Yeah. Doesn't mean I haven't been careful and tried to cover myself, but, yeah, I think I do."

"You think?"

He turned back and smiled at Jimmy. "Yeah, I think."

"You sure you don't want a second opinion on whatever it is you're about to step into?"

"Too late. It's happening as we speak. Which means you gotta go."

"You're sure you don't need me?"

"I'm sure."

Jimmy didn't move.

"Okay," Eddie said, "so get the hell outta here, and don't look back. Understand? I'll call you when it's over."

"When's that gonna be?"

"Tonight, I hope, but don't expect to hear for a few days, maybe more, after I see how it goes and I get to where I'm going. Okay?"

Jimmy reached out and shook Eddie's hand. "Keep your cool, man, like the old days."

Eddie nodded. "Sorry I forgot your sweaters at the hotel."

Jimmy tightened his grip. "Later, when it's over. You come to the house, and we'll have a few drinks and a home-cooked meal, and I'll tell you all the lies about how I conquered the Alps and looked damn good doing it. Okay?"

"Okay." Eddie hesitated a second before releasing Jimmy's hand. "So, okay, get the hell outta here."

Jimmy stepped out of the car, then looked back. "Stay cool," he repeated.

Nine o'clock, exactly. Eddie could sense the nerves in his stomach and feel the muscles in his chest tightening around his lungs and forcing deep breaths that sounded like sighs. The pressure was building in his head until he could almost hear it. It was that school-night feeling, the night before the oral book report was due, that hopeful-dreadful-fanciful feeling that somehow the inevitable was evitable, that somehow time could be stopped, that Miss Greenhalgh wouldn't actually call on him, and he wouldn't have to stand in front of the entire class stumbling through things he didn't understand—not the way he was supposed to understand it. Who cared what it meant? It was just a damn story. Why should he stay up all night just so Miss Greenhalgh could embarrass him again, just so she could watch the red heat of humiliation rise in his face, just so she could stand there listening to the snickering sneak through the class before saying, "Now, now, that isn't nice. What criticism can we offer to help Edward?" Bitch!

But life was inevitable, and he did stay up all night, and he was called upon, and they all snickered. Everyone except Becky. Becky Raines never snickered. She'd just lower her chin and avoid his eyes and turn a little red herself, because she was embarrassed for him. And then, later, in the corner of the schoolyard where he was humming rocks at a rusted fencepost, Becky came up to him and said she thought he was right, it didn't mean anything, it was just a dumb old story, and he said, "Yeah, well, fuck it. Who cares anyway?" and again she turned red and lowered her chin and her eyes and walked away, and somehow, after that, he never found the nerve to go up to her and say thanks and to tell her he was sorry. He wondered whatever happened to Becky Raines, where she was, and how she turned out. However she turned out, though, he was absolutely certain it was better than this, better than—

"Yo? You listenin' to what I'm sayin'?"

The long black limousine turned west onto Massachusetts Avenue and slowed a bit. Eddie Nickles sat up and turned to Jean St. Jean Toussaint, sometimes known as Johnny Easy, sometimes Johnny Two Cheeks, the man Eddie called T. "What?"

"What I'm askin' is if you're listenin', if you're payin' attention?"

Eddie let his head drop back on the seat and sighed. "No, matter of fact I'm not listenin'. Look, man, we've been yackin' 'bout this for days. How much talkin' you need to do? It'll work or it won't, that's all there is to it."

"You see? That kinda talk what's making me nervous. Like real nervous you know? I mean like this is not your standard business transaction, you know what I'm sayin'?"

"So, T," Eddie said, distracted by other thoughts, "this part of your personal fleet or what?"

T slumped back in the soft, black leather and turned his stare out the smoked-glass window, shaking his head. "Man, you think I'm stupid or somethin'? You think I'd use my own ride for somethin' like this? No, sir. Times like this you call on a friend. You know what I'm sayin'?"

"Indeed I do, T. Indeed I do."

T looked to Eddie again. " 'Sides, with the money you're payin' me, I can afford all sorts of luxuries. Which, by the way, I been meanin' to ask. Like where alla sudden you come up with this kinda cash?"

"Like you, T, I got friends."

"Yeah, man, looks like it. But we're straight, right? I mean, this is business we're doin' here."

"Absolutely. You got your money up front."

"I got half. You remember that. I got half."

"That's right, and when we finish doing what we gotta do, you get the other half."

"Plus expenses."

"Plus expenses."

"And you got it, right?"

Eddie reached into the pocket of his rumpled raincoat and pulled out a key. "Like I told you, the end of the night, we're all still alive, I give you this key and the case it goes to. You know I'm not gonna short-change you."

"So, you got all this cash, why don't you get yourself a decent coat?"

"What? What's wrong with this coat?"

"Man, I seen better on dudes beggin' quarters on the street."

"Yeah, well, it works for me," Eddie said, and T again just shook his head.

They traveled several more blocks before Eddie sat up and said, "Tell him to slow down. That's it. Up there on the right." He pointed to a small restaurant, and T opened the sliding glass window between the driver and passenger compartments. "Slow down, James. It's up there on the right."

"You see the sign?" Eddie asked. "The small sign there? Two Quail?"

James said, "Yeah, I see it. So do I pull up or what?"

Eddie turned to T. "You sure no one can see us in here?"

T answered with an annoyed frown. "Man, you see shit when I picked you up? Why do you think the smoked glass is for? Relax. You're gettin' me jumpy. I never seen you so? . . . so? . . . whatever."

Eddie leaned forward and spoke to James. "No, the man's not there. Go around the block. No! Wait, wait, slow down."

"Man, I'm as slow as I can get without stoppin', you know."

"All right, all right, it makes sense you'd pull up and wait."

"So you want I should—"

"Yeah, yeah, pull up." Eddie turned to T. "No one can see, right?"

T looked at him worriedly. "Muthafucka, what's wrong with you?"

"All right. Okay. Just checking. Okay, so pull up. We'll just wait. Okay, we'll just wait here a few minutes."

T slid the privacy window shut and turned to Eddie. "Man, what's wrong with you? Don't go lettin' James see you losin' your cool. Nothin' worse. Gotta show confidence, you know?"

"Man, don't lecture me. I know what I'm doin'. Just a little nervous about the timing. Got too many balls in the air, you know?"

"Yeah, well, two of those balls is mine, so I don't want no fuckups, 'cause you're gettin' freaked."

"T, you ever see me freaked?"

"Wouldn't be here if I did. All I'm sayin' is you're makin' me nervous. And if I get nervous, then James is gettin' nervous, and if James is gettin' nervous. . . you know what I'm sayin'?"

"That's him!" Eddie said, suddenly. "He just came out. There, on the steps?"

T reached for the privacy window and slid it open. "James," he said quietly. "The dude in the suit, up on the steps there."

"Yeah, I got him," James said.

"Okay," said T. "Make it simple and polite. Just say, 'Excuse me? Are you the gentleman who has an appointment with Mr. Brecht?' And when he says yeah, you say—"

"Yeah, yeah, yeah, fort'een times you tole me. I got it."

James, neatly dressed in a black suit and chauffeur's cap, turned back and smiled at Eddie. "You ready?"

Eddie nodded. "Yeah, James, I'm ready."

"Cool," James said and stepped out.

James was a large man who looked every bit the professional football player he could have been had not a gang fight and a nine-millimeter bullet just above the left kneecap ended his career when he was a sophomore in high school. Now he was every bit the part he was playing, the polite chauffeur who tipped his hat and bowed his head ever so slightly to the target, who returned the gesture with a neat European bow of his own. "Nice touch," Eddie whispered under his breath, as James gestured an offer to carry the man's briefcase; the man shook his head, and James then gestured to the waiting limousine.

Eddie looked to T, who nodded as Eddie slid to the middle of the back seat, away from the door. A moment later, the door was opened and the man ducked to step in, then hesitated. Eddie lunged quickly, grabbing the man's coat and dragging him into the back of the car, shoving his face to the floor, and holding him down by the back of his neck.

James quite deliberately picked the man's briefcase up from the street and tossed it in the car. He then closed the door and, as if he were in no hurry at all, stepped around to the driver's side, got in the car, and drove slowly away.

Eddie released the man's neck. "This is Mr. Bolles," Eddie said to T, "otherwise known as Arkady Treshkov."

T smiled. "Yo, man, what's happ'nin'?"

Treshkov looked up, his small eyes widening, his small mouth gaping.

Eddie planted his fist hard in the middle of Treshkov's face, and Treshkov went out. Trickles of blood began seeping from his nose and upper lip.

"Man," said T, "what the fuck you doin'? That's gonna cost you extra. I don't run no car-cleanin' service, you know? Gonna cost you extra if the man bleeds on this car."

"Sorry, man," said Eddie, flexing the pain from his hand. "It just came over me. Whatever it costs, just give me the bill."

r

Five blocks from the District of Columbia Courthouse, on the edge of Chinatown, Yury Khavkin, as instructed, took the hotel's elevator to the third floor, walked to the middle of the hallway, and knocked twice on the door to room 312. No one answered, and he knocked again. Again, there was no answer.

He stepped back from the door and looked toward the elevator, then turned and looked toward the other end of the hallway, where a bright-red exit sign glowed over a door with a small wire-mesh-reinforced window in its center. He saw nothing.

He took a deep breath, then knocked again. "Brecht?" he asked quietly. He waited a moment more, and when there was no answer, he stepped back and took a compact cellular phone from his pocket.

Suddenly the exit door at the end of the hall opened and Arlis Brecht poked his head out. Khavkin raised his chin in recognition and slipped the phone back into his pocket. Brecht signaled with his hand for Khavkin to come to the end of the hall, where Brecht slipped a key into the door of room 328. "I couldn't be sure you'd come alone," Brecht said when Khavkin joined him.

Khavkin smiled at Brecht. "We have our bargain, Mr. Brecht. You should not distrust everyone."

Brecht shrugged and opened the door. Khavkin stood back to let Brecht enter first and then followed him. "I admire your caution, but—"

Yury Khavkin stopped at the sudden sound of a pistol's hammer being cocked and the cold feel of metal against his right temple. "So," a deep voice came from behind the pistol, "this the right dude?"

"That's him," said Arlis, a bit nervously.

Khavkin did not move, but only stared at Brecht. "You have made a big mistake, Mr. Brecht. A very big mistake."

"Shut the fuck up," came a voice from the open bathroom door to Khavkin's left, a voice accompanied by the display of a second semi-automatic pistol.

Within seconds, Khavkin was handcuffed and hustled into the stairwell behind the exit sign and the door with the wire-mesh window, and all he heard were a series of "okay"s from voices below him, voices signaling that each level of the stairwell leading to the underground garage was clear.

In less than a minute, Yury Ivanovich Khavkin was safely and silently packed away in the trunk of a car making its first turn onto the ramp which led to the street which led to the freeway which led to Anacostia.

❧

Philo Machus had been in the business far too long to leave anything to chance. His agents had been assembled; a few good men, they were, men who were independent and of proven reliability, men of discretion who followed instructions and asked no questions and did not care to know who they would be tracking or why, men with signal locators and tracking devices and phone tracers and wireless communicators the size of a matchbook, men who would disappear the moment the quarry had been captured. The plan had been set, his objective was clear, and all Philo Machus had to do was wait.

Arlis Brecht was anxious. Machus could hear the man's nerves even over the phone. He heard the slower cadence of his speech, as if Brecht's words had been so carefully planned, the subtle drop in the register of Brecht's voice, and the unmistakable quaver of nervousness disguised as a sudden cough. Helen Grehm wanted to stop looking over her shoulder, Brecht had said. She was prepared to turn over whatever information she had, including all codes and account information, in exchange for guarantees that she could simply disappear with her life, and, of course, with the money from the scandium trades, to which she claimed title as reparations for Toddy's murder. But it had to be done on her terms and through Brecht. She would not meet Machus—or anyone else, for that matter—face to face. Brecht was to be her cover and her insurance.

Brecht was angry, he claimed, angry to have been made a fool by her, angry to have been used by Machus to further whatever schemes he had afoot, angry and tired of the whole bloody business, and he wanted out. He wanted to be out of it completely, and he wanted to be out of it forever, and he had his own plan. He would play the middleman, he would facilitate her scheme, but in the end, whenever and wherever the exchange took place, it would be Machus and not him who would make it. He did not care or even want to know what disposition Machus had in mind for Helen Grehm. He wanted nothing more than to be left alone, and assured Machus that he could count on him to do the same.

What a foolish man, thought Machus. Imagine Arlis Brecht thinking he was equipped to play the game. Imagine his thinking he was man enough and mind enough to play for a fool Philo Machus, the man who had made him, the man who had trusted him, the man who had forgiven his sins and his silliness, the man who had covered his back when others wanted to stick the knife deep. And for what? This courier, this messenger woman, this thief, this whore? He, Philo Machus, played by the likes of Brecht to save *her*? It was beyond foolish. He had always known of Brecht's weakness, but for Brecht to throw away his career, his future, to throw away his very life for her? Could there be any greater fool?. . . Well, Trevor Grehm, perhaps. Yes, all of them, the Grehms and Brecht, too, they well deserved their fates.

r

"Where is Brecht, by the way?"

"He ain't here?"

Eddie sat up. "What?"

T looked up from the other end of the table and stopped pouring the apple brandy into his plastic coffee cup. "What's happ'nin'?"

"Brecht didn't come back with you?" Eddie asked.

Elijah Roddy, aka Red Bone, aka Reds, one of the more trusted lieutenants under the command of Jean St. Jean Toussaint, looked suddenly concerned. "No. The man said 'Later,' y'know?"

Eddie's eyes squeezed shut, and his hands clenched into tight fists. "Shit!"

T walked over and sat on the edge of the table in front of Elijah. "What happened?" he asked carefully, his voice quiet and unalarmed.

Elijah shrugged. "You know, after we snatched the man like you said, the Russian guy, the other one, Brecht, you know, after we had the Russian in the trunk, this Brecht says 'Later.' "

"Whaddaya mean he said 'Later'?"

"Like I asked him, y'know, weren't he s'pose to go with us, you know? 'Cause that's what I thought you said. But he says no, y'know, like he'd catch up later. Said somethin' 'bout needin' to go back up to the room, y'know, in the hotel there, and he'd catch up later. So what was I s'pose to do? Like the man's one a y'all, so, you know, what was I s'pose to do?"

"You just left him there?" Eddie asked, standing quickly and beginning to pace. "In the garage? You just left him in the garage?"

"Yeah, well, you know, y'all said not to call 'less it was a 'mergency or whatever, and the man seemed cool about it, you know, like I'm the one got something wrong, and so I said cool and c'mon back here." Elijah looked at T and spread his hands imploringly. "So what was I s'pose to do?"

T turned to Eddie. "So this is a problem?"

"Is this a problem? We're in the middle of the game and the man holding the key to everything skies on us, and you wanna know is this a problem?"

"Yeah, man, like I wanna know is this a problem? What you think? I'm here running my mouth for exercise?"

"It's a problem."

"How bad a problem?"

"I don't know." Eddie sat down again and began massaging his temples with his fingertips.

T stepped close to him and spoke in quiet voice. "Then maybe you oughta find out like how bad a problem."

"Whaddaya suggest?"

"Maybe call the hotel room. Like maybe see if he's still there or whatever."

"I dunno if that's such a good idea."

"Why not?"

"What if something's gone wrong we don't know about? Like what if he changed sides? I call him and he's turned, or maybe the other side has snatched him, or whatever, they'd trace the call, know where we are."

"You mean he don't know already?"

"No, he doesn't know." Eddie stood up suddenly and T backed away. "Like you," Eddie said, "I operate on one part trust, ten parts cover-your-ass, you know what I'm sayin'? That's why he was supposed to come back with your people."

"Yeah, okay, that's cool, but just use your cellular. They can't trace a cellular. I mean, the number, but not where it is."

"I don't have a cellular."

"What?" T asked with obvious alarm. "Whaddaya mean you don't have a cellular?"

"I don't have a cellular phone, that's what I mean."

"Man, what the fuck you mean you don't have a cellular? How can you not have a muthafuckin' blind cellular and 'spect to work like this? So what's this man s'pose to do if there's a problem? Send you smoke signals?"

"For one thing, you use a cellular and everyone from here to Toledo can listen in."

"So whaddaya care if they're listenin'? Long as you don't act the fool and tell 'em where you are, whaddaya care? Man, you use the hard line, them bad boys'll be here before you hang up."

"We're using a cutout. There's a problem, he's suppose to call the woman and the woman calls me here. Can't trace that."

"Yeah, mebbe, long as this lady's cool. But what if she turns, like this Brecht?"

"She's cool."

"Yeah? As cool as this Brecht that just skied on you?"

Eddie paused a long moment to emphasize his point. "She's cool," he said.

"So, you're so sure, then why not do it backwards? Call the lady to call him."

Eddie shook his head. "He was suppose to make the call to Machus from the hotel, then come back with your people." He turned to Elijah Roddy. "The man say anything about making a call?"

"No."

"He make a call anytime while you were up in the room?"

"No. He didn't make no calls."

"Shit!"

"See?" said T. "This is why you need a cellular. Don't matter if they're listenin' long as they don't know where you are. Man, I thought you knew better'n this."

"Give me yours."

"Give you what?"

"Your cellular."

"Yeah, man, I'm gonna give you mine. Throw in my house and car to boot. Maybe I'll give you the winter place in Jamaica and have my ol' lady cook you Thanksgivin' dinner, too. Yeah, I'm gonna give you my cellular."

"Man, we haven't got time for this bullshit. What's the problem?"

"Man, what are you talkin' about, what's the problem? You're tellin' me these folks are all CIA or whatever, got all this fancy shit. They might not be able to track where the call is comin' from, but sure as hell they'll know what number it is, and that number is mine, ya unnerstand? Man, I'da thought you'd known enough to cop a phone that couldn't be traced to you. You tole me I didn't have to worry 'bout no shit like that. You tole me you were covered. No, sir, my phone I use to make my calls to my people 'cause no way my people connected with your folks. No way I use my phone to call those crazy muthafuckas or your side. No, sir!" T glanced over at Elijah, then back to Eddie. "Now, listen to me. We gotta straighten this shit up. My man Elijah, here, he's cool. But I'm tellin' ya, word goes beyond this room this deal beginnin' to look like the Minor Leagues, and we're gonna have a big problem on our hands. You know what I'm sayin'?"

Eddie stepped away from T and again started to pace. "Okay, this is the situation. Nobody but me and your people know where we are. Brecht doesn't know, the lady doesn't know. We made sure everyone knew only their part. That way, something goes wrong, we're covered. The problem, like I said, is that Brecht was supposed to make the call from the hotel and then come back with your man."

"Yeah, so, okay, just so's we're clear," said T. "Even if this Brecht went south on us, he don't know where we are."

"That's right . . . unless we've been set up. Unless Roddy's car was followed."

T turned away and shook his head and spoke in a soft and even cadence. "Mo-ther-fuck-er!" The audible pace of Elijah Roddy's breathing quickened as T turned to him.

"No, man, no way," Roddy said. "We were lookin' the whole time. I don' care who they are or how good they think they are, I'm tellin' you no one followed us. Shit, man, we been tailed by the best. You don't think we'd spot it?"

Eddie met T's stare. "How 'bout a signal locator?"

Roddy stepped forward. "Listen to me, man," he said to Eddie, his voice turning almost mean. "This ain't no bullshit amateur night with the muthafuckin' *po*-lice. You hear what I'm sayin'? I know what I'm doin'. That car was covered the whole time. No one got anywhere near it that weren't s'pose to. Unnerstand? No one! And I'm tellin' ya for real, nobody—and I mean *nobody*—followed us here. 'Sides, think about it. If'n they'da traced us here, our ass'd been gone twenty minutes ago. Am I right?"

"He's got a point," T said.

"Yeah, I guess," said Eddie, who turned to Elijah. "I wasn't try-ing to insult you, man, just trying to figure the possibilities."

"No problem, man, we're cool."

"So, you trust this lady?" T asked.

Eddie stopped and paused a long moment. "Yeah," he said, but with a hint of hesitation.

"So why not call her?"

" 'Cause maybe—"

The phone rang suddenly, and all three men jerked at the sound. It rang again, and T nodded at Eddie. "Go ahead, man."

Eddie picked up the receiver. "Yeah?"

There was a long silence while Eddie held the phone to his ear, and his eyes moved back and forth to meet the stares of his two companions.

"So what does that mean? . . .

"You believe that? . . .

"So what's your take on it?"

Another long silence.

"You're sure? . . .

"When? . . .

"Trust you or him?"

A short silence.

"All right, when?"

Eddie looked at his watch, then looked up at T. "Your people ready?"

"At the garage?"

"Yeah."

T pulled his cellular phone from his pocket and dialed. "Yeah, it's me," he said after a moment. He turned his back and spoke in a mumble. A moment later he turned back to Eddie and said, "They're ready."

"The car still there?"

"The car still there?" T asked whoever was on the other end of his call. He nodded to Eddie. "Yeah, it's still there."

"It's still there," Eddie repeated into his phone, then listened a moment.

"Okay, tell me exactly what he said."

Again Eddie looked at his watch. "Ten minutes?" he asked.

"You're sure about this? . . .

"If you're wrong? . . .

"All right? . . .

"Yeah, you, too."

Eddie hung up.

T held the mouthpiece of his cellular phone to his chest. "So?"

"Brecht made the call."

"So, where is he?"

"She doesn't know, exactly."

"So what's that mean?"

Eddie stared at T for a long moment. "It means he did his part and figured that's all he could do."

"Which means what?"

"Which means we're a go."

Jean St. Jean Toussaint and Elijah Roddy exchanged glances.

"It's my ass, too," Eddie said, "and I say we go."

"You're trustin' this lady?"

"I got no choice, T."

"I do."

Eddie moved over and sat on the edge of the table and spoke quietly. "You're right, T. You got a choice here. No question you've done your part, you've earned your half. You wanna fold your hand, I understand. But I'm askin' you. I'm askin' you to trust me on this. I know it's not right to bring it up like this, but, just the same, I'm askin' you just like you asked me that night on Acker Street. Trust me, man."

T stared at Eddie for a long moment. "You're sure 'bout this?"

Eddie paused, then nodded slowly. "Yeah, I'm sure."

T took a deep breath and lifted his phone to his lips. "Okay, ten, maybe fifteen minutes."

r

It was nearly ten o'clock when Philo Machus stepped into the directorate's communications room. Arlis Brecht's call had come a few minutes before, but Philo Machus was in no hurry. He would set the schedule. He would set the pace. He would take his time and enjoy the thought of Arlis Brecht pacing back and forth at their assigned rendezvous, wondering and worrying whether something had gone wrong, wondering and worrying if he had really pulled it off, if his betrayal had remained his secret, if he had really managed to insure his scalp for the paltry premium of the lives of Helen Grehm and this bothersome cop Nickles. No, Philo Machus would take his time. He would pop in and say hello to the boys in the communications room, chat them up a bit while relishing the vision of Arlis Brecht coming closer and closer to completely unraveling.

The two men on duty looked up from their card game, and froze in mid-play. "Relax, boys," said Machus with a rare smile. "I know it can get pretty boring up here."

"Yes, sir," said one of the men. "Everything's real quiet. Nothing but the standard check-ins all night."

"Well, Friday night, the weekend, and, like they say, no news is good news, right?"

"Yes, sir, I guess so."

"Well, go ahead with your game. I was just about to leave and thought I'd check one more time on our man in Prague."

"Nothing new has come in since this morning. But, like he said, he didn't expect to hear anything himself for at least a few days."

"Right, well, just checking." Philo Machus suddenly realized that he had absolutely nothing to say to these people, and so he smiled and started to back out of the room.

"Good night, sir. Have a good weekend."

"Thanks, you, too."

Yes, everything was as it should be. Quiet. No alerts or inquiries were circulating the networks, no one was reporting unusual movements, no one was expressing concern or curiosity. The end was in sight. There was nothing more to do but alert his men and get on with it.

What a fool Brecht was. What an absolute fool. If only he had controlled his libido as he had controlled his investments. But, thought Machus, Brecht certainly was not the first, nor would he be the last, to toss away his life for a few fleeting moments of carnal pleasure. A shame really, but there it was.

Machus returned to his office, where he made a single phone call. "Yes," he said after exchanging a terse and precoded greeting and reconfirming the location Brecht had set for their rendezvous. "I'm leaving now. Allow ten minutes, then listen for the signal locator. I'll activate when I'm in my car. I should be passing you at Eighteenth and Pennsylvania in no more than fifteen minutes." He then forwarded his calls to the bank of phones, tracers, and recorders in his home, donned his coat, and left the building.

"G'night, Art," he said to the guard at the side door, as he did every night, and Art, as he did every night, touched one finger to the brim of his cap and said, "Yes, sir, have a good one."

Again, as he did every night, Philo Machus took the narrow brick walk to the narrow iron gate, where he entered his code and heard the lock click open. The gate clicked shut behind him, and he started down F Street toward the parking garage where his six-year-old Buick awaited him, as always. Winter was coming, he thought, and he pulled the coat's warm wool collar high against his neck. Behind him he could hear the sounds of college students beginning their Friday-night rituals, and ahead of him were the fading sounds of commercial Washington folding up for the weekend. He walked one block, then turned north and entered a parking garage.

"Where's Roberto?" he asked after the attendant usually on duty up to eleven, the man who invariably parked and retrieved Machus's car for the two-dollar tip Machus considered extravagant but worth the personal and preferential service he always received.

"Roberto? He's trying to start the lady's car downstairs."

Machus glanced at the well-dressed woman standing nearby and shivering. She shook her head and said, "It's taking forever."

"What kind of car you got?" the attendant asked.

In its six-year lifetime, Philo Machus's Buick had not suffered a single scratch or dent, of which he was inordinately proud, and to which he partially attributed the special care and attention the car received at the hands of Roberto. "I'll wait for Roberto," Machus said.

"Okay, man. Whatever."

Machus smiled at the woman, who was still shivering, both with the cold and with apparent impatience. "I'm sorry if I'm holding you up," she said to him. "The fella's been down there almost twenty minutes. I don't know what he's doing."

Machus turned to the attendant and asked, "How 'bout handing me my keys? I know where my car's parked."

The attendant looked skeptical. "You got a ticket?"

Machus did not have a ticket. He never had a ticket. What he had was a special arrangement with Roberto, who gave Machus a special parking rate in exchange for Machus's always paying him in cash. As far as Machus was concerned, whatever Roberto did with the cash he received was strictly between Roberto and his bosses. "Roberto knows me," said Machus. "I'll settle up with him." The attendant remained skeptical. "Look," said Machus, "it's the keys up there on the upper right." He pointed to his special place on the pegboard.

The attendant looked up at the board. "Oh," he said, as if he recognized the special peg of privilege. "Yeah, okay, I gotcha. Roberto's spot, right?"

Machus nodded.

"You want me to get your car? I know where he keeps his special customers."

"No, that's all right, I'll get it myself. I know where it is."

"That's cool," the attendant said, handing Machus his keys.

Several minutes later, a gray, four-door Cadillac came up out of the garage and stopped at the landing next to the attendant. The passenger door's window slid down and a man in a black leather coat reached out and without a word, handed the attendant a set of keys. The attendant took the keys and returned them to the peg of privilege, as the Cadillac drove off.

The well-dressed woman was no longer shivering, and the attendant smiled and said, "Catch you later, Zell."

"Later, Keith," the woman answered, and both left the garage, walking in different directions.

Philo Machus, bound and gagged and stuffed in the trunk of the gray Cadillac, was on his way to Anacostia.

r

Miss Wendy Berksmere turned toward the man sometimes known as Harry Walmsley of the Government Printing Office. "What do you think?" she asked.

Harry squirmed a bit to relieve the stiffness of having sat for more than an hour behind the wheel of the car, waiting for Eddie Nickles to arrive. "I don't know," he said. "He may have spotted the backup."

"You think?"

"Maybe."

"He's got the telephone number?"

"Yes."

"Then why not call?"

"Afraid of a trace. You got to remember, he can't be all that mobile if he's sitting on the woman."

"Maybe we ought to release the backup."

"Ma'am, I don't think that's a good idea."

"I don't want this meeting blown."

"I understand, but I still don't think it's a good idea."

"As I recall," said Miss Berksmere, "your analysis was that he was not 'inherently dangerous.' "

"Neither's a rat unless you corner him."

"Yes, but who's got who cornered here? Seems to me we're playing his game by his rules."

"True," Harry said, "but from his perspective it's been our game and our rules that dragged him into all this in the first place. The past few months have not been happy ones for our Mr. Nickles. And don't forget Brooklyn."

"You really think he killed Samoilov?"

"I don't know, but I don't have any doubt that, if pushed hard enough, he'd be capable of it."

"Well, we can't wait all night."

Harry did not respond, suddenly focusing on a lone man, bundled up in a heavy coat, his head lowered against the cold, his hands in his pockets, and walking toward them. He did not miss a stride as he approached along the sidewalk, then suddenly stepped onto the street and came to the driver's window. Harry released the safety of his pistol sitting on the seat beside him.

The man, who looked to be barely out of his teens, leaned close to the window and tapped on it gently. Harry slowly displayed his pistol as he opened the window halfway.

"Yo, man, relax. Like I got a message, you know?"

"A message?"

"Yeah, like this dude paid me twenty dolla to tell you, you know, like you wanna do biznes, you know, like lose the dudes in the black Ford back dere in the alley."

"I beg your pardon?"

"That's it. Y'all have a good night."

"Wait!" said Harry. "Tell me again, who gave you the message?"

"Man, I ain't tell you in the first place, 'cept the dude gave me a twenty dolla."

"What'd he look like?"

"What do I look like? *The Datin' Game?* I got my Jackson, you got your message. So that's that." The young man turned and walked away, continuing his casual stride down the street.

Harry turned toward Miss Berksmere, but kept his eyes on the rearview mirror, watching the young man fade into the darkness. "Should we snatch him?"

Miss Berksmere stared straight ahead. "No, leave him alone."

"But—"

"Let him go, and do what he says."

"Are you sure?"

"Do what he says," Miss Berksmere snapped.

"Excuse me, ma'am, but—"

"Do it!"

Harry reached under the dash, then sat back and keyed the microphone to a radio telephone set to a special frequency. He released the key and looked again at Miss Berksmere, his expression filled with concern.

"Do it," she said quietly.

He keyed the mike. "Gentlemen, your shift has ended."

"Say again?" came the reply.

"Your shift is over. Back to the stable."

"On standby?"

Again, Harry looked over, questioning. Miss Berksmere shook her head. He keyed the mike. "No, your job's done. Go home."

There was a long pause.

"Code black?"

He keyed the mike. "Code green."

Another pause. "Copy, code green."

Nearly twenty minutes passed before Harry broke the silence with an impatient sigh. "I gotta tell you, ma'am, I don't like this. I don't like this at all."

Miss Berksmere looked at Harry, her expression calm, her eyes steady. "I do. I like this man's style. The problem has been ours all along. We kept underestimating him."

"And now?"

"He's holding the cards. We play his game."

It was shortly after midnight when Harry looked up and saw Eddie Nickles in his rearview mirror, walking toward them. "He's here."

Wendy Berksmere turned around and looked out the rear window. "On foot and alone? Interesting."

Eddie approached the driver's-side window, which Harry lowered. "Hey, Harry, it's you. So, how's it goin'?"

"Hey, Eddie," Harry said, as he closed his hand around the semi-automatic pistol by his side.

"Ah, Harry, relax. Put it down. What? You think we're gonna have a shoot-out here on the street?"

"Put it away," said Miss Berksmere, and Harry slipped the gun into his coat pocket and showed his hands on the steering wheel.

Eddie took his hands out of his coat pockets and started rubbing them together. "So, Harry, how're things at the Government Printing Office?"

"Oh, just swell, Eddie. We're putting out a new pamphlet on gumshoe techniques. You're chapter one."

"Really? I'm flattered. Be sure and send me a copy."

"Absolutely. But, look, I'll need your new address."

"Not a problem. Remind me before you leave. In the meantime, I guess we got some business to conduct."

"Here?"

"No, no, no, too cold. It's just a few blocks from here."

"You want a ride?"

"I thought you'd never ask."

"You mind if I check you out?"

"Man, I'm insulted. I thought we had an understanding, you and I. You don't hear me asking for that nine-millimeter in your pocket."

Miss Berksmere continued to look straight ahead. "Open the door for Mr. Nickles," she said.

Harry tapped the electric lock button and Eddie slipped into the back seat. " 'Preciate it, ma'am. It was gettin' a mite cold out there."

Miss Berksmere cocked her head to address Eddie over her shoulder. "Mr. Nickles, my name is Wendy Berksmere."

"Yes, ma'am, I know."

"Yes, I imagined you would. Well, sir, you have certainly led us a merry chase."

Eddie leaned over the seat and pointed up the street. "Take a right at the corner, go to the next corner, and take a left." He sat back. "Well, Miss Berksmere, to tell you the truth, it's been kinda hard figuring out exactly who's been chasing who."

Miss Berksmere chuckled. "Yes, it has seemed that way, hasn't it."

"So, Miss Berksmere, I hope you don't take this the wrong way—excuse me; Harry, right up there, take a left at the stop sign—anyway, like I was saying, ma'am, I hope you don't take this the wrong way, but you're not at all what I expected."

"And what were you expecting, Mr. Nickles?"

"Oh, I don't know. Kinda nasty business you're in. But you look to me like a nice lady. Real attractive. I know we're not supposed to say things like that these days. Give a lady a compliment and they turn around and sue you. But you kinda remind me of my Aunt Mabel when I was a kid."

"I'm flattered, Mr. Nickles."

"You should be. My Aunt Mabel was a fine woman. Used to treat my sisters and me to ice cream almost every Saturday. She was real pretty, too, as I remember."

Miss Berksmere turned almost fully around and looked directly at Eddie. "Why, Mr. Nickles, I had no idea. You wouldn't be one of those men my mother used to call 'silver-tongued devils,' would you?"

Eddie laughed. "Oh, no. Like I say, you ladies have made that a thing of the past."

Miss Berksmere smiled in return. "Yes, I suppose we have, haven't we? A shame, isn't it?"

"Yeah, I guess—Harry, take a right at the next corner. You'll see an auto-repair sign. Pull up right next to it."

Harry followed his instructions and pulled up in front of a failed auto-repair shop, its garage door boarded up, its single side door darkened, its only sign of life a weak light shining from a second-floor window. The street itself, like the repair shop, seemed all but abandoned. It was only a block long, and from one end to the other there was no sign of life: not a single car, not a single person, and both streetlights were out.

Eddie stepped out and stood by the passenger door, offering his hand to Miss Berksmere. She accepted his hand and stepped from the car. Harry quickly came to their side. "Relax, Harry," Miss Berksmere said.

"Yeah, Harry, relax." Eddie stepped forward to the door next to the garage. He took out a key, opened the door, then stood aside. "After you, ma'am," he said. "It's kinda dark, so watch your step. Just take the steps there."

Miss Berksmere stepped forward and Harry said, "Excuse me, ma'am. Eddie, how 'bout you leading the way."

"Whatever," Eddie said, and he stepped through the door.

Miss Berksmere and Harry followed, and just as they reached the second-floor landing, two men stepped out and pointed semi-automatics, one each at the heads of Harry and Miss Berksmere.

Harry flinched, and the man holding the gun on him pressed it hard against the side of his head and said, "Don't! Whatever you're thinking, man, don't do it!"

"His right-hand coat pocket," said Eddie. "A nine-millimeter. He's probably carrying more, so check him carefully. His car keys are in his other pocket."

"You're a car thief, too?" Harry asked through clenched teeth.

"Ah, Harry, don't get yourself in a snit," Eddie said with a smile. "Maybe I'm wrong, but I suspect you have all sorts of little toys in that car. You know, the kind that'll tell some clown sitting in a van somewhere exactly where your car is and all that. I thought maybe your boys could use a little practice in the art of tracking, and there's a coupla fellas downstairs who really like driving around in fancy new cars like that. Maybe they can all have some fun together."

Miss Berksmere did not move, but neither did she seem shocked or disturbed, a steady expression on her face and in her voice. "Mr. Nickles, now, what would your Aunt Mabel say about all this?"

Eddie shrugged, "Well, Miss Berksmere, I think she just might say 'Well done.' I don't know for sure, but I wouldn't be a bit surprised if that's exactly what she would say."

Miss Berksmere and Harry were led to the front room, which had the stale, dusty smell of having been closed off for a long time. The room was littered with paper and equipment apparently brought in for the occasion: a typewriter and a portable photocopier, two Polaroid cameras, a photographer's floodlight, and a stack of fresh film, ink pads and rollers and blank fingerprint cards, and neatly stacked piles of computer paper, each stack containing individual sheaves, each individually bound with a thick rubber band.

Miss Berksmere and Harry were taken to separate corners of the room, where they were thoroughly searched for weapons, wires, recorders, or any other unusual items. Their clothes were removed, Miss Berksmere being searched and assisted by the well-dressed woman who had earlier stood shivering at the entrance to Philo Machus's garage. The clothes were taken down to their car, placed in the trunk, and driven off by the young man who had earlier brought Harry the message. Each was provided a set of blue prison jumpers, which they put on. Then, one at a time, they were taken to a table where they were fingerprinted by a young man obviously well acquainted with the process, who could not stop giggling as he inked the pad, then inked their fingers, which he placed one by one within the appropriate boxes on the fingerprint cards Jimmy Legget had provided. The young man rolled each finger carefully, then printed all five fingers together, then their palms.

Harry and Miss Berksmere were next handcuffed and stood in

front of a man who took their photographs, full-faced and side-viewed. The man waited for the Polaroids to develop to check his success, then repeated the process, and said, "Thank you." He handed the photographs to a young woman who was typing entries onto some forms.

Each was then blindfolded and gagged and led to a second room; here they were seated in individual chairs, their feet tied to the legs, their cuffed hands secured to the back rails. "I hope you're not too uncomfortable," Eddie whispered to Miss Berksmere, as he was about to leave the room. "It's gonna be a little while before I get back."

It was more than an hour before Eddie returned to the room, alone. But for him and those seated in their chairs, the building had been emptied of all the people and equipment. Eddie turned on the single overhead light and went around the room, removing first the gags and then the blindfolds. It took some time for the captives' eyes to adjust, but one by one their eyes did, and they each looked about the room and at each other. There in a circle sat Wendy Berksmere, the chief of internal security and finance for the Specials Projects Directorate; her boss, Philo Machus, Special Projects' chief and reputedly the youngest Marine ever to be promoted to colonel; former head of West European Operations for the KGB and current entrepreneur, Arkady Treshkov, aka Garland Bolles; former colonel in the Soviet Special Forces turned black marketeer, Yury Khavkin; and the man who was still known only as Harry of the Government Printing Office. Each looked at the others in their blue jumpers, and all but Miss Berksmere reacted with clenched jaws and angry expressions. Only she seemed not to react at all, a certain calm fixed in her expression.

Eddie began slowly to circle the ring of chairs, watching each set of eyes follow him. He made one complete circle before starting with "You're probably wondering why I called you all together." He stopped and waited for a response, but none came. He shrugged it off and continued, speaking slowly as he circled. "Well, we'll get to that in a moment. In the meantime, I would suggest that you listen carefully and consider the wisdom of playing by a whole new set of rules, which I am about to explain to you.

"First . . . well, I might as well come right out and say it. None of you people—not a single one of you—has been very nice lately. You've been chasing people who don't deserve to be chased, killing people who didn't deserve to be killed, scaring people half to death, ruining careers, lying, cheating, stealing, and, forgive me for saying it, generally just being real assholes. Now, tonight, that's all going to change."

No one said a word, and after a long pause, Eddie continued.

"Okay, first, you will notice that there on the floor in front of you is a stack of papers. Computer printouts and such. There is one complete package for each of you to take with you. Frankly, I don't pretend to understand all of what's there, but I will tell you this. In each of those packages are computer runs and tracings on more bank accounts and money transfers than I've ever seen before. And with each of these computer runs there are notes and explanations to guide the reader to certain transactions, and account numbers and code names and whatever, all of which is designed to make it rather easy for anyone to see who stole what from who—or is it whom? Anyway, basically, it's a shorthand guide to who cheated who, how and for how much, and where it all went. Plus, as an extra added attraction, there are many notes and explanations of exactly what your various organizations were doing, are probably still doing, who gave the orders, and who profited. Like I say, it's all too complicated for a simple guy like myself, but I am told there are people out there who would just love to sit around a roaring fire with a glass of wine or whatever and spend hour after hour reading through these documents.

"You'll want to read it yourselves, because the fact of the matter is that none of you have been entirely honest with one another. It's all been a very messy business, but one thing is clear. All of you seem to be under the mistaken impression that you really understood who was on whose side and what the hell the whole pack of you were up to. Now, I've never been a spy or whatever it is you guys call yourselves, and I've never been in a mob, but I have been in government, and seems to me that the mind-set's much the same. I've watched people in government sometimes get a little too full of themselves, start thinking that whoever they are or whatever they do is just a little more important than it really is. People get confused, you know, and sometimes egos take over and common sense sorta goes out the window. I understand all that.

But you guys! Jesus Christ, I mean, I've seen some hard cases in my day, but, damn, I've never seen so much double-dealing. Hell, I'll bet, right now, if your life depended on it—which, by the way, it very well might, by the time this is over—not one of you could really say who's on who's side. Now, you people want to go on sticking your knives in each other's back, be my guest. Maybe one day you'll just wipe each other out and the rest of us will be a little better off for it. In the meantime, however, I'm not about to let you and your little war games, or whatever, screw up my life and the lives of people I care about. You understand? You see where you screwed up? You let the game get outside your little circle, and now you gotta pay the price. Understand?"

Eddie stopped and looked around, but no one uttered a sound.

"Okay, so here's what's gonna happen. First, in addition to the packages you see sitting on the floor there, my associates have made a whole bunch more copies of the same thing. Those copies are this very moment being hand-delivered and mailed to all sorts of people in all sorts of places for safekeeping. Understand?"

Again, no one spoke or even gestured.

"Now, the people with whom these packages are being placed have explicit instructions to the effect that, if anyone, and I mean *anyone*—me or any member of my family, or Helen Grehm or Arlis Brecht or Hans Talpa or any of their families or close friends or whatever, or any of the good people who assisted me tonight— if any of them get even a hint of a hassle about any of this ever again, well, these packages will be distributed to those on a little mailing list I and my friends have put together.

"Actually, it's not a small list at all. The postage alone would be a killer, since it was suggested that we include all kinds of politicians and bureaucrats and news types and whatever, including a bunch of people in Russia." He looked at both Yury Khavkin and Arkady Treshkov. "Y'all have something called the SVR, is it? And the Interior Ministry and Internal Security and whatever?"

There was no response.

"Well, the point is, it's a long list, and you know how expensive it is to send packages overseas, so I do hope you'll all cooperate here. And, of course, along with copies of the packages you see there, we are right now making up an equal number of copies of your rap sheets, as it were, which include the photographs and fingerprints you were all so kind to provide us tonight. You know, it'll just make it easier for people to put a face and fingerprints together with the names, whatever the hell your real names are. So, are we all clear? Everyone understands? . . . Yes? No?"

Eddie watched their eyes travel back and forth between one another, but, again, no one spoke.

"Well, I'll just assume you have the gist of what's going on. Now, to end our little session together, I thought I'd try an experiment, just to see if you children can't learn to cooperate and play nice with one another. Just this once. I mean, it would seem to me you have more than enough incentive, right? I mean, just one of you screws up and does something stupid, well, then, everyone takes a fall. Right? . . . Am I getting through here? I know I've never been much at making speeches or whatever, but I gave this little talk a lot of thought. An occasional nod or whatever would be nice. . . . No?"

Nothing.

"Well, it's getting late, and you all have a lot to think about. Probably want to be alone to share your thoughts and feelings with one another, so—" He stopped and cocked his head. "Oh, I almost forgot. One more thing." He looked first at Miss Berksmere and Harry, who were seated next to one another, and then at the others. "Those outstanding warrants for me? Take care of them, and quickly. I don't care how you do it or whose arms you have to twist. Just do it. Off the records, they never happened. Second, Birshstein's crowd in Brooklyn. Make sure that slate gets wiped clean. Any hassle from them will be considered a hassle from you. Again, I don't care how, just get it done." He looked at Treshkov, then turned toward Philo Machus. "Do we understand one another?"

Miss Berksmere was the first and only one to react. Her expression never changed, but she nodded to Eddie. It was single nod, and a barely perceptible one at that, but it was a nod all the same.

"Okay, so where was I? Oh, yes. Well, I guess we're all tired and getting a little cranky, so why don't we just cut to the chase."

Eddie reached into his pocket and retrieved several keys, which he tossed on the stack of papers in front of the group. "Those, gentlemen—and lady—are your handcuff keys. They will free each and every one of you if you choose to cooperate with one another."

He then reached to the small of his back and took out the nine-millimeter pistol taken from Harry of the Government Printing Office. He took his handkerchief and carefully wiped the weapon clean. "This, people, is a fully loaded weapon." He tossed it on the papers as well. "I am leaving it for you because, unfortunately, this is not the safest of neighborhoods, and a bunch of white folks running around in prison jumpers might just attract some attention. Unlike yourselves, there are people out there with an attitude, you know? So I'm leaving this with you—for your own protection, you understand—and because I know you'll all do the right thing and cooperate with one another. We all understand the ground rules, am I right? No one is going to do anything stupid like trying to take unfair advantage over anyone else. Correct?" No one spoke, and Eddie just smiled and shook his head. "Well, whatever. Like I say, I'm kinda tired. So you all have a good night, good luck, and I truly hope for your sakes and mine that I never, ever see or hear from any of you again."

Eddie had turned for the door when he heard Miss Berksmere speak up. "Mr. Nickles?"

He stopped and looked back. "Yes?"

"Well done, Mr. Nickles. Well done, indeed."

*

Out on the street, Eddie smiled. "I must say, Mr. Toussaint, you are a class act. Yes, sir, I mean a real class act."

T smiled, too, as he took a small key and a large briefcase from Eddie and laid the briefcase on the trunk of his limousine. "Organization, man. All it takes is the right people and organization."

"Well, you got that. No question."

T opened the briefcase and took a moment to decide which of the many individually wrapped bundles of hundred-dollar bills to inspect. "So tell me, man," he said, picking one bundle finally and counting the bills. "One thing. Why you goin' through all this just to tie 'em up and walk away? I mean, shit, might as well have just dropped a dime and let the government take care of it for you."

"T, when's the last time you saw the government take care of anything without causing more problems than they were trying to fix?"

"Yeah, well, but still."

"Plus, think about it. If something like this ever went public, me and the lady, everybody, man, we'd be hounded to death with investigations and trials and Hill hearings and every pissant reporter and politician crawling all over themselves to see who'd get the bigger headline. And in the end nothing would change. A few more lives would get screwed up, but nothing would change."

"So, Eddie, that's a nice speech 'n' all, but for real, man, you got some serious money coming outta tonight, am I right?"

Eddie laughed. "Yeah, T, you always could see through the bullshit."

T smiled as he shut the briefcase and opened the car's trunk to toss it inside. "I like your style, too, Eddie. You know, you and me, we could do things together. No lie. You and me, man, we put our heads together, do some serious business."

Eddie smiled and shook his head. " 'Preciate the offer, but I think I'm gonna retire for real this time."

T shut the trunk lid just as the muffled sound of a single gunshot came from the second floor of the repair shop. They both looked up, and then at each other. There was a brief silence, and Eddie shook his head. "Man, those people are incorrigible. You know what I'm saying? I mean really incorrigible!"

T, too, shook his head. "White folks!"

Eddie chuckled.

"So, you need a ride?" T asked.

Eddie nodded, and both men turned quickly and got into the limousine.

"So, T," Eddie said, as they sped away, "how's your daughter doin' in college?"

EPILOGUE

It was an extraordinary morning in the nation's capital, a morning filled with an air of renewal, autumn crisp and fresh like the beginning of a new semester. The sky was clear and the sun bright, and a light breeze carried away the exhaust of free-flowing traffic. People strolled rather than hurried to their jobs, stopping at street-corner carts and pastry shops for hot coffee and fresh-baked buns. They offered greetings to total strangers and smiled with patience for the tourists who stood in the middle of side-walks to be photographed with the life-sized cutouts of the president and his wife. The tourists smiled, too, if at times their expressions seemed glazed by a certain reverent, if confused, wonder at the massive stone warrens where each and every day dark-blue suits and bright silk ties gathered with scuffed brown shoes and miracle-fiber shirts, with flower-print dresses and patterned panty hose, to plan and regulate their agriculture and commerce, their health and their welfare, to wage their wars and police the peace, to mete out their justice and take in their taxes. Still and all, as they wandered the tree-lined avenues and manicured parks and marbled halls, they could not help suspecting that perhaps the Chicken Little press and predictors of doom might just be wrong, that here in *their* city of Washington, in *their* District of Columbia, a place once derided among the capitals of the world as "a mud hole equal to the Great Serbonian Bog," that maybe, just maybe, everything was proceeding according to plan.

Even in those corners where the air was stale and sun did not shine, the mood was the same. A new day had arrived, one born of narrow escapes and newly cleared horizons. In the private dining room of the very private Sequoia Club, Miss Wendy Berksmere looked over her coffee cup to the expression of satisfaction that came over the chairman of the Joint Operations Committee.

"Quite remarkable," the chairman said with a rare but genuine smile. He laid aside the thick sheaf of papers which Miss Berksmere had provided him, a thoroughly and imaginatively edited and unattributed version of the documents prepared by Arlis Brecht and Helen Grehm. "Absolutely remarkable."

Miss Berksmere said nothing.

"Tell me, just how long do you think it will take to close down Iberia without raising eyebrows?"

"The covert side is down. The legitimate side will take a few months or more, but we've managed to arrange a buyout that will cover us completely."

"And the covert side?"

"If the committee approves the plan, it should take no time at all. Since we'll be using established fronts and controlling everything from inside headquarters, we could be reinvested almost immediately."

"And the capital loss?"

"Best estimates are somewhere between twenty-seven and thirty million. It'll crimp a few programs for a while, but it's within the acceptable range."

"This includes the cost of closing down F Street and relocating?"

"Yes, sir."

The chairman shook his head in wonderment. "No sign of Machus, I take it?"

"No, sir, not yet, but eventually we'll find him."

"I applaud your optimism, Miss Berksmere, but frankly I doubt it. As I've said before, I suspect the opposition may have already exacted its revenge."

"Well, that could be, but I still hope we get to him first. I'd like to know what else might be out there."

"I understand, but if this reorganization works out, it won't much matter, will it? Except for losing a little money, we're all well covered, correct?"

"Yes, sir, the footprints have all been wiped clean."

"Including those of Arlis Brecht?"

"Yes, sir."

He nodded appreciatively. "Now, about this problem in Konstanz," the chairman asked, referring to reports that yet another shipment of weapons-grade plutonium 239 smuggled out of Russia had traded hands near the German-Swiss border. "Any possibility Treshkov's back at work?"

"I don't know," said Miss Berksmere. "As you read in the cover brief, no one's seen or heard of either him or Khavkin since Machus disappeared."

"But you do think they're still out there."

"Again, I really don't know what I believe. We've certainly sent enough back-channel signals, but whether Moscow has any interest in pursuing them is anyone's guess at this point."

Again, the chairman nodded. "Well, if nothing else, it's some comfort to know that we're back to business as usual."

Miss Berksmere smiled. "Yes, I suppose that's right."

The chairman sat back and folded his hands across his midriff, a curious, almost whimsical expression coming over him. "You know, I always thought that one day I would come face to face with Treshkov—or more, I always wished that someday I would. I always wondered how much we might have in common. Do you know what I mean?"

Miss Berksmere paused, then cocked her head. "Yes, well, I can certainly understand the curiosity, but for myself I'm quite satisfied for them to remain nothing more than names and faces in a file. It keeps things simple, at least for me."

The chairman stared at her for a long moment, then smiled. "Yes . . . I see your point. Well, no matter, I suppose, with all that's happened, there's little chance that either one of us will ever have the chance, whether we'd want it or not."

"I suspect you're right," she said.

"Well, there it is." He smiled again. "You have done a remark-

able job here, Miss Berksmere. I—that is, we, the entire committee—we are all both pleased and quite impressed with what you've
been able to accomplish in very short order."

"Thank you, sir. I appreciate that."

"There is, however, one thing more you can do for us."

"Yes, sir?"

"Are you free for dinner this evening?"

"Well, yes, sir, I guess I could be. May I ask what the occasion is?"

The chairman leaned forward and smiled conspiratorially. "I
suppose I shouldn't be telling you this, but I'm sure you'll act ap-
propriately surprised."

"Sir?"

"As I say, the entire committee could not be more pleased with
how you have handled what could have been a very unpleasant
situation. Early this morning, the committee met and approved
your reorganization proposal."

"Well, I am pleased."

"*And,* Miss Berksmere, we would like you to join us over
dinner, where you will be both the guest of honor"—he paused to
allow the moment to build, while Miss Berksmere lifted her eyebrows in anticipation—"and we will be asking you to take over
the directorate, with a substantial raise in salary and benefits.
Congratulations!"

Miss Berksmere sat back with appropriate surprise. "Well, I'm
not sure I know what to say."

"You don't need to say anything but that you'll do it."

Miss Berksmere laid her hand upon her heart as if to still it.
"Well, certainly, I am flattered."

"It's not flattery, Miss Berksmere, simply the recognition that in
my opinion is long overdue. We know you are the one person who
will be able to lead us back from these unfortunate problems. I
urge you—repeat, *urge* you—to accept. We need you. Your country
needs you. The business of the directorate is far too important to
let it slip away over what admittedly have been some troubling
times, but ultimately were nothing but minor misfires in an otherwise smooth-running machine."

The chairman sat back and raised one finger in emphasis. "I
need not tell you how ephemeral are the politics of our presi-

dent—of all presidents, for that matter, and their part-time policy-makers. The security of this country cannot depend on the ebb and flow of public opinion and pollsters and TV populists. No, no, the nation's security must take priority over all of that. And we, madame, we are the last bit of marrow left in the backbone of that security.

"Unfortunately, we seem to have fallen prey to the evangelists of good feelings, to the illusion of safety so readily and naïvely embraced by the insipient believers in the so-called family of man. We are becoming a population of Candides, if you will—as Voltaire once said, this 'mania of maintaining that everything is well when we are wretched.' But we, Miss Berksmere, we, of all people, know differently, don't we?"

"Yes, sir."

"Yes, we do. And that is why the work of the directorate is so vital. It is the sustaining force behind our efforts to protect our people from themselves, from their naïveté, from their self-destructive illusions. And you, dear lady, are critical to that effort. Please say you'll accept."

Miss Berksmere paused and took a deep breath. "Of course, I'm honored to accept."

"Excellent! I'm so pleased."

"But . . ."

"Yes?"

"Well . . . forgive me for asking, but . . ."

"Yes, what is it?"

"At this dinner party?"

"Yes?"

"I was just wondering . . . what shall I wear?"

*

Eddie Nickles sat back on the long wooden bench, his face lifted to the noontime sun, his eyes closed and his mind occupied with nothing but the warmth of the air and the soft lapping of the water behind him. He heard the pickup's approach across the gravel lot but did not look up until its tires locked and it slid to a stop a few yards in front of him. He glanced at his watch. They had only a few minutes to spare.

He watched Helen jump out of the truck and hurry to the back, where she retrieved a small duffle, while Marta stepped down from the driver's seat. Helen dropped the duffle and the two women embraced, then stepped back and spoke words Eddie could not hear. He watched as both wiped tears from their eyes and again embraced, as if each were afraid to let the other one go.

Finally, they parted, and Helen picked up the duffle and walked up to Eddie. "Y'all set?" he asked.

She took a very deep breath. "Yes, all set."

They stared at one another for a long moment.

"Look, Eddie Nickles," Helen said at last, "I don't want an argument from you, okay?"

He looked at her curiously.

She reached into the pocket of her skirt and pulled out an envelope, which she quickly stuffed in his shirt pocket.

"What's that?"

"It's a bank account in your name, and your name only. All the instructions are there."

"Oh, no, I—"

"Stop it!"

"No, really—"

"Stop! Listen to me. It's all legitimate. . . . Well, as far as anyone will ever know, it is. I've covered everything, so you don't have to be afraid to answer any questions or whatever, not that anyone will ever ask them. Everything you'll ever need is written down there."

"Helen, you don't need to do this."

"Of course I don't. I know that. But I want to, and the only thing you could do to disappoint me right now is to say no. Please don't disappoint me."

Eddie dropped his eyes to the ground and shuffled one foot.

Helen laughed, then threw her arms around him and held him close. "You saved my life," she whispered in his ear, then kissed him on the cheek and stood back, wiping fresh tears away. "So," she said in a sigh, looking around, "no bags?"

Eddie blushed. "Ah, well, no. Actually, my daughter's flying down in a few days. We're gonna spend some time together down in the Keys with her brother."

She smiled. "Good for you," she said, then cocked her head as if she suspected there was more.

"And, well, you know," Eddie stumbled, "in the meantime, I thought maybe I'd just hang around. You know, get a little sun or whatever."

Helen lowered her chin and looked at him suspiciously.

" 'Sides," he said, "I got a dinner date tonight."

Helen hesitated, then turned and saw Marta leaning against the pickup's fender. Marta shrugged and rolled her eyes in confession. Helen shook her head, then took Eddie's face in her hands and kissed him. "You, Eddie Nickles, are one dangerous fella."

The ferry whistled its warning that it was about to leave the dock, and Helen again grabbed her duffle. Eddie reached out and touched her arm, and she stopped. "You're gonna be okay?" he asked.

"I'm going to be fine."

"You promise?"

"I promise."

"You know where I am if you ever need me."

She nodded, then dropped her bag and hugged him again. "You take care, Eddie Nickles. I love you!" She released him and quickly grabbed her duffle and started running toward the ferry.

"Helen?" he shouted as she jumped on the ferry's platform and turned back, but Eddie didn't know what to say.

She nodded, as if she knew, then blew him a kiss and turned and disappeared toward the front of the ferry as it pulled from the dock and churned eastward toward the mainland.